SOMETHING
REAL

SOMETHING
REAL

Heather Demetrios

Henry Holt and Company
New York

For Menendian, who taught me how to write
And for Zach, who always believed I could

Henry Holt and Company, LLC
Publishers since 1866
175 Fifth Avenue
New York, New York 10010
macteenbooks.com

Library of Congress Cataloging-in-Publication Data
Demetrios, Heather.
Something real / Heather Demetrios. — First edition.
    pages   cm
Summary: Since the cancellation of her family's reality television show, seventeen-year-old Bonnie Baker, one of twelve siblings, has tried to live a normal life with real friends and a possible boyfriend, until her mother and the show's producers decide to bring "Baker's Dozen" back on the air.
ISBN 978-0-8050-9794-8 (hardback) — ISBN 978-0-8050-9796-2 (e-book)
[1. Reality television programs—Fiction.   2. Family life—Fiction.]   I. Title.
PZ7.D3923So 2014   [Fic]—dc23   2013030798

Henry Holt books may be purchased for business or promotional use.
For information on bulk purchases, please contact the Macmillan Corporate
and Premium Sales Department at (800) 221-7945 x5442 or by e-mail at
specialmarkets@macmillan.com.

First Edition—2014 / Designed by Ashley Halsey
Printed in the United States of America

1 3 5 7 9 10 8 6 4 2

All happy families are alike;
each unhappy family is unhappy in its own way.

—Leo Tolstoy

You reel me out and then you cut the string.

—Radiohead

Disclaimer

The views expressed in this memoir do not necessarily reflect those of the MetaReel Entertainment Corporation, *Baker's Dozen*, *Baker's Dozen: Fresh Batch*, or the Baker-Miller family. Bonnie™ Baker is a registered trademark. Any misuse is a violation of applicable laws.

Click on a name below to find out more about each member of the Baker family! Don't forget to check out the Baker blog here.

THE PARENTS:

Beth Baker-Miller   Hometown: Bartlett, New Hampshire

Kirk Miller   Hometown: Fresno, California

THE KIDS:

Bonnie™ Baker   Age: 17   Country: USA (biological child)

Benton™ Baker   Age: 17   Country: USA (surrogate mother)

Lexie™ Baker   Age: 17   Country: USA (surrogate mother)

Farrow™ Baker   Age: 15   Country: Ethiopia (Adopted)

Riley™ Baker   Age: 14   Country: Cambodia (Adopted)

Gavin™ Baker   Age: 13   Country: Peru (Adopted)

Tristan™ Baker   Age: 12   Country: Russia (Adopted)

DeShaun™ Baker   Age: 10   Country: USA (Adopted through foster care)

Deston™ Baker   Age: 9   Country: USA (Adopted through
                                              foster care)
Lark™ Baker   Age: 8   Country: India (Adopted)
Daisy™ Baker   Age: 7   Country: China (Adopted)
Violet™ Baker   Age: 7   Country: China (Adopted)
Jasmine™ Baker   Age: 7   Country: China (Adopted)

Click here for more information about former cast member
Andrew Baker (seasons 1–13).

SEASON 17, EPISODE 1

(The One with the Cameras)

*I*t took me four years, seven shrinks, three different hair colors, one Zen meditation retreat, and over six hundred mochas to get to this moment.

I step up to the blue velvet backdrop and face the camera. When the photographer isn't paying attention, I wipe the back of my hand over my damp forehead, then clutch my fingers behind my back, like I'm a two-year-old with a secret. I shouldn't have worn the sweater-shirt. The wool is itchy, and I'm about two seconds away from breaking out in hives. God, why won't he just take the damn picture? It's not like this is *Seventeen*. The last time they shot me, we'd spent four hours on my hair and makeup and another three in front of the camera. This is nothing compared to that, but it feels so much worse.

I want to bolt so bad, and this guy's taking forever, longer than he took for anyone who was in line ahead of me. But I have to stick it out. I've been psyching myself up for this all summer. A senior photo is an important pastime for a normal girl. And I'm a normal girl.

Finally.

I can do this. *Breathe.* It's not even a *camera* camera . . . it's just a photo. One photo. That's it. And the name that will be underneath it in the yearbook? Totally unremarkable. Nothing *Us Weekly* would care about. Chloe Baker's a nobody.

The scruffy photographer crouches down behind the camera, like a sniper looking through a scope. The panic that had started out as a slight queasiness in my stomach is pushing past my ribs, pressing against my lungs.

The sweater itching. Sweat on my forehead. Nails digging into my skin. *Keep it together. Just a few more seconds.*

I'm a freaking basket case.

"All right, Chloe," he says. "On three. One, two—"

I smile as the flash goes off, and the photographer gives me a thumbs-up, then turns to the kid behind him. "Next!"

My first voluntary picture in four years.

I grab my backpack off the floor and throw it over one shoulder as I walk out of the makeshift photo studio. Giddiness wells up in me, like I mainlined a Pepsi Freeze and got a little too high on caffeine and sugar. I want to do something to commemorate the day—bake a cake or put a sticker on my calendar. Light a candle.

Behind me, a long line of seniors wait their turn for the yearbook photos, but since my last name is at the beginning of the alphabet, I'm among the first to go home on this rare half day. Thank God for long faculty meetings.

"Proud of you, sis."

My brother, Benton™, also a senior, gives me a hug. I knew he'd been waiting for me after he took his photo, which, because he's a well-adjusted person, is no biggie for him.

4

"Is that relief I see in your eyes?" I ask him.

He shrugs. "Maybe a little."

"Someday, you'll be proud of me for doing something that's scarier than a yearbook picture."

He gives my ponytail an affectionate tug. "Baby steps." We walk away from the line together and then he jerks his thumb toward the locker room. "I'm meeting Matt, so you can take the car, 'kay?"

"Have fun."

He gives me a wicked little grin. "We get his house to ourselves until he has practice at three."

I feign shock. "Scandalous!"

He laughs and then jogs off to meet his boyfriend, while I go the opposite way, toward the parking lot.

Maybe not freaking out is proof that I'm no longer a paranoid schizo. I mean, if my classmates haven't figured it out by now, they never will. Right? Right. It doesn't matter if they look at me all day long or have ten yearbook pictures of me. It doesn't. They'll only see *Chloe* Baker.

Still. A tiny part of me wants to turn around and demand that the photographer delete my photo. It isn't too late. But I keep walking, one foot in front of the other, out of the gym, through the parking lot, and to the car Benny and I share—a used silver Hyundai with dark-tinted windows, as unremarkable as I want to be.

It's one of those rare perfect fall days that we only get, like, three of in central California. The sun is shining, but the breeze bites, and even though the trees don't really change here, not like back home in New Hampshire, a few across the parking lot have turned golden or rust-colored. I smile at them, like we're old friends. Then I slide into the driver's seat, and when I turn the key, the radio starts blaring Lily Allen's "Smile," and really, how freakin' perfect is that?

My cell rings, and I put it on speaker as I back out of my spot.

"Chlo. You still coming over?" It's Tessa, one of my two best friends.

"Yeah," I say. "Just going home to change. This sweater makes me want to rip my skin off."

"Yikes." I can hear the heavy buzz of students all around her—her last name's Lee, so she'll be in line for a while. "Well, don't hurry. After this, I have to make sure the paper's good to go. There are about five articles that I know right now, without the benefit of psychic powers, are going to suck."

Tessa is the editor of the school paper, and it pretty much takes up her whole life. It sort of works out that my friends are super-busy overachievers—it gives them less time to ask questions I can't answer.

"Don't you have underclassmen minions to do your bidding?" I say. "Make someone else proofread for a change. It's a half day!"

I pull out of the parking lot and head north, toward the highway that leads to the new housing developments out in the boonies.

"Can't. The paper's my baby. Leaving it in their hands is like child endangerment," Tessa says. "Call you when I'm done?"

"Sounds good."

I hang up and sing along with Lily Allen, reveling in the noon sun. Now that the photo's over, I can't wipe the smile off my face. I'm tempted to call my therapist from last year and be like, *I'm cured!!* but I wouldn't want to give her the satisfaction. She always used the phrase "that's understandable" whenever I told her about the stuff that happened to me, and I was like, *No, actually, none of it's*

6

understandable. That's sort of the whole point of why I'm here. But like everything else, that's in the past.

Twenty minutes later, I slow down in front of the big metal gate that leads into our driveway. It's exactly like the one we had in New Hampshire four years ago—built so that paparazzi can't see in. I press the control attached to my sun visor, and the gate creaks open. As soon as I pull into the drive, my good mood is gone, like someone came over and kicked it out of me. I hit the brakes and stare.

The telltale signs of my childhood are everywhere: vans with satellite dishes on top, the Mercedes with the familiar BRN4REEL license plate, and ropes of thick black cables that crawl around the house like prehistoric predators, squeezing everyone inside until they suffocate.

The living room curtains are closed. Hot lights seem to burn up everything on the other side of them, the fluorescent quality of the inside mixing with the sunlight outside.

As if the two could coexist.

This is the moment where I'm supposed to visualize something positive. Go to my happy place. Meditate. Instead, I just sit there, numb, with the car running, and try to remember how to breathe. This can't be possible—not when I'm finally in school and have friends and can go to the mall without Vultures hiding in planters, stalking me. Mom promised. She fucking *promised.*

But a voice inside whispers, *Yeah, Bonnie™, but parents break their promises—you know that better than anyone else.*

I close my eyes and beg the universe to pleasepleaseplease let this be a really extreme flashback. It's not real. Not real. Not.

I open my eyes—this is really happening.

7

The car feels suddenly small, like the metal sides are warping and shrinking. My sweater-shirt is full of millions of little teeth eating away at me, and I struggle with my seat belt as beads of sweat pile up under my bra, against the tight waistline of my jeans, and trickle down my forehead. Dammit, this seat belt won't freaking open, it won't—

Two guys on the roof stare down at me as I stumble out of the car, and I know they're surveying the neighborhood, seeing if there are any good shots they can get from up there. A crew is already working on making our fence even higher, and security details are mapping out the perimeter of our property. Five hours ago, they weren't here. They were probably driving up from LA just as I was leaving for school. Funny how your whole world can go to hell within three hundred minutes.

"Excuse me," someone calls, "didn't you see the sign? This is private property."

I turn around and shade my eyes against the sun as an unfamiliar figure walks up to me.

"Yeah, I know," I say. The woman has a cell phone in one hand and a Starbucks cup in the other. I've never seen her before. "My stepdad put up that sign. Who are you?"

As she gets closer, she gasps. "OMG! Bonnie™?" A look of recognition passes over her face. "It *is* you. Wow! You look like a totally different person! I love, love, *love* your long hair—so different from that cute little bob you always had, and the color—awesome. Oh my gosh, you were, like, my little sister's *idol*. For reals, she is going to FLIP when she sees how grown up you are. This is so freakin' out of control!"

She! Loves! Exclamation! Points!

"Who *are* you?"

"Oops!" She flips her hair back like she's in a shampoo commercial. "Sorry. I'm Lacey—the head production assistant for *Baker's Dozen: Fresh Batch.*"

I already hate Lacey Production Assistant Who Talks to Me Like She Knows Me.

"*Fresh Batch?*"

My tongue feels thick, and the words come out sounding like I've been drugged. My stomach gets that car sickness sort of feeling, and the world begins to tip on its axis, vertigo style.

Just then, Mom and Chuck come out the front door—Chuck of BRN4REEL fame, MetaReel's head producer. He hasn't changed a bit. His paunch strains against his shirt, and he walks toward me like a strutting peacock, his weight on his heels, his arms swinging freely at his sides. Lacey scurries away, and two seconds later I realize why; she doesn't want to get in the shot. My hands fly up to block my face—my kingdom for a pair of dark sunglasses and a ginormous hat.

"Mom! What is this?" I shout. The last word echoes across our huge driveway, *this . . . this . . . this.*

I can feel eyes on me—the camera, the dudes on the roof, the crew peeking out the windows of my house.

"Bonnie™, why aren't you in school?"

Mom's out of practice—back in the day, she would have been able to hide the note of panic that's creeping into her voice. To her credit, she has a super-stricken look on her face, but right now I hate her more than Lacey Production Assistant.

"Who cares? What's going on?"

"*Bonnie™,*" she says, pursing her lips and inclining her head ever so slightly toward the camera.

As if I could forget it's there.

Chuck's small, glittering eyes are on us, but he hangs back, letting the cameras take in all our drama. There's a movement to my right, and I see three little pigtailed heads peering out at me through the slightly open front door—my youngest sisters, our triplets from China: Daisy™, Violet™, and Jasmine™. I was hoping they wouldn't have the childhood I did, but I guess they will after all.

"Mom, *please*—" I stop because my voice is getting that high, constricted I'm-trying-not-to-cry sound, and I'll be damned if I'm going to give the cameras what they want. Also, I don't want to freak out my sisters.

Mom looks at me—really looks at me—and her eyes are sad and stressed, and I think how much they look like my brother Benny's. Then she squeezes the tip of her nose between her thumb and index finger, which is Mom Speak for *shitshitshit*. She turns to Chuck.

"We can't film this—we agreed Kirk and I would get to tell all the kids in a controlled environment. I told you it would be difficult with her. I told you, Chuck."

The camera focuses on me as Chuck whispers in Mom's ear. She starts shaking her head.

"I don't care!"

My feet start moving on their own, closer and closer to the camera. I barely register the guy holding it. I reach out my hand and touch the glass lens—nobody's really paying attention to me anymore except for the camera and the man behind it. You know those tribal people who believed a camera could steal your soul? Turns out they were right.

"I'm sorry, Beth. It's in the contract—MetaReel has full access to all public spheres of the home. The driveway is a public sphere. What do you want me to do?" Chuck asks. I can see him reflected in the lens, giving his little shrug and faux it's-out-of-my-hands frown. It's an expression better suited to a sitcom. He loves playing hapless—he's anything but.

"Bon-Bon, come over here," Chuck says, his voice wheedling. "Four years, and I don't even get a hug?"

I can't believe I used to like that nickname.

"Bonnie™," Mom calls. I can hear her heels grinding the gravel underfoot as she comes after me. *Hurry, hurry,* my blood whispers.

I look right into the camera. My face is practically pressed up against it. America will be able to see my smudged eyeliner and the zit on my chin. They'll probably show a Cover Girl commercial after this segment—I'll be a cautionary tale for teen skin care.

I open my mouth to say something—*screw you, America!*—anything, but I go mute. Typical.

Mom yanks me back, hard. Child Protective Services hard.

"Ouch!" I say it louder than I need to.

The front door opens wider, and Kirk, my stepdad, comes outside. His sandy gray hair is slicked back, and he's wearing pressed khakis and a button-down. He looks like a totally different person without the paint-splattered Dickies and ratty T-shirts he usually wears.

"Bonnie™, sweetheart. Let your mother explain," he says.

For a second, I just stand there and stare at him. *Bonnie™—et tu,* Kirk? I feel like he just walked onto the porch and slapped my face as hard as he could. Up until about three seconds ago, he was one of only two people in my whole family who were willing to call me Chloe. He'd understood why the name Bonnie™ was repulsive to me. He'd said he wouldn't want to be a brand, either. But now he's sauntering toward us, relaxed—like he's having fun. I look from Mom's perfect hair to his easy grin; this was always going to happen again, wasn't it? Stupid, *stupid* me.

"Bonnie™, go inside." Mom's still holding my arm, and I can almost feel my skin bruising underneath it, turning me purple. I shake her off, but she doesn't notice. She and Chuck are having a staring contest.

I give the camera one more glare before I jump back in my car. The keys are still in the ignition, so I peel out of the driveway James Bond style, ignoring my mother's shouts and the coffee that Lacey Production Assistant has dropped onto the front of her shirt in her haste not to die.

I can't believe it. Despite all her promises, my mom has finally given in to MetaReel. After four camera-free years, the cast of *Baker's Dozen*—my family—is back on the air.

Fireside Chats with Kaye Gibbons

INT—BAKER HOME—NIGHT: A cozy living room with a fire burning in a fireplace. Thirteen framed photos are set up on the mantel. Three of them are empty. [KAYE sits in a wingback chair beside the fire, ankles crossed. Her bob is hair-sprayed to perfection, and she wears a mint suit.]

KAYE GIBBONS: Good afternoon and welcome to another episode of *Fireside Chats With Kaye Gibbons*. Ten years ago, America—and the world—opened up their hearts to a very special family. For the past 3,600 days, we've shared in their joys [CUT to image of couple in a hospital delivery room holding a baby] and their sorrows [CUT to picture of orphanage destroyed by an earthquake. CUT to KAYE GIBBONS]. Though their circumstances are extraordinary, and they have millions of fans all over the country [CUT to image of a packed book-signing, then CUT to KAYE GIBBONS], not to mention a number of highly successful product lines, they're still just as down-to-earth as when we met them. Today we have an extra special *Fireside Chat* with Beth and Andrew Baker, and—of course—little Bonnie™, Benton™, Lexie™, Farrow™, Riley™, Gavin™, Tristan™, DeShaun™, Deston™, and Lark™, stars of the hit MetaReel reality show, *Baker's Dozen*. To celebrate the show's tenth anniversary, I'm here at their beautiful five-acre property in Bartlett, New Hampshire, where they live, work, and play. Beth and Andrew have agreed to take a few minutes out of their busy home life to tell us why thirteen is still their lucky number.

[The BAKER FAMILY enters the room, and they arrange themselves around the fireplace. BETH and ANDREW sit in wingback chairs across from KAYE. BETH holds a baby boy and sets a stroller holding two toddlers beside her as ANDREW wrangles two little boys on either knee. The other five children alternately sit or walk around the room. One, BONNIE™, approaches KAYE and gives her a hug.]

KAYE GIBBONS: Well, hello there. I know you! Bonnie™, you have gotten so big since the last time I came to visit!

BONNIE™: [grins] Today's my birthday—I'm ten!

KAYE GIBBONS: I *know*. And guess what? We have a *very* special gift for you today. You want to know what it is?

BONNIE™: [nods] Uh-huh.

BETH: Bonnie™, what's the magic word?

BONNIE™: [clasps her hands together] Pretty please with a Sweet Sparkles™ cherry on top?

ANDREW: [laughs] Good girl, Bon-Bon!

KAYE GIBBONS: Well, since you asked *so* nicely . . . ["Happy Birthday" begins to play as three production interns enter the room, pushing three identical baby strollers. BETH gasps, her eyes filling with tears.]

ANDREW: [clutches the boys in his arms and stands] Oh my God. Oh my God!

BONNIE™: [runs to the strollers and peers inside, then looks up in confusion] But I wanted a bike.

KAYE GIBBONS: Well, Bonnie™, we thought we'd get you something even better. Remember when your mommy and daddy were so sad because the little babies from China couldn't come?

[BONNIE™ nods.]

KAYE GIBBONS: Well, we have not one, not two, but

three baby sisters from China, flown here special just for your birthday!

[BONNIE™ begins to cry, but the camera pans to the joyful faces of ANDREW and BETH.]

ANDREW: We've got our baker's dozen!

[CUT to opening credit sequence of *Baker's Dozen*. The theme song, "Recipe for Love," plays as three more pictures are added to the credits, superimposed over chocolate chip cookie designs.]

VO: KAYE GIBBONS: This has been another *Fireside Chat with Kaye Gibbons*. To keep up with the escapades of the Baker family, tune into MetaReel on Tuesday nights at eight or watch the twenty-four-hour live feed on MetaReel.com.

SEASON 17, EPISODE 2

(The One with Bourbon and Cigarettes)

The dirt in the orchard is a little damp, but I sit on it anyway. Withered pieces of fruit lie scattered around me like forgotten toys, and the branches they've fallen from shiver in the brisk November wind. The scents of rotting apples, manure, and chimney smoke fill the air, and for a second, I can almost imagine I'm back in New Hampshire. Dad would be cooking dinner at home. Mom would be . . . still Mom. Probably doing a book tour and going on talk shows to sell her clothing line. And, let's be honest, I'd still be in the New Hampshire equivalent of this abandoned field—wearing more than the thin sweater I have on in California, but still running away from MetaReel, ditching the craziness at home.

I lean against the gnarled trunk of my favorite tree and take a deep breath. I think the idea of fresh air making things better is a myth. It doesn't take away pain—it sharpens it. I pull my knees up to my chest and press my eyes against my kneecaps until I see a fireworks display of color against my lids. Doesn't work. The image of my mother with her camera-ready face and doe eyes won't disappear. I want to open my mouth up to the sky and scream as loud as I can, but this is no time to turn into the tabloid disaster that was "Bonkers Bonnie™."

My mind spins, a pinwheel that never stops turning round and round. Just like it did in the days before my parents pulled the plug on the show, just like it started to in the driveway, which was why my fight-or-flight response kicked into overdrive.

Powder your nose and put on some lipstick before you head home. Don't cry! Puffy red eyes will only add to the misery that is your face. Remember, the camera adds ten pounds. Uglyuglyugly don't look at me, please, don't look at me.

I open my eyes. No cameras. No crew. Just me and the trees and the wind. I remind myself that I'm *Chloe* now—history doesn't have to repeat itself. I even have the yearbook picture to prove it.

My phone starts vibrating, and I fish it out of my pocket—Tessa. My finger moves to the little answer icon, hovering over it. There's no way I can go over to her house, not like this, and I know if I hear her concerned voice, I'll start sobbing and blab everything. The phone pulses against my hand: *liar, liar.* I clutch it in my fist until the vibrations stop and the screen tells me I missed a call.

My leg's cramping, so I'm starting to stand up, when I hear the crunch of gravel as a car pulls into the turnoff from the highway. Heart in my throat, I slide back down the tree trunk. I'd parked my car behind an old fruit stand, but it's easy enough to spot from the road if you look longer than three seconds, which most people don't. Lacey Production Assistant must have put some sort of high-tech tracking device on my car while I was busy going schizo on camera. Soon they'll be following me around, and that will be it—I'll have to start taking those pills again, the ones that make me feel like Lucy in the Sky with Diamonds. Happy pills for unhappy girls. *Shitshitshit.* This has to be illegal. I need a lawyer. I need a—

The ignition turns off, and I hear the door creak open, then slam shut. Footsteps come my way, and my stomach does a flip. Bastards. MetaReel cameramen are notoriously relentless—I know that better than just about anybody. I have thirty, maybe sixty seconds before they're on me. I crouch and run deep into the orchard, barely feeling the cuts that low-hanging branches scratch into my face as I fly past them.

I hear footsteps behind me, and my chest does this thing that reminds me of all those panic attacks I used to get, like it's on a roller coaster that jumped off its track, so I veer off the path and slide down to the ground, smearing mud all over my new jeans. I clutch at my knees and gulp in air until my heart stops trying to wring itself out.

Breathe. Breathe, dammit.

My body's on red alert, and I have to bite my tongue hard or else I'll start giggling. It's a horrible nervous habit—very straitjackety.

"Chloe—what the hell? Where are you?"

Benton™.

The adrenaline slips out of me and melts into the earth. It's just my stupid big brother who I love more than anyone else in the world. No cameras. No strangers. My legs are lead pipes, and I have the shakes of an addict, but I stand and make my way back out to the path.

Benny's standing a few feet away, holding a pack of American Spirits in one hand and a bottle of Maker's Mark in the other.

"Dude, why didn't you call?" he says.

The subtext here is *thanks for letting me get ambushed by a camera crew, etc.*

I shrug. My eyes are getting all weepy again, so I can't see the expression on his face.

"Oh, hell. Come here."

I tumble into his arms, and Benny wraps them around me. I squeeze him tight, and I hear the air whoosh out of his chest as he kisses the top of my head. He smells like woodsy cologne with a faint whiff of cigarettes underneath, and that Bentonness that is sort of indescribable but always reminds me of coconut macaroons. He hugs me tight and proceeds to curse out our parents, Kirk, MetaReel, and a number of other people, but because he's Benton™, it sounds like a soft, reassuring lullaby more than a tirade.

"Did Mom tell you what I did?" I ask.

I feel him nod. "'Sokay. I'm sure they won't air it," he says.

Uh-huh. Riiiiiight.

"Okay, I'm lying. I'm sure they'll air it in the most sensational way."

I wish I'd had the guts to say something into the camera. Now I'm just going to look like I was having another mental breakdown. Maybe I was. Maybe I am.

"I thought you were MetaReel," I mumble into his chest. "Did they follow you?"

Benny drops his arms and shoves the bourbon into my hands, then opens his pack of cigarettes.

"Dunno. Matt had to get back to school for football, so he dropped me off outside our gate, as usual. I took one look at the insanity and jumped into Mom's car. Then she calls as I'm driving away and proceeds to give me a lecture about driving while talking on my cell phone—for the benefit of the cameras, natch—and then is like, 'Oh, by the way, the show's back on, and Bons just freaked.' I knew you had to be here, so I came right over."

The flame from the lighter catches in Benny's eyes, and it's like I'm looking at two little pools of hopelessness. This is going to be equally hard on both of us, just in different ways. He takes a drag of his cigarette while I take a swig of the Maker's Mark. The fire feels good as it courses down my throat, but I grimace anyway because, God, it's disgusting.

"Where'd you get this?" I ask.

"Had it in my backpack. I'd left it at Matt's house last time I was there, and I was gonna put it back in Kirk's stash, but . . . I think we have better uses for it."

"Do you think they'll have an episode with an intervention? You know, 'the Dangers of Teen Substance Abuse,' blah, blah, blah."

The look on his face reminds me of season eight, when he convinced my sisters and me to "decorate" Mom and Dad's bedspread with his permanent markers.

"As the eldest in the family," he says, "I can assure you I will take full responsibility for all illegal activities conducted on or off the set by our persons."

The set. Our house is not a home anymore, it's *the set*.

"Eldest," I say, brushing the air with quotation marks.

"Two months, baby. While you weren't even a twinkle in Mom's eye, Lex and I were already rocking out in another woman's womb."

That would be the surrogate mom my parents lassoed to help them have Benny and Lexie™ before my mom was able to get pregnant with me. They're twins, but Benny's older by sixteen minutes and eight seconds. We'll all be eighteen by the time we graduate in June, which, considering recent events, cannot come soon enough.

"Ho," I say.

"Slut," he counters.

I sock his arm, and he kicks my butt with the side of his foot, like he's playing Hacky Sack, then he grabs the bottle out of my hand and gulps down a few shot glasses' worth. He passes the bottle to me, and I take a tiny sip. We weren't old enough to consider drinking last time around, but I did other things to dull the weirdness and pain. I run my hand over the bottle's cream label, feeling kinda freaked out that I'm, what do you call it, self-medicating? I only know this phrase because it's what the tabloids said about me four years ago. Benny seems to read my thoughts.

"This is just for today, 'kay?" he says.

My answer is another, larger, sip to drown the image that comes to mind of Tessa waiting for me at her house.

"Wasn't that fun?" I ask.

"What?"

"Having friends."

Benny twists the bracelet his boyfriend made for him last summer. "Yeah," he says, so softly I barely catch it.

I can hear Dad just like it's yesterday: *No more cameras. I promise, Bon-Bon. Just please don't hurt yourself again. I'll even come home, if that's what it takes.*

He didn't, though. Come home. Instead, Mom got full custody, moved us to the other side of the country, and married the contractor working on our new house. Dysfunction meets function. Or something like that.

Benny kicks a clod of dirt, and it bursts against a tree trunk. I feel like that's what just happened to my life in the past three hours.

"Dad's gonna flip his shit when he finds out," he says.

"Not like we would ever know," I mutter. His condo in Florida might as well be on Mars.

Benny flicks the ash off his cigarette and takes a long drag. "Oh, I'm sure the media will tell us what he has to say about the whole thing."

Yeah, that *would* be how we'd know his reaction. A celebrity gossip blog, a segment on *Entertainment Tonight*. Though I haven't spoken a word to him in four years, it's fairly easy to keep up with his B-list-celebrity self. Last I heard, he was doing some lame-ass charity golf thing in Hawaii.

I shiver and gaze at the tree branches overhead. I used to play this game where I'd look up at the sky and imagine that I was somewhere else in the world—Rome, maybe, or Thailand. And I would marvel at how the sky looks the same wherever you are on the planet, give or take some pollution. If I didn't look down, I could be anywhere but here.

Benny shakes his head. "It's gonna be so much worse than before."

"That bitch," I say, throwing a rotting apple down a path of trees. I rub my arm where Mom had grabbed me. "I can't believe she'd do it without telling us first. Not after . . ." I trail off, not wanting to actually talk about *It*. "Why didn't they tell us sooner?"

"Why did they make us be on this crazy fucking show in the first place?"

Suddenly, a lot of things start coming together: Mom's insistence last month on my getting that expensive haircut and the hour-long consultation at the department store makeup counter. That recent family portrait that she'd had us all take and Kirk's frequent business trips to Los Angeles. They'd been planning this for a while.

Benny takes another huge swig of bourbon. The bottle's only half full now.

"Okay, Dionysus, lay off the booze." I put the cap back on and start pulling him toward the car.

He stumbles over some roots in the path and nearly falls flat on his face, but he catches himself and looks up at me, his cigarette clamped between his two front teeth.

"Oh, my, what *would* the bloggers say if they saw me now?"

I give him my best look of disapproval. "You have to quit smoking, you do know that?"

"What, and take away an opportunity for Beth to show off her parenting skills?"

"But she's just a regular mom," I say, doing my best Beth Baker-Miller impersonation.

"Yes, and we can read all about it." He holds up his phone. "Preorder for only $24.99."

I look at the web page he's pulled up. "No." There's my mom's famous shaggy bob, her red hair vibrant against a plain white background. *Recipe for a Happy, Healthy Family.* I look up. "She wrote a cookbook?"

"*Au contraire.* This, my dear sister, is a tell-all. Convenient that it's coming out just a few weeks before the show starts up again, isn't it?"

He grabs his phone before it slips out of my hands.

~ ~ ~

Lexie™ picks us up, a ride I know comes with about five thousand strings attached.

"This is the last time I play chauffeur to your two drunk asses," she says by way of hello.

Benny struggles into the backseat, singing through the Beach Boys' greatest hits. "*I wish they all could be California girrrrrls,*" he croons.

Lexie™ rolls her eyes.

If my sister were a character in a Victorian drama, she would be the snobbish rich girl with a penchant for talking shit about everyone behind her fan. For the record, this is the *only* time she has ever picked up our, quote, two drunk asses. But who's counting?

"You know, Bonnie™, you don't want to come off as a total dropout," Lex says. "What were you thinking, getting all up in the camera like that? Super psycho, if you ask me."

She checks her side mirror as she pulls out, but it's more because she misses her reflection than any attempt at driver safety.

"I didn't ask you," I say, changing the radio from pop to oldies. "But you've always been the expert on making love to the camera, so maybe I should have."

"I was *twelve*. That's a healthy age to explore your body," Lex snaps. She puts the station back to Power 105.1—Today's Hottest Music!

I arch one eyebrow, a skill I perfected during season ten. "Is that what we call masturbation these days?"

Benny howls with laughter. "Ohmygod, I totally forgot about that!" He adopts the tone of a voiceover actor: "*Will Lexie™ be able to resist humping the living room couch? Or will her raging hormones get the better of her? Find out next week on Baker's—*"

"Shut up, Benny. At least I wasn't a nudist. Or did you forget that your boy parts had to be blurred out for all of season seven?"

"I heart my body," he says, making a heart with his fingers à la Taylor Swift.

Lexie™ ignores him, slowing down as we near our house.

"Keep driving." I put my hand on the wheel, but she pushes me off.

"Don't do that again, Bonnie™." There's a threat hiding in the silky folds of her voice, and I wish she would just freaking get over season thirteen.

"You know, I thought you'd be a little nicer to me now that the show's back on," I say. "Isn't this, like, the happiest day of your life?"

I hope I'm not a mean drunk. Am I? In so many ways I am my father's daughter. I switch the station back to oldies, just because.

Lex's eyes shift to me for a second and then she just shakes her head. "Forgive me if I'm not super quick getting over being on house arrest since we were thirteen. It's not like I was famous before or anything. And, you know, I totally love lying to my friends every day. And forget having a serious relationship. But whatever. No problem."

Instantly I'm furious, like I'm breaking out in a sweat, but instead of sweat, it's just pure, unadulterated rage oozing through my pores because, *God*, can she push my buttons, and I just want to freaking punch her face.

"Oh, I'm sorry, Lexie™," I say, my voice sticky sweet. "I had no idea I was keeping you from having a serious boyfriend. You mean all this time you didn't *want* to sleep with half the guys at your school?"

I know I've gone too far. Something like hurt flits across her face, but it's gone before I can feel too bad. It's not like she's ever held back to spare *my* feelings.

"Well, one of us has to get laid," she spits.

Maybe I deserve that for essentially calling my sister a whore, but it's still a low blow.

"Can you bitches *please* shut up?" Benny groans from the backseat.

"Well, now that the show's back on," I say, ignoring Benny, "you can stop blaming me for every problem in your life."

"Great. I'll just pretend the past four years haven't happened. Thanks, Bonnie™, I feel a lot better now."

I hate her because she's right. And because all of it's my fault— and *none* of it is. It was never just about protecting me. It was about what Dad did and the media storm and what people were saying about all of us and a million things I really don't want to, really *can't*, think about right now.

"Mom and Dad were the ones who canceled the show—" I start, but Lex's voice cuts through me.

"Because someone had to go all drama queen and eat half the medicine cabinet."

Then, "*Lexie™.*" It's just her name, but Benny's stacked a serious threat behind it.

For a second, it's just this heavy silence with the Mamas and the Papas' "California Dreamin'" playing on the oldies station which, you have to admit, is pretty ironic.

When I can't take it anymore, I adopt an I'm-going-to-be-the-bigger-person tone and say, "Lex, we can't go back until we give Benny a chance to sober up. Maybe we can grab some food or, I don't know, but I told you that on the phone—"

"My car. My rules. I didn't agree to anything," she says. "Besides, don't you think filming will be that much better with a little booze in you?"

Benny throws up his hands and starts laughing maniacally. Maybe I'm overreacting, but I think it's safe to say day one of filming is going to be a total disaster.

SEASON 17, EPISODE 3

(The One with the Retake)

*a*s soon as Lex pulls up to the front door, it swings open, spilling a rectangle of light onto the driveway. My little brothers and sisters—all ten of them—press their faces against the front window and crowd in the doorway as Mom rushes down the stairs, arms outstretched. I guess I have to open my door now. The blood rushes to my head as I step out of the car—that extra swig of bourbon was probably a mistake.

"Bonnie™! Benton™! Are you guys okay? I've been worried sick."

I take one look at her perfectly coiffed hair and fresh coat of lipstick and think, *Uh-huh.*

"We're fine."

My tone is borderline don't-screw-with-me, but all it gets from Mom is a twitch of her lips. The word *fine* covers up a multitude of sins, doesn't it?

A cameraman steps through the doorway and swoops down on us. I avoid him like he's a boy I seriously regret making out with.

I keep my eyes down, hair pulled forward. Then I duck past Mom to dodge the smothering hug she really wants America to see. I'm sure the doting mother angle would be great for book sales, but I'm not interested in being part of her PR machine again.

"No, you're not okay, Bon-Bon. It's been a long day for all of us." Lex bestows her sweet-as-sugar smile on me. "C'mon, sis. Let's get you upstairs."

She puts her hand up to block my face from the camera and wraps her other arm around my shoulder in the sort of protective embrace you see in tabloid pictures of stars walking out of courthouses or rehab.

I shrug her off. "Lexie™, what was that you were saying about not wanting to be my chauffeur?"

Cue evil glare from my oh-so-concerned sister.

Benny stumbles on the stairs, but he's able to grasp the railing just in time. Mom flutters around him, making maternal-sounding clucks and coos.

"I'm al-all right. I just gotta . . . uh . . . 'scuse me." He pushes past the cameraman who's suddenly in his face and grabs my hand, pulling me away from Lex and Mom.

As we make our way into the house, I stop in the hall, blinking. When I'd left this morning, there'd been a wall along the right side of the narrow hallway, sectioning off the kitchen. The wall is gone.

"Whoa." Benny stares with equal surprise at the lack of wall.

I hear a duet of giggling behind me. Farrow™ (fifteen, from Ethiopia) and Riley™ (fourteen, from Cambodia) grin at our shock. Back when the show was filming, the two of them were labeled the "bookworms." Quiet and withdrawn, they've been able to weather the storms by escaping into other worlds. Sometimes at night I still hear them whispering in their bedroom, reading aloud to each other.

"You should see your face right now, Bon," Farrow™ says. Her eyes are sparkling, and I'm pretty sure she's wearing makeup, which bothers me for some reason.

Riley™ socks Benny on the arm. "Crazy, huh?"

Benny just nods, still shell-shocked. A pointed look from me, and they scamper off toward the dining room, books in hand. There's a window seat in there where I know they'll hide out for most of the night.

My eyes sweep over the newness. There's not a bit of dust or tools or anything. It smells like paint—enough to get my head throbbing a bit—but when I touch my pinkie to the wall, it's already dry.

"This is just creepy," I mutter. Benny grunts his assent.

I peek into the kitchen, which is suddenly super shiny, with new appliances and bowls overflowing with fruit. There are even happy-happy photos of all of us on the fridge. I wonder if it's like this in the rest of the house. My bones turn to liquid when I think about the diaries hidden throughout my bedroom.

We keep walking, and when we reach the living room, I stop, dumbfounded. I can see my reflection in the bay window overlooking the backyard, and there're about twenty kinds of shock on my face.

"*What?*" This is all I can say.

Because I don't even recognize it. I mean, I literally could be in someone else's house. In the few hours since I left for school this morning, they've totally redecorated. It looks like someone robbed a Pottery Barn, then stole a bunch of paint from Home Depot. Mom brushes past us and corners Kirk, handyman slash stepfather extra-ordinaire. He's putting the final touches on a new entertainment center, doing something with power cords. Kids are running in and out of the room—someone must have given them soda or something because they're at a ten on the hyper scale—so Mom doesn't notice that I'm eavesdropping while pretending to check out the new photos on the mantel. Thirteen frames all lined up, holding those fancy portraits we recently got.

"Benton™ smells like a liquor cabinet," Mom whispers. "Can you get him somewhere private and sober him up? This is *not* how I want to start the show. We can't have—"

Mom shuts up as a burly guy sticks his camera into the archway that leads into the living room. His scuffed leather boots leave tracks on the cream rug, and he's wearing one of those OLD GUYS RULE T-shirts. He gives me a curt nod as he focuses on Mom and Kirk, but is otherwise silent.

"I'll handle it," Kirk says to Mom. His eyes drift over to the kitchen doorway at the other end of the living room, and I can tell he's looking at the cabinet above the sink where all the booze is. He purses his lips and looks in our direction.

I give him a wan smile and pull Benny back down the hall, toward our bedrooms upstairs.

"Oops," Benny whispers in my ear.

I hit his arm, and he stifles a giggle. My brother is a terrible drunk, but he's just as goofy when he's sober. Really, you can't take the kid anywhere. We go up three steps before we hear a "Wait!"

I turn around and—*wonderful*—it's Lacey Production Assistant. "Hey!" she says. She's like the Hollywood version of those girls who are always trying to get people to sign up for school clubs. Her toothy smile and eyes say, *C'mon! It'll be so much fun!* She was probably born with a clipboard clutched in her arms.

She gestures with a walkie-talkie toward what used to be a wall. "Chuck really wants to keep you all downstairs right now. So, if you wouldn't mind going into the kitchen—"

"Actually, I *would* mind—" I start, but Benny's already pushing me away from the stairs.

"Dude, I need some water," he says. "And I'm not going in there without you."

Chuck grins as we come into the warm light, his hands spread out with benevolent Jesus-like welcome. I guess this is how it's going to be, the head producer of MetaReel hanging around my house, acting like *I'm* the guest.

He's surrounded by a mass of kids who are positively glowing from the excitement of having the cameras in the house again. Boxes of pizza cover the table—most of them empty—and I see some bags from the mall piled in a corner. As usual, Chuck's playing Santa Claus. *He sees you when you're sleeping, he knows when you're awake. . . .*

"Hello, hello. We saved a pie for you," Chuck says. "Hungry?"

Benny and I shake our heads. I feel like I'll never be hungry again. Lex maneuvers her willowy frame so the cameras will catch her every perfect angle.

"I already had a salad, but thanks, Chuck," Lex purrs.

A couple of sound crew guys are leaning against the new granite counter, and they stare at her ass appreciatively. Lex gives them a little wink that makes me want to wring her neck. One of the guys grins, and his sound boom inches closer.

"Observe the phallic symbol as it stalks the rare sex kitten," whispers Benny in his spot-on Australian accent.

I snort/laugh louder than I would have if I hadn't been sipping on bourbon, and Lexie™ turns a snow queen glare on me. I smile like, *Who, me?*

My phone vibrates, and I pull it out. My mouth makes an O, and I show Benny the screen.

WTF Chlo? I've called you fifty times. I'm coming over.

"Oh, hell no," Benny mutters.

"Be right back," I say, racing past the cameras. I don't see the thick black cord running along the floor between the kitchen and hallway, and I trip over it, my knee coming down painfully on the carpet.

"Whoa! You okay there?" asks a sound boom guy.

Face flaming, I mumble a "yeah" and then limp to the downstairs bathroom. It's bad enough falling like a three-year-old in front of strangers, but that awfulness multiplies by about a billion when you know it just might make national headlines.

I breathe a huge sigh of relief when I finally close the bathroom door behind me. This is the safe zone—no cameras were ever inside unless Mom told them to film us doing makeovers or something horrible like that. I'm assuming the rule still stands. I rub my throbbing knee, then put down the toilet seat and call my best friend.

Tessa's never seen my whole family together. Even though Kirk is a new addition to the *Baker's Dozen* clan, we're immediately recognizable en masse. My teachers and friends have never met my mom— they would absolutely know her from the cover of her bestseller *There Are Never Too Many Cooks in the Kitchen: How Being Mom to a Baker's Dozen Changed My Life.* It's crazy, but no one has figured out who we are. Change a few names, keep a low profile, homeschool everyone until junior year—we've kind of created our very own witness protection program.

I don't have a good excuse for not coming over, but I tell Tessa there's drama at home, and I'm sorry I didn't call, and no, she really shouldn't come by tonight. She's never been inside my house, but she knows where I live from the occasional ride home. Tessa's not a gullible person, but she's always bought my excuses: my parents are really strict, they're not home much and I can't have guests if they're not around, I have to babysit. I'm used to bending and stretching the truth until it morphs into something socially acceptable.

"But you're still coming with us to the Tower District on Saturday, right? Before Mer's party?"

Meredith is the third in our trio, a vivacious drama girl whose theatrical antics somehow balance out Tessa's no-nonsense academia and my wallflower status. We have plans to go to Hand Me Downs, our favorite vintage shop in the arty area of downtown, before Mer's birthday extravaganza. It seems like forever ago that we'd had that conversation, but it was only yesterday.

"Yeah." I hope I'm not making promises I can't keep. Now that Chuck's in charge, I'll practically need a MetaReel release form to hang out with my friends.

Someone knocks on the door.

"Just a minute!" I yell. "I gotta go," I say to Tess. "I'll meet you guys there at one?"

"Okay . . . well, text me or something if you're bored."

"For sure."

I splash some cold water on my face because I'm definitely feeling like I had a bit too much to drink in the orchard, and I need to be sharp tonight so I don't humiliate myself any more than I already have. I groan into the towel as I dry my face off, then open the door. When I get out of the bathroom, Chuck is micromanaging everyone. He glances at the cell in my hand.

"Tomorrow we're issuing you new phones."

Translation: no more private calls.

My heart deflates until it's like one of those flat, useless helium balloons that gradually sags until you have to pop it to put it out of its misery.

Chuck starts to walk away, but I step in front of him. "You're not gonna bring cameras to my school, right?"

He leans back, just a little. His eyes narrow, reptilian, like he's not used to being challenged. But all my desperation warrants is his little shrug. "You know how it is, Bonnie™. I never know what's going to happen until it does."

"Well, I just . . . can we not do that? Because it's hard enough—"

"I promise I'll give you a heads-up. Could be fun, you know." His eyes hatch plots, but his smile is easy and reassuring. Well, it's intended to be reassuring.

"But—"

He's already walking away.

"Chloe."

Kirk, the stepfather I now equate with villains from Marvel comics, is standing near our bookshelf, which is bursting with the self-help books he loves to quote. He's into motivational stuff with words like *power, future,* and *success* in the titles.

I raise my eyebrows. "I thought I was *Bonnie*™ now." And it isn't until I hear the hurt in my voice that I realize how betrayed I feel about the whole name thing.

A pained look crosses Kirk's face. "I'm sorry about that, hon.

36

Chuck insisted we call you Bonnie™. I need to choose my battles with him so I can protect you kids and your mom."

I fold my arms across my chest. It's so clichéd, right? But it feels safer somehow. "Kirk, the best way to protect us is to keep the cameras out of here."

It's hard to explain to people who didn't grow up with them. Even Mom doesn't understand how being in front of a camera all the time twists and warps you. How one second it makes you feel unbelievably alive and the next publicly strips you down until all that's left is one big question mark.

Kirk leans against the bookshelf. "Trust me, sweetie, I realize that. I do! But your mom and I can barely keep a roof over our heads. There are fifteen mouths to feed, three of you going off to college next year. . . . The grocery bill alone is taking up most of my paycheck."

This gives me pause. I hadn't really thought about the financial logistics of the deranged venture that is my family. I mean, maybe on the periphery of my consciousness I've been aware that our family is big and has a lot of expenses. But being a TV family, money is something we always just seem to have. Money and lots of random swag. So where did it all go?

"What about my dad?"

Kirk snorts. In his world, Dad is up there with corrupt CEOs and people who kick dogs.

"I'm not letting Andrew take care of my family. He made his choice."

I instinctively flinch at the use of the possessive pronoun. *My.* I like (liked?) Kirk, but I'm not his daughter. Not for the first time, I wonder what guy in his right mind would sign up for this gig. *Thirteen* stepchildren and one crazy-ass wife.

Kirk puts a large hand on my shoulder. "No matter what happens, Chloe, your mother and I love you very much. Remember, only *you* have the power to control your response to challenges."

I barely resist the urge to roll my eyes.

"Bonnie™?" calls a woman with a sleek black pixie cut.

"Yeah?" I shade my eyes to see past the glaring white light that's set up on a tripod next to me.

It's Sandra, another producer from back in the day. She practically lived with us during the show, running around with curling irons and clothes from sponsors, getting us all spiffed up for special episodes and appearances. She's the one who designed all the clothing lines with our trademarked names and helped Mom develop her RealMom™ brand of household crap that sold at Target during our show years. To me, Sandra was never crew; she was like a big sister, favorite aunt, and girlfriend all rolled into one.

And this is the first time I've seen her since our last day of filming.

"Sandra!"

She grins and throws her arms around me. "You're quite a young woman now, aren't you?" she says. She smooths back my hair and straightens my shirt—old habits die hard.

"It's so good to see you," I say.

And I really mean it. When the show was canceled and the crew went home, it was like we'd lost half our family. These people I'd spent my entire childhood with just disappeared one day. Like they'd punched out at the end of a long shift at work and couldn't wait to get home. I have a hard time imagining that we were just a job for Sandra, that the show's cancellation was like getting transferred to another branch of the same company. But maybe that's what it was. How else do I explain why I haven't seen her in all this time?

"And it's *great* to see you." She kisses the top of my head and then hands me a bag of clothing. "We need you to change, hon."

How many times have I heard those words? *We need you to change.* Be thinner, be prettier, smile more, why can't you be like Lex, you're too emotional. . . .

"I like my clothes," I say. I hold the bag away from me, like it's poison.

"No corporate logos—you know that," she says, pointing to my hoodie. There's a tiny Adidas symbol on it. I'd changed into it while we were waiting for Lex, no longer able to handle the sweater-shirt from woolen hell.

"Also," she adds, "we'd like to keep you in dark tones. You know, the camera adds—"

"Ten pounds," I mutter. Here comes the no butter, no sugar, no deliciousness diet I remember from my youth.

"More of you to love," she says, giving my arm a friendly squeeze. Someone calls her from another room, and she throws her hands up in the air, already frazzled. "We'll catch up later, sweetie."

I trudge back into the bathroom. The clothes are a perfect fit but not my style at all. I like clothes you can paint a house in, and these threads scream teen pop star. In the left corner of the off-the-shoulder blouse, I see a silver embroidered *B.* My hands shake as I peel the shirt off and look at the inside label: BONNIE™ LASS DESIGNS. I throw the shirt onto the floor and shove my hoodie back on. I refuse to go back to being trademarked, to only being known by a name that is a brand. I stuff the clothing back into the bag and throw it into the little trash can next to the toilet.

When I go into the living room, Chuck is rubbing his hands together, looking every bit like the ringleader of our circus. My siblings stand around in a big circle—the bookworms, the triplets with their pigtails, and my five other brothers who alternate between being disgusting and adorable. Then, of course, there's Benny and Lex and me. A baker's dozen.

Sandra catches my eye and mouths, *Too big?* as she takes in my hoodie. I make a face and shake my head. She whips out her phone and starts typing on it. I may have won the battle on this one, but not the war.

"Okay, everyone, let's get started," Chuck says. "Now that we're all here, I'd just like to say that MetaReel is delighted to be invited back into the home of this wonderful family—with a great new addition, of course," he says, nodding to Kirk. Kirk smiles and gives a little wave at the scattered applause from the crew.

I know Dad was a cheating bastard, but I feel strangely offended. It feels wrong that Kirk's here, slipping into Dad's shoes like this. I keep thinking I'm in an episode of *Buffy the Vampire Slayer* and I'm going to find out this is all the result of an unfortunate voodoo curse.

"And I just want you all to know that Kirk and I hope you make yourselves at home," Mom says to the horseshoe of strangers around us. "The kids and I always felt like the crew was our extended family, and we hope that can continue."

We? No, I most certainly *do not* hope that can continue. But I see Sandra over in the corner, and I think about the old days and how the crew once baked me a homemade birthday cake and helped me play practical jokes on my siblings. For just a moment, I let myself sift through those memories. I've locked them away for so long; Hal dressing in drag for an impromptu fashion show, Dan teaching me how to waltz. Liz making finger puppets with me on a rainy day and Len telling us the same groaner jokes, over and over. I can't imagine it ever being like that with the people in our living room. I know it's illogical to assume the old crew could just leave their lives and come film my family, but I can't help but feel hurt that it was so easy for them to pack up and never look back. Not once.

"Thank you, Beth, we're delighted to be here," Chuck says. He turns to my siblings and grins, clapping his hands like a carny touting his ride. "Now, kiddos, it's time for our first interview of the season!"

The little ones don't know what this means, so they start jumping around. Those of us who've reached puberty look at one another and shrug. Interview segments blow. They always ask inane questions or want you to just riff off of whatever when all you want to do is relax in your own home.

"Chuck, some of us have homework. Can this wait?" Benny asks.

Kirk steps up to Benny and gives him a little clap on the shoulder. "It'll just be an hour or two. Besides," he adds, with a hard look, "seems like it might be tough to concentrate on homework after your antics this afternoon." Busted. Benny's eyes slide over to mine, and I give him a sympathetic frown.

Kirk points to the stairs that lead to the basement. "Down you go," he says.

Benny shrugs a *whatever*, but we're standing so close that I feel his whole body tense up.

"Matt's gonna freak," he says to me in an undertone. "He's starting tomorrow night, and he is so not gonna understand why I'm not at the bonfire. I'm supposed to be there in half an hour. I knew it was a mistake to date a jock."

Poor Matt. It makes me sad to picture him at the bonfire rally thing that the football team has the night before big games, scanning

41

the crowd for Benny, pretending it's no big deal because everyone at school just thinks they're best friends. They're both in the closet, but for different reasons. Matt's family is super religious and would probably think they could de-gay him. Our family knows (*has* known for years and years) and doesn't care, but Benny has no desire to be the next poster boy for gay rights. The media would just eat that up, analyzing old episodes to see what they'd missed all those years.

"I'd cover for you, but there is no way I'm letting you drive," I whisper back.

Benny sighs and starts rapid-fire texting Matt.

"Are you gonna tell him?" I ask.

"Not this way," he says, meaning text. "I told him I got stuck with babysitting, but now he wants to know why you won't do it."

"Tell him I have a date." My stomach flutters as Patrick Sheldon's face comes to mind. Unrequited love sucks.

"Bonnie™, think of a realistic excuse," Lex says.

"Why do you have to be such a bitch all the time?" I snap. Of course, this is the moment the camera decides to be focused on me.

"Do you mind?" I ask the dude behind it.

I don't care if he's just doing his job—his "job" is to ruin my life, and I'm not going to pretend I like it. His face is expressionless, and he keeps the camera trained on me because, I don't know, maybe Bonnie™ will lose her shit. Again.

Mom moves in front of the camera and flashes a strained smile at all of us. "Okay, kiddos, let's get downstairs."

Tristan™, the family jock, vaults down the stairs like it's an Olympic event. Maybe his birth parents were Russian gymnasts. The seven-year-old triplets—Daisy™, Violet™, and Jasmine™—form a little train and hold on to one another's waists as they make their way toward the basement. The rest of the younger boys—Lark™, Deston™, and DeShaun™—horse around behind them. MetaReel deemed them "the wild things" back in season eleven, and I've never been able to decide whether it was a self-fulfilling prophecy or a keen observation. Magazines and TV show hosts used to say they were ADHD or whatever, but here's the thing: that's just a label MetaReel got people to use so no one would say, *Hmmm, maybe they can't concentrate for shit because there are cameras on them 24/7.* But what do I know?

"Woo woo, chuga chuga chuga," shrieks Daisy™.

"Get this, get this." Chuck nudges a cameraman with a mop of sandy red hair and Pumas. Puma Guy gives Chuck a silent thumbs-up and slowly follows my siblings. A sound guy is behind him, trailed by Lacey Production Assistant, who's gripping her clipboard like it's the last life preserver on the *Titanic*.

Much as I hate to admit it, it's a good TV moment. I look at the kaleidoscope of kids all heading down the stairs, making a big, beautiful multicultural caboose. Mom and Kirk look on, their arms around each other, and I get this sudden flashback of how it used to be, with us kids running around and Mom and Dad chasing after us, laughing. A lump forms in my throat, and I think of Dad watching the show from wherever he is, not a part of it anymore. Even though it's totally his fault everything's so screwed up (mostly, anyway), I wish he were here.

The younger teens—Farrow™, Riley™, and Gavin™ (resident musical genius)—stumble down the stairs, trying to be cool but really just as excited as all the others. Then there are the bios (Benny, Lex, and me—the biological children of my mom and dad): we sort of shuffle along behind the rest with varying degrees of awkwardness, and it takes about ten hours for us all to get into the basement. Other than the bios, the rest of the kids come from all over the world or foster homes in the U.S. We're like the poster children for alternative families. And broken homes.

I can tell from the shouts downstairs that more surprises await us. I want to be rebellious and brave and refuse to listen to the Man as played by MetaReel, but I'm exhausted, and I can tell from the defeated slump in Benny's shoulders that he is, too. The adrenaline rush of the past few hours is over, and I can already see that I've lost.

The basement has been transformed into a lounge filled with beanbag chairs and hammocks that hang from hooks in the ceiling. Posters cover the walls, and a new foosball table sits in the corner next to an enormous TV. There's even a fancy keyboard for Gavin™. He bolts to it and starts filling the room with the hopping trill of a ragtime he learned earlier this week. If he doesn't become a screwed-up child star with a drug habit by the time he's twenty, the kid might play at Carnegie Hall.

Four stationary cameras are set up so that the whole room can be televised 24/7 on MetaReel.com. Benny and I lean against a wall, watching as the kids check everything out while Lex flits around, playing Perfect Sister. The new lighting shines on her wavy blond hair like a halo, and when she smiles, you can almost forget she's heinous. Almost.

Benny cracks his knuckles one by one. "I need a cigarette."

"I need . . ." Something. But I don't know what. "I need to not be here," I say. That much is clear.

"Bonnie™? Benton™? Can you guys come up for a minute?"

Kirk is at the top of the stairs, motioning for us to follow him.

"Yep. I was wondering when this moment was going to arrive,"

Benny says. He's got the look of a man who knows the jury's gonna say "guilty."

"Coming," I call up. I turn to Benny. "Sucks."

"Oh, yeah."

When we get upstairs, Kirk and Mom are sitting on the new couch in the living room, where the lights are now turned down low. A few candles are lit, and their flames create little shadows all around the room.

"Mom . . ."

There's a plea in my voice. It says, *Can we please have this conversation in private? Can we not do this right now?*

Mom looks down at her hands and starts pushing against her cuticles with her fingernails. I can tell Kirk's not used to being on camera like the rest of us because as he gestures to the longer part of the new L-shaped sofa, he makes the rookie mistake of compulsively looking at the nearest camera out of the corner of his eye.

"Let's get it over with," Benny says with a sigh.

I plop down as far away from the parentals as possible. At this point, I'm not sure what makes me more wary—the argument we're about to have or the presence of the cameras. There are three set up at various angles. I see we have Puma Guy, Old Guys Rule T-shirt guy, and one of the dudes from the kitchen.

"I'm sorry we didn't tell you earlier," Mom says.

She clasps and unclasps her hands, and I wonder what this must be like, to have to parent people on TV who are practically adults themselves. I almost feel sorry for her, but then her recent book cover flashes to mind. I raise my chin and decide that silence is the best policy. She deserves to sweat a little.

Kirk puts a hand on her knee. "Beth, let me handle this." He turns to us, his steely eyes never leaving ours. "Before we discuss anything else, I think Benton™ has something he needs to explain." He holds up the Maker's Mark like he brought it for show-and-tell. Damn. He must have searched Lex's car.

Benny sighs and shakes his head. "It's true. My name's Benton™, and I'm an alcoholic."

I snort, and Benny grins.

Kirk's face goes red. "Drinking is no laughing matter, son."

"I'm not your son," Benny says. His voice is harsh, like it belongs to somebody else.

"But you're under *my* roof—"

"Dammit," says one of the camera dudes. "Hey, guys. Can you hold on a minute? I gotta re–white balance with this candlelight."

"What?" I say, incredulous.

Chuck peeks in as the guy holds up a light meter and adjusts his camera. "Looks like we'll have to do this scene again. Kids, can you just go back from your entrance? This is looking great."

Benny and I glance at each other, and I know he's thinking the same thing: hell. We are living in hell.

Praise for
Praise for
Recipe for a Happy, Healthy Family

"A triumph. Beth Baker-Miller gives a raw and honest portrayal of a family's struggle toward hope."
—*Modern Woman Magazine*

"A must-read for fans of *Baker's Dozen*."
—*Celeb Weekly*

"A fascinating look at a unique and inspiring family."
—*Good Life Magazine*

"Beth Baker-Miller knows what it's like to be a Reel
—and a *real*—mom."
—Janet Clark, author of *It's Never Too Late:
Starting Over After Forty*

Seventeen years ago, Beth and Andrew Baker started a family. Believing that there was nothing more important than to "Fill Your House with Laughter™," they decided to have thirteen children—a baker's dozen. What began as a private wish soon caught the attention of MetaReel head producer Chuck Daniels, who took it upon himself to make the Bakers' wish come true. Over the next thirteen years, the Baker family grew, delighting audiences across America with their precocious antics and fun-loving playfulness. But all good things must come to an end. Here, in her first memoir since the cancellation of the show, Beth details how Andrew's infidelity and the media frenzy surrounding their crumbling marriage affected her children—and gave her the courage to move on. With never-before-seen photos and a first-ever look into the life of the Baker family since the show's cancellation, *Recipe for a Happy, Healthy Family* will reunite you with America's favorite family . . . and introduce you to their newest addition.

SEASON 17, EPISODE 4

(The One Where I Ditch School)

My eyes skim over the pages of *1984*, but it's hard to concentrate on totalitarian England, even though my house is currently being taken over by Big Brother. I didn't do the reading last night, and I'm trying to catch up so that I don't look like a dumbass when Schwartz starts discussing it. But after spending the night staring at my bedroom ceiling, all I can see in front of me is a pile of letters and punctuation. Then one sentence catches my eye.

I grab my pen and underline *Nothing was your own except the few cubic centimeters inside your skull*. I bet I'm the only person here who really understands this.

I glance at the clock above the whiteboard. Its simple white face and black numbers say *steady job*, *data sheets*, and *uncomfortable ties*. So not inspiring to young, inquisitive minds.

One fifteen: Schwartz is late again. You can pretty much depend on an extended lunch for the first ten minutes of gov. Usually I love the noisy chaos of the room before Schwartz ambles in, but all I can think of is MetaReel. Every time the door opens, I tense up, waiting for Chuck and a camera dude to walk through it. But it's always another student, adding to the euphoric *It's Friday!* conversations about tonight's game, dates, and movies.

Tessa's sitting next to me, finishing up her calc homework. Every now and then, she curses under her breath or gives her long black ponytail an angry pull—typical grouchy Tessa. It's comforting, that bit of normal. I want to tell her that a MetaReel camera filmed me eating my Cheerios this morning. I could just lean over and say it, like it's something of note. *Weirdest thing*, I'd say. *It seems America is going to be interested in my breakfast habits.*

"Poor eraser," I say instead, flicking the red bits of rubber that cover her desk.

Tessa just shakes her head. "Poor *me*. Kelson's a sadist. I can't believe he expects us to actually answer these questions."

The door bangs open and I jump, my hands clutching my copy of *1984* as if it has the power to ward off evil production companies. Mer catches sight of Tessa and me and stomps over in her knee-high Doc Martens. With red curls frizzing all around her and a dark green scarf draped dramatically around her neck, she looks like an irate Celtic goddess bent on some serious destruction.

"I've decided that Hamlet is a total douchebag," she says, plopping down at the desk in front of me. "Why is Ophelia into him?"

"Because he's a prince?" I say.

"Because she's a doormat," Tessa mutters.

Mer holds up a well-worn copy of *Hamlet*. "The NYU audition is next month, right? So I chose Ophelia, only I can't get into the part *at all* because I would never want to be with some mopey emo dude

50

like Hamlet." She throws the play onto her desk, then slams her fist on the cover, like she's punishing it. "I should have done Juliet."

"So you'd rather be with a mopey emo dude like Romeo?" Tessa says.

"At least he wants to marry her! Hamlet's all 'get thee to a nunnery.' Asshole."

I trace invisible shapes on my desktop. "Total douchebag."

"Or maybe he's just misunderstood?" a familiar voice says.

Every cell in my body suddenly becomes hyperaware, like I'm on the red carpet at the Emmys, and the camera flashes are hot and bright, and my face hurts from smiling, and I know the whole world is watching. I turn around. Patrick Sheldon is slouched in a desk in the back corner, arms crossed. He's a patchwork of threadbare flannel and thrifted denim, and his hair is greasy, like he hasn't washed it since the seventh grade. God, I want him.

"Misunderstood?" I repeat. *Wantwantwant him.*

"Yeah," he says. "Dude's got a lot on his mind. What with his dad being murdered and all."

"Oh, come on—" Tess starts.

Mer points at him. "Mopey Emo Dude."

Then she shoots me a too-obvious look that says, *We so don't have the same taste in men.* I give her the evil eye.

Patrick shrugs. "Labels." He points at Mer. "Bohemian Drama Girl." Then to Tess. "Overachiever."

Tess raises a fist. "Asian pride."

Patrick looks at me. He cocks his head to the side, then the ghost of a smile dusts his lips. "Enigma."

Is that good or bad?

I know I should look away. This is the part where I look away. *Look. Away.* I grab my book, my eyes shifting to the cover.

"As fascinating as this discussion is," I say, holding up *1984*, "Schwartz is totally gonna pop-quiz us in about three minutes."

I turn to the front of the room, but Patrick exhales—a soft, derisive little snort.

"What?" I ask, with a quick glance behind me. "Is it so crazy that I have negative zero interest in bombing this quiz?"

He smiles. Just a twitch on the left side of his lip, but it's a smile. "There's no negative zero."

"Whatever." My lips turn up a little, though, and his eyes hook mine.

I hold his gaze until my cheeks grow warm and then I pull away and stare at the whiteboard. Sometimes Patrick and I slip into easy conversation, where I forget all about my secrets, and it feels like I'm just a normal girl talking to a boy who makes her insides flutter. Other days, I can hardly say a word, too scared I'll let something slip. I used to talk to everyone, everyone in the whole world.

But that was before.

I drown out Tessa and Meredith as they continue their *Hamlet* discussion until it's like I'm sitting underwater in the deep end of my pool and they're somewhere above me—far enough away for me to pretend they're not really there. This lasts for approximately four seconds.

"Hello . . . Chloe . . . Earth to Chloe," says a voice above me.

I blink twice. "Huh?"

Jason Calloway is holding a digital camera and snaps a photo before I can come up with one of my customary excuses.

"Jason, what the hell? Give me that!"

I lunge for the camera and grab it out of his hand before he can dart out of my way.

"Whoa, settle down, Baker," he says. "It's just a little shot for the senior yearbook spread."

"Not anymore," I say.

I bring up the last picture on the screen and hit the Delete button, ignoring Jason's muttered curses. I watch my surprised face turn into a blue screen that says "No Image." I wish I could do that to every *Baker's Dozen* DVD in the world.

"What's your problem, Chloe?"

"My problem," I say, dumping the camera into his outstretched hand, "is that you can't just go around taking pictures of people without their permission. It's, it's . . ."

I trail off, struggling to put into words what every part of me knows to be true.

"It's a violation of privacy," says Patrick.

I shoot him a grateful look. He just shrugs.

Jason holds up his hands and takes a dramatic step backward. "Don't sue me!" he says. I flip him off, and he grins. What a little bastard.

Tessa poses for Jason. "How about a picture of the only member of the Taft High Korean-American club?" she asks.

Jason laughs and takes the photo while I slink farther down in my chair and stick my head in my backpack, pretending to search for something inside. God, like, fully half the class is looking my way— why did I have to make such a big deal about the damn picture?

Cue the perfectly timed entrance of Mr. Schwartz. Behind him is one of the kids from the AV club, carrying a tripod in one hand . . . and a camera in the other.

What is up with this week? Have I offended the gods or something?

The paperback in my hand starts to warp under my palms, and the room begins to shift slightly, shimmering like a mirage. I wish I could remember all those weird affirmations and breathing exercises my therapist from last year taught me, but right now all I can think is, *Don't lose it, Bonnie™, don't lose it. CHLOE, don't lose it.* Oh hell oh hell oh hell. I've slipped into using my old name. Bad sign. Very bad sign.

Schwartz organizes some papers on his desk while everyone watches the AV kid set up the camera. The red light blinks at me, and it's like everything I've been trying not to think about since first period just floods back in, all at once, until I'm drowning in it. I'm dying, and nobody notices. They're doodling in notebooks and texting under their desks, and just when I wish somebody would see me, I'm suddenly invisible.

"Okay, folks—*1984*," Schwartz says, waving around his copy of the novel. "Imagine that this was in every class." He points to the camera. "In every room in your house. How would it make you feel to have Big Brother watching you twenty-four, seven?"

Schwartz sits on the edge of his desk and folds his hands over one knee, letting his gaze sweep over us, a shark looking for a victim. I can't breathe, I can't breathe, I can't—

"Like shit," I blurt out.

I did not just say that out loud. I did *not*.

For some reason, I look back at Patrick. Our eyes lock, and something in his agrees with me, says *yes*. My face gets sunburn red, and I turn back around, but now I see that they're all looking at me, and right now, I almost miss the Bonnie™ era. If I were two-dimensional again, I wouldn't have to see the expressions on my classmates' faces. If I were enclosed in flat screens, the high-definition broadcast version of me could believe they weren't even there at all.

"Okay. . . ." Schwartz looks at me for a long moment, and I can tell he's trying to decide whether to welcome my passionate response and riff off of it or say I have to stay after class.

I don't wait to find out. I grab my backpack and run out of the room, and I don't stop until I reach my car. My hands are shaking so bad that I can barely get the key in the lock, and I check over my shoulder about fifteen times to see if the campus security dude in his little go-cart has spotted me yet. Fifty hours later, I get inside the car and somehow make it out of the parking lot without any red rent-a-cop lights flashing behind me. It isn't until I'm on the highway that I realize, *Holy shit, I just ditched school.*

SEASON 17, EPISODE 5

(The One with Uno)

I drive until the constant buzz of incoming texts gets to be too much.

"Okay!" I yell at my phone.

I swerve into the next strip mall and park in the middle of the half-full lot. I don't know if MetaReel has bugged my car or not, so I get out and cast a furtive glance over my shoulder, as if the police are hot on my trail for playing hooky. I glance at my phone: ten texts.

"Damn."

I run across the lot and into Cleo's, a little café with dessert and coffee that I've been to a few times with Tess and Mer. It's perfect, full of dark corners meant for lovers. I know I'll be able to hide out here for a couple hours. A college kid gives me a bored hello, and I say hello back, wondering if it's obvious I'm supposed to be in school right now. I try to look nonchalant as my eyes sweep over the menu behind the counter, but my mind keeps playing my psychoness in Schwartz's class on a loop. I can't believe I said *shit* in class. And then ran out. *God.*

I order an oversized peanut butter cookie and a mocha. I only picked at my lunch, and I'm sort of looking forward to drowning my sorrows in sugar and caffeine. I check my texts while the barista makes my drink. Tess and Mer sent simultaneous WTF texts followed by worried texts followed by *seriously, call me right now* texts. They must have gotten hold of Benny because he sends me one, too. Unlike them, though, he gets why I'm being a weirdo. All he says is:

Will meet you after school. Where you at?

I text him back and, when my mocha's ready, I head over to a huge velvet chair, where I spend the next two hours alternating between trying to read *1984* and staring off into space. I think about how maybe it's time to go back to homeschooling because I'm not sure I'll be able to show my face at Taft again. Like, *ever*.

At three ten, Benny walks through the door. He's my lighthouse. Always has been. No matter how lost I feel, he's there to guide me back to myself.

"Lay it on me, sister."

I tell him everything, and the tears come only when I can see the sadness around his eyes and the way he tries to hide his worry by fidgeting with the stuff in his pockets.

"It won't happen again," I tell him, my voice colder than I intended. "*God*." I look out the window, but instead of the parking lot I'm seeing orange plastic bottles lined up in my parents' cabinet.

Season thirteen sits between us, lonely as a buoy in the middle of the sea. Benny swallows. Stares at the palms of his hands.

Disappointment crashes through me. "It's just . . . I got the yearbook picture taken, you know? I thought—"

"I know," he says. Gentle.

I fold and refold my napkin. "It's like normal's never gonna happen."

"True story." He stands up and grabs my backpack, then holds out a hand to help me up. "Let's go home."

Home.

I'm not really sure where that is anymore.

~ ~ ~

"Bonnie™, I need you to help your brother with babysitting tonight," Mom says.

She'd called me into her bathroom while she was getting ready, which is *Baker's Dozen* code for *I don't want the cameras to hear this*. It's the reality TV equivalent of spy movie tactics, except we don't need to turn on the shower or play really loud music to hide our voices.

"What about Lexie™?" I ask.

"She has a date—and didn't get drunk last night."

I open my mouth to protest, but she shakes her head. "I could smell it on your breath. Do it again, and you'll be babysitting until the triplets graduate from college."

I sink onto the toilet seat and wish, not for the first time, that I'd been one of those kids people abandon on church steps.

"You're just gonna leave us here with MetaReel all night?"

Mom pulls at her wrinkles, frowning at her reflection. "No. The cameras will be gone in half an hour. We're just getting some dinner with Chuck. Should be back by ten or so. Jasmine™ has a cough, so don't let her run around too much, and Deston™ needs to do his homework. Make sure Farrow™ doesn't spend too much time online and . . ."

There's no way I'll remember her specific instructions for each of the ten kids. My definition of a successful night of babysitting is that no one died and the house didn't burn down.

". . . and don't forget about the laundry. It's in the dryer, but it needs to be folded."

I stand up. "Okay. You'll be home by ten, right?"

There's a scream downstairs. "MOM!"

"Oh, God. Now what?" She pushes past me on her way out the door, then turns around and squeezes my shoulder. "Thanks, Bons."

"Uh-huh."

She hovers in the doorway, looking uncertain. "I'm sorry about yesterday," she says.

I don't say anything, just stare at the chipped polish on my toenails.

"I know it's a major adjustment, sweetie. But it's for the best. I promise."

From downstairs again: "MOM! Tristan™ took my doll, and he won't give it back!"

She sighs. "Okay, then. We'll talk later."

We won't. We never do.

"MOM!"

As she leaves the room, I think about how Mer and her mom have a standing lunch date every Friday. I've always been jealous of that—other than little snatches of time like this, I haven't been alone with my mother since I was in the womb. I'm about to run after her, tell her I'm sorry for being angsty, when I remember that she just wrote a memoir she didn't bother to tell any of us about.

My phone starts vibrating—Tessa.

I close the door behind me and sit back down on the toilet seat. I hit the green button on my phone before I can change my mind. "Hey."

"Chloe! Are you okay? I've been trying to get ahold of you for, like, ten hours."

I sigh. "Yeah. I just . . . it's a really long story." Like seventeen years long. "Is Schwartz super pissed?"

"No. I think he was worried, more than anything. He asked me after class if there was something going on." She pauses, and when I don't say anything, goes, "Chlo, you're freaking me out."

I should tell her. That would be the smart thing to do. But I can't. A crazy part of me is hoping this will all go away. The other part just wants to hold on to Chloe for a little while longer before Bonnie™ takes over.

"I know. I'll try to keep the psychotic episodes to a minimum, okay?"

She ignores my joking tone. "*Chloe*. Spill."

I clutch my cell phone and rest my forehead against the cool bathroom wall. "It's stuff at home," I say. "And I can't talk about it. Not right now. But I promise I will when . . . when I'm ready."

There's a long silence on the other end of the line. I can hear the growling, guttural voice of Amanda Palmer playing in the background and the sound of Tessa tapping her pen against her desk.

"You know you can tell me anything, right?"

I'm not Catholic, but I can sort of see why people go to confession. It must feel so amazing to be able to tell someone who you really are.

"Yeah," I whisper.

Someone pounds on the bathroom door. "Bonnie™! Mom says you have to come down now!"

Violet™—one of the triplets.

"Who's Bonnie™?" Tess says.

"Oh. Um. My sister's going through an invisible friend phase. Hey, so I gotta go babysit. Sorry for the freak-out."

"See you tomorrow for Hand Me Downs?"

I'd forgotten. "Sure. Sounds good."

I hang up, open the door, and plaster a smile onto my face. Violet™'s dressed in a pink tutu and a mini football jersey, and there's a camera behind her—Old Guys Rule T-shirt dude.

"You silly girl," I say, pulling on one of her pigtails. The camera loves this shit. I hate how trying to please it is so ingrained in me.

I am puppet, watch me dance.

"Look what I can do!"

Her version of a cartwheel involves her knees being parallel to the ground, but I applaud and then we go downstairs to where a mob of children are scarfing down half of the local KFC.

The cameras are weaving in and out, zooming in on little arguments, pulling away to get the full effect of our chaos. One of the cameramen smells like sweat and French fries, and my stomach turns. Benny mimes shooting himself in the head; I pretend to hang myself. When the cameras finally leave and Mom and Kirk follow them out, it's as if the house suddenly gets bigger, brighter. My face hurts from trying to make it look normal, and my limbs feel heavy from my lack of sleep and the endlessness of this day.

Lex comes down the stairs wearing a skintight black dress and red hooker high heels.

"Working tonight?" Benny asks her.

"Very funny," she says.

There's something resigned in her expression, as if she's playing a part MetaReel cast her in long ago. It occurs to me that Lex might feel just as abandoned by our mom and dad as I do. Maybe what I always thought of as willful sluttiness has actually been an attempt to fill the gnawing parent-shaped hole we all share. Too many times, I've seen her creep in well past midnight, lipstick smeared, her underwear peeking out of her purse. She never looks happy. Just tired and ready for one of her cucumber masks.

"Lex," I say, putting a hand on her arm.

She startles at my touch—that's not something we do. Touching, I mean.

"What?" She narrows her eyes, the blue lakes of them reduced to two thin streams.

"If you get back early, maybe the three of us can . . . watch a movie or something?"

She looks at Benny, and he shrugs. He's got two boy monkeys hanging on him and one of the triplets trying to apply lipstick to his cheek.

"Yeah, I don't think so," Lex says. "I'd say the time for sibling bonding is pretty much over, wouldn't you?"

She pushes past me and throws open the door just as a red sports car pulls up with Jay-Z blaring out the windows.

"Don't wait up," Lex says over her shoulder. She slams the door behind her.

"What was that about?" Benny says. I know he's talking about my impromptu invitation—Lex's bitchiness has been the new normal since season thirteen.

"I don't know. I was feeling charitable. Stupid me." I rub my hands over my face and shuffle into the living room. "Who wants to play Uno?" I ask.

~ ~ ~

It's close to midnight, and Mom, Chuck, and Kirk still haven't come home. By now, all the kids are asleep, and Benny and I are sprawled on the living room couch, watching an old episode of *Sex and the City*. The past twenty-four hours have left me numb. If called upon, I'm not even sure I'd be capable of doing basic math. Uno with the kids had been fun, though. I knew it would be one of the last times I'd get to hang out with my siblings without a camera capturing every moment, so I'd tried not to get annoyed or bored, even when my brothers decided it would be really fun to play Fart on Bonnie™.

"I wish Stuart wasn't so gay with a capital G," Benny gripes, as one of the show's characters sashays across the screen.

I sock his arm. "Don't discriminate against your own people."

"But look at him. I mean, *plaid*? Ugh." His cell phone goes off, and he jumps up. "It's Matt."

"Matt wears plaid," I say.

"Shut up."

I give him a little wave as he heads toward the stairs and up to his room. When I hear the garage door open a minute later, I change the channel to PBS so Mom doesn't know what we were watching, then turn off the TV. The living room is now completely dark. I stand up and am trying to pick my way through the maze of toys and games on the floor when the door opens and I hear my name. I freeze, listening.

"—going to be hard for Bonnie™. That's what I'm most worried about."

Mom.

"Kids?" she calls.

I crouch down and crawl into a corner as I hear Mom's heels on the wood floor. I feel like an idiot, but I can't waste an opportunity to find out what new hell Chuck is planning for us. I'm tired of being caught off guard all the time.

I see Mom's reflection in the living room window as she steps into the hallway. A forty-year-old version of Lex. If Lex had red hair. She rests her hand on the banister and looks up the stairs.

"All quiet on the western front," she says, then returns to the kitchen. "Guess they're up in their rooms."

"I'm gonna turn in, honey," Kirk says. "Gotta be up early tomorrow for that Redding job. For what it's worth, I think you're making the right decision."

Right decision—about what?

She sighs. "I hope so. 'Night."

Chuck and Kirk exchange good nights, and I hear the stairs creak under Kirk's weight as he goes up to the master bedroom. A chair scrapes against the floor and the fridge opens, then closes. A clink of glass, the hiss as a bottle opens. The pop of a wine cork.

"Thanks," Chuck says.

I don't need to see them to know Chuck is drinking one of Kirk's Heinekens and Mom's downing a glass of Chardonnay.

Chuck: "Look, I love Bonnie™ as if she were one of my own kids. You know that. We're not supposed to have favorites, but she's always had a special place in my heart."

Screw. Him.

"But, Beth, you've got *twelve* other children. Are you going to agonize over every decision about this show because one of them has become a little camera shy?"

Camera shy? I guess that's what we're calling me wanting some goddamn privacy.

"Of course not," Mom says. "But even you have to agree that this isn't just any episode."

I wish I'd heard the beginning of this. I consider walking in there and demanding to know what they're talking about, but that's Bonnie™. Going in with guns blazing always backfires on her. Chloe has to play this smart.

I ease over to the little decorative cutout in the wall. From here, I can see their faces as they sit at the kitchen table. Chuck's folded hands and serious expression make him look like a Sunset Boulevard Yoda. Mom's organizing the art supplies the triplets left on the table, putting crayons back in boxes and stacking construction paper as she talks.

"The rest of the kids will be okay with it," she says. "Maybe even excited, once they get over the shock. But Bonnie™ . . ."

"Bonnie™'s a teenager, Beth. She's going to be hormonal about anything we do."

Why do people think it's okay to chalk all teen emotion up to hormones? As if they're less real or something.

My phone starts vibrating in my pocket, and I frantically push buttons to get it to stop. It sounds like a freight train. I duck down just as Chuck's head begins to turn in my direction. After a second, he continues pontificating, and I let out a silent sigh. I look at the screen—Mer. She'll never know how bad her timing was.

"Beth, this is going to be a beautiful episode. It's a great way to kick off the show. All heart."

I peek over the ledge of the cutout in the wall. Mom is running her finger around the rim of the wineglass, her lips pursed.

65

"What if people think this is just a stunt?" she says. "I'm doing this show because I love my kids and I want them to have everything I never had. But the tabloids are going to say I'm exploiting them— you know they will."

"I hear you, I really do," Chuck says. "It's a dramatic beginning. But we gotta think of the ratings, Beth. It's how we keep you on the air."

I wish Benny were here. Maybe he'd be able to decode this better than I can. Something big is going down for our first episode. Something Mom's convinced I'm not gonna be happy about. But what? *What?*

"You're right," she says. "I know you are. I just think we need more boundaries than last time, and I'm not sure this isn't crossing one."

Chuck nods. "I couldn't agree more. Trust me: you are the final word on how the world sees your family."

Mom pinches her nose with her thumb and index finger. After a minute, she lets her hand drop. "I'm terrified of our audience losing sight of what this family is about."

Chuck leans forward, resting his elbows on the scratched surface of our huge kitchen table. "Love, Beth. It's about *love*. The best kind—messy and imperfect and *real*. People are gonna watch the show because you've taken everything the world has thrown at you and you've still come out on top. Stronger than ever."

I don't think my parents getting a divorce is coming out on top. Apparently, neither does Mom.

"But everything with Andrew . . . how is that inspiring? How is that about love?"

I think of my dad, doing whatever it is he's doing in Florida. Does he know the show's back on? Or will he find out like the rest of the country—from commercials and magazine ads and talk-show interviews?

"But that's just it, Beth. You're a single mom who got dealt an impossible hand. Then you were so brave, willing to love again, after everything Andrew put you through. This is an *American* story. Half the women watching *Baker's Dozen* have had their marriages fail. You're showing them . . . you're showing them how to fail *well*."

Wow. Chuck Daniels, ladies and gentlemen.

Mom laughs, a bitter, tired sound that flicks at the air. But it's at herself, not him. He drains his beer, then sets it down. The sound of the bottle against the wood is like a gavel—Chuck's word is law.

"Growing pains, Beth—that's all you're feeling. MetaReel's gonna take good care of your family. That's a promise."

He stands up and gives her an awkward pat on the back. "This'll be your best season yet," he says. "You'll see."

When the front door closes behind him, Mom presses her fingers to her skull and starts massaging her temples.

"Okay, okay, okay," she whispers.

As if saying the words could magically make them come true. But I already know that whatever Chuck has planned, it's not *okay*.

SEASON 17, EPISODE 6

(The One with the Retro Sunglasses)

*B*enny talked me off the ledge when I told him about the conversation between my mom and Chuck, but I still feel like jumping off a building. Preferably a tall one.

"You can't control everything, Bons," he'd said. "MetaReel's gonna do what they're gonna do. It's all about how we respond to it. Us getting wasted . . . not the best response."

And because of that bottle of bourbon we shared, neither of us is really in a position to negotiate with Mom. I know if I bring up my eavesdropping with her, she'll see it as more proof that I'm getting out of control. And I can't have her think I'm going off the deep end again. That will just give Chuck more episode ideas.

Still, I can't stop replaying the whole thing. I feel sick just thinking about the first episode. Why would it be particularly bad for me? I've gone through all kinds of possibilities in my mind, but the only thing that would truly mess me up would be if the cameras came to school. The worst part is, I have no idea when it's all going down.

Our show doesn't air until the end of November, but they're shooting the footage now.

"Oh, hells *yes*! I am so wearing this tonight," squeals Mer.

I snap back to reality. Mer holds a mod red dress against her body, then runs behind the leopard-print curtain in the tiny dressing room at the back of Hand Me Downs.

"That's hot," I say, belatedly.

My words sort of hang in the air, and I smile at Tess to cover up their clumsiness.

"You okay?" she asks.

"Yeah," I lie. "You know how it is when parentals are nuts. It's all good."

She gives me a concerned look across the vintage accessories table, and I busy myself with a rack of sunglasses. I've been two beats off all afternoon, tone deaf to their bubbly, glittery Saturdayishness. Even Tessa, our resident grump, has the Saturday bug.

So far she and Mer have been cool about not pushing me to tell them what's going on, but I know it's only a matter of time before they stage an intervention. Hastily, I grab a huge pair of seventies sunglasses and model them for Tessa, my voice peachy-keen light because I'm fine fine fine.

"Like?"

Tessa grins. "*Love.* You so have to buy those." She holds up a vintage tee that says *The Too-Loud Polka Parade* with cartoon drawings of a polka band. "I can't resist this."

"It's perfect for your collection." Not that she needs any more—Tessa has three drawers full of offbeat T-shirts at home.

I check my reflection in the gilt mirror over the 1920s hat

display. The frames are see-through mauve, with dark lenses that take up half my face. They're perfect for when the Vultures descend: movie star sunglasses that put a thin, plastic wall between me and the flashing cameras.

The dressing room curtain opens with a flourish. "What do you guys think?"

Mer's in the red dress, her long auburn hair falling in waves over her shoulders, and she juts out one hip and rests a hand on her waist. All she needs is a catwalk and a pair of white, knee-length patent-leather boots.

"Hello, 1965," says Tessa. "Two enthusiastic thumbs-up!"

I point at her with a lace parasol. "That dress has 'It's My Party and I'll Cry if I Want To' written all over it."

"Yes!" She dances back into the dressing room singing one of her goofy, made-up songs. *Parents out of town! Cha-cha-cha. Party at my house. Cha-cha-cha.*

Tessa rolls her eyes in Mer's direction and calls, "Don't quit your day job."

"What-ever!" Mer sings.

The clerk bites her lip to hide an amused smile—she probably thinks we're silly little teenagers. She looks like the kind of girl who might carry her own flask, a regular Tower District type. Tattoos snake up her arms, and her lips are vixen red. It's a cool contrast with her 1950s housewife dress, and I wish, not for the first time, that I had the guts to look like that. But then people would look at me, which is sort of not the point of trying to be wallpaper.

Finished changing, Mer sashays toward us, the dress over one arm. "You guys ready for some Vicenti?"

Vicenti is heaven on earth—an amazing Italian deli with dirt-cheap sandwiches and creamy gelato. On warm summer evenings, the line snakes out the door and around the block.

"Oh, yeah." Tessa glances at me. "You're gonna get those, right?"

I take the glasses off. They'll draw attention, but they also scream *personal bubble*.

"Yeah."

We pay for our stuff and head down the street. It's a chilly afternoon—for California, anyway—so the usual buskers aren't serenading pedestrians with their guitars. This strip features some of the only independent businesses in our suburban town, where there's a Walmart or McDonald's every few blocks. The Tower District's a mishmash of boutiques, coffee houses, performance spaces, and thrift stores. Everyone who doesn't fit in comes here, the San Joaquin Valley's own little slice of San Francisco.

"Chloe!"

I jolt as Mer shouts my name, certain that a MetaReel camera must be pointed right at me. But no. When I follow her gaze, I go warm all over. Patrick Sheldon's behind the counter at Spin, the only indie record store between LA and San Francisco.

"Mer, don't stare at him," I growl.

"You know, I was looking for a David Bowie record. Maybe—" Tessa starts to cross the street, but I grab her.

"We are *not* going into Spin. We're going to Vicenti." There is no way I can face Patrick after acting like a lunatic in gov yesterday.

They both ignore me and sprint across the street.

"You guys suck!" I say, catching up to them.

Tessa swats my arm. "No we don't. We love you. And you *loooooove* him. So we're going in there."

Just seeing him with his elbows on the counter and his head in a book makes me swoon. The way his hair gets in his eyes and how he bites his lip in concentration . . . yum.

"I don't know what you see in that dirty brainiac, but *comme tu veux*," says Mer. That's Mer's French for *suit yourself*.

"I disagree," Tessa says. "He's got this *je ne sais quoi* about him." (They're both in French III.)

Tessa opens the door and practically shoves me inside. Patrick immediately looks up and breaks into a startled grin.

"Baker!"

It's a Schwartz thing—he never uses first names in class, and the people who get his weird fabulousness (he once asserted that the Declaration of Independence was sexy) take up the habit. You always know a Schwartz devotee by the use of last names.

"Hey, Sheldon," I say.

He puts a scrap of paper between the pages of his book (*1984*) to mark his place.

"Lee, Mason," he says as Tessa and Meredith come in behind me. "What's up?"

"Mopey Emo Dude! I didn't know you worked here," feigns Mer. "This is *so* what Hamlet would do if he wasn't a rich-ass prince."

Patrick shrugs. "I basically get paid to read and listen to music all day. It's pretty excellent."

"Um." Tessa glances around. "My dad's birthday is coming up so I'm gonna . . ." She points in the general direction of the store.

"If you need help, just, you know." He gives a little wave of his hand.

"Got it. Thanks. Mer, can you show me that album you were talking about?"

"Yep. This way."

And just like that, they're waltzing toward the rock section.

I think I'm about to have the longest conversation I've ever had with Patrick—well, the longest one where it's just us. I smile at him and point to the book.

"What part are you at?"

He flicks his hair out of his eyes (want want *want* him) and says, "I might spoil it for you—where are you at?"

"The first time Winston and Julia go to the apartment."

"Kills me."

"Right? It's like you just *know* it's not going to end well. I mean it can't, but I love how for a little while, they just don't care," I say.

"Have you read it before?"

I shake my head, and he pulls a pack of Wrigley's spearmint gum out of his front pocket.

"Man, are you in for it, then," he says.

"That bad, huh?"

"Oh, yeah."

He offers me a piece. As I reach for it, our fingertips brush against each other, like two dogs touching noses. It's only for the span of a heartbeat, but my blood instantly turns fizzy. I stick the gum in my mouth and busy my hands with folding and refolding the wrapper.

We're silent for a minute, but it's a good silence. I can hear Tessa and Mer murmuring at the back of the store, no doubt theorizing on what our body language suggests about the potential for coupledom. I gasp when Radiohead's "Talk Show Host" comes on.

Patrick nods his head to those first shivery opening chords: a slow, melancholy dance between bass and guitar. "It's a good one, huh?"

"It's been in my head all day—this is so weird." The first line is *I want to, I want to be someone else or I'll explode.* So, yeah. In my head all day. "It's one of those songs that make me stop whatever I'm doing and just . . ."

"Yeah. Yeah."

So we listen for a while, me leaning against the counter, Patrick lightly tapping its surface in time to the music with his finger. Thom Yorke's wild, crazy, beautiful voice serenades us, and I think, *Not bad, Chloe. Not bad at all.*

"Chloe."

"Hmm?"

"Yesterday in class . . . I mean, you don't have to talk about it if you don't want to, but . . . are you okay?"

I think the noise I make is a nervous laugh, but I'm worried it might sound more like a bray. Then I start talking, because I have to answer, right? And it's like I'm on speed, each word rear-ending the next in its haste to spew out of my mouth because I want to skip over the me in this and just be a normal girl talking with this boy who gets under her skin in the best kind of way, but it's unavoidable, what I did, and I wish I could go back and undo it, but I can't. And so that's why Patrick Sheldon will never, ever be my boyfriend and I hate, just completely *hate*, my life. I want to be someone else or I'll explode.

I say, "So stupid, huh? I had to get out of there, and it seemed like a dramatic way to, uh, ditch. I was thinking about that dumb yearbook picture Jason took and was sort of like, *agh*! And then Schwartz was waiting for an answer, and I thought, Hey, what the hell—it's true, isn't it?"

74

"What?" he asks, eyebrows drawing together, so so cute.

"That it would feel like shit. To be on camera all the time."

"Oh. Yeah. Definitely."

Shut up, Chloe aka Bonnie™, shut up. But I can't. I have to fill the dead air between us, because the silence is dangerous now.

"I mean, hypothetically true," I say. "Obviously I don't *know* know, I just—"

"Chlo, ready for some lunch?"

Saved.

I turn around and flash Tessa a grateful smile. "I'm starving. You got what you needed for your, er—"

I can't remember the excuse she gave and, apparently, neither can she. Her eyes widen, and my stomach jumps into my chest. There's a scary five seconds in which I'm certain Patrick's going to be all, *Oh. She likes me. Poor girl.* But Mer saves us.

"Sheldon. My house—tonight—eight P.M. My parents are out of town, ergo *party.* Are you free?"

My heart starts beating a *say yes, say yes,* but I know that even if he comes, I'll probably get nervous and avoid him. What's the point when in a few weeks' time, everyone will know what a freak I am?

He looks over at me. "Are you going?"

My eyes widen, and there are internal fireworks, and all I can say is, "Um. Yeah."

Tessa and Mer elbow each other none too subtly.

Patrick smiles his crooked upturn of the lips. "Then I'll see you later tonight."

He grabs the record out of Tessa's hand and raises his eyebrows. It's a ninety-nine-cent Weird Al Yankovic album.

Tessa shrugs. "It called to me."

He laughs and puts it in a bag after he rings her up.

"See you tonight," Mer chirps.

Patrick picks up his book and nods. "Later."

My eyes snag on his, but I can feel a blush creeping up my neck, so I say a quick good-bye and stumble out the door.

"Success!" Tessa says, pumping her fist as we walk down the street. "I *knew* he was into you! Haven't I been saying that for months?"

"You guys are shameless," I mutter. They don't buy my grouchiness. I can't hide the goofy smile that snuck onto my face as soon as I left the store.

Mer shimmies down the sidewalk, ignoring the amused glances of passersby. "*Parents out of town! Cha-cha-cha. Party at my house. Cha-cha-cha!*"

Tessa gives me a long-suffering woe-is-me look. "This is *before* wine coolers. She's going to be out of control tonight."

Mer turns around and grins. "I'll hold your hair back if you hold mine."

We pass a newsstand where glossy tabloids yell at us with words like REHAB, CHEATING, and EXPOSED on the covers. It feels like someone just threw a bucket of cold water on me. Like, *Wake the hell up, Bonnie*™. How many headlines will I have this time? Which trashy magazines will put me or someone from my family on the cover?

Patrick better not be crushing on me right when everything changes and I can't have him.

~ ~ ~

I take a sip from Benny's red plastic cup and grimace. "*Bleh*. How can you drink this stuff?"

"Because I'm so manly." He puffs out his chest, and I can't help but laugh.

We're hiding out on Mer's back porch, away from the spilled beer and loud laughter.

"Whatever," I say. "Just . . . don't get crazy. Camera phones are not our friends."

I don't trust people I barely know to resist the temptation to sell a story or a picture to *Us Weekly*.

Benny takes another drag of his cigarette. "MetaReel rears its ugly head."

"Yeah."

He snorts as a few of Mer's drama friends fall into a pile on the trampoline that takes up most of her backyard. They laugh and shriek and crawl all over one another with tipsy affection. The old, familiar ache comes back, pulsing and raw. I wish I could laugh so hard my stomach hurt. Don't remember the last time I did.

Benny blows his smoke away from me, out the side of his mouth. "I can see the headline now: *Benton™ Baker, Raging Alcoholic?*"

We shouldn't have come.

"Let's skip out," I say. "If Chuck saw us leave the house, there could be cameras on their way and—"

"He didn't see us!" Benny's voice is laced with frustration. I've been a nervous wreck ever since we got here, wondering if Patrick will show, half hoping that he won't. "We were careful, trust me. Just . . . enjoy being out while it lasts."

The sliding glass door opens, and the sounds of the party dance in the air: Kanye West, drunken laughter, hollering.

"There you are," says Tessa. She's wearing the hilarious shirt she bought on her last trip to Korea with her family that has pictures of smiling flowers around the words *Life is beautiful. Be my happy place.*

Her lips turn up in an impish smirk. "He's here."

My body reacts as if it just jumped out of a plane—elation followed by sheer panic.

Benny gives her a puzzled look. "Who's here?"

"I'll answer that with a riddle: what walks on two legs and is the object of Chloe's affection?"

He laughs. "Ah. Sheldon." He turns to me. "Get your ass in there, Chloe."

My voice goes whiny. "Can't you go with me?" He takes a particularly long drag as if to say, *Nope. Nada. End of Discussion.*

"*Please?* You guys are friends, you can make it less weird."

"Chlo, Sheldon's not gonna make a move if your big brother is standing right next to you," he says. "Now, *go.*"

He swats my butt, and I sock his arm before Tessa drags me inside. The smell of beer and a million different perfumes and colognes hits me as soon as I enter the living room. In the half hour I've been outside with Benny, Mer's house has filled to bursting. I recognize almost everyone, but that doesn't make it any easier for me to carry on a conversation. I don't know how to do teenager. Every time I try, it's like I'm a thirty-year-old cast in an after-school special.

"Tess—"

I spin around, scanning the crowd for her jet-black mane, but Tessa's been absorbed into the fray. I can't believe she ditched me. Out of the corner of my eye, I see Patrick. We're separated by at least fifteen people, but my whole body is attuned to his, as if after all these months, we're finally on the same frequency. His lanky frame moves smoothly through the sea of bodies, somehow avoiding being jostled. He's encased in a bubble of cool. Me? I'm standing here, turning around in circles like I'm in one of the Mad Hatter's teacups at Disneyland. I lose sight of Patrick when a group of football players pushes past me to get to the backyard.

"Excuse me. Sorry. Oops, sorry. Thanks," I mumble, trying to orient myself.

"Chloe."

I feel a slight tug on my sweater, and there he is, looking down at me.

"Patrick—hi."

Damn. The way his lips twist, like he's got a secret but isn't telling, gets me every time.

"I'm guessing this isn't really your scene," he says. Is that because I'm wearing only jeans, a T-shirt, and a comfy sweater when every girl here is dressed to kill?

I shake my head. "Not so much. But it's Mer's, so . . . I'm here," I finish lamely.

"So what is your scene?" he asks, shouting a little, to be heard above the Lady Gaga mix the lead in this year's school musical just put on.

"I don't have one," I say. "What's yours?"

He laughs. "I don't have one, either."

A couple of Mer's show choir friends start doing an improvised cheer while a guy from my English class gets ready to do a keg stand.

Patrick shakes his head and leans close so I can hear him. "Don't you ever feel like they're all on a different planet or something?"

"*Yes*," I say. I start laughing as I look around me. "I'm so glad you're here. Usually I just hide in a corner and play on my phone until Tessa or Mer rescues me."

"Anytime, Baker."

I point to the dining room. "Thirsty?"

He gestures for me to lead the way, and I take him to the cooler on the dining room table. I grab a Coke and Patrick takes a beer and says something to me with an adorable smile, but I have no idea what, because two guys next to us have decided to play a violent version of thumb war that involves reciting a litany of every curse word known to man.

"What?" I shout, over a particularly creative string of expletives.

Patrick looks at the guys and rolls his eyes, then moves his lips close to my ear and says, "I was saying that I'm really glad you came into Spin today."

I shiver a little as his warm breath touches my ear. "Me too."

There's about eleven seconds when I feel like we could almost kiss, but then Mer's shouting in the living room for everyone to gather round.

"Looks like the birthday girl's going to make a speech," I say. My eyes flick up to his, and I hear myself saying, "Keep me company?"

"That's why I came."

I bite my lip to keep my grin a respectable size, and he follows me to the living room. Why wasn't he flirting with me last year, when I was relatively normal? Tessa says it's my fault he hasn't asked me out yet because I'm the human version of the shower in her downstairs bathroom; hot one minute, cold the next. But Patrick's not like other guys. He's really hard to get a read on, so I never know where I stand with him. I mean, compare yesterday in Schwartz's class with today—totally different, right?

Mer is holding court on top of the coffee table, a copy of *The Vagina Monologues* in one hand, a bottle of cheap wine in the other.

"So, some of you may know that I'm auditioning for NYU next month." Everyone cheers, and she shakes her hips. "So I'd like to practice one of my monologues, because it's my birthday and that means you all have to listen to me. Am I right?"

Cue drunken *hell yeahs* from the kids sprawled on the couches.

Mer catches sight of Patrick and me, and a diabolical grin spreads across her face. Her cheeks are too red, and her eyes have an unnatural brightness.

"Chloe Baker and Patrick Sheldon! This one's for you. It's called 'Because He Liked to Look at It.'"

I give her a not-so-subtle look of death and pull Patrick toward the kitchen, my face redder than Lex's hooker stilettos.

"She's wasted," I mutter. I can't even look at him. "Sorry. Mer's—"

"Bohemian Drama Girl?" he says. He seems more amused than anything. Still, I'm going to kill Mer the first chance I get.

"Right. She's definitely dramatic."

We're standing close, in a little corner off the kitchen, and I'm getting distracted by the way his hair hangs into his eyes. I need to stop staring at him and think of something to say so that I can drown out Mer's impromptu performance. I wish she'd done Ophelia.

"So . . . how long have you been working at Spin?"

"About a year. I'm saving up for a post-graduation trip."

"That's awesome." Someone turns up the music, and I have to shout. "Where are you going?"

He shrugs. "Don't know yet."

"I'm dying to go on a road trip. My brother and I have talked about it, but . . ."

Now that's not going to happen. Not with being recognizable again.

He cocks his head to the side. "But . . . ?"

I shrug. "Who knows? June's far away." Cue subject change. "You have bio with Benny, right?"

"Yeah. We're lab partners." He bumps my shoulder with his in a friendly way. "He talks about you all the time."

I groan inwardly. My brother as matchmaker. "Good stuff, I hope."

His eyes never leave mine. "Definitely." Then again, maybe I don't mind Benny talking me up. "Do you have any other brothers or sisters?"

I choke on my soda. "Sorry," I cough, "wrong way." I think of the thirteen framed photos on the mantel in my living room. "Uh, yeah, a couple. Hey, do you know what the homework was for Schwartz's class? I didn't get a chance to, er, write it down yesterday."

"What with the hasty exit."

"Right."

Someone pushes against me and, for just a moment, I grab onto Patrick's arm to keep my balance. Best two seconds of my life. He looks down at me, and everything gets all effervescent and fluttery, and he has the most amazing lips, they're perfectly shaped, and I can't help but wonder what it would be like to—

I let go of his arm, but he's still looking at me with this we-have-a-secret smile. After a few more seconds, he says, "What were we talking— Oh, yeah. Homework." He runs a hand through his hair, like he's clearing his head. "It's a current events report and—Chloe?"

I don't move, I don't even breathe. All I can do is stare at the camera that has materialized behind Patrick. They found me.

Patrick turns around, then looks back at me, confusion etched in his face. I barely register him. I'm a deer in headlights that's got a few seconds to live. I have to warn Benny. But just when I'm about to run to the backyard, the camera moves past me and I see that it isn't MetaReel after all—it's just Simon from the AV club.

"Yay! Simon's here," shouts Mer. "Guys, he's getting footage for the senior video. So make love to the camera!"

I'm an idiot. I try to shake off the panic that is threatening to show Patrick and half the senior class what a madwoman I am. It probably only takes a few seconds for me to ball it up and hurl it somewhere deep inside me, but it feels like forever. Finally, I put my Coke on the counter behind me and look up at Patrick.

"Sorry," I say. "I, uh, was just thinking about—never mind. I actually have to go, but, um . . . yeah. I'll see you?"

My escape plan is lame.

I start to walk away, but Patrick grabs my arm. His hand is warm, and for a second all I can think is *he's touching me*.

"Chloe. Did I say something or—"

I shake my head, mortified and freaked out. I can feel . . . can feel the panic attack creeping up on me, like some Navy Seal hit squad with camo paint on their faces and night vision binoculars. "No! God, Patrick, no. I'm just tired and, you know, curfew. . . ." I roll my eyes like, *ugh, parents*. "Sorry. I better get Benny—"

"Wait." He pulls out his cell. "What's your number?"

I open my mouth to tell him, but then I remember what Chuck said about our phones. "Um. I'm actually getting a new number, so . . . maybe, could I have yours?"

"Okay, hold up."

He grabs a pen out of his pocket and an old receipt and writes his number on the back. Then he folds it, reaches for my hand, puts it on my palm, and closes my fingers over it. I wonder if his skin is tingling as much as mine.

"I really want you to call me. Will you?"

I stare at the paper and nod. "Yeah."

"And I don't want to do the whole wait-a-few-days game." He smiles. "Maybe if you're up for it, we can do something tomorrow."

I think Patrick Sheldon just asked me out on a date. I forget all about the impossibility of him and me and grin, wishing I hadn't made up that dumb excuse about having to go home.

"Yeah, that'd be . . . great."

"Excellent. I'll talk to you tomorrow then."

"Okay."

I stand there for a minute, certain I must be levitating, I'm so freaking high on this boy. Then I push through the crowd, gripping his number. I look behind me, but all I see is his back heading toward the door. He'd come to the party only for me.

On Monday, Benny and I get to school way before the first bell. MetaReel's not allowed on campus, so I actually wake up early just to hang out in the Taft parking lot. The first episode doesn't air for three more weeks, but I already feel tense, every muscle in my body poised to run at the sight of the paparazzi. Even though they haven't released our photos, MetaReel is already promoting the show; on our way to school, we passed a new billboard that has a picture of thirteen stick figures with two bigger ones off to the side. It says, THEY'RE BACK, with the MetaReel logo in the corner. It would only take a little bit of detective work and a couple of gossipy Meta-Reel employees for the media to know where we are.

My eyes hungrily scan the familiar school buildings, and I feel a pang of—this is going to sound so strange, but it's the only way I know how to explain it—I feel a pang of *homesickness*. More than any place in my life, Taft has been mine, uncorrupted by the pervy camera eyes and the crew and my parents and my million siblings. Before this weekend, I had actually started to feel *normal*. It was delicious. But now I'm already saying good-bye. Soon, every moment will take on significance. It's going to be a month of lasts. There will be a last class, of course, but also a last opening of my locker, a last caf lunch, a last trip to the weird world of camaraderie in the girls' bathroom . . .

Benny's voice punches into my reverie. "Penny for your broody thoughts?"

"Leave me alone. I'm busy wallowing in self-pity," I say.

"Thought as much." He tries to make his voice sound light, but I can hear the nervous energy underneath it.

We press our fingers against the heater, watching the student body sleepily make its way into the parking lot.

"Where's Matt?" I finally ask, taking a sip of my extra-scalding mocha. Usually they meet up during our Starbucks run, but today Benny had insisted on the drive-thru.

"Freaking."

I curl up on my side and take in the dark circles under Benny's eyes.

"But you're still together," I say gently. Part of me is jealous—I haven't been able to tell anyone about this crap, but Benny not only has someone, he has a significant someone.

"For now," Benny says. "But when it all starts really happening . . . I mean, I'd be fine if people found out I'm gay, but if the Vultures go after Matt . . ."

I nod. The cultlike megachurch where Matt's family goes is most definitely not supportive of the Benny and Matt persuasion. Case in point: his pastor had recently said that God made Adam and Eve, not Adam and Steve.

"Subject change: what did Sheldon have to say when you called him on Sunday?" he asks. I hadn't mentioned anything about a date, just that Patrick had given me his number.

I was really hoping to avoid this conversation. "I didn't call him."

I jump as Benny shouts, "*What?*"

"I couldn't! All I have is my MetaReel cell. I can't call Patrick on a bugged phone! I tried to leave the house, like, five times to get to that old payphone they have at the gas station, but Chuck kept making us redo all those shots."

And, okay, I psyched myself out. The more my attempts to call Patrick failed, the more certain I became that this was a sign from the universe. It's not meant to be.

"Tell me you contacted him in some way," Benny says.

I shake my head.

"E-mail?" Benny asks.

Another shake.

"Text?"

Nope.

"Smoke signals?"

I sigh. "I like him too much to lead him on, Bens. It wouldn't make sense if I was all of a sudden like, Oh hey, I can't ever see you, but I like you, too."

"So write each other love letters! He's old-school—I bet he only listens to vinyl and shit like that."

I start tearing at the sleeve of my Starbucks cup, just to give my hands something to do.

"Benny. Even if he doesn't care about our crazy-ass family, I could never go on a date with him—I'm not interested in inviting Chuck and the rest of the crew along to dinner and a movie. So there's no point in leading him on."

He shakes his head. "Seventeen and never been kissed."

I shove him. "Low blow, Benton™ Baker." I drain my mocha and put it back in the cup holder. "This will be a moot point after the show airs."

"Why?"

"No more Taft High," I say. "It'll be homeschooling until we can get the heck out of Mom and Kirk's house." Kirk had converted the garage into a classroom, complete with whiteboard and projector. From nine to two every day, the Baker School for Children on Home Arrest is in session.

I throw some faux sparkle into my voice. "I can't wait to have one of the Hulks try to teach me Spanish. On the plus side, I bet we'll get to do art projects with pipe cleaners and fingerpaint."

The Hulks are these two ladies who teach my brothers and sisters five days a week, so named because they're both over six feet tall.

Benny's eyes widen. "Did Mom seriously say we'd have to quit Taft?"

"No." I shrug. "But I can't imagine coming here after the show airs. That would be, I don't know, suicide."

Benny's face darkens. "Not funny, Chlo."

Right. Season thirteen, episode nineteen, "The One Where I Get My Stomach Pumped." I kiss my fingers and place them against his forehead.

"You know what I mean," I say. I'm not interested in hanging around Taft once my family's dirty laundry starts airing every Tuesday at eight and streams 24/7.

We both jump as someone raps on the back windshield. Tessa waves, and I start to open my door, but Benny puts a hand on my arm.

"You've got to make it right with Patrick. I won't live with lovesick Chloe for one more second. He wants you. Just . . . go for it, already."

I point to a handsome boy across the parking lot, a young Taye Diggs in a football jersey. Benny was right—Matt looks freaked. "You first," I say.

Benny follows my finger and sighs. "See you later."

As I get out, Tessa practically pounces on me. "Aghhhhhh!"

"Aghhhh." Tessa ignores my mocking tone, probably taking it for embarrassment. She knows I hate being the center of attention, which is fine because she and Mer are always happy to take on that burden.

"What did he say? Did he confess his undying love? Did he say he has wet dreams about you?"

"Eww! God, Tessa, it's like seven thirty in the morning. Can this line of questioning wait until I've digested my breakfast?"

"You eat coffee for breakfast. Now, spill," she says.

This was one of three things I was dreading today. The other two were running into Patrick (shocker) and going to Schwartz's class.

"There's nothing to spill. I was busy, so I didn't have time to . . . call him."

"What?"

People have got to stop looking at me with that expression and saying "what?" Mer spots us as we enter the hallway and pretends to be a cheerleader doing a victory cheer. Have I mentioned she's an exhibitionist?

"Gooooooo, Chloe!" she yells.

A few people look my way, and I send up fervent prayers that a hole will mysteriously open in the ground and swallow me up. As usual, God ignores this kind of thing.

Tessa takes me by the shoulders. "What is going on with you?"

I can't look her in the eye, so I stare at my All-Stars like, *Oh wow! I have shoes on! Cool!*

"Seriously. It was craziness at home. I told you that," I say.

At least this isn't a lie. It was total mayhem yesterday. Chuck put us through what amounts to a reality TV bootcamp, going over all the dos and don'ts for Kirk and the kids who are too young to re-member about acting natural when a camera's in your face and not talking about the show outside the house and yadda yadda yadda.

I shrug off Tessa's grip in a friendly kind of way as the bell rings. Thankfully, she's got AP math and science classes I'm not smart enough to take (it's true—TV rots your brain, especially when you're on it), so I won't see her until lunch.

"Don't forget I'm a journalist, Chloe Baker. I'll get to the bottom of this!" she says as I make my way up the hallway, toward English lit. I've no doubt she'll try—she isn't the editor of the school paper for nothing. I raise my hand in a backward wave as I continue walking away. I don't have to turn around to know she's scowling at me. Honestly, I'm not sure which is more complicated: high school or being on TV.

I'm sure my outburst in Schwartz's class is why I keep getting weird looks from random people in the halls, but I try to convince myself this is a good thing; it's like I'm cross-training for the marathon of shame that's coming up in three weeks' time. If this regimen of people staring at me, friends grilling me, and me avoiding a certain absurdly sexy boy continues, I will be in great shape for our pilot episode that airs on Thanksgiving night.

I'm two hours into the day, and I already need more caffeine. Trying to be invisible is exhausting. I see Benny and Matt having an intense discussion by the lockers between second and third periods, and Benny shoots me a tortured look before going back to their conversation. I must have a similar expression on my face too. It feels like it looks like that.

"Hey," a voice says.

I look up, and my heart stops, then clenches. Patrick cocks his head to the side as he takes me in.

"Hi," I mumble.

This is one of those eloquent conversations that are super painful to watch on teen dramas, when you want to throw something at the TV, because why can't anyone just say what they mean? Here's the thing: I'm dying to just tell him everything right now. And I wonder what it would feel like to have my cheek pressed against his flannel shirt, to have him wrap his arms around me—

"You okay?" he asks.

"I'm fine!" My voice when I say this is high and fluffy. A cotton candy voice.

He falls into step beside me as I make my way to the gym for third period.

"I didn't take you for an 'I'm fine' kind of girl," he says.

I have internal squirming and, I hope, external calm. I like to think I've become what he'd called me that day in gov—an enigma—during these hermitlike years away from the camera.

"Well, I am. Fine. I'm not sure what an 'I'm fine' kind of girl is like, but . . ."

I make the mistake of looking up, and for just a second, I let myself fall into his brown eyes. I don't want to be one of those girls who's like, *Oh, his eyes, his eyes*, but damn. They really are fantastic. Golden sand and deep brown earth all mixed together. He smiles, which in my current circumstance is like someone shoving a knife in my stomach.

"Why didn't you call me?" he asks.

This is the thing about Patrick: he asks in this totally nonjudgmental way, like I could tell him I thought he was ugly or that I'd love to just find a backseat—any backseat—and make out with him right now, but I happen to be really busy and can I get a rain check? I feel like he'd take either response in stride, but something glimmers in the corners of his eyes that makes me think he wants it to be the latter.

"Patrick . . . I'm sorry, I wanted to but—"

"Don't listen to a word my sister tells you, Patrick Sheldon. Unless it's that she wants you."

I. Am. Going. To. Kill. My. Brother.

Ever calm, cool, and collected, Patrick gives me a sardonic raise of his eyebrows, then he turns and flashes Benny a half smile. "Excellent."

I try to shoot daggers at Benny, but he throws me a look that says I'll thank him later. He's bigger than me, which is so unfair, because I'd love to beat his ass right now.

I turn to Patrick. "Well, I guess there's nothing left to say then, is there?"

Patrick shrugs. "Unless your brother's a liar."

"Yep. Totally pathological."

I'm not sure how he takes this or how I even want him to take it. A few hours ago, no, a few *minutes* ago, I'd been committed to telling him in a demurring kind of way that I'm not dating right now. But then I had to go look into his goddamn eyes. And I lost all my nerve. Even if Benny hadn't walked by, I really don't know if I could have done anything but bat my eyelashes and say yes, yes, and more yes.

I stop in front of the girls' locker room. "This is my unfortunate destination. You?"

"Bio."

"Lame."

He nods in agreement. "See you in gov."

He doesn't say anything more about me not calling him, and I pretend like I've forgotten. I flash him my easy breezy beautiful Cover Girl grin and then push through the wide double doors that lead to the locker room. I sneak a look over my shoulder to watch him lope down the hall, his ratty backpack slung over one shoulder and one hand in the pocket of his worn jeans.

Sigh.

~ ~ ~

Schwartz's class turns out to be fine because there's a sub and we have mindless bookwork to do in preparation for Friday's branches of government test. Nobody says anything to me about my freak-out, and once I've dutifully reddened and ignored a few looks, everyone goes back to not seeing me. Patrick sits behind me because someone had already taken his seat in the back corner (Right? Or is it because he wanted to sit here?). Other than the usual pleasantries, we don't talk much. It could just be me being hyperaware of him, but it feels like something's different between us now. My skin wakes up when he's around. Every noise I hear behind me—a cough, the scrape of a chair, the sound of a pen tapping—feels like a love letter in code.

"Gum?" Patrick asks, tapping me on the shoulder.

He holds out a single stick of Wrigley's Spearmint.

"Thanks."

He gives me that mysterious hint of a smile that made me fall for him in the first place and then goes back to mindless bookwork. I slip the gum out of its outer wrapper and open the foil. As I fold back the thin silver paper, I see that what he's given me is more than just a stick of gum. It's hope, and fear, and plain old giddiness all in the form of a note written in perfectly precise letters:

For the phone phobic: thisispatrickleaveamessage@gmail.com

The bell rings, and as I leave the classroom, I catch his eye and hold up the gum wrapper with a smile. *Good*, he mouths.

My new Chuck phone vibrates, and Sandra's face flashes on the screen. I'm tempted to let it go to voice mail, but I know Sandra. She'll just keep calling me until I answer.

"*Hola, mija,*" she says.

"Hey, Sandra. Um, I'm at school. I can't really talk right now."

"That's okay, I just wanted to let you know that you have to be home as soon as school is out. You and the girls have a photo shoot today."

"I can't. I'm busy," I lie. Photo shoots are Lex's thing. "And I don't want my picture taken, anyway. I already told Mom that."

"Bonnie™, we need shots for the promos, the website, the show credits . . . don't worry. No *Seventeen* or *Teen Vogue*. Although I think you'll change your mind about that once we get into the swing of things."

I sigh as I struggle to open my locker. "Fine."

"XOXO," she singsongs.

I roll my eyes and hang up just as the final bell rings. Now Señora Mendoza is going to make me explain in Spanish why I'm late.

"Dammit," I mutter, grabbing my Spanish book and slamming my locker shut.

I could ditch. But I wasn't going to let MetaReel steal my last few days of high school.

*T*essa and Mer are the only friends I've ever had, but not once have I assumed they would take my secret in stride. If I were to visually represent the lies I've told them for the past year, they would look like those concentric rings inside an ancient tree trunk, the circles getting bigger and bigger as they expand toward the outer bark. The closer to the present, the bigger my lies. I've invented my entire past, down to weird details like breaking my arm in fifth grade (never happened) and saying half of my siblings are cousins (wishful thinking). I've created family vacations out of stardust and childhood friends out of 100 percent pure fancy. I don't need to imagine the hurt looks my best friends are going to have on their faces when they find out who I am; I've seen those expressions before, when people realize their spouse is cheating on them or their father isn't coming home. Betrayal.

Now Benny and I are huddled in a deserted corner of a huge book-store, poring through copies of Mom's book, which just hit bookshelves today. We considered buying it, but that would mean giving money to an evil cause.

Mom made a mysterious trip to LA, but Benny and I Googled her and figured out she had some big book launch where MetaReel RealStars™ from *Monster Parents* and *Sweet Sixteen Mom* were pretending to be excited about her book.

"Is it true that Dad tried to hit Mom *on several occasions?* Have I blocked this out or something?" This is what chapter seven says.

Benny shakes his head. "That never happened. I mean, sure, Dad cheated on her and he drank too much, but he was never, ever violent."

From the time I was nine until I was thirteen, all I can remember from my parents' interactions are arguments. Sometimes loud, but always in front of the cameras. They usually ended with one of them stomping off into the interview room to bitch about the other. Still, we'd just been kids. We didn't know what went on behind closed doors.

I read out loud from the chapter. *"Andrew was so sweet with the kids, but only a year after we got the triplets from China, he was hurling insults in my direction every day. It wasn't until he pushed me against a wall that I knew for certain that he hated me. It took me four more years, but I finally found the courage to kick him out. It was only a matter of time before he started hitting the kids. I didn't want to be a statistic."*

Benny leans his head against a stack of art books and briefly closes his eyes. "I don't know what to believe anymore."

I run my fingers over the glossy photos with captions underneath that imitate a family album in the middle of the book. There's me, being born—on camera. There's the day when Ronald McDonald installed a fry machine in our house. There's Dad, giving me a bouquet of flowers on my twelfth birthday. There's Lexie™, posing for the camera like a preteen *Playboy* model.

I flip back to the table of contents, hoping I won't see—but there it is. Chapter fifteen: "Death on Our Doorstep."

"Benny."

I'm gutted. Compared to everything Mom's done, this is the worst. How could she do this to me? To all of us?

He scoots closer to read over my shoulder, abandoning his own copy.

The night Bonnie™ overdosed was the most terrifying of my life. We'd already had to deal with her cutting—

I hiss as all the air leaves my chest, but keep reading. I have to keep reading. Benny squeezes my shoulder.

Andrew had moved out the week before and was at the house for a visit with the kids. I think Bonnie™ took it harder than the rest—she'd always been very attached to her father. I come from a broken home, too, so I knew how hard this would be on the kids . . . but I never thought my daughter would try to commit suicide.

I shake my head. "I told her that's not what it was."

Benny stays silent, and I look at him, accusing.

"You still don't believe me?"

He says each word as if it's a stone, gently turning over each one and inspecting it before it leaves his mouth: "I think if you were upset enough to put all those pills in your mouth, you might not have been the best judge of your real intentions."

I slam the book shut with disgust. "That's comforting, thanks," I spit.

I don't know how to explain to him—to all of them—that I seriously wasn't trying to kill myself. I've never seen the episode where

I swallow nearly all of the random pills in my parents' medicine cabinet, but I'm sure it was portrayed as a suicide attempt. At the hospital, there were social workers and therapists and lots and lots of family. It was hard to breathe, that's what I remember most. Bright fluorescent lights, everything stark white, people hovering. But I was lucky to be breathing at all. I know that now. I know it was so stupid. Beyond stupid, obviously. I just wanted my parents to hear me, and it seemed like no matter how much I said or how loud I said it, they were never going to let me have a normal life. To make friends, to meet boys, to go outside the confines of our high-definition life. And then Dad left.

Oh, Bon-Bon, they would say, *you have no idea how lucky you are.*

But why would such a "lucky" girl take those pills?

A few customers pass by, and I lower my voice. "I'm not a coward, Benny. I was just trying . . . you know what? Never mind."

Benny tries to grab me, but I'm too quick for him. I drop the book and race down the Fantasy aisle, losing him among castles and warlocks. I push past the Mystery section, skirt the bestseller table, and practically knock down a display of crossword puzzles. My chest constricts, and it's getting harder to breathe. Waves of panic roll over me, and my arms begin to tingle. I push through the heavy glass door and ignore a startled woman's glance. When I'm in the sunshine and cool air, my throat unclenches just a little. I stand behind a large planter that blocks me from the parking lot, my hands on my knees, my chest heaving.

You are in control, I repeat, over and over. My therapist from before told me I should practice saying this when I feel a panic attack coming on. *You are in control.*

But I'm not, am I? That's the problem.

"Hey." Benny's kneeling down, and his hand starts to rub my back.

"Hi," I choke out. I don't want him to see me like this. He's got a suicide-watch look in his eyes, and the last thing I need is for Meta-Reel to find out I'm still having the attacks.

"How long have these been back, Chlo?" I can hear the worry in his voice, and I know it's because he loves me, but they're mine, these attacks, and I hate that everyone thinks they can talk to me about them.

I shake my head, try to get my breaths even. I hated being on the medication: the antidepressants, antianxiety, anti-*me* pills. And even though it felt like such a victory to stop using them, right now I could go for some. Anything to wipe that look off of Benny's face. Guilt settles in my lungs, cold and heavy. It must suck having me for a sister, never knowing if I'm gonna lose my mind again.

"I'm fine, Bens." He purses his lips, and I force myself to stand up straight. "Really. That was just, you know, unexpected."

Keep it together, Chloe. I love and trust Benny more than anyone in the world, but if he thinks I'm anything like season thirteen Bonnie™, nothing will keep him from alerting Mom.

"I don't know . . ."

I grip his arm, hold his eyes. "Benny, I'm okay. Seriously. Please don't say anything. It's the last thing any of us needs."

I can see the argument inside him, the way his jaw tenses as he looks past me, off into the busy parking lot. I know he's weighing it all, imagining what Chuck could do with this tidbit, remembering that night he found me, unconscious and barely breathing.

"I won't say anything for now," he finally says.

"Thank you."

He grabs my shoulders and holds me away at arm's length. "But you've gotta be straight with me, Chloe. If it's too much, if you maybe need meds, you can't hide it from me. Because if I find out you are, I'm going straight to Mom."

I nod and he engulfs me in a bear hug. I feel something hard against my stomach and pull away.

"Benny," I say, looking down, "what's in your shirt?"

He looks over his shoulder, then quickly pulls my mom's book out of his waistband.

"Benton™ Andrew Baker!"

He shrugs. "Serves them right for selling this trash."

"And you're worried about *me*?"

~ ~ ~

When I get home, the camera crew is MIA. They can't film inside the home unless Mom or Kirk is here, but the live streaming cameras have already been mounted on the walls of every "public" space in the house (basically, not the bedrooms or bathrooms). Once the first episode airs, the streaming cameras will be activated and fed onto our website. That way if any pervy dude watching wants to see what I'm up to at any hour of the day, he can just get online. I wish I was being paranoid, but it's true. Every single kid in my family has gotten skeezy fanmail, and there are more than a few creepy blogs dedicated to us. I shudder, imagining those sickos getting off on my sisters play-ing dress-up in the living room. In season ten, I remember getting a letter that obviously no one had checked, because it said the most disgusting things I've ever seen in print. The fact that it was written in crayon and had stickers on it is what still makes my skin crawl. That was the episode where I asked my mom what a blow job was.

The house is eerily quiet, like it's bracing itself for tomorrow. Earlier this week, Chuck had informed us that *Good Life* magazine is featuring the Baker-Miller clan on its January cover, and they're going to be here with their crew and our crew and our big-ass family all day. I look out the sliding door that leads to our backyard; the little kids are running around with the new nannies, their cries of delight muted because of the thick glass door. In addition to the Hulks for homeschool, we now have two nannies who hang around from six A.M. until all the little kids are in bed. I haven't bothered getting to know them—in my eyes, they're just part of Chuck's entourage. Like everyone else, they've had to sign some serious legal paperwork promising not to gossip about us to the tabloids, which is all I really care about.

As I step into the kitchen, the toe of my shoe gets wedged between those stupid camera cords again, and I nearly fall on my face. I throw out my hands and catch myself on the counter. I *have* to stop tripping over this thing before we start streaming. I give the cords a vicious stomp before I grab a glass of water and head toward my room. Some of the older kids are in the basement—from the sounds coming up, I can tell they're playing that blood-and-guts game Chuck surprised them with yesterday. Lex's car isn't in the driveway, and Benny's out with Matt; after I'd had my panic attack, I told him I needed to be alone for a few hours.

Being home doesn't feel any better, though. My anger at Mom's betrayal has morphed into this ugly black thing, like tar is coating my insides, filling me up with hatred. *Hatred*. I think it's actually come to that.

I take the stairs two at a time and push my bedroom door open, then lock it behind me. Mom had finally agreed to install a lock on my door after one too many kids ransacked my room. Now I'm more grateful than ever for the privacy it affords me. I don't even care that it's cramped and tiny—Lex and I were going to have to share, but Kirk divided the room in half by literally putting a wall in the middle of it. When we lived in New Hampshire, I'd had to share with her and Farrow™, my fifteen-year-old sister. I guess there are perks to having a contractor as a stepfather.

My room is my favorite place in the universe, because if I run my fingers over the walls, I literally have the world at my fingertips. Every square inch of space is covered with glossy photos from travel calendars. Since we moved here, I've been ordering them online—old ones, so they're super discounted. Just across from me are Morocco, India, and Japan. Someday, I'm gonna take these down, pack them in a suitcase, buy a plane ticket, and go. Far, far away—that's where fairy tales happen, right? *In a land far, far away.*

I grab my laptop and plop down on my bed, leaning against a stack of pillows. Normal people would scour the Internet after their mother wrote a tell-all. But I don't need to Google myself to know that it's not going to be pretty.

Instead, I open my e-mail, feeling hopeful. Patrick and I have had this back-and-forth all week. Little stuff, like a link to a favorite website or a homework question. I smile as I see that something from him is already waiting for me. He must have sent it right after school today. At first, I don't open it. Instead, I try to savor our cyberspace flirtation, my body humming with this bit of happiness that comes from just seeing his name there. Knowing that, right now, he likes me for who I am. Well, for who he thinks I am.

Finally, I can't take it anymore. I click on the e-mail, then turn to sparkly mush as soon as I read it.

Three Things I Thought About Today

1. You
2. This weekend
3. The park

My fingers hesitate over the keyboard, ready to evade him again. But my pulse quickens as I remember the silence in the house, the absence of the crew. This might just be my last chance to have a date in high school. I reply:

Re: Three Things I Thought About Today

1. You
2. Tonight
3. The park

I hesitate before hitting Send. What if these were isolated thoughts, and I somehow misunderstood? I must consult an expert in the field. I dial Mer's cell.

"Hello, stranger," she says. "What's up?"

I can hear the cast of *Oklahoma!* in the background. She's one of the big parts, I forget which.

"Am I interrupting a chorus line?" I ask.

"Hilarious." Her dry tone makes me smile.

"I have a question," I begin.

"Uh-huh."

"So I think Patrick is trying to set up a date—"

I have to pull the phone away from my ear as she squeals. I have not perfected this excited girl sound, but she manages to do it loud and long enough for both of us.

"OMG, first date, maybe first kiss. What are you going to wear?"

Good old Meredith. "Okay, first, I'm not sure if he's actually asking me, hence my phone call."

I read her the e-mail, and I imagine her nodding on the other end of the line, twirling one of her red curls.

"Yep. This is cryptic boy speak—even more so because it's Patrick and slightly artistic. However, in my professional opinion, he is so asking you out."

For a second, everything is beautiful. Show schmo, I don't care. I, Chloe/Bonnie™ Elizabeth Baker, have a date.

"So, my e-mail response is good: you, tonight, the park?"

"Totally," she says. "I have to go perfect my crotch-revealing high kick, but listen. Wear a button-down shirt and put on some makeup. I want a FULL report as soon as you get home. In fact, I'm texting Tessa right now. We're having a sleepover, so just come right over as soon as he kisses you good night, 'kay?"

I hesitate, but then remember my parents are out of town.

"That's hopeful," I say. I can't even believe—me, a kiss, Patrick. "Okay," I say. "Wait, why a button-down?"

"You'll see," she says, her voice going low and flirty.

Oh.

"Love you!" She hangs up before I can respond.

I hit Send on my e-mail and stare at the screen until Patrick e-mails me back. When he does, I throw down my laptop and jump around the room—Mom's book, the show, and the pills all but forgotten for the time being.

SEASON 17, EPISODE 9

(The One with the Zombie Apocalypse)

*G*lenview Park is in one of the older suburban areas of town, tucked off a side street. When I arrive, the playground is draped in shadows and milky moonlight. Instead of pulling into one of the many empty spots in the parking lot, I leave my car across the street. Patrick said this way, the cops won't bother sweeping through the park as they drive by. Since it's past ten, the park is closed. Across the grassy lawn where, I imagine, picnickers usually lounge, the bright fluorescent lights of the tennis courts suddenly shut off. As I get out of my car, I can hear shouts and laughter from the baseball diamond on the other side of the tennis courts. Those lights, too, have turned off, and I can just make out a small group of boys trudging away from the sandlot, jostling one another as they head toward idling minivans.

I wait until a car passes, then dash across the quiet street so that I can get under cover of the large, sleepy trees bordering the park as quickly as possible. For a second, I lean against a tree and try to calm my breath, which is hard because my heart is pounding against my chest like it's been buried alive. I know Patrick is waiting for me at the top of the apparatus in the playground, and I can just make out the large wooden structure up the stone path that weaves through the trees.

Isn't it considered a bad idea to have a first date with a boy you barely know in a deserted park after ten o'clock at night?

Yes. But this is Patrick Sheldon, not some shady-ass guy at a party with roofies. Still, I get a bit of a thrill, walking on the wild side. For the past year, I've been wallflowered, trying to rein in every inclination to make noise, be noticed, get a laugh. Bonnie™ died hard. Even though by the end of season thirteen I'd hated doing the show, living my life in front of the camera had fashioned me into a total ham. Before, I could stand in front of crowds of people or hang out on the set of *Good Morning America* like it was my own living room. I went to movie premieres, did photo shoots, whatever. Never nervous or shy. Now just the thought of any of that makes my stomach churn.

I pick my way out of the shadows and move up the path, the ground growing soft beneath my feet as I get to the sand that marks the playground's territory. I shiver, both from cold and anticipation. The empty swings move eerily in the breeze, faint starlight glinting off their thick metal chains. The apparatus looms before me, a sturdy wooden structure consisting of a hut enclosed on three sides, a slide, monkey bars, and a tiny net of rope for climbing. We used to have one just like this in our backyard when I was a kid. I remember falling off the monkey bars, the air whooshing out of me with frightening speed. Our nanny at the time was too busy preening for the cameras and so, for a long minute, nobody noticed me. Finally one of the cameramen heard me gasping, but by then I was so frantic that it took almost an hour for me to calm down. That was the episode where the nanny got fired. I think it was season six.

"Hey."

I hear a soft whisper, and when I look up, Patrick is dangling from the monkey bars. As he hangs suspended above the sand, I catch a slight glimpse of the bare skin between the waist of his dark jeans and the hem of his flannel shirt. I look away, blushing.

"Hi," I say.

He jumps down and comes over to me, our mutual nervousness hanging in the air between us, heavy and cumbersome. He reaches out and grabs my hand, pulling me toward the swings. I wish I wasn't wearing mittens—I want to feel his skin against mine.

"Will you tell me the moment you start freezing your ass off?" he asks.

"As soon as I experience a numbing sensation in that general area, I will let you know," I assure him.

"Excellent."

He lets go of my hand when we get to the swings. I wonder if this is a cool thing to do on first dates or if it's a Patrick thing. I'm guessing Tessa and Mer will let me know.

I twist my swing until the chain gets all tight and wound around itself. Then I pick my feet up and let it spin me. I feel dizzy, but I'm not sure if it's the swing or being alone with Patrick.

"So do you live around here?" I ask.

I instantly regret this question because now he'll want to lob it back my way.

"Yeah. Up the street a bit. You don't though, huh?"

I shake my head, and he doesn't press the issue. For a while we're quiet, pushing ourselves into the sky, letting the cold air wrap around us. What does one *say* on a first date? I can't have conversational filler with Patrick. I want a deep thought, a witty observation, something that will not be off the picked-over carcass of Getting to Know You.

"Your three favorite words: go," he says.

(How totally wonderful is he?)

I lean back and pump my legs, climbing higher and higher. I had forgotten how fun something as simple as a swing set could be.

"Ummmm," I say. Obviously stalling. I want good words. I want the right words.

"Don't think. Just, you know, whatever comes to mind first."

"Okay," I say. "*Serendipitous*."

He nods, but doesn't say anything.

Was *serendipitous* not good? I find our being in the same government class very serendipitous indeed.

"*Malicious*."

"Nice," he says.

"And . . ." I swing higher, until my feet go past the roof of the jungle gym and kick the stars. "*Brazen*."

"Brazen," he repeats, like he's tasting the word, seeing if he has the right palate for it.

"What about you?" I ask, my breath coming out in puffs of autumn smoke.

Immediately he says, "*Gloaming*."

Oh, I love that word.

"Cool. Number two?"

"*Paperweight*."

"Paperweight?"

He nods. *"Paperweight."* He pumps his legs a bit faster, and just as he catapults into the sky, releasing his hands from the swing, he yells, *"Yawp!"*

I laugh, my stomach in my throat as he lands on both feet.

"You're insane!" I shout.

I let my legs dangle so that my swing slows, descending toward the ground in graceful back-and-forth swoops. Patrick's eyes are shining as he comes toward me.

"So you sound your barbaric yawp over the roofs of suburbia?" I ask, quoting a millennial version of the Walt Whitman poem he'd referred to. We'd had to do a report on it in English last year.

He laughs. "Something like that."

He reaches out his hands and grabs my swing, bringing me to a stop. I tilt my head up to look into his eyes. Suddenly I'm realizing that this might be a terrible idea. Am I really going to let myself proceed from harmless crush to bone-crushing feeling just when I should be keeping my distance? He must see some vestige of that worry in my eyes, because he drops to his knees, his chest leaning ever so slightly against my knees.

"What's got you freaked out?" he asks.

What is he? Aren't boys not supposed to notice things like this?

I open my mouth to say, *Nothing, I'm fine,* but then, unexpectedly, "It's really complicated. I mean, I can't tell you. Not . . . right now."

"Do you want to be here?" he asks, his voice soft.

I nod. Vigorously.

"Is somebody gonna kick my ass for being here with you?"

I think this is his way of asking if I either A) have a boyfriend or B) a violent dad. I shake my head.

He holds out both of his hands and smiles. "Well, then, we're ready for stage two of our park adventure."

~ ~ ~

Patrick has turned the fort at the top of the playground into a cozy little campsite, complete with a camping lantern, S'mores Pop-Tarts, and sleeping bags. When we get up there (via the rope net), he immediately points to the sleeping bags and says, "I'm not shady. This just isn't the most comfortable place in the world to sit."

I pretend to look horrified. "I don't think this is at all appropriate."

He grins. "I promise to be a gentleman."

I roll my eyes and look away. The swings were so much easier than this sudden closeness. We're squeezed into a space intended for people who still play hand-clap games, and though I don't mind brushing up against Patrick (quite, *quite* the opposite), it feels like the closer we are physically, the harder it will be for me to tell him outright lies.

"Convenience store ambrosia?" he asks, holding up a bottle of Pepsi.

I nod and take it. "You should have told me to bring some hot dogs to grill or something," I say.

"Oh, no," he says, "this feast is on me."

I smile and break off a piece of my Pop-Tart. "So do you hang out here a lot?" I ask, gesturing to the park around me.

He nods. "Yeah. Well, once the under-four-footers are gone. It's a good place to be alone."

I want to ask him what his parents are like, if he has brothers or sisters. Does he need an escape or just a diversity of hangout locations? Instead, I keep my eyes on my Pepsi and nod. "I have a place like this, too."

We talk, and the words flow between us, sometimes in rushing torrents, sometimes in lazy, slow-moving streams. I skirt around topics I don't want to answer and he brings up random questions like "How do you like your eggs?" When I have enough courage, I sneak looks at him. His face has sharp lines sketched with a quick, sure hand. The dim light from the lantern catches in his eyes, glints off a silver band on his middle finger. He sits slouched against a rolled-up sleeping bag, and with his longish hair and threadbare second-hand couture, he could be a beat poet, Kerouac or one of his friends. He looks like the kind of boy who would jump trains, strum a guitar, and pass a joint.

We sit facing each other, our legs propped against opposite walls of the fort so that our knees occasionally knock. Once again I notice the quiet energy humming within him, just under the surface of his cool nonchalance. It's like his ghost of a smile is the only thing standing between him and wild abandonment.

"Tessa says you're an anarchist," I say, after explaining, per the question he'd just asked me, what I would do in the event of a zombie apocalypse (avoid malls). I don't know what being an anarchist means exactly, but I like the sound of it. Being totally free.

"Hmm," is all he says.

"What's 'hmm'? Is that code for 'I'd Tell You But I'd Have to Kill You'?"

He chuckles. "So you've talked to Tessa about me?"

My face grows warm, and I lift my chin to counteract that tell-tale sign of *eeek!* "I can't help but notice that you're avoiding my question."

He sits up and leans closer. "Sorry," he whispers, his voice all low and bedroomy. "I got distracted."

Cue sweaty hands and short breath and warmth in strange, un-expected places. Is this what it feels like, falling hard for someone? Is it supposed to turn you inside out?

He smells like pine needles and dryer sheets, and it makes me happy to think he put on some clean clothes and cologne for me. Obviously I'm super into dirty I-don't-give-a-fuck Patrick, but I like that he wanted to impress me.

I let myself move into the electric space between us, feeling like there actually is a zombie apocalypse and we're the last people on Earth and, dammit, why won't he just kiss me already?

And then he does.

This is what I will always remember about my first kiss:

- Soft lips and the taste of Pepsi and cinnamon
- Patrick's firm, gentle hands snaking through my hair
- The faraway sound of mariachi music, from a house up the street
- Warm honey filling every cold, lonely, confused, scared place inside me

He pulls back for a minute, and I can't help it, I say, "That was my first kiss."

He grins, this goofy sort of delighted smile that makes me not feel so dumb for telling him.

He says, "It would be wrong to leave it at just one, then."

I nod and he's kissing me again, and this kiss lasts longer and for a while I feel like I've become a long-term visitor on Planet *Ahhh*.

When his lips finally leave mine, his fingertips stay on my cheeks, and he looks at me—really *looks* at me—for a long time. Five seconds? Minutes? Centuries? Maybe it's the feeling behind his eyes or the way the warmth of that kiss slowly slips back on the tide of our breath, but I suddenly feel like I need to leave. Now.

"I have to go." I disentangle my hair from his fingers and move away.

"Chloe—"

I shake my head, my feet already on the wobbly rungs of the rope ladder.

"Chalk this up to irrationality, okay?" I say.

He looks like he wants to say something, but then nods. When I get to the last rung, I look up into the dimly lit hut. He's leaning over the edge, looking down at me with this unnameable expression. Disappointment? Confusion? Hurt? I really don't know.

I can't cry in front of him, so I smile through my already blurry eyes and stumble away. I can feel his eyes on me until I finally reach the deepest shadows of the tree-lined walkway. Then I run to my car and don't look back.

Baker's Dozen, Season 13, Episode 2

INT—BAKER HOME—NIGHT: [BETH screams into a phone while ANDREW administers CPR to someone lying on the floor of the master bedroom.]

BETH: I don't know, I don't know! Andrew, is she breathing yet?
   [CUT to ANDREW.]

ANDREW: C'mon, Bonnie™. C'mon, sweetheart. One, two, three, four, five. Shit! C'mon, baby.

BETH: Andrew! Is she breathing?

ANDREW: One, two, three, four, five, six—

BETH: Andrew!

ANDREW: No, goddammit! Tell them to get over here!

BETH: [speaking into phone] No. No. I don't know how many pills. The bottles were all over the floor.

What? I can't remember . . . I don't know. My husband had surgery last year, he had a lot of painkillers.

[The sound of sirens grows louder. BETH drops the phone and runs to the front door. CUT to PARAMEDICS rushing into the house. CUT to ANDREW sobbing over BONNIE™.]

BETH: In here!

PARAMEDICS put BONNIE™ onto a stretcher. CUT to BENTON™, standing in the doorway.]

BENTON™: [screaming as PARAMEDICS rush past him with BONNIE™] Bonnie™! Don't die, Bonnie™, please don't die.

SEASON 17, EPISODE 10

(The One with the Scones)

I don't go to Mer's house. Instead, I text her after I get home, claiming my mother is pissed I'd gone on a date without her permission and now I'm grounded. She seems to buy it, but I know it's only a matter of time before I'll be forced to recount every last detail of the date. Just to torture myself, I check my e-mail to see if maybe Patrick sent me something. Even a *whaaaa?* kind of e-mail would have been preferable to the vast emptiness that is my in-box. It's like the Siberia of in-boxes.

I decide to indulge my tragic inner nature by lying on my bed in the dark, staring at the ceiling. There's just enough light from outside to see the vague outline of my ceiling fan, but the room is otherwise cloaked in heavy black swaths of night. It's almost four in the morning, but I'm still wide awake, letting my anger build.

After my Sixty Minutes Hate, I hear a car pull up in the driveway. When I look out of my second-story window, I can see the back of Kirk's SUV slip into the garage. The sky is already starting to stretch and yawn, and I sit there for a minute, watching the deep blues of early morning slowly lighten into the watercolor hues of dawn. Venus shimmers, and the moon sort of backs out of the sky, like it's reluctant to leave but doesn't want to overstay its welcome. I'm almost enjoying this rare glimpse of five A.M., but I don't linger. When I hear the front door open, I leave my bedroom and pad downstairs.

"—have to get everything together before the crew comes. God, I'm exhausted."

Mom's voice. I stop on the stairs.

Kirk: "Maybe after this weekend, we can get you a massage or something."

"Mmm, sounds nice."

Gross over-forty-adult kissing noises ensue. I hover on the stairwell, uncertain. On the one hand, I really, *really* don't want to do this without coffee. On the other, I *have* to talk to my mom.

"I'm gonna jump in the shower," Kirk says.

I tiptoe down the stairs and into the living room, barely escaping a brush-in with this guy I used to think was okay even though he wasn't my dad and who now I can't trust at all. It has been surprisingly easy to turn against Kirk; calling us out for drinking on national TV was more than a rookie mistake. It was a violation of trust and respect that I won't be forgetting anytime soon. Sure, we shouldn't have done it. But he enjoyed his little moment in the sun—I could tell.

I wait until I hear the door to the master bedroom close, then I step into the kitchen.

"Bonnie™! What's got you up so early?"

Mom's measuring coffee into this fancy new coffeepot, and even though it's the butt crack of dawn, she's got perfect hair and makeup. Just like the good old days.

"I couldn't sleep," I say. I lean against the counter opposite her. My stomach—traitor that it is—grumbles.

Mom reaches into a canvas tote on the table and takes out a plastic container of scones.

"I have more in the bag if you don't want blueberry." She crosses to the fridge. "OJ?"

"I'll wait for the coffee."

Mom gave up the coffee-stunts-your-growth fight long ago.

"So . . . how was LA?" I ask.

"Great!" Mom's voice gets high and peppy, which means she's hiding something. "Maybe we can all go down there together sometime. Get some sun."

"Huh. So what were you up to?"

Mom starts opening the cabinets, pulling out all the fancy platters we use only for holidays. "Oh, you know . . . businessy stuff."

The coffee gurgles, and I get up to pour myself a cup. I take my time choosing and decide on an old Valentine's Day mug with hearts and cupids. It's ugly as sin, but we keep it because guess how easy it is to get stuck with no cup at all in a house with fifteen people?

"So Benny and I were at the bookstore yesterday."

I have rehearsed this a few times, and it comes out sounding less casual than I wanted it to.

"Uh-huh," is all Mom says.

She's not even listening.

I look over at her. "I said something?"

"Sorry, honey, I missed that. What about you and Benton™?"

I take a sip of coffee, then put the mug down because I don't want to throw it.

"I *said*, Benny and I were at the bookstore yesterday."

Now she hears. She looks at me for what feels like the first time since I entered the kitchen.

"You saw the book."

I nod.

"You're angry."

I nod.

"Well, sweetie, I don't know what to say." She throws her hands up in the air and lets them fall against her thighs. *Smack*. "It's important that I advocate for our family, and this was the best way to do it."

Advocate? What are we, a nonprofit?

I shake my head. "So talking about the pills was, what, an attempt to prove what a great family we are?"

Mom's tone gets hard, defensive. "I am trying to *protect* you, Bonnie™. It's important that we have the last word on the matter. I'm not stupid. The tabloids are going to dredge all this up again. The last thing people remember about the show is what you did to yourself—"

"What *I* did to myself?" I'm shouting already, but I can't help it. This is just so Mom. You try to confront her about something, and it's like you threw her a boomerang. It always *always* comes back to you. "Because living out my entire life on television didn't contribute at all to my depression."

Mom purses her lips. "I'm not going to let you use me as your punching bag anymore." This, I think, sounds suspiciously like a Kirkism. "*You* made the choice to take those pills," Mom continues.

"*You* made the choice to blame me for it, and for a while, I was okay with that. I blamed myself. But I don't anymore. Honey, I love you, but I refuse to carry around your guilt any longer."

Now I'm shaking. Like somebody replaced my blood with carbonated AGHH!!!!!

"Mom. Have you ever asked yourself why your thirteen-year-old daughter wanted to swallow a bunch of pills? Maybe—just maybe—it was because I had a *psychotic* childhood—"

"Bonnie™. We have been over and over this. You put this family through hell, and now, just when things are starting to get back to normal—"

"This is normal? Strangers in our house, shoving cameras in our faces? I have to use a fake name at school and lie to everyone I know. What's normal about that?"

"I'm sorry you're upset," she says. She pinches her nose between her thumb and forefinger and briefly closes her eyes. Like she can't stand the sight of me. "I know your father and I said we wouldn't do the show again. But circumstances change. This was the best decision I could make for our family, to provide for us. I know you don't understand it—I don't expect you to. I hope to God you never have the financial concerns we do. But I need you to respect my decisions, and someday, when you have kids, you might cut me a little slack."

"You promised! And you didn't even tell us. I got home from school, and they were just *here*."

"What do you want from me, Bonnie™? Please, tell me. Because no matter what I do, it's never enough for you!"

Now she's shouting. Soon enough—yep, there's the sound of doors opening. I hear one of the triplets say, "Mommy?"

My eyes are getting hot, and God, I don't want to cry. "I want you to admit . . . I . . . Why are you doing this to me?"

My voice cracks on *me*, and I want to punch myself, I'm so freaking frustrated with my inability to keep cool.

Mom's voice goes low. "Nobody is doing anything *to* you. There are fourteen other people in this family that I have to think about. *Fourteen* people I have to feed, and clothe, and buy toys and books and everything for. Do you know how much toilet paper we use in a month, how many bars of soap? Don't even get me started on groceries! I'm sorry, Bonnie™, but the world doesn't revolve around you. Writing the book, doing the show, running around the country for PR and having a million meetings—this is *my job*. I'm sorry I'm not a doctor or a lawyer, but this is what you're stuck with."

"Nobody asked you to have a million kids! It's not our fault!"

Her eyes narrow, and I wonder if maybe I've gone a little too far.

"Which sibling of yours did you want me to give up for adoption?"

(Lexie™.)

"I'm not even going to answer that," I say. *WTF?* "You can't make me do the show. Whatever sick thing you and Chuck are planning for the first episode, I won't do it. It's, like, child abuse."

Mom looks at me like I just sold American secrets to the Russians. "How can you say something like that? You have no idea how—"

"Lucky I am. I know, I know. You've already told me that a million times," I say. "But what's lucky about not having a real life? What am I supposed to do when all my friends find out I've been lying to them for the past year? How do you think it feels to know that everyone at my school can read all about the Pill Night?"

Mom's face softens, for just a moment. "I know it must be hard to—"

"No. You don't know. You don't know what it's like because you *want* this. I don't want this. I want a life, I want . . . I . . ." *Want.* So much. No. So *little.*

I hear a shuffling noise behind me, and when I turn around, I see myself reflected in the glassy eye of a camera.

"What?" is all I can say. Confused, like a polar bear is sitting at the table drinking tea. I hear my mom sigh, and I whirl around, flinging my words at her. "Has this thing been here the whole time?"

"Bonnie™ . . ."

Notice that she doesn't deny it.

I stand there for a minute, dazed. I want to scream and shout at the camera, rip it out of this stranger's hands and take a baseball bat to it. But I don't. I can already feel the mask I've learned how to wear since I was finger-painting settle over my face. I become plastic, expressionless Bonnie™. Then I turn on my heel and brush past the camera.

~ ~ ~

"If we refuse to participate, Meta will go the whole troubled teen angle."

I nod. I know Benny's right, but the thought of going out there, getting back in front of those cameras after the fight I had with my mom this morning . . . *ugh.* I prefer to stay here, on my bed, with my bedroom door locked. Forever.

"What if we go live with Dad?" I ask. I'm not really sure how I want him to answer that.

"Okay . . . One: you haven't spoken to him since the show ended. Can you imagine living alone with him in some douchey bachelor pad?" (I couldn't.) "Two: That fucker ditched us for a nineteen-year-old receptionist. Three: I'm not leaving Matt, and you're not leaving without me."

"Benny, I can't do this. I mean, I feel like I literally *can't*. And after this fight with Mom, there's just no way I can homeschool again. Which means I'd have to go to Taft. Which sucks great big fat balls."

Benny laughs—one loud, sharp guffaw. "You did not just use the phrase *great big fat balls*."

I put a pillow over my face. "I want to die."

He grabs it and hugs it to his chest, his eyes darkening a bit. "No you don't. You want to have sex with Patrick Sheldon."

I smile to let him know I'm kidding around—it's tricky using the D-word around my family. "Okay. And *then* I want to die."

"If you do it in that order, you'd be the first human in the known universe to go to heaven *before* they die." Benny licks his lips in the kind of lascivious way that is totally inappropriate around one's sister.

"Boo . . . Hiss . . . Don't quit your day job," I snark.

"Okay, but, seriously, that first kiss sounded . . ." Here Benny shivers from head to toe.

"Benny, did you take an extra gay pill this morning?"

He throws the pillow at my face. "Did you take an extra bitch pill this morning?"

"My subconscious *sabotaged* my first and only date slash kiss. I think I am allowed an extra bitch ration for the day."

"Okay, but that doesn't solve our problem."

We sit in silence for a few minutes, the house waking up all around us.

"We have to do the show, don't we?" I ask miserably.

He frowns. "Yeah."

"After we graduate, I'm immediately moving out. Even if I have to hook to scrape together the money."

"Or you can write a tell-all. There's just as much whoring, but you can work from home."

"But I wouldn't get to wear pleather stilettos and get beaten up by my pimp."

Benny sighs. "Decisions, decisions."

These are the kinds of pep talks reality TV kids have when the cameras aren't rolling.

SEASON 17, EPISODE 11

(The One with the Photo Shoot)

Benny puts his arm around me as we make our way down the stairs. *Good Life* magazine is waiting. DeShaun™ and Deston™ (both fated to be professional wrestlers someday) career past us, whooping and shouting.

"Yo! Walk!" I yell.

Deston™ flips me off, and I stare at him, aghast.

Benny just shakes his head. "Chuck should never have given those fools Killer Kombat Five," he says. I'm imagining what will happen to these boys, with their crazy reality TV life and dumbass video games.

"Don't you think people should have to create, I don't know, a mission statement or something when they start a family?" I ask.

Benny trips, cursing as he nearly breaks an ankle on a Barbie doll left on the stairs. He picks it up and hurls it down the hall, and there's a satisfying *thunk* as it hits a door.

"Something like, *We at Baker, Inc., think that a child should be raised in the most stressful environment imaginable. That's why we firmly believe in having so many children that you can't remember all of their names* blahblahblah?" he asks.

"Yep. Sounds about right to me."

When we step into the kitchen, all hell has broken loose. The triplets are sitting at the table arguing over the pros and cons of using OJ instead of milk in one's cereal. The tween boys are shoving one another around (natch), and the tween girls are flitting in and out, casting shy glances toward the cameras. Farrow™ has spilled a bottle of nail polish on the new rug, and Tristan™ looks like he's about to cry as he holds a crushed Lego superhero thing in his hands.

"Tristan™, it's okay," I say, wrapping an arm around him.

He just looks at the mangled body, shaking his head like he's the only kid who's not going to get adopted. He's sensitive, and Mom worries he's falling behind developmentally. Which is, of course, why she's now agreed to have him filmed 24/7. I wonder if he wishes a different American family had adopted him.

"We'll fix it later, I promise," I say. He leans into me, and after a minute or so, I feel his thin body shudder against my side. I kiss the top of his head—it smells like Play-Doh.

Mom gives us a frazzled wave as I pass her, apparently deciding to forget the whole argument for now, and then turns back to Sandra, who goes back to plucking at Mom's eyebrows with a medieval torture device. Puma Guy starts to shadow me as I struggle to get to the refrigerator, like he's a shark following the scent of blood.

"Where should we set up wardrobe?" asks an arty-looking woman.

"Uh, let's do it in the family room," says Sandra.

"Great," the woman says. She opens the front door and shouts, "Family room!"

127

Two seconds later, racks of clothing wheel by, followed by a couple of carts with boxes labeled SHOES and ACCESSORIES.

"Props in the dining room!" calls a lanky man of utter fabulosity.

I can see that over his shoulder our dining room is being transformed into the kind of chic, glossy space you see in magazines. A girl pushes past me, holding bags from Whole Foods.

"Sorry!" she calls over her shoulder.

"No problem," I mumble.

"So, like I was saying, we don't have anything you'd call a 'quiet day,'" my mom is saying to a thin, fashionable woman with a mini tape recorder in her hand.

"How do you manage it all?" she asks.

"Well, I'm pretty organized. Kirk and I have synchronized calendars on our phones, which we update constantly. I have a whiteboard over near the kitchen table where I write announcements. I have to admit, I have literally e-mailed some of my older kids before!"

I pull open the fridge and pretend to have trouble choosing the kind of yogurt I want so that I can hear what Mom's telling her.

The reporter laughs and looks down at the list in her hand. "So why have you decided to do the show again?"

This should be good.

"I want to reach out to other women like me. Women who are having trouble creating families of their own or struggling to move on after a divorce." Her voice grows soft. "I want to encourage them not to give up. At the end of the day, there's nothing better than being surrounded by your kids. *Nothing.*"

It's weird thinking about us Bakers influencing people, considering we're probably America's most dysfunctional family. I almost feel bad for anyone who watches us and can feel *inspired*. That's ten kinds of messed up.

I grab a yogurt, then fish around in a nearby drawer for a spoon. Mom calls Daisy™ over so that she can braid her hair while she interviews.

"Last question," the reporter says to Mom. "As I'm sure you know, the *New York Times* recently reported that since your adoption of Deston™ and DeShaun™ through the foster care system, there has been a forty percent increase in foster parent applications. How does it feel to know you've touched so many lives?"

Mom's lip trembles a little. "You know, when Andrew and I decided to work with foster kids after so many international adoptions, it was a scary step. But it was so rewarding. I love my sons, and I'm incredibly thankful that they're a part of our family. I'm so happy that our experiences have encouraged people to open up their homes. There are so many kids in need."

"And it wouldn't have happened unless you'd done *Baker's Dozen*. No regrets?"

Mom gives a firm shake of her head. "None. I wouldn't have any of my children without MetaReel's help, and that's the truth. This show gave me my family. I'll be forever grateful."

I'm guessing she means MetaReel footed the bill for all the expensive adoptions and procedures, but it's crappy to know we wouldn't exist as a family without a major corporate sponsor.

"Excuse me, Bonnie™?"

I turn around, prepared to scowl, but the guy with the fancy camera around his neck is kinda hot. Like rugged, foreign correspondent hot.

"Yeah?" I say, wishing I had at least run a brush through my hair.

"I'm Eric. I'll be doing some candid shots throughout the weekend. I just wanted to say hi and see if it's okay if I get you in some of them."

"Um, sure. Yeah, that'd be fine." I can see Benny snickering out of the corner of my eye, so I tilt my head so I can't see him.

"Great," Eric with baby blue eyes and sexy tattoos says. "I just figured you probably get sick of people shoving these in your face all the time."

I grin. "You have *no* idea. I appreciate you asking."

He smiles and walks over to where Tristan™, DeShaun™, and Deston™ are arm wrestling.

"I appreciate you asking," Benny says in a falsetto, batting his eyelashes.

"Oh, shut up."

"Do you think you should play Two Minutes in the Closet with him before or after we break for lunch?"

"How," I ask, "are you always so horny? My God, doesn't Matt do enough for you?"

"A gentleman never tells," he says.

Lacey Production Assistant walks in, a clipboard pressed against her chest and a walkie-talkie strapped to the waist of her skinny cords. She and Lex are doing the girl compliment game, where you go back and forth and say "Oh, I like your (fill in the blank); where did you get it?" until one of you runs out of things to point and squeal at.

Chuck waddles into the room, all three hundred pounds of him, and claps his hands to get our attention. "Okay, folks, let's get started!"

The room goes as silent as it can when there are thirty, no, wait, here are six more, and I haven't even counted the camera dudes—

"There are forty goddamn people in this house right now," I whisper to Benny.

He rolls his eyes.

Chuck is still talking. "Today and tomorrow are going to be pretty hectic around here. Let's not forget that this is a *home*, so please clean up after yourselves. A quick reminder that the second floor is totally off-limits to the magazine crew. Now, I'm going to turn it over to Melissa Shapiro from *Good Life*."

The woman with the tape recorder smiles and waves. "Hey, everyone. We are *so* excited to have you on our January cover! I promise we're going to have a lot of fun this weekend."

Benny coughs, but I know I'm the only one who hears him say *bullshit*.

"Now," she continues, "we're going to do a big family shot outside and then after lunch we'll do a dinner scene in the dining room. No eating the props until after we're done!" The room fills with polite chuckles. "Tomorrow we'll be at Harvest Studios for the actual cover shoot. I need all the ladies to hair and makeup, which is in the kids' classroom for today, and, guys, we need you in wardrobe. Let's have a great shoot!"

Everyone claps, but I just busy myself with a scone in between texting Tessa and Mer. No, I tell them, I can't go to a movie or the mall.

Chuck: "Bonnie™, can I have a quick word?"

I sigh and put my phone in my back pocket, following him to the front porch. He stops a few feet away from the tent that MetaReel has already put up at the side of the house. This is where the monitors are—one for each camera. Crew I rarely see sit in front of them in director's chairs, their headsets on, oblivious to the world around them as they focus on the filming inside.

"What's up?" I say.

Little beads of sweat line his upper lip, and his eyes flit over me like he's an appraiser who finds I've come up short.

"Well, sweetheart, I feel like we got off on the wrong foot. I can see this is hard for you, but I hope you know I'm on your team."

I want to say, No, Chuck, you are *not* on my team, but I just stand there and shrug. I'm gutless like that.

He sighs, like I gave him the wrong answer to a test question. "Look, hon. I hope you're thinking about the big picture here. Because the show is a great opportunity for you to set the record straight about all that nonsense back in season thirteen. It's your chance to show the world you're not still that little girl who overdosed."

The sucky part is that, in his twisted universe, he's kind of right. I could morph into the Bonnie™ everyone used to love or a new Bonnie™, who's clever and witty and explains away the most painful night of her life with a roll of her eyes and a self-deprecating joke or two. It'd be that easy. But I don't want to play by Chuck's rules. In his world, you have to sell your soul to gain your dignity. I don't think that's a fair trade.

"Chuck, I don't care about setting the record straight. I just want it to go away. I was a kid, and I made a mistake. It's over."

But it's not. It won't ever be.

He cocks his head to the side, trying to catch my eye. "I hope your mother wasn't mistaken when she said all you kids would be happy to do the show. It'd be a shame to have to cancel the series because one person out of fifteen doesn't want us here."

"Two," I say. Chuck raises his eyebrows. "Benny doesn't want to do it, either."

He sighs and his hands jangle whatever's in the pockets of his massive cargo shorts.

"This is what I'm talking about, Bonnie™. This attitude. We've done this before, Bon-Bon, haven't we?"

His eyes stray to the big front window, full of laughing, smiling kids. And, once again, I'm the piece that doesn't fit. The one on the outside, looking in. Why can't I just let all my angst over this go? Mom and Kirk are beaming, and cameras snap snap snap. I catch Benny being his usual affable self, and I know that if it weren't for me, he'd be making the best of the show, doing whatever anyone wanted him to.

"There's a lot of good that can come out of this for you," Chuck says. "For all of you. But we need you to cooperate, okay?"

"I am," I say. "I'm here. I'm doing the shoot."

Chuck shakes his head. "You know what I mean. We need to see the Bonnie™ America fell in love with."

"Or what?" I ask.

His voice grows hard, and I remember he's not the highest paid, most sought after television producer in the world for nothing. "Or we cancel the show and sue your parents for signing the contract under false pretenses. I'm not sure how they'd be able to afford a lawyer with thirteen kids—three going off to college—but that's not really my concern." He smiles. "But I know you'll make the right choice, hon. The camera just loves you."

He's doing it again, I realize. What he did over and over when I was a kid.

"Is this like when I was a little girl and you told me that I had to stop saying I didn't want to do the show if I wanted my parents to stay together?"

He holds his hands up, palms out, and tries a sad little frown on for size. "And what happened to them, Bonnie™?"

My breath rushes out and my insides cave in, like they've been bulldozed. He stares me down as I slowly disintegrate. I need to say something, but the words won't come.

A *Good Life* woman opens the door and starts beckoning to me.

"There you are!" she says. "Let's get you into hair and makeup."

"Just a second," I say, turning back to Chuck.

But he's already walking toward one of the MetaReel trucks in our driveway. "Have a good shoot, Bonnie™," he calls over his shoulder.

Translation: If I *don't* shut up and be a good little monkey and make love to the camera today and every day, then it'll be my fault that my family gets sued by one of the largest corporations in America.

Just like it was my fault when Dad left.

~ ~ ~

"You've got beautiful bone structure, you know that?" says the girl putting on my makeup.

"Is that industry for You're Not Pretty But You Have Nice Qualities?" I ask.

She laughs. "You always were funny, weren't you?"

Okay, that creeps me out. I'd forgotten how people talk to us; they watch you every week for thirteen years, and they feel like they know you. It's weird.

"No," she continues, "I'm not bullshitting you. You look stunning. This eye shadow really brings out the green in your eyes. And your hair . . ." She sighs and tries to fluff up her limp locks. "Did you know that women in India cut off hair just like yours and sell it to American salons?"

I wrinkle my nose. "That's sad. Like 'The Gift of the Magi' but without the warm fuzzies."

She laughs again.

Soon we're in the backyard, perched on this brand-new fancy jungle-gym thing that some company donated to the show. On Wednesday they'd done all this filming with Kirk and the delivery dudes and my brothers trying to build it. I'm sure it will be one of our episodes, something like *Kirk and the boys try to build a Kidz Zone™ playground, but will they finish before it starts raining?*

"Bonnie™, can we get you perched on the monkey bars?" asks some non-Eric entity with a camera.

"Like, swinging?" I ask.

Patrick's skin, peeking out from under his flannel shirt.

"No, maybe reaching out like you're going to swing?"

This is going to look so dumb.

"I guess so," I say.

They made me wear a skirt, and I feel like a poor man's Marilyn Monroe with all this freezing wind—also, I never wear skirts. They make me feel three years old. I climb up the net rope to get up to the bars, and all I can think about is the startled look on Patrick's face last night as I ran away from him. I reach for the bars and smile through the kids whining, my mother's snapping, and the millions of tiny adjustments the camera dudes are shouting out. There are a couple of bounce cards set up—white circles that have something to do with lighting. They're catching the sun, and the light jumping off them is blinding and gives me an instant headache. Kirk just grins, his teeth super white and—I'm just noticing this—his skin much tanner.

"Did Kirk get beauty treatments in LA?" I ask Lex.

She's posed on the edge of the platform beside the monkey bars, her legs crossed, sitting pretty. She flips her blond hair away from her face, then leans forward to look past me, her breasts heaving against her too-tight shirt.

"Maybe," she says. "Weird, huh?"

"Understatement of the year." I let go of one bar, cursing as I shake out the pins and needles in my arms.

Lex rolls her eyes. "Okay, tell me you're not having fun at all," she says.

"I'm not having fun at all."

"Whatever." She flashes a grin in the general direction of everyone looking at us. "That Eric guy is super hot. I have dibs."

Typical.

"Aren't you remotely pissed about Mom's book?" I ask.

She adjusts her skirt, keeping her eyes on the cameras. "I looked through the copy Ben brought home. Doesn't seem too heinous. I mean, the stuff about Dad was . . . but, whatever. It's good publicity for the show. Mom said we could go to some of her book signings, too."

"You're unbelievable," I mutter.

"I'm going to take that as a compliment."

We stay there for about an hour while various strangers keep coming around to move our bodies or shove light meters in our faces. My breath tastes like hair spray, and the wind is making my eyes water, so now I have this irritating makeup-in-my-eye thing happening.

"Lexie™, Bonnie™, why don't you put your arms around each other for a few of these?"

Lex throws an arm over my shoulder, and I let go of one of the monkey bars. Smile!

"Okay, everyone," shouts a girl with long black hair and oversized geek-chic glasses. "Last one. Ready? CHEESE!"

The little kids scream "cheese," and I purposely close my eyes.

"Okay, folks, lunch!"

The kids cheer because there'd been a pizza rumor. My arms feel like jelly, and my hands are raw from the cold. I jump down from the apparatus, then throw my hair into a messy bun, forgetting that someone had spent an hour making it look all supermodelish. Eric snaps a shot, and I feel slutty because I kind of grinned at him in a slightly come-hither way even though less than ten hours ago, I was kissing Patrick.

"Dude, I need a cigarette," Benny says.

I rub my arms to get the blood circulating again. "I need a massage."

He glances at my outfit. "We look like we just ran away from prep school."

It's true. We're wearing sweater vests. And plaid.

"Screw sweater vests," I say.

He gives me a nod, his face serious. "Before we ceremoniously burn them, wanna come with me to the gas station? I finished my last cig this morning."

"I thought you were going to quit."

"Yes, because it's easy to quit smoking on days like this."

"Okay, let's go before anyone catches us."

We slink behind Kirk's elaborate barbecue and into the front yard, which is pretty hard to do because it's basically rigged up like a freaking CIA safe house. There are about a gazillion cameras mounted onto the walls, plus the high security fencing around our whole property.

"Oh, good, I was afraid they'd be blocking me in," he says, as we slip into our car.

I click the gate opener, and the tall metal doors slowly creak open. Benny does a twenty-three-point turn, which takes about ten minutes because there are a ton of vehicles parked all over our front drive. I fiddle with my iPod, trying to find the right song to counteract my schizo morning. As Benny pulls out of the driveway, he slams on the brakes, hard.

"What the hell?" I shout, throwing my hands against the dashboard.

"Chlo. Look."

I glance across the street.

"Shit," I say. "Back, back," I yell, holding up my hands to block my face.

Benny reverses our Hyundai, nearly crashing into Chuck's Benz. I throw my head into my lap as the gates close, hoping they weren't able to get a clear picture of my face.

Benny hits the steering wheel. "How did the goddamn paparazzi get our address?"

I shake my head, staring at the closed gate. The Vultures were circling again.

www.metareel.com/bakersdozen /comingsoon

INT—BAKER HOME—AFTERNOON: The *Baker's Dozen* theme music plays. [BETH BAKER-MILLER sits with KIRK at the Baker-Miller dining room table.]

BETH BAKER-MILLER: How can I describe the past four years? [sighs] Hard. Terrifying. There were nights I would just lie awake, missing Andrew, feeling lost. Being a single mom to thirteen kids is the hardest thing I've ever done. But I love them more than anything in the world. They're my everything.

[Images of the BAKER FAMILY before the show's cancellation]

KIRK MILLER: [standing on the Baker-Miller front porch] Being the stepfather of thirteen kids is . . . [chuckles and shakes his head] Well, it's a truly unique experience. Sometimes I sit back and watch Beth and think, How is she sane? She's amazing.

LEXIE™ BAKER: [sitting on her bed] When the show ended, it was like losing Dad all over again.

[CUT to image of ANDREW BAKER with the children. CUT to BETH, sitting beside KIRK in the Baker-Miller dining room.]

BETH BAKER-MILLER: [tearful, dabbing at her eyes] Worst memory? When we almost lost Bonnie™. There is nothing worse than having a doctor tell you your baby might not make it.

[CUT to clip of BONNIE™ being put on a stretcher.]

VO: LEXIE™: I know Bonnie's ashamed of what happened in season thirteen. I think that's why she's afraid of the cameras now—she hasn't gotten over it. I mean, how do you get over trying to kill yourself?

[CUT to clip of BONNIE™ in the kitchen with her mother.]

BONNIE™: Mom. Have you ever asked yourself why your thirteen-year-old daughter wanted to swallow a bunch of pills?

[CUT to KIRK standing on the Baker-Miller front porch.]

KIRK: Andrew left a big gaping hole in the heart of this family. I don't pretend I can fill it. The wounds these kids feel are deep. They'll never get over what he did to them.

[CUT to BENTON™ in the Baker-Miller living room.]

BENTON™: My name's Benton™, and I'm an alcoholic.

[VO plays over recent footage of the family.]

VO: Tune in next week for a special two-hour live episode of *Baker's Dozen: Fresh Batch*. [Theme music]

SEASON 17, EPISODE 12

(The One in the Janitor's Closet)

o, yeah, the secret is totally out. Once the Vultures found us, MetaReel immediately put our photos up on the website and began airing the promo for the first episode, which, apparently, is going to be live. Benny said that must have been what Mom and Chuck were talking about, but that still doesn't make sense. Chuck said there would be "joy" on my siblings' faces. The thought of a live episode is doing nothing but making all of us jittery. It's one thing to have cameras taping you. It's quite another to know that *at that moment* there are millions of people watching.

These are the texts I got about three hours after the Vultures snapped our photos:

Tessa: You need to call me. Like NOW. My little sister just saw your picture on celeb.com.

Mer: Um. I just looked on MetaReel's website. WTF? You're Bonnie??

Darren (dude from my English class): Hey. This is Darren from

English. We did that Kafka project together in Sept.? RU really Bonie Baker?

Yeah, *B-O-N-I-E.*

~ ~ ~

Mom, on Sunday night, after the magazine people finally leave: "KIDS, DOWNSTAIRS!"

"Oh, so now they want to talk about all this crap?" Benny grumbles.

I resist the urge to pull my hair out. "This day is never going to end."

Our fifteen-hour picture marathon in the studio is finally over, but that doesn't seem to be reason enough to cancel our weekly family meeting. It's always a clumsy ballet of scheduling and chore assignments, peppered with complaints and arguments.

"How many texts have you gotten so far?" Lex asks, falling into step with us. She's glowing. I may have been born on camera, but Lex was born *for* it.

"More than I wanted," I say. And none from Patrick.

"OMG, everyone from school is going to be fuh-reak-ing out," she says.

But her walk is bouncy because Lex can't wait to lord her celeb status over the plebes at Sequoia Arts.

"*Fame! I'm gonna live forever. Baby, remember my name,*" Benny sings.

"Jazz hands," I stage-whisper, waving my fingers around.

Lex just raises her eyebrows. "And *that* little impromptu performance is why I go to an arts institution, and you go to a lame-ass public school."

143

I roll my eyes. "She says, her eyes glittering with malicious intent." My heart skips at the word, and I have to force myself not to replay that part of my date with Patrick.

"Grow up," she growls, pushing Benny aside as he executes some surprisingly limber Rockettes kicks.

"I'm surprised she doesn't get a sunburn from the rays of her own awesomeness," Benny says as Lex heads to the first floor.

"It's a problem that has stumped scientists for years."

When we get downstairs, everyone is seated at the dining room table. There are fresh flowers in the vase and lit candles. I guess I have to get used to my home being a set—all the world's a stage and yaddayaddayadda.

"Okay, guys," Mom says, holding her cell phone and typing into it as she speaks. "The Meanies are back, and we have to stay away from them as much as possible."

"Meanies!" shrieks Jasmine™, aka the Triplet Whose Voice Can Break Glass.

Daisy™ and Violet™ giggle, their little hands covering their faces.

"Who are the Meanies?" prompts Chuck.

He's off camera, just behind Old Guys Rule Dude.

"The Meanies," Mom says, "are the paparazzi. They've set up camp outside our house, and now Kirk and I have to find a way to make sure the kids don't get harassed. This is my number one priority right now."

I think if she hadn't written that book, we might not be having this problem until the first episode airs, but I don't say that because we're barely on speaking terms right now. Plus, there's the whole Chuck-threatening-me thing. I feel like he's watching every word I say, waiting for an opportunity to screw my family over.

Kirk clears his throat. "It's important that we don't acknowledge them."

How the hell does *he* know how to act?

Mom nods. "Benton™, Bonnie™, and Lexie™, I'm sorry but you're probably going to be seeing them a lot. They're not allowed on campus at your schools, but they'll set up shop across the street. Just don't give them the time of day."

The rest of the kids are homeschooled, so they only need to worry about it when they go out with Mom or Kirk. I nod and play with my cuticles, pushing them down, pressing against my nails. I go to my happy place during times like this. I'm on a beach, the waves are licking my toes, I'm— Okay, my happy place is currently unavailable.

"So let's talk about tomorrow," Mom says, opening up her massive day planner.

I tune Mom out and lean back in my chair. Part of me wants to go online and see what people are already saying, just so I'll be prepared. The other part of me wants to never open my laptop again. I picture Tessa, Mer, and Patrick Googling me, and I have to bite my lip to keep the tears back. Mom drones on forever, pointing to the big whiteboard calendar that's on the kitchen wall. I hear the words *book tour* and *Kaye Gibbons Show*, and I mentally vomit.

"Great, thanks, everyone," Kirk says. "Meeting adjourned."

Lacey Production Assistant comes up to me right away. "Hey, Bonnie™?"

When I look at her she backs away a little, like I'm a rabid beast. Maybe I'm glaring, I don't know.

"Um. We need you for a little one-on-one. Can you come down to the basement?"

"It's been a really long day."

"Just a quick chat," she says in a voice that makes it clear she's not asking. I look over toward Chuck and he nods.

I shrug off the hand Lacey puts on my arm and start toward the stairs. When I get down there, the camera is facing a plush couch that has a table next to it with a pretty little lamp and a vase of fresh flowers. I sit down on the couch, cross-legged, and Lacey sits to the right of the camera, on a stool.

"Hey, Bonnie™," Puma Guy says. "Long day, huh?"

I should really learn his name. I can see he's trying to be nice. Maybe he even feels bad for me.

"You know it," I say.

"Okay, ready?" he asks. The red light is blinking.

"Yep, I guess."

"Okay, and five, four, three, two—"

Puma Guy points to Lacey, and she glances down at her clipboard.

"So, Bonnie™, tell me a little bit about how it feels to see the paparazzi again."

I know they will edit out her voice so it seems like I'm just chatting, sitting here and dying to tell America all my feelings. I shake my head.

"If you want to know how it feels to have people point cameras in your face and not care at all that they're freaking *vultures* and to have your friends texting you being like, who *are* you?, then I would have to say it feels like crap."

Lacey closes the big O she's making with her mouth and kind of coughs.

"Um. Okay. So . . . how do you think it's going to be at school tomorrow?"

I grip the little throw pillow on the couch and shrug. "Guess I'll find out when I get there. My prediction is that it's going to suck a lot. Speaking of . . . I have to get up in five hours, so I'm gonna go. 'Night."

I don't wait for permission. I just get up and walk past the camera.

~ ~ ~

"I resent that the Vultures wouldn't even let us go through the Starbucks drive-thru in peace," I say, slamming the passenger-side door.

Good thing we left the house a little early—the student parking lot is almost full, which means the bell for first period will be ringing soon. So much for being early enough to explain myself to Tessa and Mer.

Benny sets his latte on the roof so he can throw on his coat. "Guess we'll have to invest in an espresso machine," he says.

"God, we sound like spoiled assholes, don't we?" I say.

He raises his cup to me in a toast. "I like to think of us as inmates of a comfortable prison."

"Hey, hey. If it isn't my favorite celebrity friends," says Matt.

He and Benny do the fist-bump, half-hug combo that guys do. This is how in-the-closet boyfriends greet each other in public. I wonder, will this change once people start paying more attention to Benny? Maybe they will finally have to be who they really are—or will Matt say he can't handle it?

"Hey, friend," I say, accepting his bear hug.

"Are you sure you want to be seen with us?" Benny asks. He says this seriously, like he's finishing a conversation that started a week ago.

"Yes." Matt's voice is firm, and I feel a tiny prick of jealousy when I see the way he looks at Benny. I wish someone would look at me like that.

"I'm gonna . . ." I point in the general direction of the school.

"Love you," says Benny.

"XOXO," I singsong, mimicking Sandra's voice.

Benny rolls his eyes as I make my way to the front door. My face is already hot, and I keep my eyes down and hide behind my hair. If it weren't so cloudy, I would be wearing the retro sunglasses I bought in the Tower District.

"Chloe."

It's Tessa. She's standing near my locker, holding on to both straps of her backpack. No hug.

"Hey."

I had sent both her and Mer a long e-mail, detailing all the reasons why I hadn't told them the truth. It was apologetic, full of ellipses, and probably the e-mail equivalent of a kicked puppy's whine. Pathetic. Neither of them had gotten back to me.

Tessa just sort of looks at me, like I'm an alien. "I don't know what to say."

I kick at the dirty linoleum. "Um. Did you get my e-mail . . . ?"

She nods. "Yeah. Yeah. It's just so . . ." She kind of waves her hands around.

In a way, I feel so much better, knowing that she knows. Even if it means we can't be friends. Because I always knew I'd have to tell her someday, if we were ever going to have any kind of real friendship. But I just wish I had been in control of the when, where, and how.

"I know this is shitty," I say. "And I totally understand if—you know. I mean, whatever you want to do."

The bell rings, and she kind of shuffles backward.

"Okay. Right. I'll see you, uh, later, I guess."

I'm not sure if that means *please don't eat lunch with me*, or what. It's not like I was planning on doing anything other than hiding out in my car.

"Cool. See you," I say. I open my locker and shove a book into my bag. I don't even know which one it is, I just have to do something with my hands.

There should be a class on where to put your hands during awkward moments. Like, no other animal has to stand around with these ridiculous appendages that make everything worse. Hands are awkward as hell. I watch Tessa disappear down the hall, belonging, being absorbed into the crowd.

I feel disoriented trying to get to class. People are staring, a few obnoxious guys shout "Bonnie™!" as they bolt down the hall to their classes. I don't even know them. It dawns on me that I'm living my worst nightmare. I literally have had almost this exact dream. Except that just when I would reach the feeling of total panic that is beginning to poison my system right now, I would always wake up. Sweating and shaking, I would look around my room and smile into the familiar shadows. But here, now, I don't get to breathe that sigh of relief and fall back against my pillow.

Who am I kidding? I can't do this. I'm about to turn around, back toward the entrance and the student parking lot beyond that, when I see him walking toward me. I can't help it—I stop dead in the center of the hallway, the bodies around me parting like the Red Sea. If this were a movie, Patrick would stop too. We'd stare at each other, breathless, with longing in our eyes.

But he doesn't stop.

I look down and turn around, walking fast. I know he's caught up to me only when I feel his hand slip into mine. I jump, startled by the unexpected touch, but he doesn't let me stop. Instead, he kind of drags me down the hallway, and I stumble after him, confused and a little bit ecstatic because he's *holding my hand*.

"Um. Patrick?"

He looks at me for a second, but he doesn't say anything. I can't get a read on him because his eyes dart away too quickly. The hallway is emptying out, and I keep waiting for a teacher to yell at us to get to class, but just before we reach the door that leads outside, he makes a sharp right, into a tiny hallway I've never noticed before. Probably because it's dark and the door off the side of it says STAFF ONLY.

Patrick opens the door and pulls me inside, shutting it behind us. We're in the kind of darkness that obliterates everything in it, and my heart is doing all kinds of uncomfortable things, and I can hear my blood pumping in my ears, and what is going on? I hear a chain pull and then the little closet flickers with wan light from an overhead fluorescent tube. As the light sputters, it kicks slivers of incandescence around us, some of them cutting into Patrick's face and eyes. When he lets go of my hand, cold air hits my palm. It's important to note that I don't ask why we are in a janitorial closet. Actually, I don't ask anything at all. My voice seems to be malfunctioning.

"So this is what you meant in the park when you said 'it's complicated'?" he asks.

I nod. We stand there, sharing air, listening to the scurrying outside in the hallway. It smells like bleach and Pine-Sol and mold.

It's heaven.

"Should I call you Chloe or Bon—"

"Not the other name." It would feel like defeat, if this boy called me by my MetaReel namesake. "I hate . . ." I shake my head. "Just Chloe. That's my name. I mean, to me. It's my name to me."

He sets his backpack on the ground and leans against a big sink that takes up a third of the closet.

"Are you okay?" he asks, his voice quiet. Serious.

Outside, I hear a locker slam, then it's silent. I wonder if he saw the 911 episode or read the articles about me getting my stomach pumped.

"I'm fine," I say, smiling a little. I'm an "I'm fine" kind of girl, after all.

I can tell he remembers our conversation from last week, because his lip turns up and he gives his head a slight shake.

"Those paparazzi seem rather *malicious*," he says.

"They're *brazen*, that's for sure." I want to find a way to work in *paperweight*, but I can't.

Are we flirting? Where's the moment when he remembers he's supposed to totally ignore me? Heels click on the linoleum outside, and Patrick puts his finger to his lips. I immediately tense up, but the sound of the possible teacher or other adultish person fades away.

"I have three questions," he says.

I slip off my backpack and rest against the wall, next to a huge shelf filled with cleaning supplies.

"I might have three answers." I feel my walls go up, higher than usual.

"Fair enough."

Okay, I need to mention that he's wearing this flannel shirt that's rolled up to his elbows, and he's got this soft gray beanie that gives him a collegiate I Just Got Out of Bed look, both of which really increase his hotness factor.

"One." He holds up a finger. "Why did you leave after I kissed you?"

"Wow. You couldn't start with something easier like, *What's it like to be on a reality TV show?*"

I'm stalling, and he knows it.

"Well," he says, "I assumed that a girl who likes her eggs over easy wouldn't really dig being on a reality TV show," he says. "So . . ."

It's quiet and warm and dim, and I really don't care that it smells weird. This is the safest I have felt in weeks. I'm totally off the radar—MetaReel has no idea where I am.

"I left because . . ." I look up at the ceiling. Oh my God, why am I always almost crying around him? "Because, it's . . . I didn't want to lie to you, and it felt like, um. Like you were kissing someone that wasn't who you thought you were kissing?"

Patrick straightens up and walks the two steps it takes to get to me. I make the mistake of looking into his eyes, and the tears trickle out, tickling my cheeks as they slip down. He wipes them away with the backs of his fingers, and I become this soft, malleable thing under his skin.

"Question number two," he says, almost whispering. I nod. "If I kissed you now, would you A) kiss me back, B) run away, C) tell me this isn't going to work because you're famous again, or D) all of the above?"

"What was A?" I ask. Because I'm now wondering if my mind has

152

created a defense mechanism wherein I invent alternate realities in order to escape the pain of my existence.

"Kiss me back."

"I choose A."

He moves closer and then we're kissing, and for a little while I forget that my entire life is completely insane. I just let myself fall into him, and there's only our breath and the soft sound of our lips and the slight drip of the faucet. My third kiss ever, even better than the first two.

I pull away first. "What was number three?"

He blinks, then leans his forehead against mine. This is better than the kiss. This is the kind of thing that says, *I really like you, I'm not just trying to get in your pants.*

"Number three: I'm not into bullshit relationships—"

"That's not a question," I say.

His lips find mine, quickly. Kissing Patrick Sheldon is better than a grande mocha from Starbucks. Better than the best Radiohead song. Better than just about anything. He pulls away, his lips only centimeters from mine.

"I know," he says. "It's a preface to my question. I'm not into bullshit relationships. By which I mean, I don't want to play games. And I know these past few weeks you've been dealing with unjust amounts of craziness, so maybe what seemed like games was really just confusion. But I really . . . I've been wanting to ask you out for a while now, and I wish I'd done it earlier, before all this happened, but I wasn't totally sure . . . I mean, one minute I'm convinced you feel the same way, and the next you hardly talk to me. But that day you ran out of class, all I wanted to do was follow you. I couldn't handle seeing you upset like that. Um."

He kisses me again. I think this officially qualifies as making out. I am making out with Patrick Sheldon in a janitorial closet. After a while, he pulls away, but slowly, like he doesn't want to, but time is of the essence.

"Sorry. What was I saying?"

"You wanted to follow me."

This is the best day of my life. Which is weird, because it was maybe the third worst about five minutes ago.

"Right. So. My question is, how do you feel about boyfriends?"

Best. Day. Ever.

"I feel . . . do you mean boyfriends in general or specific boyfriends?"

"Very specific."

"Isn't there an order to this? Aren't there steps that we're skipping—"

"Screw steps. I want to be with you."

I grin. I mean, there is just no one like Patrick Sheldon. I reach my hands up and trace the tips of my fingers along his jawline. I open my mouth to say YES YES YES! but then my life comes crashing back down on me. I imagine his picture on the cover of *US Weekly*, or MetaReel trying to make an episode out of my parents meeting him.

"You don't want to be with me, Patrick."

"Funny, because I'm pretty sure I just said the opposite." He smiles, like he knows he's already won.

I let go of him and walk to the sink, keeping my arms crossed.

"You saw the paparazzi out there, right? And MetaReel knows where I am twenty-four, seven. So when we were at the park, imagine that on camera, for all of America to see. I mean, you can't even call me. My phone is bugged. What kind of girlfriend has a bugged phone? It's worse than a dad with a shotgun."

Patrick's lips form a thin line, and he shoves his hands in his pockets. "What about your brother and Matt? What are they gonna do?"

I stare at him. "I don't know what you're talking about."

"Chloe. I'm not an idiot. Unlike most people around here, I actually pay attention to what's going on."

Wow. Not even Tessa or Mer have guessed that one.

"Besides," he adds, "Ben and I are friends. We talk. They know I know."

I make a mental note to WHAA? to my brother next time we're alone.

"I don't know what they're doing," I say. "I mean, I can't imagine Benny without Matt. It would kill him if . . ."

"Is it that you don't trust me? Like, do you think I want to be some kind of pathetic B-list celebrity and I'm going to leech onto you—"

"So you think I'm pathetic? Or my family is?"

This is the thing: I can talk shit about my family, but no one else is allowed to.

Patrick's quiet for a minute and then he puts his hands on my shoulders and leans down so we're eye to eye.

"I'm not going to let you do this."

"Do what?" I ask.

"Push me away so I'll get angry and give up."

I shake my head. "I'm not trying to!"

"So you don't trust me, is that it?"

155

"It's just . . . I feel like, so much is happening, and I have liked you for, I mean ever since I got here, right? And I'm freaking out because I'm so used to people only being nice to me because I'm famous. So I feel . . ."

Suddenly he wraps his arms around me so that the warmth of him seeps into the coldness of me. He smells like dryer sheets and pine needles again.

"I don't want to push you," he says.

"Yes you do," I say, my voice muffled against his shirt.

It occurs to me that I am living out my fantasy, right here, right now. Minus the janitorial closet. Maybe this is the universe's way of making things up to me: Patrick in exchange for a messed-up childhood.

"Okay, you're right. But only because I know we'd be great. And I don't want to wait for you to figure it out."

I think about the night at the park. How he's the only person who's ever asked me how I liked my eggs, except for waitresses.

"So what are the responsibilities of Patrick Sheldon's girlfriend?" I ask.

I can hear the smile in his voice. "She has to be willing to jump into janitorial closets at a moment's notice. This is absolutely essential."

I laugh. "Okay . . ."

"She has to trust him and know he will never, ever screw her over and that he has absolutely no aspirations for fame. More on that later."

"Uh-huh."

"She has to sometimes be willing to do totally insane things."

"Like what?"

"Like ditch school all day today. I've instructed Ben and Matt to meet us behind the gym in five minutes, by the way."

"How—"

"Just say yes."

"To what?"

He kisses my forehead, then his lips move to my ear. "Are we together?"

I shiver. "Do you promise never to Google me? I mean, I'm sure you already have, but, like, never again?"

"I didn't Google you," he says. "My mom read about your family somewhere and asked me if I knew the famous girl who was hiding out at my school. I've never seen your show."

I bite my lip. "So you don't know about. Um. There was something that happened, a few years ago—"

"And you can tell me about it if you want to." He tucks my hair behind my ear. "You can't convince me to be un–into you."

In the dim light I can see hints of the feeling in his eyes. I know that if I want to understand what it means to let someone in, someone other than Benny, I'll have to take a risk. I have to hope that he won't let me down. That he can be a person who is a place—a place where I can go and call a time-out on all the uncertainty and awfulness of my life.

"Okay. Yes."

He tilts his head to the side, unsure.

"I'll be your damn girlfriend."

He doesn't even try to hide the excitement in his voice. "Excellent."

I narrow my eyes. "So when you set things up with Benny, you were pretty confident that you could get me to agree to this in ten minutes?"

He frowns. "I was hoping five, but Ben said you'd put up a fight." He checks his watch then gives me that crooked smile I love. "But we still have two minutes."

"Hmmm . . . what's a girl to do with—"

Patrick doesn't let me finish the sentence.

SEASON 17, EPISODE 13

(The One with the Pepsi Freezes)

"*Y*ou are scarily good at evading school officials," I tell Patrick.

It had taken the four of us a while to surreptitiously cram into his car, but we're finally moving. I'm currently lying in a fetal position in the backseat of his mom's SUV, hiding from the Vultures. Matt's in the front seat with Patrick, and Benny's hunched up on the floor next to me, his knees drawn up to his chest.

Patrick looks at me in the rearview mirror, and his eyes crinkle up a little as he smiles. "It's all about the execution. You just have to act like you're supposed to be doing whatever it is you're doing, and few people question it."

"I fully recognize that I'm already enjoying the fringe benefits of your relationship with my sister," says Benny. "However, I draw the line at you turning her into a criminal mastermind."

"Damn. I thought we were all going to rob a bank or something," I say.

Patrick laughs. "Oh, that's for this weekend."

"There are a million dudes with cameras out here," Matt says. "You guys really *are* famous."

I can't see, but we must be turning out of the parking lot. Thank God Patrick's mom opted for tinted windows.

"They probably want to get a picture of my alcoholic self," Benny mutters. "So much for getting into a decent university."

Ever since he saw the "intervention" spot on MetaReel's website, Benny's been freaking.

"Everyone loves a reformed sinner," I say.

He snorts. "Matt, be a dick and take a picture of them with your camera phone—let them know how it feels."

"Don't these guys have anything better to do?" Patrick mutters.

I hold my breath as the car turns out of the lot. I can picture the paparazzi out there, with their long black telephoto lenses and their cigarettes and cups of gas station coffee. They were the first thing I saw when I pulled out of my driveway this morning. They'd followed us to the drive-thru at Starbucks, then finally camped outside our school. *Fifteen* photographers, shouting my name whenever they saw me. Which, I smile to myself, is not right now.

"Okay, we're out," Patrick says. "It doesn't look like anyone's following."

"Benny, did you turn off your phone?" I ask, my voice panicked.

"No. Why?"

"Um. MetaReel tracking us with GPS?"

"Shit. It's like, it's in my . . ." Benny struggles to get it out of his back pocket. He bangs his elbow against the door. "*Ow*. Okay, got it. Off." He rolls his eyes, and I nod as if to say, *Yeah, I know.*

Patrick does something with the radio and then old-school

Weezer comes on—the song, "Island in the Sun," is the perfect soundtrack for our little adventure: *We'll run away together.*

"Where are we going?" I ask.

Patrick risks a look back at me and smiles. "Where do you want to go?"

It doesn't take me too long to think of a first stop. "Can we get Pepsi Freezes?"

"Your wish is my command," he says, turning onto Summit Avenue.

"Side note: I love Pepsi Freezes almost as much as I love Matt," says Benny.

"Excuse me?" Matt turns his burly Abercrombie-esque body around. "Pepsi Freezes are not about to frolic with you in a media shit storm, Benton™ Andrew Baker."

I've never heard them be so open about their relationship with anyone but me. It's beautiful and disorienting, and I'm just going to burst with how amazing this day is becoming.

"Yo! Turn around! You have to keep up appearances," Benny says, shooing at Matt with his hands. "Remember, two members of the Baker family are not lying in extremely uncomfortable positions in the backseat of a pseudoanarchist's car right now."

"Pseudo?" Patrick says. "I resent you pseudo-ifying me."

"Oh, you've been . . . whatever you just said," Benny says.

"Chloe." Patrick catches my eye. "Am I required to frolic in said shit storm as well?"

" 'Fraid so," I say.

"*Ob-la-di, ob-la-da*," he says.

Matt furrows his brow. "Huh?"

"Beatles," I say. It gives me a little thrill, knowing I speak Patrick Sheldon.

Patrick pulls into one of the gas stations in town that sells Pepsi Freezes, which are basically Pepsi Slurpees, but way better. Plus, this was a secret test of mine to determine our true compatibility; only one of the three gas stations in town that sell Pepsi Freezes actually gets the Pepsi-to-Freeze ratio right. Patrick passed.

"Okay, we're here. Be right back," Patrick says.

"Baby, can you get me a pack of American Spirits?" Benny asks Matt.

"Um. Sure. Because I really like watching my boyfriend kill himself," Matt says, opening the door. I love that Matt's refusing to use his fake ID for Benny's nasty habit.

"So that's a no?"

"Shhh," I hiss. "We're not supposed to be here right now."

Matt gets out, and I hear Patrick laughing as they walk away.

I give Benny a look. "When were you going to tell me that you guys came out to Patrick?"

He shrugs. "I was never a hundred percent sure that he was into you. I mean, I was pretty sure, but then some days it seemed like when your name came up, he wanted to change the subject. Now I know it's because he didn't know how *you* felt about *him*. I just didn't want to complicate things."

"How would that complicate things?"

"Because if you knew he knew, it might make you fall harder for him, and I didn't want that to happen unless he felt the same way." He notices my confused glance and adds, "Tolerance is irresistible."

"So, he's known about you and Matt since . . . ?"

"A long time. But he didn't tell me he knew until September."

I shake my head. "So how long has he liked me?"

"You don't wanna know."

I look past the neon signs advertising processed food and coffee to where Patrick and Matt are filling up huge cups with thick brown liquid. My heart does crazy pirouettes because *my boyfriend is buying me a Pepsi Freeze*. "I wanna know," I say.

"Since last fall, when you guys had English together."

I groan and throw my head in my hands, but Benny just laughs. "Whatever. You guys are together now. Speaking of, on a scale from one to ten, ten being the level of a Justin Bieber fan who gets to take a picture with him backstage, how happy are you right now?"

I laugh. "Okay, I'm going to go with a seven because we're still doing the show and it was super weird with Tessa this morning."

"Seven's good," he says.

I nod as I see Patrick come out of the gas station with two Pepsi Freezes in hand. "Seven's good."

~ ~ ~

"I vote the pink one," Benny says.

Patrick frowns. "I don't know. I sort of prefer the green, actually."

"Matt?" I hold up the two wigs, and he shakes his head.

"I am so not qualified to make a judgment call on this."

We're in the dollar store, surrounded by random crap made in China that has provided us with over forty minutes of uninterrupted entertainment. It is my new favorite place in the world.

"I'm going with the Groucho Marx look," Benny says. "There's no way the Vultures will recognize me with these on."

"Nice," I say.

I throw a floral gardening hat on Patrick's head. "We can call you Patricia," I say, as Benny and Matt wander off.

"This doesn't make me more conspicuous?"

"Hmm. Maybe a little. Are we trying to blend in or be so outrageous that they assume there's no way it could be us?" I ask.

Patrick takes off the hat and puts on a pair of googly eyeglasses. "Hey, you're the expert on this, not me."

"Chlo, they have mini Christmas trees!" Benny shouts from a few aisles over.

I see the cashier crane his neck in our direction.

"Ten bucks says he kicks us out in the next fifteen minutes. He probably thinks we're gonna steal something," I whisper to Patrick.

He grabs a pair of neon blue sunglasses and sets them on me. The cheap lenses turn everything brown. "Are you kidding? We're the most exciting thing that's going to happen to this store today," he says.

He leans in and gives me a quick kiss, googly eyes and all. "Look, two hours as my girlfriend and you already have green hair and outrageous sunglasses."

My hands find their way around his waist without me telling them to go there, which is kind of cool. "I like that word."

"Outrageous?" he teases, leaning in again.

"Chlo!" Benny stage-whispers.

"Christmas calls," I say.

Patrick groans, but follows me over to aisle five. On our way, we pass a display of Thanksgiving tablecloths, and my stomach immediately clenches; in two and a half days, we'll be shooting our live premiere. As if it's not bad enough that we have to do the show in the first place, Chuck has decided that our first one should be as stressful as possible. No pressure, it's just millions of people watching. In his words, "It's like you're a distant relative people haven't seen in a while and you're inviting them all to celebrate the holidays with you!"

"What's up?" Patrick asks.

His eyebrows come together in a frown, and he reaches out, brushing a stray lock of hair out of my eyes. My heart plays hopscotch as it hits me again that he and I are together. Somehow, with all the crap at home, something seriously wonderful is in my life.

"I was just . . ." I see a multi-pack of Wrigley's Spearmint and grab it. "I'm buying you this."

"You know I have about a thousand of those at home, right?"

I lean in closer. "Yeah, but not from *me*."

By the time we leave the dollar store, we're armed with various useless disguises, copious amounts of off-brand candy, and a mini Christmas tree.

"Hungry?" Patrick asks.

"Where can we go that someone will not take camera phone pics of us?" asks Benny.

"My place?" Patrick suggests.

"Whoa. Already taking my sister home to meet the parents, eh? This is getting serious. I haven't even had the birds and the bees talk with her yet."

I hit him. "Ohmygod, Benny, *shut up*."

Patrick's lips snake up a little. "They're at work. I might have great parents, but they wouldn't be particularly thrilled that I ditched school."

As Patrick pulls into his family's garage, happy anticipation fills me, like when I'm in a crowded movie theater and the lights go down. I never get over going to other people's houses—it feels crazy intimate to me, like I'm getting to see this private part of their existence. Before the show started filming again, sharing my home with someone would have meant telling them my biggest secret. Just casually being in someone's house feels like I'm reading their diary.

"Okay, you two. It's safe to get out," Matt says.

Benny groans. "Oh, thank you, sweet Jesus."

The door opens, and Patrick helps me out, keeping his hand in mine as he leads us inside the house. I still don't know what the outside looks like, but the inside resembles Tessa's: a two-story house in one of the older developments, cozy and lived in. Patrick gives us a quick tour and laughs good-naturedly when Benny and Matt give him shit about all the pictures of him on the walls.

"I can't even comprehend being an only child," I say.

What would it be like, to be the center of your parents' universe?

"Well, I can't comprehend having enough siblings to populate a small island nation," he says.

Benny shakes his head. "Oh, man, you have no freaking idea."

Patrick opens a door at the end of the hall on the second floor. "This is my room."

"Which my sister will only see when chaperoned."

"Really, he's always like this," I mutter to Patrick. "Doctors have been searching for a cure, but . . ." I shrug, and Benny sticks his tongue out at me.

Patrick's room is much more organized than I imagined it would be, but it is still very much a Patrick kind of room. Everything in its right place. A stack of Wrigley's spearmint gum sits on his desk, and his bookcase is full of books like *On the Road* and *Fear and Loathing in Las Vegas.*

"These are random and awesome," I say, pointing to a series of black-and-white photos on the wall. A Ferris wheel, a car from the thirties, workers in a field.

"Oh, yeah. I found them in my grandparents' basement last Christmas. My grandpa took them when he was a kid. He grew up around here, too."

There's a black-and-white poster of the Empire State Building and another one of—I step toward it for a closer look—the caption says it's the Walt Disney Concert Hall in LA. It's futuristic and wild, made of metal that looks like waves. It's not a building, it's a giant sculpture.

"I like that you don't have supermodel posters or baseball trophies," I say.

Patrick laughs. "No, none of those."

"Holy shit, Sheldon," says Matt. He holds up a brochure. "Columbia?"

Patrick reddens slightly and shakes his head. "Parental hopes that are going to dash on the rocks of . . . fill in the blank with something poetic. Lunch?"

"Changing the subject?" asks Benny.

Matt's stomach growls, and we laugh away some of the awkwardness.

"We're gonna raid your fridge," Benny says. He grabs Matt's hand and ushers him out of the room, giving us some privacy.

"Did you already apply?" I ask.

I hope I sound nonchalant, like I'm just oozing with idle curiosity. This is hard to fake because the last thing anyone wants to find out within the first two hours of a new relationship is that their boyfriend's possibly/maybe moving across the country in less than a year. I can physically feel the turn in our conversation sap the bright, happy enthusiasm I've been splashing around in since we got off campus. Now I feel like I'm in dirty bathwater that's growing cold, when it seemed like only seconds ago it was all warmth and rainbow-colored bubbles.

"Yeah, I applied a few weeks ago." He fiddles with the blinds next to his bed, adjusting them so the sunlight isn't in my face. "But, I mean, it's *Columbia*. The chances of . . ." He runs a hand through his hair, embarrassed. "I mean, they have one of the best architecture programs in the country."

That explains the sketchbooks on his desk, the cup of perfectly sharpened pencils.

He moves closer to me. "What about you?" he asks, his voice soft, like he can sense my mood just walked into an industrial freezer. "When you graduate, you're free, right? No more show?"

I don't think so. For the rest of my life I will have to carry around my past. My whole childhood can be downloaded, streamed, or purchased in a boxed set of DVDs on MetaReel's website. Then there're the books Mom wrote and the books other people wrote and articles about me that are just out there in the ether, waiting for someone to stumble upon them. *Free* is not in my vocabulary.

My eyes scan the walls, roam over his record collection. "This is the room of someone who knows who they are and what they want." I try to smile at him. "I don't have a room like this. I'm just trying to get through high school."

My room, with its pictures of travel destinations, is all about escape. It's the only dream I've ever really had. But you can't major in running away.

He wraps his arms around me, and I can't believe it's almost

168

starting to feel normal, but it is. My head automatically falls against his chest, and my hands press against his shoulder blades as he rests his chin on top of my head.

"I think you might be the coolest person I know," he says. I snort, and he tightens his grip on me. "Seriously. Every time you spoke in class I was like, *yes*. Plus, I've been watching you from afar in a totally noncreepy way, and I can say with certainty that you have never seemed like you don't know what you're about. You're, I don't know, you're this composite of awesomeness."

"Good band name," I say against his chest.

"Yeah. The Composite of Awesomeness. Let's do it. Can you play an instrument?"

"No."

"Sing?"

"Definitely not," I say.

"Then let's be one of those bands that are really shitty but because we say we're artists people will be afraid to criticize us."

I laugh. "Okay. Maybe we'll throw a little Nietzsche in there to intimidate the haters."

"Excellent."

"Hungry! Dying of starvation! There is a famine in the Sheldon kitchen!" yells Matt.

"You better not be on his bed!" adds Benny.

I pull away. "Coming!"

Patrick grabs my hand again as we start toward the kitchen. It's warm and solid, something I want to hold on to for as long as I can. "Six more months, and the world is your proverbial oyster," he says.

I want to believe him. I really do. But, somehow, I feel like I'll be carrying the weight of my family around for the rest of my life.

MEET THE BAKER'S DOZEN!

<u>Bonnie™ Elizabeth Baker</u>

Age: 17

Favorite Color: Pink

Favorite Movie: Anything with Jude Law

Favorite TV Show: *Big, Bad Baby Mamas* (www.metareel.com/baby)—MetaReel's new show!

Favorite Quote: "Dance like everyone's watching and you don't care." (Denise Henshaw, cast member of MetaReel's *High School Drop-Out*)

Favorite Food: Beauty Bar™ from Health Nutz™

Fun Fact: Bonnie™ is the only one of her brothers and sisters to be born on national TV! Watch the episode <u>here</u>.

What she wants to be when she grows up: A fashion designer (and a RealMom™)

What she's most excited about: The Bonnie Lass™ halter dress in "Turquoise Dream" and getting to graduate this summer!

Favorite *Baker's Dozen* Episode: Season 11, Episode 17: The one where she got to learn how to ride a horse at Horsin' Around™ in Malibu, CA. Watch this and all of her fave episodes <u>here</u>.

Her Scrapbook: Click <u>here</u> to see photos of Bonnie™ since she was a baby! And don't forget to check out the family <u>blog</u> to keep up with all of the Baker's Dozen.

SEASON 17, EPISODE 14

(The One with the Skittles)

The next day at school, Tessa and Mer are waiting by my locker. When they see me, they both wave, and some of the despair huddled in my chest disappears when I see the hopeful smiles they give me. I haven't talked to either of them since yesterday morning, when Tessa could barely say two words to me. I came to school today assuming I didn't have friends anymore and had planned to be that sad girl who has to eat lunch by herself in her car. I hug my books tighter against me and push through the crowd. I'm almost to them when the first taunting of the day happens.

"Hey, Bonnie™!" says this little twerp I've never seen.

"Fuck off," say Tessa and Mer at the same time.

The three of us look at one another, the kid forgotten, and burst out laughing. Tessa throws her arms around me, and Mer hugs both of us, and we become this blob of blubbery forgiveness in the middle of the packed hallway. I want to cry or laugh or maybe do both at the same time, but instead I just breathe them in, the men's cologne that Tessa wears and Mer's watermelon-scented lip gloss.

"I'm sorry for being such a bitch," Tessa says into my hair. "I just didn't know what to think. We're the crappiest friends ever."

"We suck at life," Mer agrees.

I shake my head. "I lied to you guys. I didn't want to, but I did. Seriously, I understand. You were hurt—it's okay."

Tessa pulls away and takes a long look at me. "No, it's not."

And from the look on her face, I can tell she's not just talking about her behavior. She's talking about my life. I can picture her sitting at her desk, researching my childhood as if it's one of her AP History projects. Instead of making me angry, the thought adds to my relief.

"I'm glad you know," I say. And she nods like she understands I mean the show *and* the pills.

"Well, I feel like a frickin' idiot for not recognizing you," Mer says. "My mom used to watch your show all the time. Like, how did I not put your face and last name together?"

I have a flash of Mer's mom watching me throw a tantrum or seeing my parents get into one of their epic fights, and I try not to judge her. She didn't know she was watching one of her daughter's future best friends. To her, we were just another TV show.

"I'm glad you didn't recognize me," I said. "If you had, I totally would have gone back to homeschooling. When I first got here, I thought there was no way it would work—becoming Chloe, hiding my family. But four years off the air is like four hundred in reality TV years, you know?"

"I never watched the show, but I'm still surprised I didn't

172

recognize you from all the magazine covers." Tessa gently pulls a lock of my hair. "You look better as a brunette, by the way."

I agree. "Yeah, they say blondes have more fun, but that's so not true."

The bell rings for first period, and the students around us surge toward the classrooms. I grab my books out of my locker, and the three of us walk down the hall.

"Hey, where were you yesterday?" Mer asks, just before she peels off for chem.

"Playing hooky," I say.

I see Patrick up ahead with his friend Max. He catches my eye, and his grin holds all kinds of delicious promises.

"Okay . . . what's *that* about?" Tessa asks.

My face goes through about ten different shades of red before it settles on desert rose.

"I'll tell you at lunch."

I walk into first period, too high on having my friends back to care about the way the air seems to suck out of the room as soon as I enter it. Let them stare and whisper and update their Facebooks and Twitters.

Right now, they can't touch me.

~ ~ ~

Diane Finchburg is pretty nice. I want to hate her, but it's sort of hard to be against someone with an unlimited supply of Skittles. A half hour into our session, I'm still sitting in her sunny office, munching on my second Fun Pack, staring out the window behind the cluttered desk with the DIANE FINCHBURG, SCHOOL COUNSELOR nameplate on it. My punishment from Mom for ditching school yesterday is to start seeing the Skittle Lady so that I can, in her words, "learn healthier ways to cope with the show." When I'd pointed out that Benny had been ditching just as much, Mom gave me a look that basically said, *Benny's not a nutcase like you.* So I didn't really pursue that line of questioning because there were two producers and a camera in the room at the time.

Now I'm here, talking to a stranger about my problems. It's a little less awful than I thought it would be. She's wearing this cute sparkly headband I saw on the J.Crew website—it clashes with her rubber duckie socks, but I like that about her. Instead of being all clinical behind the desk, she's in the chair next to mine. The fact that she's not wearing any shoes somehow makes me forget we're even at school.

"So how do you think the taping will go on Thursday?" she asks in her chamomile tea voice.

I shrug. "I mean, bad, probably. It's live. Anything can happen."

"It must be hard to concentrate in class with all this going on at home."

"A little, I guess. But it's okay."

I wonder if my responses are frustrating because I'm not the spaz Mom probably made me out to be.

"Chloe, I want you to know that anything we say here stays in this room. I'm not gonna pick up the phone and call your mom. There are no cameras, no MetaReel. It's just me and you, okay?"

"Okay."

Still. I'm not going to be telling her my deepest, darkest secrets anytime soon.

"Mr. Schwartz says you're really bright. One of his best students. Have you thought about helping out with student government? He's in charge of that, you know. I could talk to him."

"I don't do clubs or anything like that. It's . . ."

I trail off because I don't want to answer, and I don't owe her one. It feels like every random person I come into contact with wants me to bare my soul. I know Skittle Lady's trying to be nice, but at the end of the day, she's just another Lacey Production Assistant without a cameraman by her side.

"Are you afraid people won't accept you for who you are? That they'll only see you as Bonnie™?"

I roll a purple Skittle around in my mouth. "Maybe. I don't know."

Clubs are for people who belong. I don't. It's almost as simple as that. Almost.

She makes a steeple with her fingertips. "What about your dad? What does he have to say about all this?"

"Kirk?"

"No. Your biological father."

"He's not on the show anymore."

If one of us died, we'd probably say it like that. *Oh, so-and-so's not on the show anymore. Didn't you see episode twenty, the One with the Funeral?*

"Your mother mentioned you might want to talk about him."

"Why? *She* never does. Unless it's in a book half the country's going to read."

Ms. Finchburg nods like she understands, which, let me tell you, she most certainly does not.

"How does that make you feel?" she asks.

Psych 101 rears its ugly head.

"It makes me feel like she's glad he's gone."

"Are *you* glad he's gone?"

How many times have I asked myself that question? The answer changes every day. Yes. No. I don't know. I hate him. I hate her. I hate me.

"I'm glad they're not screaming at each other all the time." I point to a picture on her wall. "That's really cool." Patrick would like it, I think. It's a black-and-white photograph of a bunch of guys eating lunch on this tiny beam high above New York City. It makes my hands sweat, just looking at it.

Diane Finchburg glances at the print for a second. "Thanks." Pause, then, "So have you spoken to your father recently?"

She's good about not letting me change the subject, I'll give her that.

"Okay. Ms. Finchburg—"

"Diane."

"*Diane*. I really appreciate that you're, like, trying to aid delinquent youth and everything, but I'm just not comfortable talking to you about my dad. He's not around, he hasn't been for a long time. That's really all you need to know."

"Okay, sure." She shifts in her chair, crosses her legs. "Why don't we talk a bit about the panic attacks. Your mom said you used to get them a lot. Had any lately?"

I shrug.

"I used to get them in college," she says. "I have a little trick that gets rid of one before it starts—wanna hear it?"

"I guess."

She tells me that as soon as I get that heart attack feeling in my chest, I should close my eyes and take a deep breath while counting to ten.

"When you get to ten," she says, "exhale and imagine all that panic leaving you."

"Simple as that?" I say. My old shrink made me read self-help books and suggested I get in touch with my spirit guide. I'm not holding out much hope for deep breathing.

She smiles. "It's all up to you. I'm guessing by now you know that there isn't really much about life that's simple."

I snort. "You could say that."

The bell rings, and I get up.

"Have a good lunch, Chloe," she says.

"Yeah. Uh. Thanks for these," I say, holding up the Skittles.

"Anytime."

I slip out of her room, thankful that no one in the front office sees me come out of there. All it takes is one person, and the tabloids will be all, *BONNIE™ BAKER: Unstable Already?* Or something like that. When I step into the hallway, Patrick is waiting for me.

"Did you Apparate here or something? The bell rang two seconds ago."

He laughs. "I have class across the hall." He puts an arm around my shoulders as we start walking toward my locker, and I love how this broadcasts our togetherness to the world. "How was it?"

"Sugary," I say. "Taste the rainbow?" I shake the bag of Skittles.

He holds out his hand, and I pour a few onto his palm. "I hope we're eating more than this for lunch."

"Can lunch happen far away from my peers?"

"Chloe!"

I turn around, and Tessa's eyes kind of widen as she notices Patrick's arm around my shoulders.

"Okay, we don't hang out for *one* day, and you guys are PDA'ing?"

"Um . . ."

She looks from me to Patrick. "So is this an official thing or a we're-taking-it-slow thing?"

I look up at Patrick. "Excuse her frankness. She's a journalist," I say.

"Official," Patrick says, squeezing my shoulder. "Unless you've already left me for another man?"

I shake my head. "A movie star tried to sweep me off my feet last night, but I turned him down."

For a second, it's just Patrick's sandy eyes and my arm tightening around his waist and—

"I'm still here," Tessa says. "Just in case you guys are going to start making out or something."

I blush, and Tessa grins, holding up a key. "Schwartz said the gov classroom can be ours every day during lunch, as long as we open it back up five minutes before class."

"Whoa," I say. "How'd you manage that?"

I know Schwartz likes us, but this is all kinds of favoritism. Not that I'm opposed to it.

"I told him I was a terrible friend, that I had deserted you in your time of need, and that I could maybe buy back your trust with a place to have lunch without everyone snapping pictures of you with their phones. And I threw in a Snickers to sweeten the deal."

I smile, suddenly lighter than air. "Thanks, friend."

She squeezes my arm. "I really am sorry."

"Me too." It feels so good to stop lying to my best friend.

I turn to Patrick. "Do you want to come, or are you gonna hang out with Max and Derrick?"

They're his closest friends at Taft, but I see Patrick driving alone off campus almost as much as I see him eating with them. Not that I've been keeping track of him or anything.

He grabs my hand. "Lead the way."

After lunch, I can hardly concentrate in gov.

I'm actually really into Schwartz's lecture on dictatorships, but all I can think about is that my family's shooting our live episode in less than forty-eight hours, and I want nothing more than to contract a horrible contagious disease. I wish My Life Sucks wasn't my brain's default.

"So who can relate the Heisenberg Uncertainty Principle that we discussed yesterday to *1984*?" Schwartz asks.

Tessa's hand is up in half a second, of course. He nods. "Lee?"

"The whole Heisenberg thing is basically saying that once something is observed, it changes. So if we apply it to *1984*, we could say that since Big Brother is watching everyone twenty-four-seven, this would mean that the characters in the book are changing how they would normally act—like, if they weren't being watched, they'd probably behave differently. There are cameras on them all the time—er."

Her face flushes red, and she casts an apologetic look my way. Suddenly I'm the elephant in the room.

"Anyway," Tess says, her words tumbling over one another in a flustered race, "Wilson and the other characters, they're aware that Big Brother is tracking everything they do, so we don't really know *how* they would act if they were just . . . living a normal life."

Schwartz catches my eye to see if I have something to say, and I shake my head, just a little, and he nods. I was hoping school would be an escape from the kind of crap I'm thinking about all the time, but apparently not. I sort of can't wait until the *1984* unit is over. Bring on early colonial law or apartheid or something.

"But the Heisenberg Principle applies to all of society," Patrick adds.

Schwartz leans against his desk. "Explain."

"I mean, you don't need a camera on you to be observed, right? School, for example. We're all probably different at home, but when we're here, everyone's under a social microscope. So our behavior alters to conform and fit in. We might not even know we're changing the way we act. It just happens naturally. The trick is to be true to yourself, no matter who the hell—er, *heck*—is watching."

I reach my hand back, and he clasps it under his desk.

"So everyone's observing everyone all the time, which means we don't really know who the *real* version of anyone is?" Mer asks.

Patrick nods. "Yeah. And so, basically, Big Brother doesn't have to watch us because we're watching each other."

One of the slackers on the other side of the room, Michael Ingraham, gets this look on his face, very lightbulb-going-off.

"So, like Facebook, right?" he says.

Schwartz nods. "Care to elaborate a bit, Mr. Ingraham?"

"I mean, like, we're always saying who we're with, where we are, what we're doing. It's like we're spying on each other."

"Oh my God," Mer says. "That's legit creepy."

I so don't have a Facebook. For obvious reasons.

Someone in the back of the room groans. "This is hurting my brain."

Schwartz laughs. "Okay, okay. Good insights here. For homework tonight, I want a page on how the Heisenberg Uncertainty Principle applies to one character in the novel. Give examples."

The bell rings, and I gather up my books.

Tessa puts her hand on my arm. "Chlo, I'm sor—"

I roll my eyes. "I'm not made of glass, Tess. It's cool, don't worry about it."

Patrick leans close to my ear. "There's going to be a very important meeting in the janitor's closet at precisely 2:47 P.M. Attendance is mandatory," he whispers, planting a quick kiss on my cheek.

Before I can answer him, he sweeps out of the room. If things like that could just keep happening, I would never have to think about the show again.

"Janitor's closet?" says Tessa. "Scandalous!"

I laugh. For once, this is a scandal I am totally okay with.

SEASON 17, EPISODE 15

(The One That's Live)

"Bonnie™, we really need to see you in the blue dress. It's one of the signature items from your new collection!"

I look at Sandra, clasping my hands together in supplication. "Please don't make me wear that thing. It makes me look like an American Girl doll."

It's frilly and has black velvet ribbons and capped sleeves.

"Nonsense. Now take off those jeans."

I sigh and do as she asks. Because I am spineless and nervous. And maybe Kirk is right—maybe to get through this in one piece, I'll have to choose my battles. Sandra does stuff to my hair and face and then pronounces me gorgeous and ready to entertain twelve million viewers. I clutch at my stomach and try to eat a few more saltines. I don't know if I'm actually coming down with something or if it's just nerves, but I've been nauseous since I woke up this morning. I've never had stage fright before—being born on national television and then spending your childhood in front of a camera pretty much eliminates that possibility. But here I am, feeling like a total rookie. I still have no idea what Mom and Chuck are planning for this episode—it's MetaReel, so anything can happen.

Lacey Production Assistant sticks her head in my room. "Hey, Bonnie™. Oh! Cute dress."

I take in her jeans and T-shirt. "Trade you."

She laughs. "We're going live in fifteen minutes, okay? Your mom wants you downstairs."

"All right."

I take one more look in the mirror and then make my way to the nucleus of the Baker-Miller household. The chaos meter is at a ten, except we all look nicer than usual. I stop two fights and give three mini lectures before I get to the front hallway. It's times like these that I'm thankful to be a big sister to ten siblings—it's the best birth control out there. You won't see me on MetaReel's *Sweet Sixteen Mom* anytime soon.

"Hey, hey," says Benny, when I finally enter the kitchen. He's wearing so-not-him clothes. He looks around, then lowers his voice. "Is Patrick watching?"

I nod. "Yeah. I told him this is the only episode he'll ever get to see. I just feel like . . . I need to know at least one person out there isn't a hater, you know?"

Lex saunters in, looking like a pop star. "So who's this Patrick guy I keep hearing you two whispering about?"

"Just a guy from school," I say.

She'd never understand my adoration of a boy with ratty T-shirts and unwashed hair. Lex goes through guys like they're ChapStick, each of them variations on the Ken doll.

"Right," she says, unconvinced. But she doesn't push it. Maybe the holiday season is bringing out the decent in her.

"Anyone having fond memories of Thanksgivings past?" Benny asks, pointing at the turkey in the oven.

"Are we talking season eleven?" I say.

"Oh, God," Lex moans. "That was a disaster."

Three words: Rachael Ray, Dad, wine. Basically, he got drunk and hit on Rachael Ray, celebrity chef, while she was trying to teach him to make a turkey. It probably would have gone over all our heads if he hadn't tried to cop a feel. That was the year we ate McDonald's for Thanksgiving.

"What a bastard, huh?" says Benny.

Mom comes in, holding a turkey baster in one hand and a glass of white wine in the other. Does she have the same memory every Thanksgiving? She must, right?

"Oh, there you are!" she says.

A frilly apron sets off her girlish figure, and her hair is blow-dried to perfection. She has the kind of haircut that women all over America will be asking their hairstylists to give them for the next year, a shoulder-length deal with lots of layers.

Mom pulls me against her for a hug that smells like chardonnay and gravy. "Truce?" she asks, her voice a whisper in my ear. When I don't say anything, she pulls back and gives me a hangdog expression. "It's Thanksgiving."

"Okay," I say, feeling like a traitor to myself. I don't want to pretend that everything's fine, but even the bloodiest battles have a cease-fire now and then.

Mom looks me up and down, then nods in approval. I feel like our little moment is something she had to cross off a list. "Why don't you go in the dining room? Someone will tell you what to do."

I maneuver past a camera and practically bash my head into the wall when I trip over the same freaking cord. Finally I make it into the dining room, which has a few of the kids' art projects on the walls: turkeys made out of construction paper hands, Pilgrim hats, and Native American headbands with feathers.

"Okay, everyone, we're about to start filming!" Chuck calls. He dabs at his face with a handkerchief and takes a swig of his Red Bull as he looks into the kitchen, one finger counting us off. We must all be present and accounted for because he nods, satisfied. "Remember, this is LIVE. No matter what happens . . . the show must go on. Break a leg!"

"I find that foreboding, don't you?" Benny whispers, sneaking a corn muffin off the table.

"Right?"

Sandra hands me some forks. "Just go slowly around the table with them. We want to get a shot of you helping set up."

"Okay."

"But don't start until Chuck says we're on air."

"Got it." I smile as nicely as I can, and she rushes off to corral the little ones.

A Christmas CD starts playing in the kitchen. "Someone has gotta tell Mom Christmas comes after Thanksgiving," Benny says.

"Are you kidding me? The woman listens to it in *July*." Lex squeezes both our arms. "*Merde*," she says, and flits away.

I give Benny a look, and he says, "It's what dancers say for luck. It means 'shit' in French. Don't ask me how I know this."

Figures that's what Lex would say to us. The chaos begins to look more organized as the minutes slip away. My stomach rolls, and I clutch at the table. What if I totally freak out on TV and give an epic demonstration of the Heisenberg Principle—*breathe*. I try to take a deep breath and count to ten like Diane Le Shrink suggested, but the smell of the food is just making me feel worse. Maybe it's not nerves—I could have something highly contagious. But even if that were true, I doubt I'd be able to convince Chuck it's a health risk to have me down here. I'm pretty sure he'd expose everyone to the bubonic plague if it got him the shots he wanted.

"Doesn't it feel weird knowing Matt's watching this?" I ask.

Now that it's almost time, I'm wondering if I should have told Patrick to boycott the show. Will seeing my family freak him out?

Benny nods and kind of blushes. "We have a little secret message worked out. So he'll know I'm thinking of him or that I, like, need him to send me some good vibes."

"What is it?"

"*Cantaloupe*. Every time I say that, it's for him."

"Benny, when the hell are you going to have an opportunity to say *cantaloupe* during Thanksgiving dinner?"

"No, it's brilliant. See, if it were something more normal, he wouldn't be sure. Like, if it was *potato* or *fork*—"

Chuck: "And we're live in five, four, three—"

The first thirty minutes of the two-hour special fly by. Everyone is given Thanksgiving duties or kid-wrangling duties or kids-running-around-being-cute duties. The cameras follow me as I set the table, peel potatoes, and scold the triplets for getting underfoot. Violet™ gets her finger slammed in the bathroom door, and I have to kiss it and make it better. Riley™ and Gavin™ keep doing disgusting fart noises with their armpits while ignoring my I'm-going-to-kill-you looks. Because there're so many cameras, I never know when I'm actually on TV. Chuck is upstairs, engineering the whole thing—he's Big Brother in the flesh. I just keep picturing people I know watching—especially Patrick—and it makes me so self-conscious that I keep bumping into things and being generally klutzy.

Now I'm back in the kitchen, buttering the mashed potatoes, and I concentrate on making them as fattening as possible, like it's my calling from God. Benny's carving a ham in the dining room (and I hear him say, "I've seen *cantaloupes* bigger than this thing!"), Mom's doing something at the counter involving cinnamon and sugar, and Lexie™'s trill of a laugh scampers in from the living room. Apparently, her job is to be charming.

"How's high school, Bonnie™?"

Lacey's asking me this off-camera, as usual; America will hear her voice but never actually see her. I would love to trade places with America.

"Good," I say. *Salt, salt, butter, pepper, a little more butter.*

How to be here and *not here* at the same time? I need a happy place my mind can go to.

"Have you made friends?" she asks. She has to practically shout over the whir of the handheld mixer. I turn it up to high speed. Mom shoots me a frustrated look, which I ignore.

Add milk. "Uh-huh."

"What did they do when they found out who you were?" she yells.

The camera behind Lacey draws closer and this dress is so freaking tight and itchy, and I can feel sweat building on my upper lip, which is totally unattractive, and I know I shouldn't be thinking about such shallow things, but does the camera really add ten pounds and, if so, how bad do I look on the flat-screen TV at Patrick's house?

"—who you were? Bonnie™?" Lacey says.

I look up, startled. Crazy how you can check out like that on live TV. "What?"

Mom comes over and unplugs the mixer. "I think those are good and whipped, Bonnie™." She gives me a hard look with her back to the camera before returning to her end of the kitchen.

Lacey looks down at her clipboard, an uncomfortable cough escaping from her glossy lips. "So, I have a question here from June Bailey from Springfield, Ohio. She's seventeen like you and a huge fan. She says she feels like she grew up with you, and she's glad the show's back on. Her question is, *What do you miss most about* Baker's Dozen?"

For a minute, I just stand there, feeling torn. I don't want to insult June Bailey from Springfield, Ohio, but I am the wrong person to ask this question. I don't miss anything, except for the childhood that was denied me. I open my mouth to say that or some version of it that is politically correct, but something I haven't wanted to admit for a long time comes out instead.

"My dad," I whisper.

"Dinner!" Kirk calls.

I didn't realize he was right behind me. He gives me a tight smile as he hefts the turkey platter in both hands and walks into the dining room. I didn't mention my dad to hurt his feelings—I hadn't even wanted to say what I said. I turn away from the camera, jumping as the doorbell chimes. I have literally never heard it before, since we've lived in virtual isolation for the past four years.

And I know. This is it. The big surprise Mom is certain I'm not going to like.

She walks into the entryway, wiping a towel on her hands. "Did one of you guys invite someone?"

For a minute, I have this horrible vision of Patrick being on the other side of the door. What could be worse than discovering that this sweep-you-off-your-feet boy had turned out to be a fame-hungry mortal after all? But when Mom opens the door and just stands there, her whole body rigid, I begin to understand the limitations of my imagination.

"Hello, Beth."

"Daddy?" shouts Lexie™, running in from the living room.

I can't see him, but I don't need to. I'd recognize his voice anywhere. The room gets spinny, and the camera in the kitchen nudges closer to me, a predator sniffing half-dead prey.

"Hi, sweetie," he says to Lex.

Kirk brushes past me and stands in the doorway, blocking my view. I edge away, into the dining room, out of sight. A camera stays on me, ignoring my personal bubble, so I focus on the uncomfortable ballet flats Sandra made me wear. I'm trapped—the only way upstairs or out of the house is past him. Past my dad.

"You must be Kirk," Dad says. I hear the rustle of shopping bags, as if he were some normal guest who brought wine or a pie or something.

Kirk grunts in assent. "What are you doing here?" I can tell from his voice that he's crossing his arms, looking stern.

What utter and complete bullshit. He knew Dad was coming— was the memorized script Chuck's idea, or is Kirk just getting into his role as Replacement Father?

"Honey," Mom says, "it's okay—"

"No, it's understandable," Dad says. "I'm sorry for just dropping in . . . I wanted to see the kids on Thanksgiving. I was in the area, and you weren't answering your phone. I took a chance."

I lean against the wallpaper in the dining room, closing my eyes to stop the spinning. I should have seen this coming, should have known that Chuck would cook up something guaranteed to get the ratings through the roof.

"Hanging in there?" says a soft voice.

I open my eyes and nod. Benny gives me a hug. We hide in the dining room, listening to the disembodied voices in the hallway.

"Who's he?" Jasmine™ asks.

Ouch.

"I'm your daddy, sweetheart."

"No you're not. Kirk's our daddy."

It's so sad and deranged, my life. This little bubble of hysterical laughter starts making its way up my throat, and I have to clamp my hand against my mouth to keep it from escaping. The camera keeps its unflinching gaze on me, and I stare at the carpet. *One, two, three, four*—

I can't do the counting thing. My chest tightens. *One, two, three*—

"Well." Mom coughs. "Um. We're just about to eat, so . . ."

"Oh. Of course. I'll come back another—"

"No!" Lex practically shouts. "We have room at the table. He can stay, can't he, Mom?"

I feel Benny's arms stiffen around me, and he swears, just loud enough for me to hear. America holds its breath—will Andrew Baker be invited to join his family on Thanksgiving, or will he be left out in the cold to contemplate the disaster he made of their lives?

"Of course," Mom says.

Thirty seconds later, my dad is in the dining room.

We look at each other for a long time, the cameras crowding us, wanting those precious close-ups. He looks different. His hair has gotten grayer, and he has a slight paunch. His clothes scream bachelor—nothing about him seems fatherly. He's trendy. His eyes begin to fill up with tears, but mine are surprisingly dry. I don't know what I was expecting to feel when I saw him again. I thought it'd be something more than this cold, dull ache.

"Look at you," he whispers. "You're all grown up."

Daddy, Daddy, look! I'm an angel! I'm in the backyard, staring at the sky and carving wings into the snow. He smiles. *You've always been my little angel*, he says. I reach out my arms, and he picks me up and twirls me around.

When I find my voice, the only thing remaining of that memory is the winter in my tone. "That's what happens when you don't see someone for four years."

"*Bonnie™*," Mom says.

Dad blinks, like he's wondering what I did with the Bonnie™ he remembered. He's playing his part well—I wonder how much coaching Chuck had to do.

"No, it's okay, Beth. I deserved that," he says to my mom. He turns back to me. "I understand why you feel that way, sweetheart. But I want another chance. I want to be a part of your life."

Benny's voice slashes the air. "But you only wanted that chance if it could be on TV?"

Dad sighs. "Ben, you have no idea how many times I've tried . . ." His voice breaks, and I ignore the sympathy that's trying to push its way into my heart. Nothing he says could make up for leaving us. Nothing. "It's the only way your mother would let me see you."

"What?" I don't know if I say this out loud or not. I guess I can always watch this episode if I really want to know.

Mom throws her towel on the table, nearly knocking over one of the lit candles. "That is absolutely not true! How *dare*—"

"Oh, so I just imagined that restraining order? Or what about all the returned mail? How many times have you changed your phone number or—"

The room erupts, sixteen voices talking all at once, smacking against one another, trying to be heard.

Lex: "Mom, what's he talking about? Did you—"

Mom: "That's not the whole story, and you know that, Andrew!"

Kirk, getting up in Dad's face: "What kind of man walks out on—"

Benny: "Kirk, this isn't really any of your business."

Lex: "Wait, are you saying—"

The chorus of children: "Mommy, I'm hungry." "Where's Chuck?" "Why are they yelling?" "Who's that man?" "He's our dad." "Huh?"

Benny, staring desperately at a camera: "Cantaloupe!"

Mom: "Goddammit, it's Thanksgiving!"

The triplets start crying, and the older kids sort of huddle around the table and watch the adults scream at one another. The cameras inch closer, and the booms circle around us like menacing birds. The sounds of my family falling apart press against my chest, and my breath leaves my body in short, agitated spurts. I look down and try to concentrate on not choking, but Ican'tIcan'tIcan't—

"I have to get this off," I mumble, pulling at my tight dress.

My skin is covered in sweat, and the nylons Sandra made me wear are cutting into my stomach. The room seems to get smaller and smaller as more people crowd into it, and I can't think, it's so loud. I push past my siblings, throw my hand up against a camera lens that blocks my path.

"Get out of my way!" I scream. I stumble blindly past bodies, tearing at the high neck of my dress, gasping for air. I'm choking, gagging. I have to get upstairs before I throw up. *Please let me get upstairs. Please, God, please.*

"Bonnie™? Bonnie™!"

I ignore my mom and tear through the kitchen, trip over that fucking cord, God, I hate that cord, and up the stairs. I don't stop until the door of the bathroom slams behind me and my knees fall painfully to the cold tile floor. I've never been so happy to see a toilet bowl in my life.

~ ~ ~

Ding!

The tone shatters the silence of my bedroom, and I shudder awake, rolling into a fetal position. The red numbers on my alarm clock say 12:35. Two hours and thirty-five minutes after the live episode. I wonder how it ended. A food fight? Teary reconciliation? My body feels worn out, and disappointment nags at me. If I'm honest, part of me had been up here waiting—hoping—that he would knock on the door. I'm realizing that's what I've wanted all along. But what he had to offer were postcards and the occasional phone call. I wanted more. I wanted a flesh-and-blood dad.

It was my choice to stop speaking to him after I took the pills. *I'll come back, baby. I promise. Just please don't hurt yourself again.* That's what he'd said, over and over, when I was in the ambulance and, later, in the hospital room, after they'd pumped my stomach. After they said, *She'll live, but it was a close call.* But he didn't. Come back. I waited, but he never did. Tonight was the first time I'd spoken to him since we moved out to California. I wonder if Mom really had kept him from us or if that was just another one of his lies. It doesn't matter. He didn't try hard enough. We weren't worth the effort.

I stare at the tray of food on my desk. Cold Thanksgiving dinner that I'd told Mom I didn't want.

Ding!

I sit up, shivering in the thin bathrobe I'd thrown on before tumbling into bed.

Ding!

I move my finger along the mouse pad on my laptop, the bright light painful after the hours of miserable semiconsciousness.

Sheldon1015: Hey . . . you awake?

Sheldon1015: Your phone is off. I think you have enough evidence if you want to tell the police you have a stalker—I left way too many anxious boyfriend texts.

Sheldon1015: Crap. MetaReel can't read your texts can they? I don't know how them tapping your phone actually works.

Sheldon 1015: Chloe.

Sheldon 1015: Chloe.

Sheldon 1015: Chloe.

Sheldon 1015: This is my cyber version of throwing pebbles at your window. Is it working?

YoSoyChloe: Hey

Sheldon1015: Hey! (I'm still working on the right term of endearment for you, so know that I'm saying more than "hey.")

Despite everything, I smile. Some warmth floods back into me, cracking the ice around my heart. My fingers hover over the keyboard. Patrick Sheldon makes me want to be clever even during a personal crisis.

YoSoyChloe: Okay, _____ (insert term of endearment).

Sheldon 1015: ☺ I want to call you. Can I? Because I think there have been clinical studies about it being really bad for your health if you don't hear the voice of the person you can't stop thinking about.

YoSoyChloe: Bugged phone, remember?

Sheldon 1015: You can pretend it's a wrong number. We'll pull one over on whoever listens in to your phone calls.

YoSoyChloe: Honestly, I . . .

YoSoyChloe: I'm sort of afraid I'll start crying. And then I'll just feel like an idiot, you know? God, you probably think I'm already a total spaz. I wish I'd told you not to watch.

Sheldon1015: You're not a spaz.

Sheldon1015: Chloe . . . Argh! Everything I want to say is going to look dumb as hell in writing. How do you feel about sneaking out of the house?

Great. Except that I'm practically on suicide watch.

YoSoyChloe: Normally, I would love the opportunity to put my ninja skills to good use, but I'm actually exhausted. Rain check?

Sheldon1015: I suppose I will put away my shining armor and save my (ninja) damsel in distress tomorrow. Are you up for a rescue around 5? 6? Movie/dinner/a shoulder to cry on?

YoSoyChloe: I'm always up for rescuing, but . . . I don't think my mom will let me out. You might be dealing with a Rapunzel situation. I'm not sure what the fallout from tonight will be.

Sheldon1015: Throw in a dragon and swordfights and I'm sold.

YoSoyChloe: ☺

Sheldon1015: Can I say one totally embarrassingly boyfriend thing? Er, type it, rather.

YoSoyChloe: I like totally embarrassingly boyfriend things.

Sheldon1015: I miss you.

Sheldon1015: Honestly, I feel . . . I just really miss you. I'm verging on pathetic here—it's been less than twenty-four hours since I've seen your face.

YoSoyChloe: Except on TV.

Sheldon1015: Right. That magnified the missing. And it made me want to hurt some people.

YoSoyChloe: Ha. Yeah, that makes two of us.

YoSoyChloe: Can I say one totally embarrassingly girlfriend thing?

Sheldon1015: Please do.

YoSoyChloe: I missed you so much last night that I chewed a whole pack of spearmint gum.

Sheldon1015: Okay, you better go before I drive over there and climb up to your balcony.

YoSoyChloe: ☺ Night.

Sheldon1015: This sucks.

YoSoyChloe: Yeah.

Sheldon1015: I am way too tempted to start quoting Shakespeare to you in proper Mopey Emo Dude fashion. I need to step away from this computer before I lose all of my dignity. Shall I compare thee—no! Stepping away . . .

Patrick signs off, but I don't close my laptop. Instead, I grab a DVD I keep in the drawer beside my bed and slide it into the disk drive. My eyes tear up again as the *Baker's Dozen* theme song plays.

Baker's Dozen: Season 10, Episode 9

INT—BAKER HOME—EVENING: Mariachi music plays in the background. [ANDREW stands in front of the stove in the kitchen, stirring something in a pot. BONNIE™ stands beside him, holding a corn tortilla.]

ANDREW: Okay, Bon-Bon, you ready to make some enchiladas?

BONNIE™: [looks into the pot, doubtful] It's still boiling.

ANDREW: [reaches for the tortilla] We'll do it together. Ready? One, two . . .

BONNIE™: Three! [they dunk the tortilla into the pot]

ANDREW: *¡Ai ai ai! ¡Caliente!*

BONNIE™: [laughing] Hurry, it's gonna break!
[They set the tortilla in a glass baking dish.

ANDREW crosses to the sink and rinses his hands while BONNIE™ sticks her hand in a big bowl of shredded cheese.]

ANDREW: [Sneaking up behind BONNIE™. He now has a sombrero on his head.] *¡Hola, señorita!*

BONNIE™: [Turns around. Her face is shocked, then she breaks out into hysterical laughter.] Daddy, you're crazy!

[ANDREW turns up the music and begins twirling her around the kitchen.]

ANDREW AND BONNIE™: [singing together] *La cucaracha, la cucaracha, la la la la la la la . . .*

SEASON 17, EPISODE 16

(The One at the Mall)

When I wake up, someone is snoring in my bed. I turn over, only mildly alarmed—this is not such a strange thing when you have a dozen siblings.

"Benny." I shake my brother's shoulder.

"Hmph." He turns onto his side, throwing an arm against his eyes to block out the sunlight.

I kick off the covers and crawl over him.

"You're awake," he mumbles.

I look at the clock. "It's lunchtime. I thought it might be a good idea to get up."

"Whereyago?" His words are muffled against the pillow, but I get the gist.

"Bathroom. Be right back."

I open my door as quietly as possible and tiptoe across the hall. I try the knob, but the door's locked. I don't want to alert everyone that I'm awake—it could result in footage of my bedhead and ratty

PJs that I don't want people to see on next week's episode. I can feel how bad I look.

But I really have to pee.

I tap on the door. "Can I get in there?"

"Almost done," Lexie™ says.

This is Lex-speak for twenty more minutes.

"Dude. I just need, like, two minutes."

The door immediately swings open, and waves of steam envelop me as Lex pulls me inside and shuts the door behind her. The room reeks of her expensive shampoo.

"Er, good morning?" I say, blinking in the mist.

"Oh my God, we have to talk."

Lex is wearing a towel around her middle and another wrapped around her hair. An assortment of creams and girl-torture devices sit on the cluttered counter. This is the official girls' bathroom, so there are about ten bottles of lotion, piles of hair accessories, five hairbrushes . . . any time of the day or night you walk in here, it looks like we robbed a Walgreens.

"Um. I really have to pee."

"Go ahead, I won't look."

I sigh and turn on the faucet.

"Hello? Hate the environment much?" she says.

"It's bad enough no one can pee in private in this family. The least you can do is let me harbor the illusion that you can't hear me."

"You are so bizarre." Lex plucks at her eyebrows and studies her face in the mirror with an intensity better suited to nuclear physicists.

"Just because I'm not comfortable running around backstage naked between act one and act two doesn't qualify as weird."

"It's a theater thing—you wouldn't understand." She closes her eyes as she dabs cream on her eyelids, and I take this opportunity to sit on the toilet.

After a few seconds, I flush and she opens her eyes.

"You obviously have some quality gossip to share, so out with it," I say, resigning myself to a lengthy Lex-a-thon. I sit on the edge of the bathtub and run my hands through my rat's-nest hair.

"So. After you went *loco*, the shit really hit the fan. I mean, it was like Armageddon in there."

"Don't look so upset about it," I mutter.

Lex gives me her fake sweet smile and turns back to the mirror. Despite being twins, Benny and Lex couldn't be more different.

"So, Mom and Dad and Kirk were going at it in a major way. Dad was all, 'You never let me see them,' and Mom's like, 'Well, it's hard to get in touch with someone who never answers their phone.' Then—and this was priceless, it's so too bad you missed it—Kirk and Dad got in this old-guy fistfight."

"What?"

God, how am I gonna show my face at school on Monday?

"Right? It was crazy."

"Did they, like, hurt each other?"

"No. I mean, it was lame, but Dad literally walked over to the turkey, picked it up, and threw it on the ground!"

"Whoa."

"Yeah. And I'm there being all, 'Mom, make them stop,' and Benny's sitting at the table with his head in his hands talking about cantaloupes, and the kids are screaming. I heard Chuck say they didn't even go to commercial, it was so good."

"What the hell is wrong with them?" I say this louder than I intend to and immediately look at the door.

"Don't worry," she says, noticing my glance. "Mom and Kirk are doing Black Friday book signings all day. Mom's gonna make a killing."

The steam is suffocating, but Lex glows in this totally obnoxious, goddesslike way.

"What about Dad?"

"Gone. He stormed out. Said he loved us and to call him if we wanted to come to Florida."

Even Lex isn't a good enough actress to hide the disappointment in her voice. She busies herself with her makeup bag, like choosing the right eyeliner is the most important thing in the world.

"If he really loved us, he would have stayed." My voice is hard, bitter. "He got himself back on TV, and now he's famous again. That's all he cares about."

Lex sighs. "I don't know what to think anymore," she says. "Maybe Mom really did keep him from us. She was pretty hurt about . . . you know." The affair. The divorce. The end of the show. End of the world.

I'm so sick of it. My whole life feels like it's in a slingshot, and I'm just waiting for whoever's in control to let go. Once, just once, I want to be the one pulling back the rubber band.

"Lex, this is so messed up. Aren't you worried about what people at school are gonna say?"

Lexie™ takes the towel off her head and sprays her long locks with detangler, half of which ends up in my eyes and mouth.

"I look at it this way," she says, running a comb through her commercial-worthy tresses. "It can only help me—I mean, people get famous for losing their fat asses or eating worms. As long as I play my cards right, I can make it on my own as soon as we graduate."

I give her what I hope is a withering look. "Lex. Spielberg's not interested in how well you fight with your family on camera."

"Look, Bonnie™. I know you have this whole anti vibe going and, whatever, that's fine. But I love the camera. *I love it.* So you can be a hater, but at the end of the day, this is what we've got. And I'm going to make the most of it."

I stand up and push past her and out the door. "I need to eat . . . or something."

"Fine. Do what you always do when someone wants to talk about something uncomfortable. God forbid you actually have to *deal* with your problems."

I look back at her. "Fuck you."

She raises her perfectly shaped eyebrows. "Right back atcha."

I really want to hit her, and I probably would if we were a few years younger. Now I just growl and slam the door. She opens it back up.

"It must be nice," she snaps.

I turn around. "What?"

"Being the only one Dad really cares about."

"That's not—"

"Watch last night's episode if you don't believe me. See the way he looks at you and tell me he gives a damn about the rest of us."

She slams the door hard, leaving me alone in the cold hallway. Adrenaline surges through me, and I think about barging back in there to tell her off, except the look on her face stops me. This wasn't Lexie™ being her usual dramatic self. She really believes Dad loves me more.

Which is totally ridiculous.

When I get back to my room, Benny is on my computer. He immediately closes the window of the web page he's on, but I catch it before it disappears.

"So what does celeb.com have to say about me this time?"

"They liked your dress."

I roll my eyes and plop back down on the bed. "Lex was in the bathroom."

"Uh, yeah. I heard the tail end of *that* conversation."

"I don't get why she said that. About Dad loving me more."

Benny crosses his arms and leans back in the chair. His hair's all mussed up, and his eyes are still heavy with sleep. "I don't think Dad loves any of us very much. Not anymore. But you've always been his favorite."

I open my mouth to disagree, but he just raises an eyebrow. "Whatever."

"So . . ." He gets up and sits at the end of the bed, giving me one of those soul-searching Benny looks. "You wanna talk about last night?"

I narrow my eyes. "Did Mom tell you to keep an eye on me?"

"Don't be a brat," he says.

I dig the heels of my hands into my eye sockets and take a long, ragged breath.

"I don't want to talk about it. But I'm sorry for not trusting your motives."

He pats my foot. "Mom and Kirk are out—Lex told you?"

I nod. "I need to find a way to get to Patrick's tonight." I peek out my window, looking past the high security fence. "The Vultures are still out there."

"Matt and I have a plan, but you're not gonna like it."

When he tells me what we have to do, I groan. "This is so not gonna work."

"Let's just try, okay? The most important thing is that Matt and Patrick don't get caught."

"Yeah." I know exactly what he means—I would never want to bring this craziness into Patrick's life. He's already in deep enough, but at least no one is blogging about him or camping outside his home.

I bring my laptop over to the bed. Patrick's online, which is good because I can't talk about this on my MetaReel phone.

YoSoyChloe: Morning.

Sheldon1015: I have my sword, but I have no idea where my trusty steed went. Are you letting down your hair?

Benny reads over my shoulder. "You guys are weird."

YoSoyChloe: Benny says we're weird.

Sheldon1015: Weird is the new cool.

"Touché," Benny says.

YoSoyChloe: ☺ So. We have a plan.

Sheldon1015: I hope it involves your green wig and blue sunglasses.

YoSoyChloe: Worse. It involves the mall.

Sheldon1015: On Black Friday? I love how certifiably insane you are.

YoSoyChloe: Sore subject.

Sheldon1015: Is Ben still reading over your shoulder?

YoSoyChloe: No

Sheldon1015: I love everything about you. Is that a sore subject?

YoSoyChloe: Um. Blushing. A lot.

Sheldon1015: So, the mall, huh?

~ ~ ~

"Okay, ready?"

I look in my rearview mirror. Three SUVs and two motorcycles. "Benny, this is not going to work."

"It will. Just run as soon as I stop the car."

"People are going to recognize us, they'll—"

"Listen. You, Patrick, possibly on or in his bed. Are you going to give that up over a few Vultures?"

He's right. That *would* be certifiable. Benny doesn't wait for my answer. He swings into a spot, and we're out of the car. I hear the lock chirp behind me as we run into Macy's, cameras in our faces, people looking. I want to cry so bad, but a surge of adrenaline courses through me as we make our way through the store and then I sort of want to laugh because it's a little bit thrilling, outrunning the paparazzi. I hear voices as we fly through the shoe department.

"Wait! Is that . . . ?"

"Where?"

"By the mannequin."

Click. Camera phones. *Click.*

I ignore the voices, the stares. Benny squeezes my hand as we split up. He's off to menswear, where Matt is picking him up at the back entrance. I'm going into the mall, but not too far in. Patrick's friend, Derrick, works at Hot Topic, and he's going to get us out through an employee hallway. I don't know if anyone has seen me yet—the mall is packed, and it smells like pretzels and sugar and new things. They're already piping in Christmas music—it's the most wonderful time of the year. *Go, go, shit, go.*

I walk fast, keep my eyes to the ground. As soon as I pass the Disney store, I see the oversized lava lamp, and I duck inside, practically knocking Patrick over.

"Hey, you," he says. He puts a protective arm around my shoulder and guides me past various goth-inspired paraphernalia to the back of the store and behind a velvet curtain labeled EMPLOYEES ONLY.

We made it. Well, past stage one, anyway. Patrick pulls me against him, and his lips find mine in the half light. For a minute, I forget I'm a fugitive because everything's turning to jelly, and it is so hot to be kissing someone in an off-limits place when people are after you. It's like we landed in an action movie.

"How'd it go in Macy's?" he asks.

I'm shivering almost uncontrollably from fear and this crazy intense *want* that's attacking my muscles. I nod, trying to catch my breath. "Could have been worse, but they got tons of pictures."

He kisses the top of my head. "I considered myself a pacifist until we got together," he says. "Now I have a mental hit list that includes all paparazzi, everywhere."

I smile and just hug him tighter. Then I let him go and pull my phone out to text Benny. I laugh and show Patrick the picture Benny just texted me back of him in Matt's car, the two of them grinning wildly.

Just then the curtain parts and Derrick slips in. "Hey, Chloe," he says.

He's wearing a vintage Star Wars T-shirt and a hat that says COL-LEGE. His nails are painted black, but I won't hold that against him.

"Hey. I really appreciate this," I say.

He grins. "S'nothing. Most exciting part of my day. I just spent the past fifteen minutes trying to explain to a mom why *Harry Potter* is not going to turn her kid into a Satanist."

I shrug. "I don't know, that sounds pretty exciting to me."

I've always wanted a part-time job. I know that's what privileged kids who are bored say, but I can't imagine that level of independence. I guess I've worked for MetaReel most of my life, but I've never seen a paycheck with my name on it. I'd take a wage slave job over reality TV stardom any day.

Patrick claps Derrick on the back. "You got it?"

"Yep." He hands Patrick a plastic card. "Just go through that door and follow the hall to the end. It'll let you out in the Dumpster area. You said you parked your car behind the cleaners, right?"

Patrick nods.

"Cool. Shouldn't take you more than four minutes, then."

"Excellent. I owe you one," Patrick says.

Derrick shrugs. "I like to see you happy, man. Later, Chloe."

"Bye."

He goes back out through the curtain, and Patrick grabs my hand. "Freaked?"

I grin. "Not with you."

He presses his lips against mine, just for a second. "I cannot *wait* to get you to my house," he says.

My face turns scarlet, and he laughs quietly as he leads me out the back door. Four minutes later, we're in his beat-up Volvo, merging onto the highway.

I hold up my phone and lean in close to him. "Smile."

I send Benny the first picture I've ever taken of Patrick and me, then close the phone and snuggle close to him as we head away from the total mayhem that is my life.

Reality TV Family Garners Record Viewers, But Child Psychologists Worried

By TIM FISHER, Affiliated Press

Last night's live taping of the MetaReel revamp of *Baker's Dozen* has already sparked a debate among child mental health experts across the nation. While nearly fourteen million Americans tuned in to last night's show, a poll conducted immediately afterward reveals that 80 percent of viewers believe the show is negatively affecting the Baker children. "The unexpected visit by their father was clearly damaging," says Tina Nolte, a professor of psychology at Fresno State University. "Personally, many of my colleagues and I feel that placing a child in these kinds of situations could classify as a form of child abuse." This is not the first time the phrase "child abuse" has been used in connection with the show. The emotional reaction Bonnie™ Baker had to her estranged father's unexpected visit reminded many viewers of the seventeen-year-old's suicide attempt just four years ago. An attempt, many believe, that was in reaction to the show itself.

"Enough is enough," says Janet Frazer, a spokesperson for the ACLU. The organization, which is suing MetaReel in a class-action suit on behalf of a number of former reality TV child stars, has been concerned about the issue of child labor in reality TV for over a decade. In addition to taking MetaReel, the nation's largest and most successful reality TV production company, to court, the ACLU is also lobbying for both state and federal protections for underage performers. "When is this nation going to recognize that half of MetaReel's shows are totally unregulated?" says Melinda Greenberg, chief counsel for the ACLU's suit against MetaReel. A spokesperson for MetaReel denies such allegations, saying, "Both Beth [Baker-Miller] and Kirk [Miller] are confident they are acting in their family's best interest. The children are having a blast and are eager to have the cameras in their home."

SEASON 17, EPISODE 17

(The One with the Movie)

Patrick's house already feels familiar to me. Even though I've been here only once, I've pictured him inside it a thousand times more. As he opens the door leading into the kitchen from the garage, the smell of cilantro and grilled chicken greets me.

"Mom?" Patrick calls.

My stomach freefalls, and I instinctively pull back, but he puts a hand on the small of my back and guides me inside.

"They're going to love you," he whispers.

His breath tickles my ear, and I shiver slightly as his lips graze my neck. He pulls away just before the female version of Patrick comes into the room, drying her hands on a checkered towel.

"Chloe!" she says.

She immediately pulls me into a tight hug. When she steps back, I try to smile, but I'm suddenly aware of every dirty thought I've ever had about her son.

"It's nice to meet you, Mrs. Sheldon."

"Oh, call me Lori. It's nice to finally meet *you*. Patrick's only been going on and on about you for the past six months."

"Mom," Patrick says, giving her a playful push.

She grins and swats at him with her towel.

"More like a year," says his father as he enters the room. "Nice to meet you, sweetheart," he says.

I immediately fall in love with Brian Sheldon. Not in a creepy way, but in an I-wish-you-were-my-dad kind of way. He's tall, like Patrick, and has the same piercing eyes. He looks like I thought a professor would (tortoiseshell glasses, tweed jacket), which makes sense, since he teaches law at the university. I shake the hand he offers me.

"You too. Um. Thanks for having me. I know it's the holidays and—"

"Nonsense," Brian says. "It's just us three, anyway. Lori's making tacos. You guys hungry?"

Patrick looks at me, and I nod. "That'd be great," he says.

Lori gestures to the tiny dining room table, which is already set for four. I can't even comprehend such a small number of people in one family.

"You guys want Cokes?" she asks. "You must be thirsty after your infamous mall adventure." She says this in a melodramatic way, which makes me laugh. I wish my mom had time to do voices.

"Yeah, thanks, that'd be great," I say.

My eyes drift around the cozy furnishings and family photos. God, this house is so quiet. I keep expecting to hear something break or kids shouting down the hall, but everyone who lives in the house is here, speaking in soft voices, focused on one another.

Patrick pulls out a chair for me, and my heart skips a few beats when he catches my eye and smiles before sitting next to me. His we-have-a-secret smile makes me feel like I'm the only thing he sees.

Brian settles in beside Patrick, a glass of wine in his hand. "How'd all the cloak-and-dagger stuff go?"

I shrug. "Pretty well, actually. My brother and his . . . um . . . his friend, got away, too. Patrick's pretty good at this—I'm sort of convinced he's an international spy."

Lori and Brian laugh.

"I'd tell you," Patrick says, "but then I'd have to kill you."

I stick out my tongue at him, and he responds in kind. I can't believe how natural it feels to be sitting with his family. They are so not dysfunctional at all. It makes me feel warm and sad and something else I can't quite name. It's the opposite of last night. Patrick grabs my hand, like he knows what I'm thinking. I'm surprised how affectionate he is, with his parents right here. They don't seem to mind, though.

"Well, I'm glad he's putting his CIA training to good use," Lori says.

They're being so nice about all of this, but there's no way they could want their son mixed up with my hot mess of a life. I need them to know that I would never endanger what they have—their peaceful dinners, their enjoyment of one another.

"I promise we wouldn't have come here if— I mean, I would never let the paparazzi know where you guys live. And I swear, MetaReel won't know anything about Patrick—"

Brian shakes his head. "Don't worry about that, Chloe. I'm just glad my son finally got the guts to ask you out." He gives me a wink and Patrick rolls his eyes.

"Thanks, Dad. I think she fully realizes how pathetic I am. Appreciate it."

Brian grins. "Anytime, son."

They banter like this during the whole meal, passing food, chatting about this and that. They absorb me into their routine without question. Without judgment. All throughout, Patrick does little things that make me internally shiver—a hand on my knee, insisting on feeding me a piece of avocado, finding moments to give me private glances that hold all manner of messages and promises. Through it all, his parents talk and laugh and make me feel like I actually belong here. They deftly avoid mentioning the show in any way, but they ask about Benny and school and our government class. Finally, Lori claps her hands.

"Okay, you two. Get outta here."

I crumple my napkin. "That was delicious. Can I help—"

"No," she says. "You two have a date. We'll be in the den if you need anything."

Patrick stands up. "You kids be good now," he says to his parents. Lori swipes at him, and he jumps out of the way, laughing.

They start clearing the table, and Patrick tugs on my hand, leading me up the stairs. We go by the family photos I remember from when I was here the last time, and each step closer to his bedroom increases my goose-bump-to-non-goose-bump ratio.

"I told you they'd love you," he says.

"They're great. Really. You guys were cracking me up."

He puts his arm around my waist, pulling me against his hip in a half hug. "You know, what they said was true. About me not being able to shut up about you all these months."

We're at his bedroom door, which is closed.

"I'm glad you finally asked me out," I say.

"Me too." He traces his finger along my collarbone, his eyes pensive.

"What?"

"It's just . . ." He sighs. "I hate to think of you in that house. My parents were good about not mentioning it, but I was not . . . okay . . . watching."

My body goes cold, and I try to step away. "If this is too weird or hard, I totally under—"

"No!" He reaches out his hands and trails them along my neck, drawing me close again. "I meant that I wasn't okay seeing all the shit you had to deal with. And I couldn't do anything. I just had to sit there."

I lean in and kiss the end of his nose. I've secretly wanted to do that for, oh, a year. "It was worse last night because it was live. And, you know, my dad showing up."

Patrick's eyes darken, and his body goes tense. "Can't you get out of it? I mean, it's got to be illegal for them to be filming you when you don't want it."

Right now, I need an escape from Bonnie™. I don't want to be in that headspace. "Let's not talk about it tonight, okay? I just want to be with you."

He looks like he wants to say something else, but then he smiles.

"Okay." He clears his throat and gestures toward the door. "So, I know we've never actually gotten to go on a *date* date, but I'm still trying to work out a strategy for that. In the meantime, since we couldn't go to the theater, I brought the theater to you."

Patrick opens his door and pulls aside a white sheet that hangs from the ceiling.

"My lady," he says, motioning me forward with a gallant twirl of his hand.

I giggle and move past the sheet into his room, which he has transformed into a private cinema. Movie posters cover the walls, and a tiny projector sits on top of his bookcase.

"Be right back. Take a look at the movies while I grab concessions," he says, shutting the door behind him.

A beam of light littered with dust motes streams from the projector to the sheet, the only light in the room save for his desk lamp. Patrick's stacked a bunch of pillows on his bed, making a sofa. A pile of DVDs sits on his desk. I flip through them, a mix of every genre and time period. Something glints beside his desk—when I look closer, I see it's an origami-like design made out of Wrigley's gum wrappers. I smile, imagining Patrick sitting at his desk, folding each wrapper.

A few minutes later, there's a knock on the door, and when I open it, Patrick's holding a bowl of freshly popped popcorn, a shopping bag full of candy, and a mini cooler with sodas.

"You're amazing," I say, helping him set everything down.

He looks at me for a minute and then reaches for something in his closet.

"This is for you," he says, handing me a box wrapped in the comics section of the newspaper.

"Patrick—"

He puts a finger to my lips. "Just open it, already."

I tear along the paper and hold the box up to the light from the projector.

"You got me a cell phone?" I ask. It's one of those prepaid ones.

He nods. "Guaranteed *not* bugged by MetaReel."

I wrap my arms around him. "Thank you," I whisper.

He tightens his grip on me. "Now I can hear your voice more."

I set the box on his desk and lace my fingers behind his neck, letting my lips fall into his. We stand like that for a long time, just kissing, until we hear laughter downstairs, and I pull away.

"Um."

He shakes his head. "My parents would never come up here and bother us. Besides, they've started an *I Love Lucy* marathon—they'll be on the couch all night." Privacy—how novel. "But we might as well pick a movie and keep up appearances, huh?"

I laugh and we look through his movie selections. We finally opt for *Raiders of the Lost Ark*, but as soon as the opening music starts, Patrick is feeding me Red Vines and his makeshift couch turns back into a bed. It is, I think, surprisingly easy to make out to the sound of treasure hunting. For two hours, we alternate between attempting to watch the movie and giving up entirely.

"This is a vast improvement on the janitor's closet," I whisper, about halfway through Indy's adventures.

Patrick nuzzles my neck, his breathing heavy. "Agreed."

His lips travel to my ear and along my jaw. My hands snake under his shirt, and he pulls it over his head in one deft movement. I hear it fall on the ground a second later. He leans over me again, one hand reaching for the buttons on my shirt. (I totally took Mer's advice about the button-down.)

"Okay?" he asks, his fingers hesitating on the top button.

Yes Yes Yes. I nod and his lips come back to mine. His fingers fumble with the buttons on my blouse, but I keep mine in his hair. I don't know what else to do with them. I can almost hear Mer saying something cringe-inducing like, "Put them on his man parts!" But the thought of trying to undo his belt buckle fills me with more fear than the red carpet on Emmy night. That horribly embarrassing episode of season seven pops into my head—the one where my family was on the *Kaye Gibbons Show* and Kaye Gibbons asked me if I'd heard of the birds and the bees yet. And I'd made that stupid comment that I didn't like bees because they had big stingers, and everyone had laughed because little Bonnie™ Baker didn't get the double entendre.

"What's wrong?"

I blink. "What? Nothing."

Patrick's looking down at me, and I can't believe how MetaReel managed to sneak into the negative space between us. "You sure?"

"I'm sure." I pull him to me and close my mind off to my family, to the past, to the nothings before this something.

We don't go far or anything, but it feels good just to have my skin against his. To have his eyes travel down the length of me. I like how his fingertips make shapes against my stomach and how mine clutch at his bare shoulders when I pull him closer. And I like how for a lot of the time, he just holds me and listens while I tell him about last night in whispers and sighs and silence.

SEASON 17, EPISODE 18

(The One with the Autograph)

"Coffee?" Benny asks.

I hold up our two thermoses and make a sad face as we leave the kitchen. "Got it. I miss Starbucks."

Lexie™ brushes past us on her way out the door. "Why are you guys not going to Starbucks?"

"Um, so we don't spend the first half of our morning dealing with the Vultures?" I say.

The paparazzi have doubled since the live episode. Now wherever we go, it looks like we're part of a caravan. Which is why we only go to school, then come right back home. It's like we're under house arrest. Movies? Forget about it. Shopping? Strictly online. Dates? Impossible. I don't think I'll ever see the Tower District again, which sucks because, A) I love it and it's where Tessa, Mer, and I used to go almost every weekend, and B) I wanted to do that girlfriend thing where you go visit your boyfriend at work and bring him treats whilst looking cute. This is shaping up to be the worst senior year in the history of senior years.

"Girls!" Mom calls from the living room. "Don't forget to come home right after school. We have our mani-pedis, remember?"

How could I forget? Mom decided that all the girls in the house were in dire need of some R and R. I suspect this is the core of this week's episode, where Beth Baker-Miller tries to reconnect with her daughters after a stressful weekend. I can't help but feel like anything my family does from here on out is at the suggestion of a producer.

"Okay," I mumble.

I ignore Puma Guy as he gets in my face, his camera trying to steal a sip of my coffee, and tuck myself into the car. Once Benny and I are on the highway, we commence with our early morning bitch session about MetaReel. The Complaint of the Day: Frosty Fun™ cereal is one of our sponsors, so we had to say good stuff about it every other bite ("Wow, Mom, this Frosty Fun™ cereal is so yummy!") and do a few retakes of us pouring it into our bowls, and it just sucked because now we're running late and my stomach is full of soggy, nasty cereal. Also—and this is really shallow, but I don't care—Lexie™ mentioned the zit on my chin in front of one of the cameras and asked if I wanted to borrow some concealer. I take that as a sign that she's still holding Dad's favoritism against me.

Bitch session over, I spend a few minutes looking out the window. There's something simultaneously comforting and depressing about the abandoned fields. We pass the orchard where I used to go to collect my thoughts. I haven't been able to go there since we started shooting. Longing for that little corner of the world I could call my own pulses in me—it would have been nice to have a place I could run away to. I hear Lex's voice on Saturday morning: *Do what you always do when someone wants to talk about something uncomfortable. God forbid you actually have to deal with your problems.*

"Benny."

"Hmm?"

"Lex said something that kind of got under my skin."

"And this strikes you as unusual?"

I frown. "She said I always run away from my problems." My orchard, after I first saw the cameras. Sprinting upstairs the night of the live taping. Taking the pills. "Is that true? Do I have trouble, you know, *dealing?*"

Benny gives me a sidelong glance, probably trying to figure out if I'm really angsting or just feeling contemplative. He must have guessed the former, because he lets out a long sigh.

"Well," he says, "I think maybe . . . yeah. A little."

I take a sip of coffee, and Benny turns onto the road that leads to school. Trees and vineyards give way to suburbia: chain stores, gas stations, cookie-cutter houses.

"I don't mean to. I'm not trying to be a drama queen."

I wonder what the tabloids are saying about me now, after this weekend.

Benny shrugs. "We all run away from stuff in our own way. I mean, when things get too intense, I know I can always see Matt or at least call him."

"Cantaloupe," I say. He smiles.

My voice grows soft. "But this weekend, when Dad came . . . why did you stay in the dining room?"

Benny steers with one hand while he takes a long drink from his thermos. "I honestly couldn't tell you. Maybe I'm a yes-man. They told me to be there, so I was there."

I shake my head. "No. You're pragmatic, maybe. But not a robot."

"Whatever you want to call it." He shrugs. "I guess I figure we've got six more months until graduation. After that, I'm out."

"I can't even imagine being free of it all," I say. What would life be like without my family, without this albatross around my neck?

"I can," Benny says, his voice quiet.

We're pulling into the parking lot, and on instinct, I keep my head down as the Vultures surge toward us. How much are our pictures worth? One Vulture jumps in front of the car for a good shot, and Benny lays on the horn as he slams on the brakes.

"Idiot! Move the hell away!" he shouts.

The Vulture smiles and snaps an angry Benny and surprised Bonnie™ photo. I can see the caption now: *Inseparable brother and sister team Benton™ and Bonnie™ Baker caught mid-fight on their way to school. Sources say the pair have been growing apart ever since their father's Thanksgiving visit.*

That's what it would be. Some big, stupid lie because they can't have the caption say we were yelling at a Vulture for almost making Benny guilty of vehicular manslaughter. When we drive onto the black asphalt of the student parking lot, I immediately relax. Thank God for the principal's strict policies about who can and cannot be on school property.

Benny pulls into our usual spot next to Jason Calloway's massive truck and turns off the ignition.

"What were we talking about?" he asks.

"Me. Running away."

He nods. "Yeah. So . . ."

I get to the thing that's stressing me out, maybe even more than the show itself.

"So if I run away so much, then why am I the only one of us who doesn't know what to do after graduation?" I ask. "You'd think I'd have some grand escape plan, but I don't. Lex is going to Hollywood, you've sent in your college applications—"

"*Chloe*. You told me you already mailed the UC applications." Benny stares at me, and I get a hint of what he'll look like when he's a father someday. "The deadline—"

"I know. I know." I hold up my hand to keep him from saying more. "My boyfriend's applying early decision to Columbia, and you'll be at USC or wherever, and I'm going to be stuck here forever, running and not going anywhere." My voice gets rubber-band tight, straining against the lump that's growing in my throat. I close my eyes and swallow until I don't feel like I'm being strangled by my own anxiety.

Benny puts a hand on my knee. "Hey. It's okay. We'll figure something out."

"I don't know, Bens. I'm—" I don't finish the sentence, but I'm scared he knows what I almost let slip: *I'm losing it. Again.* I open the door and step out of the car.

"Chlo—" I can hear the concern in his voice, the unspoken plea: *Please don't take the pills again.*

"I'm fine, Benny."

Even if he's right, even if I *am* freaking out, I resent that everyone jumps to the conclusion that I'm going to raid Mom's medicine cabinet the second life gets overwhelming. Can't I be allowed to have bad days, really bad days, without them assuming I'm suicidal? And people wonder why I don't like to talk about my feelings.

I slam the car door and head to class, hoping equations and historical dates will be enough to distract me for a few hours.

~ ~ ~

"Bonnie™?"

A little girl, maybe ten or eleven, comes up to me as we exit the nail salon. She clutches a piece of paper and a pen in her hands. "Can I have your autograph?"

Her voice cracks on the last word, and her face is fire-truck red—the same color, I'd bet, as mine. For a second, I just look at her, confused. The Vultures press close, and the snap of their cameras makes it hard to focus on anything.

"Oh, that is so *sweet*," says Mom. She gives me a look and nods toward the paper.

"Um, sure," I mumble. I take the pen and awkwardly sign my name. My signature looks scratchy, quite possibly the lamest autograph ever. I feel like a total poseur.

The little girl grins. "Thanks!"

She skips away, waving the paper at a middle-aged woman waiting beside a minivan. They smile at me, and I try to smile back, the cameras catching it all.

"Why'd she want *your* autograph?" Lexie™ asks.

I shrug and duck into our big black van with the tinted windows. This used to happen all the time, when we did meet-and-greet events, but it's so different now, being older and aware of what's going on.

Mom ignores Lex as she puts the key in the ignition. "It's a good reminder, isn't it?"

I cock my head to the side. "What do you mean?"

"That you're a role model." She gives me a meaningful glance in the rearview mirror. "Don't forget that."

I look back at the little girl as she jumps into her own van. Why, out of all of us, had she chosen to ask *me*? I take a few shallow breaths to ward off another panic attack. My chest feels like it's in a vise.

At home, I go straight to my room and call Tessa on my prepaid Patrick phone. I know she's probably still in the newspaper room working on Friday's issue, but I need *real* girl time, not Reel-sanctioned girl time.

"Hello?" I can hear the boisterous noise of the newspaper staff in the background and for a second I just want to scream, I'm so freaking jealous.

"It's me."

"Chloe?"

I'd forgotten she wouldn't recognize this number. "This is my non–MetaReel-bugged cell."

"Hey! I forgot about the sugar daddy phone. I'm gonna program it in like that: Chloe's Sugar Daddy Phone."

I laugh. "Patrick might prefer *Mopey Emo Dude* over *Sugar Daddy.*"

"Too bad," she says. "He is now Sugar Daddy. So what's up?"

"Can it be Friday already?"

A rom-com night at Mer's was in the works, if I could successfully dodge the Vultures. Otherwise, they'd be camped in front of *her* house, too, and I wasn't okay with that.

"I *know*," Tess says. "It feels like the longest week ever, and it's only Monday. I'm still all sluggish from Thanksgiving. My mom made an obscene amount of Korean food, and my parents just got a Wii so they made me and my sister spend, like, the whole weekend virtual bowling—which is so weird, by the way. And then we—" She stops abruptly. "Sorry. That was just my insensitivity gene acting up."

She had watched the show, but we hadn't had much of a chance to talk about any of it yet because she'd spent lunch working on the newspaper.

"No! Don't apologize for being normal. Besides, my weekend wasn't all bad." Even I can hear the bliss in my voice.

"I sense a Sheldon story on the horizon."

I tell her about the weekend, and she *oohs* and *aahs* and does all the things that Benny would do if he were a little gayer.

"How was the salon?" Tessa asks, after we're through psychoanalyzing my date. "Did you get claw-the-rapist nails?"

I laugh. "No. But someone asked for my autograph."

"That is just ten kinds of strange."

"Right?"

"But you have to admit, it felt a little cool."

"No," I say, a little more loudly than I'd intended. "So *not* cool." I'm suddenly moving around my room with angry strides, pacing across the thick carpet until the soles of my feet start to burn. "It was this little girl, and I just wanted to be like—*I'm nobody, okay? So just leave me alone.* It's so weird. It reminded me of before the show ended and we'd be at these book signings and kids would randomly come up to the table and say all of our names, in birth order, as fast as they could. And I'd sit there with a smile on my face, dying of embarrassment for them, for us. Just . . . wanting to run as far away from it all as I could."

There's that word again—*run*. When Tessa doesn't answer, I cringe. "I sound really snobby, huh?"

"No." There's a little hitch in her voice that tells me there's something more.

"But . . ."

"I don't know." She's struggling to find the right words, and I feel annoyed that she won't just agree with me. Why is everybody making me out to be this horrible overreacting wench?

"Forget it," I say. I should never have told her any of this. How could she possibly understand?

"Chlo, wait. I fully agree about how much being on this show sucks. But that's cool that a little girl saw something of herself in you, right?"

She sounds just like my mom. And, hello, who would want to see some of herself in *Bonkers Bonnie*™?

"Tessa, I can't be anyone's role model. You saw the show. It's a joke." I'm *a joke*. "And I don't want that kind of pressure. I just want to be freaking normal—I can't live up to millions of girls watching me for pointers on how to get through adolescence."

I hear a locker slam—she must be finished with the newspaper for the day. "All I'm saying is, I just finished writing an editorial about how screwed it is that the Taft athletics department continues to get tons of funding from the school district even though they're shutting down ninety-nine percent of the arts department. And *nobody* is going to read it or care. But you have this soapbox that's yours for the taking. I mean, the *New York Times* wrote an op-ed about you yesterday, and *Newsweek* is quoting you verbatim. If I were you—"

"But you're *not* me. You have no idea what it's like, Tessa!" I'm shouting, and I know I shouldn't be, but I can't help it. I've always made it a rule not to know who's writing about me. And now I know more than I want to—and that my best friend is reading it. "You can have my soapbox. I would trade places with you in a *second*."

For a minute, all I can hear is the wind blowing on her end of the phone and my own labored breathing. Had I always known I was jealous of Tessa? Because right now I'm practically choking on it.

"I'm sorry," I finally say.

"It's okay. I get it. I crossed a line."

I shake my head, then remember she can't see that. "You didn't. I'm just still dealing with this weekend and . . . Don't worry about it. I better go, anyway. I don't know how many minutes this phone has."

Tessa's voice is subdued, the total opposite of what it had been when this conversation started. "Sure, sure. I'll see you tomorrow."

I hang up and stare at the phone for a minute. Part of me wants to call Patrick, but I'm afraid I'll snap at him, too. And Benny is still on the guy outing with Kirk that all the boys had to go on—something involving a batting cage and pizza. I feel restless, and the last thing I want to do is Schwartz's assignment: a paper on the pros and cons of public surveillance cameras and whether or not they infringe on privacy rights. Obviously, I have a lot to say on the subject, but it's just too close to home.

I see a pair of tennis shoes in the corner of my room, and I decide to do what I always do: run from my problems. Except this time, I'm actually going to go somewhere.

When I step outside our gate, I can't help but grin. No Vultures. They must have started following the guys around town once they got their fill of us at the nail salon. I do a few half-assed stretches, then start jogging along the highway, toward my orchard. I could never run that far, of course—I'm already short of breath and the trucks and big rigs that speed by make me nervous. I want to turn around, but just the thought of it makes my legs go faster. Snow-capped mountains loom in the distance, and somewhere not too far off, I hear a faint train whistle. It's a lonesome sound, full of regret. Uncertainty. If I were to describe myself in one sound, it'd be that train whistle.

My muscles burn and my head pounds, but I push my body into the wind, my eyes stinging from the dust the gales kick up. After a while, some of the tightness in my chest loosens its grip, as if the wind itself has siphoned some of the tension off me. I'm tired and hungry and sweating, but I'm smiling. It feels good to do something on my own. I turn onto a smooth dirt road that seems to go for miles. My body finds a rhythm, and I don't think anymore, I just *am*. I'm not Bonnie™ or Chloe. I'm the essence of her, the nontrademarked person the camera can never capture and my parents have no right to sign over. There is a sovereign nation encased in this skin that MetaReel can never own.

Finally I stop and lean my hands on my knees, breathing hard. My body is soaked with sweat, and my legs have turned to jelly. After a few seconds, I turn back toward my house.

I'm done running.

Baker's Dozen: Season 13, Episode 9

INT—BAKER HOME—MORNING: The BAKER-MILLER living room. [BETH BAKER-MILLER sits on a couch, in front of a mantelpiece with thirteen framed photos.]

BETH: It seems like this is . . . the best thing. For the kids. And for us.

[CUT to ANDREW, sitting in the kitchen, at the family dinner table. He absently plays with his watch strap.]

ANDREW: I never meant to hurt anyone. It was a mistake. [His eyes take on a faraway look.] But Beth's wrong—I love my kids, and this has nothing to do with them.

[CUT to BETH, still in the living room.]

BETH: I mean, how irresponsible can he get? He brings another woman into our home, and he expects that with thirteen children running around, no one's going to notice? [Tears well, and she begins dabbing at them furiously with a tissue.] We had . . . we had this dream to . . . have a huge family and give these kids a safe, loving home. And he's just throwing it all away!

[CUT to ANDREW, at the kitchen table.]

ANDREW: I don't know, man. I guess she just changed, you know? And I did too. Fifty percent, you know? The divorce rate. I mean, it's just not fair to the kids. Beth and I, when we fight . . . it's ugly.

[CUT to image of ANDREW and BETH screaming at each other in the backyard.]

ANDREW: What do you want me to do, Beth? [Beep sounds as ANDREW curses] you.

[ANDREW stalks off and BETH stares after him.]

BETH: He's out of control. Absolutely crazy.

[Camera pans to BONNIE™ and BENTON™, wide-eyed, watching their parents. DESHAUN™ starts crying, and BONNIE™ picks him up, comforting him.]

BETH VO: I can tell this is affecting the kids. Especially the older ones. It's not healthy to see your parents in screaming matches all day long.

[CUT to ANDREW, once again sitting at the dining room table.]

ANDREW: So I'm leaving.

SEASON 17, EPISODE 19

(The One with Enchiladas)

"Chloe?"

I look up from the Q and A my English teacher, Miss Daniels, has us doing for Shirley Jackson's creepy short story, "The Lottery." Everyone else has a partner, but there's an odd number, so I'm working alone.

"Yeah?"

She beckons for me to come to her desk and hands me the pink slip of paper a student aide just left with her. I read the note once, twice, three times, just to be sure. It seems weird to see the words *your father* in a stranger's looping script. I wrap my fingers around the thin paper and squeeze.

"Make sure you write down the homework before you head out," she says.

Miss Daniels smiles at me, but all I can do is nod, feeling numb and strangely hopeful. The crumpled note in my fist says my dad is here to take me to lunch, but there must be a mistake. Maybe it's

Kirk—a babysitter fell through? That happens sometimes, me having to leave class because Mom and Kirk are overwhelmed. I throw my stuff into my backpack, my ears burning as the class watches me fumble with my coat, my books. It gets noticeably quieter—less talking, more watching. It feels like my whole life is streaming. Like, no matter where I am or who I'm with, I have an audience. Even when I'm alone, I can't turn Bonnie™ off. I push open the door and walk slowly down the hall. My thoughts scatter like confetti, swirling around, all colorful and fleeting.

As I near the office, I catch sight of him; it's most definitely my dad. My *dad* dad. He doesn't see me—probably too busy flirting with the students or charming our matronly secretary. On instinct, I duck into the closest hallway and lean against the wall, closing my eyes while the stale air flows in and out of my lungs. I pull out my phone and text Benny. I didn't see him in the office with Dad, so he must be on his way. I really don't want to go in there alone.

I just got the note. I'm in the hallway. Where are you?
Class. What note?
Dad's here.
WTF?
I guess we're going to lunch?
Why didn't I get a note?
I don't know.
You need backup?

I hesitate, but only for a second. Benny's class is right near the office. He would have gotten a note before me if he were getting one

234

at all. I don't know why my dad didn't ask him to come, but I don't want to complicate matters any further. I'm sure Benny's hurt—how could he not be?

Not right now. Thanks.
K. Gotta go—tchr.

I wipe my palms against my jeans and hover in the hallway. I don't see any cameras, but I don't trust him. After all this time, he's suddenly interested in having a relationship with me? I'm sure this has absolutely nothing to do with the fact that we're back on TV again. *Right.* And what about the rest of my siblings—why is he singling me out? Maybe it's as simple as I'm the only one of us kids my mother actually had. I was the miracle baby. Or because I'm the one who almost died. Still. It doesn't seem very fair. It's not hard for me to imagine the look on Lex's face if she finds out.

I square my shoulders and look at the door marked OFFICE. *Just go, Chloe.* I count each step to calm my nerves. After four years and one ghastly on-camera reunion, there are seventy-three steps between my father and me.

Distance between people can be marked in many ways.

As if sensing me, Dad turns around and his face breaks into an uncertain smile. I don't return it, but I pull open the door.

"Hello, sweetheart."

I grip the straps of my backpack and manage a grimace. "Hi."

The secretary watches us with poorly disguised fascination. We stand there for a few more seconds and then Dad turns to her and flashes his Andrew Baker smile. It's the one on the DVD covers of our show.

"Great to meet you, Mrs. Rose. I'll make sure to get Bonnie™ back by—"

"Chloe," I cut in.

"What?"

I just roll my eyes and start walking out of the office—Mrs. Rose already has enough gossip to last her awhile.

"Thanks again," I hear him say to her.

A minute later he's beside me.

"So, it's Chloe now?" he asks, his voice even. I can't tell if this bothers him or is merely interesting.

I keep my eyes straight ahead and walk quickly, hoping that no one in the classrooms will recognize us. The lunch bell is going to ring any second.

"Benny goes here, you know."

Dad nods, his long strides matching my short, quick ones. "I do. But I wanted a little alone time with you. That okay?"

The universe is testing my new resolve to stop running away from my problems. But there's a difference, isn't there, between running away and self-defense?

We're almost to the main entrance. "Are you parked out front?"

"Yes."

Of course he is. How could he resist letting the Vultures get a few nice shots of him taking Bonnie™ out to lunch?

"Does Mom know you're here?"

"She does." He points to a BMW a few feet away. "That's me."

"Nice car," I say, my voice dry.

Dad grins. "This one's a rental, but we've got one just like it at home. We love this thing."

"We?"

He coughs uncomfortably. "Hop in."

Is he still with her? The girl who is practically my age?

"Is MetaReel coming to lunch with us, too?"

"No. But we should hurry before they figure out where we are."

I open the door and duck inside. The new car smell makes me nauseous, and as soon as he starts the engine, I immediately roll down the window. I slip on my don't-talk-to-me glasses from Hand Me Downs as we pull out of the parking lot.

"They out here every day?" he asks, gesturing to the Vultures.

"Of course."

"So what's good around here?" He's injected some false cheer into his voice, and it's as obvious as my mother's recent Botox treatments.

"I'm not hungry."

Why am I in this car? He doesn't deserve to just walk into my life like this. I should get out.

"Honey, don't you think you've punished me long enough?"

I bite my lip until I can taste blood in my mouth. Then I stop because I don't want to go back to thinking that hurting myself makes the other pain go away. Fuck. I'm with him for, like, three seconds, and it's like all those years of therapy and figuring it out are just gone. Like *that*.

Dad purses his lips and exhales like he's rationing his air. He used to do this when he got annoyed, but was trying to keep his temper. It's the reaction I want (to make it harder on him, to—*yes*—to punish him a little), but it hurts my feelings all the same.

"Well," he tries, "I saw a Mexican place near the freeway—Don something-or-other. Wanna get some enchiladas?"

"I guess."

"Great."

Dad reaches over and fiddles with the radio.

Call now and you'll receive . . . You and me could write a bad romance . . . The Dow Jones is up three percent and market shares . . . At Crazy Dan's you're not just getting a good deal, you're getting . . . Blackbird singing in the dead of night, take these broken wings and learn to fly . . .

Finally, he just shuts it off. His hands grip the wheel, his knuckles white, and I stare at them for a moment, lost in a memory of him teaching me to write, his fingers gently guiding my own. This is the man who gave me words. But he didn't listen when I tried to use them.

"So how do you like high school?" he finally says.

"It was good until all this started up again." Now, being in the midst of the show, I know it was more than good. It was football games on autumn nights, eating lunch in the caf at long, sea foam green tables with no one staring at me. It was sleeping over at my friends' houses and knowing people liked me as Chloe, not Bonnie™.

"Your grades okay?"

Really?

"Dad, I can't talk about my grades right now. I haven't seen you in years, and you come during our *live episode* and get in a fight with my stepdad and show up at my school and—" I stop because if I don't, everything I've wanted to say will come tumbling out.

Dad pulls into the restaurant parking lot and kills the engine. I can see the Vultures in the rearview mirror, taking out their cameras. This is why I only go from home to school and back again.

"Shit," Dad says.

I don't wait for him. I shove open the door and sprint toward the restaurant.

"Bonnie™! One picture!"

"Hey, Bonnie™, how're you feeling?"

"Andrew—just one shot of the two of you. C'mon, man."

Dad walks slowly, and when I look back, he's talking to them. *Traitor.*

"Please. I'm just trying to take my daughter out for lunch. Go back to Hollywood, huh?"

I swing open the door of the restaurant and immediately go to the bathroom. I pull out my phone and dial.

"Benny?"

My voice is shaking and I'm not strong I can't do this I'm a coward why can't I just tell him to fuck off and why why why did I get in that car oh God please—

"Chlo! Where are you?"

"Don Ricardo's."

"What's going on?"

I look at myself in the mirror—dark circles under my eyes and stringy psych-ward-escapee hair. It occurs to me that MetaReel might be listening in on Benny's phone even though I'm using my prepaid one. Right now I'm too upset to care.

"I have no idea. I don't know what the hell I'm doing here."

Benny swears, and I hear him muttering to someone near him. It's lunchtime at Taft. "Hey, Patrick wants to say hi. Hold up."

I can hear the chaos of the cafeteria for a few seconds and then, "Hey, you."

"Hi," I say, my voice soft. I can hear the yearning in it—can he hear it, too?

"Do you want me to kick his ass?" Patrick's voice is dry, but the undercurrent of emotion in it suggests he's not entirely opposed to the idea.

I laugh. "Would you?"

"Actually, yes. I think I would. I'm not violent by nature, but you sort of bring that out in me. Er, not you. Rather, the people around you. Hey—hold on a sec. What?" I can hear someone talking to him, then, "Tessa and Mer say they're willing to Taser him."

I try to laugh, but it comes out as a grunt. "Well, I'll text you if it comes to that."

There's a pause and then, "Seriously. I'll come pick you up. You don't owe him anything."

Refusing is not something I've ever been allowed to do. I don't know what the consequences would be if I did. I'm tempted to take his offer, to have Patrick shield me against all the Vultures and whisk me away to somewhere quiet and safe.

"That sounds . . ." I sigh. "I have to deal with this."

"I know." He pauses, but because I can't see his face, I'm not sure what's weighing down the air between us. "Don't go home until I get to see you, okay?"

"Wouldn't dream of it."

Benny gets back on. "One call, and we'll come out and rescue your scrawny ass."

"Love you."

"Love you too."

Benny's worried. I can tell visions of me popping pills are dancing in his head. I hang up, then splash some water on my face before I go out into the restaurant. Dad's sitting at a table in the back, away from the windows. He looks anxious and a little bit lonely, which makes me sad. I realize I've never seen him alone. Ever. This seems statistically impossible, but it's true.

I look at the lime green drink beside my place setting and raise my eyebrows.

"I ordered you a margarita," he says.

I plop down into the chair across from him. "You're aware that I'm seventeen?"

He grins, magnanimous. "My father let me drink when I was a senior in high school."

My grandfather, it must be noted, died eight years ago from a busted-ass liver.

I look at the drink and then decide, What the hell? I put the straw between my lips and take a tiny sip. It's delicious—tart and salty and warm when it hits my stomach. Dad settles back and gives me a long look. I tuck my hair behind my ear self-consciously, and he smiles.

"I missed you, honey."

The mariachi music being piped through the speakers on the wall is too cheerful for this conversation.

"Your fault, not mine," I say. "I guess MetaReel made it worth your while?"

I feel like I'm getting away with murder, being this openly disrespectful.

He bites his lip and looks up at the ceiling. "They offered me *access*—access I haven't been able to get for years." I snort and let my eyes drift over the southwestern décor. "Sweetie, when you get older, you might understand a bit more."

"What's to understand? You cheated on Mom, you left. It seems pretty simple to me."

I take a big sip of the margarita and then another when my eyes start to water. I'm not going to cry in front of him. He doesn't deserve it.

"Bonnie™, I know that's how it looks, but it's actually pretty complicated—"

He stops himself as the waitress comes up.

"You guys ready to order?"

She's wearing a traditional Mexican dress that accentuates her curves. Dad meets her brown bedroom eyes and smiles. *Goddammit, can't he just be a normal dad for three seconds?*

"I'll have the enchiladas—cheese. And another one of these." He points to his margarita—he's already drained it. Typical. "Bon?"

"Cheese enchiladas," I mumble.

"La Cucaracha" plays in my head, and I wonder if he's thinking of the same thing.

The waitress leaves, and Dad puts his hand over mine. "Look at me. Please."

I take my hand away and bring it to the straw in my drink, taking another long sip.

"Go easy, hon."

I narrow my eyes. "You want *me* to go easy? I thought you were the one with the drinking problem."

Seasons ten through thirteen have well documented that. Dad sighs and leans back.

"What can I do, Bonnie™? I'm here. I'm trying. I love you—I love *all* of you."

"Then where have you *been*?" I say, the words ricocheting around the empty restaurant. "You broke your promise. You said you'd come back. But you didn't. And I've been waiting and waiting and then Mom married Kirk and—"

My voice breaks. How many times have I rehearsed this monologue? In my head, it is perfectly edited, each phrase crafted for the express purpose of making him hurt as much as I do. My words are supposed to be daggers thrown at his heart, not half-coherent complaints. I grip my knees with both hands and try to hold my body together. I'm about to rip at the seams; if I cry, everything inside me is going to fly out. When someone opens the door, pieces of me will be borne away on the wind. I'll never be able to find all of them. I'll never be whole. *I'll never be whole.*

When he speaks, Dad's voice is low, placating. "Honey, I know. I *know*. I wanted to keep that promise so badly. But I couldn't. Your mother and I . . . Bon, we hate each other. You know that. And the arguments were getting worse—you must remember how bad they were. When you took those pills—"

My dad stops, picks up his glass, and drinks half of it in one sip. He doesn't even get brain freeze. He motions for the waitress to bring another round.

"When you took those pills and we almost lost you—I blamed myself."

I roll my eyes. Right. He blamed himself, which is why he, what, ditched us?

He leans forward, his eyes bright. "I know why you took them. You wanted me to come back. You wanted everything to be like it was before . . . before I left."

"You mean before the affair."

He sighs. "I mean before your mother and I stopped loving each other."

I finish my drink and close my eyes so that I don't have to see the pain in his. Instead, I picture the amber tequila flowing down my throat and into my veins. It turns my blood into gold. I'm warm and made of rubber.

And I want more tequila.

The waitress brings the drinks and our enchiladas. I'm obviously underage—I even have my backpack with me. I wonder how my dad charmed her while I was in the bathroom. Or are these celebrity perks? I can tell the margarita is going to my head because I'm having trouble maintaining control of the cold ball of anger that was rolling around in my heart a few minutes ago. Now I just feel depressed.

Which is so much worse than angry.

When the waitress leaves, Dad takes a bite of his enchilada and smiles. "Better than mine?"

This is an olive branch. Should I accept it?

I stab at the enchilada—the taste holds so many memories. I swallow, then permit the corner of my mouth to turn up. "No. But good."

We eat in silence for a while, and I'm surprised how much of it I manage to get down. After a few minutes, I take off my sweater.

"God, it's hot in here."

Dad picks up my drink and puts it on his side of the table. It's only half finished, but he slides a full glass of water close to my hand.

"Drink that up, or I'll never hear the end of it from your mother."

Is he playing cool dad—or is this how he would have been anyway? I open my mouth to argue, but then the room starts to spin, so I bring the glass to my lips.

"I still don't understand," I say. "Why didn't you try harder to see us?"

"I did. But you always refused to come to the phone. You never answered any of my letters or e-mails. The last thing you said to me was that you hated me and never wanted to speak to me again."

"Yeah, but . . . but you're not supposed to give up!"

Dad keeps his eyes on his plate. Something about the sagging defeat in his face causes all those hurtful memories to add up.

"You never wanted this, did you? You didn't leave because of . . . because of *her*. You left because of *us*."

My voice is soft, not accusing. Maybe it's the alcohol, but I'm finally getting it. It's despicable—*he's* despicable—but I now understand season twelve, when he bought sports cars and took "business trips" to Vegas.

"It all happened so fast," he whispers. His eyes are glassy, far away, like he's watching his life play out on a big-screen TV.

"It was a joke between your mother and me—a baker's dozen! We were only twenty-two, you know. By the time I was twenty-three, we had you, Ben, and Lex."

Four and a half years older than I am right now. Shit. Here he is, a divorced father of thirteen . . . and he's only forty. Most of my friends' parents are the same age as my grandparents. No wonder Dad freaked out. Still, that doesn't make it okay to do what he did.

He looks at me, and I nod for him to go on.

"We had both just finished college, and I had a crappy job in a cubicle. Your mom wanted a baby so badly, but the doctors said it was impossible. We knew we could never afford the fertility treatments. She was so sad . . . it broke my heart. Hell, we were high school sweethearts."

That's the most depressing part about the whole thing. People who have prom pictures together should never get a divorce.

"Anyway, she wrote MetaReel, told them about our plans. I never expected them to be interested. I thought, What was the harm in letting Beth have a little hope? But then we got the call. You should have seen the look on her face. She acted like she'd won the lottery. And, I guess in a way, she had. *We* had. Once they interviewed us and decided on the show . . . I mean, it seemed like we'd be crazy to turn it down. And when the treatments worked, and we got you . . . it felt like it was all worth it. For a while, it was great. It really was."

I don't realize I'm crying until I taste the salt on my lips. Dad reaches out and touches his fingertips to my cheek, and this makes me cry harder. For just a second, I lean against his upturned palm.

"Daddy, I . . ."

Mom never has time. Even after Kirk, there's only so much of her to go around. She doesn't know about Patrick, that he even exists. I want to tell Dad how I have this fantasy of Patrick coming to my house to pick me up for a date and how he would call Dad *sir* and shake his hand. Dad would make jokes about having a shotgun and then I'd say *Dad, you're embarrassing me*. The only person who's always had my back in this whole world is Benny, and he's great, but he's not a substitute for the man sitting in front of me.

"I tried my best to be a good dad, I really did," he says. "But I was so young. It was just . . . too much."

"But we're still here," I whisper.

"Yes. You are."

We don't stay at the restaurant much longer. Though there are a million things I could say, I feel like I need to let this soak in for a while. I'm glad Dad doesn't make any promises, and I don't ask him to. Will I see him again? I honestly don't know.

"Are you sure you can drive?" I ask.

He nods. "Of course."

I watch him walk ahead of me, and he doesn't stumble or sway. He must be drinking quite a bit for three margaritas not to affect his motor skills. They made him pretty honest, though.

When Dad pulls into the Taft lot, I hesitate, my hand on the door handle. We lock eyes, and I'm surprised to see parts of myself in his face—the green eyes, the long bridge of my nose.

"I love you, Bonnie™."

I can't say it back, and I'm not sure if I believe him. Instead I nod and open the door. There's a flicker of disappointment in his eyes, but he smiles. The bell rings—if I hurry, I can make it to Spanish. I watch him drive away and then I turn back toward school and the life I've made for myself without him.

SEASON 17, EPISODE 20

(The One with the Notebook)

There's a soft knock on my bedroom door later that night. I was expecting it earlier, but Mom was busy with tantrums and dinner. My head is pounding from too much tequila—too much Dad—and I really don't want to have this conversation, but I slide my journal under my mattress and open the door.

"Can I come in?"

"Yeah."

Mom sits on the edge of my bed, and I sink into the desk chair. "You doing all right?" she asks.

I nod, but just that one motion makes me wince.

"Yeah."

She crosses her arms. "You don't *seem* all right."

I shrug. If she finds out Dad let me drink, the fallout will be fodder for next week's episode. "I mean, it was hard. And unexpected. I wish you'd told me about it."

I play with a pencil, to give my hands something to do. I don't know if Dad told her how he never wanted all of us, but now I will always see her differently. Not as a mom, but as a woman. I wonder how bad the hurt is when someone falls out of love with you.

"I couldn't," she says. "Chuck would have found out, and the cameras would have been there. I wanted to give you privacy. I felt like . . . like I owed you that." She hesitates, and I notice the lines in her face, the wisp of gray showing at her roots. "Honey, I'm so sorry about Thanksgiving."

I have a whole rant I was saving up, about how I couldn't trust her anymore and she was letting Chuck control our lives, but now it seems beside the point. I'm finally realizing that *both* my parents left a long time ago. She just happens to still live here.

"I heard you and Chuck—the night Benny and I were babysitting. You *let* him talk you into it. You knew about it." I stare at her. "How could you do that?"

She shifts her weight, looks at her hands. "I have to choose my battles with MetaReel. I really felt this was one I had to let them win." Tears spill onto her cheeks, a little river of mascara that trickles down her Lancôme mask. "But when everyone started fighting, I realized I'd made the wrong choice. And I'll have to live with that for the rest of my life."

I can feel my pulse in my head, and when I touch my cheeks, my skin burns my fingertips. The Excedrin isn't helping. I can't deal with a hangover and two broken parents in one day.

"Sure, Mom. Whatever."

There's a heaviness between us. Maybe it's always been there, but I feel it now more than ever. Because *sorry* just isn't good enough. How do you say sorry for damaging someone's life?

"Do you want to talk about lunch?" she asks, wiping at her face.

I gesture to the notebook and piles of textbooks on my desk. "I've got a ton of homework, and I'm pretty tired."

I know this is the part where I'm supposed to hug her, tell her it's okay. Give her a tissue or something.

I don't.

She stands and rubs her palms against her skirt. "All right, then I'll leave you to it." She crosses over to me and kisses my head. "I really am sorry."

I ignore her and turn to my homework, but when she opens the door, she stops. "Look, I know this is terrible timing, but I don't want you to be confused tomorrow. They're going to start assigning individual cameras to you, Benny, and Lex."

My head snaps up. "What?"

She shrugs. "Chuck thinks it'd be good to get you guys on your way to school or when you go out with your friends." Her eyes flick over my panicked face and her voice takes on that high I'm-lying-to-you tone. "It's no big deal, Bonnie™. It won't be every time. Just to give some context to the whole show. You three are gone so much."

"Mom, that is so not cool. No one is going to want to go *anywhere* with me!"

I was hoping that the Vultures would get bored with us after a while and I'd be able to go out more. Patrick and I still haven't had a real date, and I miss the Tower District and hanging out at Mer's or Tessa's.

"Sweetie, I think your friends would be really excited to have the chance to be on TV. The guys Kirk works with don't mind. The cameras are always on-site with him—half the time they forget they're even there. It's no big deal."

The condescending tone grates on my nerves, and my head hurts so freaking bad, why did I drink those margaritas, why did Dad *let* me? I don't even think, I just throw. I gasp as the notebook leaves my hand and flies toward her. She shoots out a hand and knocks it down, and we just stare at each other for a second, panting. Then she crosses the room in three quick strides and slaps my face. Hard.

I cry out—from the shock or the pain, I'm not sure—but she just stands over me, her mouth a straight, hateful line. Everything in me begs to slap her right back. I'm not sure why I don't.

"You're really turning into a little bitch, you know that?" she says.

Mom's voice slices into me, cutting away the shred of respect I have left for her. I want the world to see this, right now. This is Beth Baker-Miller in all her glory.

"You hit me," I say, hardly able to believe it. My parents have never hit me. Ever.

Mom's jaw tightens as Kirk and a cameraman step into the room.

"What's going on in here? We heard you all the way downstairs."

Me, talking over Kirk: "Get out," I say to the camera. "You're not allowed in my room. No bedrooms, no bathrooms."

But he doesn't leave.

I can see Benny and Lex and a few of the other kids crowding in the hallway. Lacey Production Assistant stands behind them, furiously texting. The word *bitch* seems to echo in my ringing ears, over and over. I put my hand up to my burning cheek.

"I'm not going to live in a house where my seventeen-year-old daughter throws things at me," Mom says.

"Then don't have strangers with cameras follow me around everywhere!" I shout.

"Bonnie™, don't speak to your mother that way," says Kirk. "You need to channel your anger into something more productive, like—"

"Who the hell are *you*? You're just some dude hitching a ride," I snarl.

I don't know if that was me or residual drunkenness speaking, but either way, it feels damn good to say.

"That's it!" Mom screams. "Do you want to go live with your father? Would that make you happy?"

"Oh, you mean with the guy who never wanted any of us in the first place? Sure, why don't I go live with him? That's a freaking *great* idea!"

Two seconds ago, I thought I could never be angry enough with her to tell her what Dad had said. What kind of person am I turning into?

Mom's face pales, and she shrugs Kirk off when he tries to put a hand on her arm. She backs away, toward the door, her eyes two sharp pieces of flint.

"Go to your rooms," she says to everyone in the hallway. I hear whispers, but I don't know what my siblings are saying.

She turns back to me, her hand on the knob. "You're grounded."

I can't help it; I start laughing. "What do you call this?" I ask, gesturing to the air around me.

She slams the door, and I flip her off, though she'll never see it. Hate is a lot like love. It's warm and fills you up until every part of you is tingling to release it.

~ ~ ~

It's Tuesday night, and the most recent episode of *Baker's Dozen* is about to start. Though I'd been grounded since Friday, Mom said I could come over to Tessa's to "study." Truth is, I'd finally decided I was ready to watch an episode of the show, but I didn't want to do it alone. Tessa's wearing her Hello Kitty killing a TV T-shirt to commemorate the event. Her parents had refused to sign a waiver, so Chuck deemed it pointless to send a camera guy with me. Small victories.

"This is kind of bizarre, watching the show with you," Mer says as she finishes up the glittery polish on her nails.

Tessa switches on the TV in her bedroom and flips through channels until she gets to MetaReel.

I nod. "Tell me about it."

Tessa throws me a sympathetic look. "Are you *sure* you want to watch this?"

I need them to watch it and then tell me that I'm not as crazy as I'm starting to feel.

"I have to see how Chuck's going to spin the fight I had with my mom last week. Matt says Coach tells him that the best defense is a good offense. So I'm being offensive. Er, you know what I mean."

Tessa scrunches up her nose. "I can't believe you just quoted Coach Hardwick."

"Desperate times . . . ," I say. I turn up the volume on the TV. "All right, let's do this."

Mer hands me my Pepsi as if it's a beer I really need, and they sit on either side of me, like bodyguards.

"This is so cheesy," I say, when our opening credits come on.

The upbeat, canned song our show has had since my childhood plays as our individual pictures fly by the screen. There's some of the footage from the studio where they made us all run and jump around, barefoot and goofy. It ends with a family photo of us all squished together on Mom and Kirk's bed and the *Baker's Dozen: Fresh Batch* logo, which looks like a recipe card.

"At least your picture looks good," says Mer.

"Are you opposed to me throwing things at your TV?" I ask Tessa.

"Um, here." She hands me a stress ball. "Just squeeze it."

Mom: "C'mon, kids, time for school. Let's go!"

Mom turns to the camera and rolls her eyes.

Mom: "I swear, those three act surprised every morning."

It's this past Tuesday. I can tell because I'm wearing Patrick's Mammoth Mountain sweatshirt, which he'd given to me during gov after the heater broke. It smells like him, so I'd refused to give it back.

Tristan™: "Mom, why can't we go to school, too?"
Mom: "You *do* go to school."
Gavin™: "At *home*."
Mom: "When you're sixteen . . ."

She's running around the kitchen, getting food for everyone. Jasmine™ reaches up to the camera, pulls it down to her level, and kisses the lens.

Jasmine™: "I loooooove you!"

She giggles and runs away. Kirk walks into the kitchen, wearing Dickies and a Fresno State T-shirt.

Kirk: "Hey, honey. I'll be home by one."

He gives my mom a peck on the cheek.

Mom: "Okay, good, because I have to catch a
    flight to Chicago for the book signing."

"Fun fact," I say. "They made them redo their conversation because Chuck wanted Mom to set up that she was doing book signings. Originally she'd just said, 'Great!'"

"So 'reality' TV," Tessa says, making air quotes, "isn't big on the
reality aspect."

I nod. "Not so much."

I'm dodging the camera, letting my hair swing in front of my
face. I've got spy hair—these are my incognito tresses. I grab an
apple and a granola bar. Benny gets our coffee and Puma Guy follows us to the car. Then the shot changes to Lexie™ giving my mom
a hug good-bye. At around that moment, Chuck and I were having an
argument about the Bonnie™ and Benton™ cam, but the editors cut
it out for obvious reasons.

Now, the focus is back on us as the camera gets in the backseat of
our car. I glare at it, then get in the front and slam the door.

"Dude, you look *pissed*," Mer says. It's a little weird—a lot
weird—to have someone say that to you while looking at you on TV.

"I was. I *am*," I mutter.

Tessa reaches over and squeezes my arm. "Just think happy
naked Patrick thoughts," she says. I'm too tense to even roll my eyes.

The show cuts to the interview area in the basement. My mom's
on the couch, looking serious.

Mom: "Bonnie™ is . . ."

She looks up, searching for the right word.

Mom: "She's still struggling with Andrew's surprise visit. It's definitely taken a toll on
our relationship. She's very distant."

They cut to my bedroom. The camera is peeking over Kirk's
shoulder. I look awful. My face is really red from where Mom had
just slapped me (of course, the camera didn't get there in time for
that). My hair's all tangled, and I'm wearing an oversized T-shirt and
sweats that make me look fat.

Kirk: "What's going on in here? We heard you
all the way downstairs."
Me, talking over Kirk: "Get out. You're not
allowed in my room."

I had said this to the cameraman, but they edited it so that it
looks like I was talking to Kirk.

Mom: "I'm not going to live in a house where my
seventeen-year-old daughter throws things
at me."

The camera zooms in on the notebook on my floor, then goes
back up to Mom and me, facing off.

Me: "Then don't—" There's a long beep covering over everything I'm saying.

"What the hell?" I shout at the TV. "I didn't curse, I didn't!"

I remember what I'd said (it was basically "Then don't have cameras following me around!"). But MetaReel made it look like I'd up and cussed out my mother *on national television*. I squeeze the stress ball in my hand, but it's not enough because my hands want to do ripping, tearing, shredding things.

"Can they do that?" Mer asks. "Just totally make shit up?"

"*Shhh*," Tessa says.

Kirk: "Bonnie™, don't speak to your mother that way. You need to channel your anger into something more productive, like—"

Me: "Who the hell are *you*? You're just some dude hitching a ride."

Okay, wow, that was harsh. My face reddens a little, but I'm still on Bonnie™'s side. I mean, my side. I blame the Heisenberg Principle—I'm not really sure I would have said that if the camera hadn't come in. Guess I'll never know. Mer and Tessa both put a hand on my knee.

Mom: "That's it! Do you want to go live with your father? Would that make you happy?"

Me: "Oh, you mean with the guy who never wanted any of us in the first place? Sure, why don't

I go live with him? That's a freaking *great* idea!"

Mom, turning to my siblings: "Go to your rooms."

The camera pans to the hallway, where my brothers and sisters are gathered looking shocked, worried, sad. Then it goes back to Mom and me.

Mom: "You're grounded."

I start laughing like a maniac, which is unfortunate because it's not very attractive.

Me: "What do you call this?"

The show cuts to Mom in the interview area again. She's dabbing at her eyes. Whatever.

Mom: "I don't know how to get through to her. I wish Andrew was more involved, but he's pretty much dropped off the face of the earth."

Chuck's voice: "Do you think she might try to hurt herself again?"

I grab the pillow I'm leaning against, stick my face into it, and scream.

Mom: "I don't know. Honestly. I have her seeing the school counselor, but she refuses to take

medication. She isolates herself when she's
home and treats Kirk and me like her punching bags."

She dabs her eyes again.

Mom: "I love my daughter, but she's tearing our
family apart. Again."

"Shut it off," I say.

Tessa grabs the remote, and the screen turns black. We sit there in the middle of her bedroom for a minute, staring at one another.

"Chlo, this is . . ." Tessa shakes her head.

"Seriously screwed up," Mer finishes. "I wish there was a way you could, like, defriend your family."

"Yeah." I feel totally unhinged, like I'm free-floating in space with nothing to hold on to. "I can't believe she would say that about me," I whisper.

My voice hitches a little on "me," but I close my eyes and take a deep breath and count to ten. I exhale, imagining the panic flowing out of me on the tide of my breath. It's thick and gray, sick-looking. I don't open my eyes until the tight feeling in my chest crumbles.

"If it makes you feel any better, I am officially renouncing all ambitions to be famous," Mer says.

I give her a wan smile. "My friend, if you didn't, I'd think you were crazier than I am."

Tessa stands and starts pacing around the room. "Chloe, this has to be illegal. You have to fight them."

I hold my hands out. Empty. I've got nothin'.

259

"How? Every time I try to talk to my mom or Chuck, they brush me off. I'm 'too dramatic,' or I need to 'go with the flow.' I mean, you saw what happened when I tried to tell my mom I didn't want the Bonnie™ cam."

We marinate in awfulness for a minute or two, but then my phone vibrates, and the sound breaks the spell. I look at it—Patrick. He promised he would never watch the show after that first live one, but he knew I was watching tonight and that I was freaked about it.

Everything all right?
No.
What can I do? Anything up to and including assassinations.
I'll keep that in mind.
Need a ride home? (That's code for I really want to see you.)

Benny was supposed to come pick me up at a gas station a block over so that we could avoid the Vultures finding out where Tessa lives.

Can't. I wish I could . . . too many Vultures. TTYL?
Yes, please.

I text Benny to tell him to come pick me up, then put my phone back in my pocket and start gathering my stuff together.

"Chloe, maybe there's someone you can talk to or—" Tessa begins, but I cut her off.

"Tess, I have no one. Seriously. My dad is a total dropout, I don't really know any of my relatives, and you saw my mom. There's no getting through to her. I just have to deal."

"But—"

I zip up my bag and head toward her door. "I love you both. But I really need to be alone for a bit before Benny comes to get me, okay?"

They nod, and I see myself out, giving Tessa's parents a quick cheerful good night before I leave. Most of the houses on her street are decorated for Christmas, but the lights and blow-up Santas just depress me even more.

She's tearing our family apart. Again.

So Mom *does* blame me for the divorce. Nice to know. Is she right? Am I the place where all the problems in my family begin and end?

"Five more months," Benny says, when he picks me up ten minutes later. "Then we'll graduate, and we're free."

But that doesn't make me feel better. I'm beginning to think I can't hold out that long.

~ ~ ~

When we get to the house, Chuck is standing on the porch, smoking a cigar. Like he's celebrating screwing me over.

It's now or never.

"Chuck, can I talk to you for a sec?"

He raises his eyebrows, but nods. I'm lucky to catch him before he leaves for the night. I stay on the porch while Benny heads inside.

"What's up?"

"I saw the episode tonight." I wrinkle my nose against the stench. His cigar smells like body odor and too-strong potpourri.

He takes a long drag and the ember glows a menacing orange. "The ratings were great. They just eat you up, Bonnie™."

A sharp wind cuts through the driveway, and I rub my arms. I wish we could go inside, but I can't have this conversation with my mom around.

"That's the problem," I say. "I *feel* eaten up. I'm not comfortable with being talked about on the show. What my mom said about me in the interview was . . . wrong."

He laughs and puts a meaty hand on my shoulder. I involuntarily flinch, and his eyes darken.

"Listen, Bonnie™, you're like a daughter to me."

I don't say anything, but this is total BS.

"When you get a little older, you'll see that all this stuff is no big deal. All teenagers fight with their moms. Trust me, kiddo, you're no different than every other seventeen-year-old girl in America."

"That's not true," I say. "And even if it were, it's still not cool to talk about my past like that. And the bedrooms are off limits, so Puma Guy shouldn't have been in there."

Chuck furrows his brow. "Puma Guy?"

"The cameraman."

"Mike."

"Yeah, whatever," I say. "Can you please not—"

Chuck holds up a hand. "You're making a mountain out of a molehill, sweetheart." I try to say something, but he holds up his hand again. "*But*, I will do my best to make sure that your past doesn't come up anymore, okay?"

It feels like he's just let out all the wind in my sails. My perfectly constructed arguments and zinger insults suddenly feel out of place, like I'm some overwrought harpy. Still. "It's not just that, though, it's—"

He gives me his it's-out-of-my-hands shrug. "I just tape what I see. You need to talk to your mother about the sort of things she says in the interviews."

He pulls out his keys and starts walking toward his Mercedes. "'Night, Bonnie™."

When I answer, my voice is hollow and small. "Good night."

I'm not ready to try talking to my mom again, so I just slip upstairs to my bedroom and pretend I'm asleep when she comes upstairs to check on me.

In the middle of the night I get out of bed to grab a glass of water, pissed that I hadn't thought to bring one up before I went to sleep. Now I'm the star of MetaReel.com, since we're streaming 24/7. When I walk into the kitchen, everything is bathed in a dim glow. The red lights on the stationary cameras are blinking, and I hurry over to the cupboard, grab a glass, and fill it with the filtered water in the fridge. Then I remember that I'm not wearing a bra under my thin shirt. Fantastic.

I'm groggy, I guess, and not paying attention, because as I walk out of the kitchen toward the stairs, I trip on that same stupid-ass camera cord that sent me onto my knees on day one of filming. My glass flies out of my hand and goes *thunk* against the carpeted stairs. It doesn't break, but the stairs are soaked, and I look like a total idiot.

"That's *it*," I mutter.

I snatch the glass out of its puddle of water and go back to the kitchen. Then I yank open the knife drawer and take out the meat cleaver. God, I'm as crazy as Annie in *Misery*. I march up to the cord, get down on my knees, and start hacking at it. It's not just one cord, but a whole stack of them taped together with thick black gaffer's tape. Even better. A few minutes later, the cords are severed, and all the cameras in the kitchen have gone totally dark. I guess I could have electrocuted myself, but whatever. I walk up to one of the working cameras in the living room and wave.

Then I put away the meat cleaver, refill my glass of water, and go back to bed.

I sleep like a baby.

~ ~ ~

The next morning, this is what wakes me up:

"BONNIE™ ELIZABETH BAKER, GET DOWN HERE RIGHT NOW."

I give the morning a grim smile. *Busted.*

SEASON 17, EPISODE 21

(The One with the Tabloid)

t's Wednesday, and we're hanging out in Schwartz's room with twenty minutes left of lunch. My mother's freak-out over the cord this morning has made me surly and Benny's not helping matters. For some reason, he's decided to get on my case about applying to some colleges during Christmas break, which starts next week.

"But you have to apply *somewhere*," he says.

"No, actually, I don't." I use my end-of-discussion voice, but Benny has been ignoring that for years.

"Sheldon. Please tell your girlfriend she has to go to college," Benny says.

I shoot my brother an annoyed glare. "Yes, because we've somehow time traveled, and now it's 1835 and I have to do what my boyfriend tells me to." I put my hand on Patrick's knee. "No offense."

He puts his hand on top of mine. "None taken."

Benny snorts. "He just wants to get some—that's why he's staying on your good side."

"Benton™ Andrew Baker—"

"If getting some were my ultimate goal," Patrick interrupts, "wouldn't it stand to reason that I would actually beg Chloe to apply to a school in New York, rather than potentially stay here?"

I can't imagine not being with Patrick, now that we're finally together. I don't know what I want to do, but in all my vague imaginings, he's always been with me. I don't like all this talk of New York.

"All right, Sheldon, you have a point. Actually, a great one. Chloe, what about New—"

I stand up and grab the remains of my lunch to throw away. "I have to go to the bathroom before class. You"—I point to Benny—"are on my shit list."

My eyes meet Patrick's, and he winks.

By the time I return, class is about to start. Patrick and I don't bring up the college discussion again, but I wonder how much it's been in the back of both our minds. He'd acted weird about the Columbia stuff Benny saw on his desk, and he's probably noticed how whenever people start talking about college, I tend to find my cell or book really interesting. When the bell rings and we walk out of the room, his fingers intertwine with mine.

"You're sad," he says. His eyes travel over my face, and he frowns.

I open my mouth to disagree, but what's the point? We've been dating a little over a month, and he can already read me like an open book. I rest my head against his shoulder as he walks me to my next class.

"Is it about the college stuff?" When I don't answer, he squeezes my hand. "I haven't made any decisions yet—about school."

I smile up at him. "You don't have to try to make me feel better."

He kisses my nose, and I turn into a puddle of melted girl. "I know." We stop in front of my class, and I let go of his hand as the warning bell rings. "Bye," I say.

He gives me a lopsided grin before heading off down the hall. It's silly, but it tugs at my heart every time we have to go our separate ways. I watch his back for a second, the way he walks with casual assurance, like he knows his place in the world. Me? I have no idea. I duck into my next class, but as soon as I sit down, my phone buzzes in my pocket. It's Mer.

Meet me in the bathroom ASAP.

I saw her three seconds ago in class—what could possibly be that important? I shove the phone back in my pocket and ask Señora Mendoza for *el baño* pass, then hurry up the hallway. When I get to the girls' bathroom, I shove open the pale blue metal door, but it's empty.

"Mer?"

"Handicap stall," she says.

I have visions of pregnancy tests or hemorrhaging, but when I get inside, she's leaning against the tile wall, a rolled-up magazine in her hand.

"What? Are you sick . . . or . . . ?"

She shakes her head and hands me the magazine. It's *Stargazer*, a trashy tabloid the Vultures love. I'm on the cover.

"I'm sorry," Mer says. "I didn't want you to find out another way."

The bold yellow headline says TEEN IN CRISIS: AN INSIDE PEEK INTO THE LIFE OF METAREEL'S MOST VOLATILE STAR. The picture is a glossy promo shot from the *Baker's Dozen* website. I'm smiling, but not with my teeth, and my eyes look lost, caged. The girl in the picture seems, I have to admit, a little volatile.

The bathroom door creaks open. "Chloe? Mer?"

"Handicap," Mer says.

Tessa walks in, a bathroom pass in one hand and her cell phone in the other. She looks at me, looks at the magazine. Then she wraps her arms around me. The magazine gets crushed as Mer enfolds both of us in her arms. I don't cry. I just shake and shake.

"Where'd you get it?" I whisper.

"A girl in chem was reading it, and I just grabbed it out of her hand and ran in here. It must have come out today."

Tessa smooths my hair. "You didn't know?"

I shake my head. "I don't think I can read it right now."

If I do, I'll be breaking my number one rule. I'd promised myself, no matter how bad things got, that I wouldn't read what people wrote about me. But now it's in my hands and the words are so close. My fingers itch to pull back the cover, but I know from experience that this is a really bad idea.

"Okay, but . . ." Mer bites her lip. "There's something you should know, like, right now."

I grip the thin pages of filth in my hand and nod.

"They have a picture of Patrick in there. With his name and everything. They got a picture of you guys kissing in the parking lot, and there's, like, this whole sidebar about your relationship."

I sit on the bathroom floor and tear through the pages until I find the article about me. Sure enough, there's Patrick and me, just this past Monday. My lips are inches from his, and we're smiling. Underneath our picture is a tiny article that Tessa and I read.

HOW SHE'S COPING

Bonnie™ Baker is all grown up. Sources close to the reality TV star say that if it weren't for longtime beau, fellow student Patrick Sheldon, she wouldn't be able to handle the stress of doing the show and trying to live a normal life. "He's already told her he loves her. They're making plans for after graduation," says a close friend of the couple. But will their relationship withstand the scrutiny of a nation? "Sheldon cares about her, but he doesn't want anything to do with the show. I just don't think they'll last," says a classmate. After the disappointing reunion with her father on Thanksgiving, it seems that Bonnie™ could benefit from a shoulder to cry on.

"Who's talking to them? Who are these 'sources'?" I ask. I look up at Tessa and Mer, but other than the pity in their eyes, they look as confused and angry as I do.

"We'll find out. There has to be a way to get them expelled or . . ." Mer looks at me, but I just shake my head.

You can't fight the Internet or everyone with a camera and a willingness to lie. My eyes skim over the pictures, landing on one of me outside of school. A yellow arrow points to my stomach. Next to the arrow it says,

Bump Alert! Is Bonnie™ pregnant? If so, how will Beth and the kids react?

"None of this is true!" I throw the magazine across the stall, and it makes a loud *slap* as it hits the tile wall. "I'm a fucking virgin! What is wrong with these people?"

I put my head in my hands, muttering over and over, "Ican'tdothisIcan'tdothis."

Just then, the bathroom door slams open. "Chloe?"

It's Patrick.

"I texted him just before she got here," Mer says to Tessa. "Handicap stall," she calls.

There's no time to be angry that Mer told him to come. He's here, and I don't have the right words to tell him that his life is about to change forever. The door swings open, and Patrick doesn't stop or say a word. He just scoops me up off the floor and holds me against him.

"What happened?"

He's asking them, not me. *Oh God, why is this happening? Why me, why now, whywhywhy?* I hear the rustle of paper as someone puts the tabloid in Patrick's hand. His body goes rigid, so I know he's reading it, but he just holds me tighter.

"We'll let you guys . . ." Tessa's voice trails off.

We've spent half the period in here. I can't imagine going back to class, even to get my stuff.

"Chloe?" Patrick's lips are close to my ear, and he speaks to me like I'm a skittish wild animal. "Let's get out of here, okay? We'll go to my place. Please."

I shake my head, numb. "Class—"

"We can get Ms. Finchburg, if you want," offers Tessa.

I know she means well, but the thought of talking to the school shrink about whether or not I'm pregnant is so not happening.

I pull away from Patrick—it's *me* who should be comforting *him*.

"I'll just . . . can you grab my stuff out of Spanish after the bell rings and bring it back here?" I ask Tessa.

She nods, and Mer pulls her out of the bathroom. When the door shuts behind them, it's just Patrick and me. I can't look at him without totally breaking down, so my eyes focus on the graffiti on the back of the stall door. Someone has written IT'S OKAY with a smiley face. I wonder who it was and why they did that. How many girls have hidden away in this stall, feeling like their life was over?

Patrick comes up behind me and wraps his arms around my waist. I lean into him for a moment, savoring this last bit of happiness.

Then I pull away.

"You should go back to class. You'll get in trouble," I say.

Patrick leans against the wall and crosses his arms, watching me. I still can't look him in the eye.

"Don't worry about me," he says.

"I do worry. I *should* worry." My voice goes suddenly hard—it stacks bricks, each word building a wall between us. "I'm not going to ruin your life, Patrick. And *this* will." I hold up the magazine. "You'll be a joke at Columbia—because you dated crazy-ass Bonnie™ Baker."

The muscles in his face grow taut, but he doesn't say anything. He just keeps looking at me, like he's waiting for something.

"This is all my fault." My voice breaks and I clear my throat. "It was so selfish of me to even think this could work. People will be asking your parents questions, and . . . I won't do this to you. We can't be together—I should have followed my instincts at the park and stayed away. God, I'm so selfish! I'll have our publicist leak it to the papers that we broke up. It'll nip this in the—"

"No."

I make the mistake of looking up. His eyes say so much more than that one word; I think of park swings and *Indiana Jones* and eating with his family. I shake my head. "I'm sorry, Patrick. But I can't run from this."

"You're running *from me*." His voice echoes against the tiles, as if a thousand anguished Patricks are surrounding me.

"Patrick, I tried to kill myself!" He flinches, and now I know for sure he really never Googled me. He didn't know. "That's why our show stopped. Because I'm seriously fucked up, and I took those pills and . . ."

As soon as I say the words, I know they're true. All this time, I've told myself it was a cry for help, a way to get my parents to see me. But in this moment of truth, that's not what I said. I tried to kill myself. *I tried to kill myself.*

"Chloe—"

I back away from his outstretched hand. "Patrick, you don't understand. This article is nothing—*nothing*—compared to what they'll start printing next."

I take a breath and will my voice to carry me through breaking my own heart. I hold his eyes, surprised by my resolve.

"All my life, I've had to deal with this. But I was always isolated— the Vultures could only hurt *me*. They didn't have anyone else they could drag through the mud. But now they know about you. *Meta-Reel* knows about you. Chuck's probably already called your house, asking your parents to sign a release form. They'll want to make us a story line, and they'll edit the show so that we won't even be able to recognize ourselves. They'll make us hate each other. They did that to my parents. I'm not going to give them that. I won't."

He closes his eyes for a second, then looks at me, his voice pleading. "Don't I get a say in whether or not we get to be together?"

I wish I had the guts to tell him I was pretty sure I loved him. But I can't say that now because it would be trite. It would sound like, It's Not You, It's Me.

"I'm sorry." My voice finally collapses on itself. I have to get out of here.

He doesn't try to stop me when I leave. I sprint down the hallway and run to my car. I don't have my keys, so I just sink down next to it and let myself sob. There is black writing on my hand, where the sweat on my palm had pressed against the tabloid. It says **all grown up.**

*T*he triplets are eating Christmas cookies at the kitchen table. The Wild Things are trying to kill one another in the living room. Everything's normal, but nothing is the same.

My mom is waving around the magazine like it's evidence in a whodunit. *May I present Exhibit A—photographic proof of the first and only boyfriend Bonnie™ Baker will ever have.*

"Who is this boy, Bonnie™?"

I don't even glance at the trash in her hand. I missed the turnoff for Caring long ago. Now I'm just numb.

"His name is Patrick. He's in my government class. It's nothing."

Nothing. I guess that is what we are now. I'll just be some girl he dated—a weird brush with pseudofame. I'll be an anecdote or, worse, a fun fact he can tell people during his freshman orientation next fall.

"This doesn't look like 'nothing.' You're kissing in the middle of your school parking lot!"

My face reddens as Old Guys Rule Dude leans against the wall, keeping the camera trained on me. Lacey Production Assistant is in the dining room, messaging our publicist.

"Can we talk about this later?" I give a meaningful glance at the camera, and Mom throws up her hands.

"Go do your homework." I dash toward the stairs. "But we're not through discussing this!" she yells after me.

I cross my room and lie on my bed, staring at the ceiling. Automatically, my hand reaches to my pocket, forgetting that I had turned off the phone Patrick gave me and buried it in the trunk of my car. It's too tempting to call him. Would he even want me back, now that he knows I'm a total nutcase?

I tried to kill myself.

Why am I suddenly able to see the truth? How many times have I maintained that it was an unconscious cry for help—no matter how loud you shout, it's hard to be heard over a dozen other voices. I thought I'd taken those pills because I knew Mom and Dad would finally listen to me. Dad would come back, they wouldn't fight anymore, and maybe we could stop the show.

It's summer in New Hampshire, and I am thirteen years old. Barefoot, cool glasses of lemonade, running through sprinklers, and jumping in pools. It's after dinner, and the sun is starting to set. The little kids are inside, getting baths, and Chuck tells me to go get Dad, that he is in the guesthouse.

Oh my God. *Chuck* told me to get Dad. Chuck *knew*—he knew all along what Dad was up to in the guesthouse. He orchestrated the end of my family. I'm only just now realizing this. I feel nauseous, and I curl into a tight ball.

I creep up to the guesthouse and peek inside, thinking I might try to surprise him, when I see that he isn't alone; he's with a pretty girl—way

275

younger than Mom. I've never seen her before, but I later hear that she is his chiropractor's receptionist. They are kissing, and his hand is unzipping her shorts. For a minute, I just stand there at the window, paralyzed. I don't want to see, but I can't move or close my eyes. I hear someone call my name—Benton™. "Bonnie™, what are you doing? We're starting the movie!" I'm terrified the cameras will catch Dad, confused about what I'm seeing, and so, so angry. Dad's head whips around, and we lock eyes for a fraction of a second. I drop my glass of lemonade and run to the house. I know things are bad between Mom and Dad— they fight all the time. The house is filled with their screams, and the silences that follow are even louder. One of the cameras has followed me outside, and they catch the aftermath on tape. It becomes one of the most viewed clips in MetaReel history. Me, running inside, crying. Dad exiting the guesthouse and trying to get the girl out. Mom, catching both of them. The fight, the tears, the sound of Mom's hand slapping Dad's cheek. Dad packing a bag and leaving. Paparazzi everywhere, Chuck yelling into his phone, the MetaReel cameras hovering.

We are carrion.

I take the pills two weeks later, after Mom and Dad tell us that they are getting a divorce. I hear her say that he is never coming back. That it is better this way. Mom says we are still going to do the show, that people will come and help us but that Dad won't be on it much. I walk up the stairs, go to my parents' bathroom, and swallow every pill in the medicine cabinet.

But I didn't want to be found. I remember that feeling now. I wanted to be alone, and I wanted everything to just stop. Forever. So I hid in their closet. It wasn't a cry for help. I fell asleep lying behind a curtain of my parents' clothing, hoping that I would never wake up.

"Mom told me you had to help wrap the Santa presents."

I blink, and Lexie™'s standing in the doorway of my bedroom, her arms full of wrapping paper and shopping bags.

I turn my head back to the ceiling. I don't want her to see me like this—I feel raw. "I'm too busy wallowing in self-pity right now."

She comes inside and kicks the door closed with her foot. "I know. Benny told me what happened."

She sets everything on the ground and then comes to sit in my desk chair, pulling her knees up to her chest.

"Sucks," she says.

I nod. "Yeah."

"Bon? You're not, *you know* . . . are you?"

"Lex, I don't have to tell you those magazines are full of shit." She raises her eyebrows. "No, okay? I'm not pregnant." My voice is pretty harsh, even though I'm not trying to be, and she flinches slightly.

"Good." Silence. Awkwardness. I really wish she would just go away. "Just, you know, if you were . . . I could help."

"Lex, if you're trying to balance out your karma, you're wasting your time. Good deeds only help you in the *next* life. So you can stop with this whole sisterly bonding thing."

Lex sighs, but she doesn't move. "Believe it or not, I'm actually really upset about the tabloid. I know we aren't close, but one, you're my sister and maybe I can be a bitch to you, but nobody else is allowed to be. And two, I would kill to have someone look at me the way that Patrick guy looks at you. Even in that stupid magazine, it's so obvious how into each other you are."

I turn my head toward her. Lex's eyes are hungry, and her fingertips rest against her lips, as if she could almost taste the want inside her. I feel like I'm looking at myself. She notices me staring, and the expression disappears. Camera-ready Lex is back.

"Plus, he's hot," she says, her voice playful. "Like, Kurt Cobain meets Johnny Depp hot."

My eyes fill with tears, and I shove the heels of my hands into my eye sockets. I can barely speak, my throat is so choked up with all the words I'd said to Patrick today. "Lex, I know . . . you're . . . trying to help me . . . but . . ."

"Bonnie™." Her voice is soft, and I feel the bed sag as she sits beside me. "Did he break up with you because of this?"

I shake my head. "I bro-broke up with . . . him."

"Wow," she says. "Your relationship is starting to look like a CW show."

This gets a begrudging snort out of me. "Well, Patrick is not a CW kind of guy, so it's just as well."

Lex puts a tentative hand on my shoulder. It's weird having her touch me, and I can tell from the stiffness in her hand that the feeling is mutual.

"That was brave of you," she says.

I look up, startled. "What?"

Everyone knows people who try to kill themselves are the antithesis of brave. If I were really brave, I'd run away or stage a protest or punch a Vulture.

When Lex looks into my eyes, I don't see any of her usual mockery or jealousy. The haughty tilt is gone from her chin. "It was brave of you to give up someone you care so much about in order to protect them." She pauses, and a soft smile plays on her lips. "But it would be even braver to give him the chance to be with you." She squeezes my shoulder. "The past is past. You tried to kill yourself. So what? I humped a couch in season twelve. We all have our skeletons."

"Wow. You went there."

She grins. "Oh, I went there."

There's a beat, and planets realign. Then we burst into hysterical laughter.

This was my day: I made national headlines, broke up with the boy I love, and decided to like my sister.

~ ~ ~

Sheldon? Really?

She doesn't look knocked up.

Do you think she'll have it?

Dude, that totally sucks.

"Chloe . . . Chloe?"

It's Thursday, and Diane Le Shrink is sitting in her usual chair across from me, her chin resting on steepled hands. I shake my head of the hallway gossip and try to focus on her.

"Sorry."

"That's okay. I was saying that I appreciate that you came to see me."

"No offense, but my mom said I had to."

"None taken." She cocks her head to the side. "But I can't help feeling like you chose to come during sixth period as an excuse to avoid Patrick."

"Why's that?"

"I checked to see who was in the class you were missing, and his name was on the list."

I shrug. "Maybe I just didn't feel like going to government."

"Well, how are you holding up?" she asks.

This has been my day so far:

- Begged Mom to let me skip school, said I felt sick, etc. She said, No, it was my decision to have a secret boyfriend, and this was the consequence of my actions.
- Got to school and saw the tabloid in half the student population's hands.
- Had ten people come up to me and ask, "Is it true?"
- Saw Patrick in the hallway, and my heart broke into a million pieces, like a Christmas tree ornament that somebody stepped on. He started to walk toward me, but I shook my head and practically ran in the other direction.
- Saw BONNIE BAKER IS A SLUT written on a bathroom stall.
- Spent lunch by myself behind the gym and decided I would rather be seen going to the school shrink than have Patrick sit behind me in gov.

But I just say, "Well, I haven't tried to kill myself yet, if that's what you're asking."

Ms. Finchburg-call-me-Diane nods. "Okay."

I stare at her socks (skull and crossbones Santas). Should I ask Tessa and Mer about what happened in gov? Do I really want to know how Patrick was acting? Diane tosses a pack of Skittles at me, and I surprise myself by actually catching it.

"So. Do you want to talk to me about yesterday?"

"It was a really bad day." I open my Fun Pack and eat the purples first.

"So, let's get the crappy stuff over with," she says. "*Are* you pregnant?"

My Skittles turn to ash in my mouth. "*No.*" God, this is ten kinds of embarrassing.

"Because, if you are, I'm here for you. I can help—"

My face is on fire. "Seriously. I'm nowhere near pregnant." Unless you can get pregnant from having your boyfriend see you in your bra, this talk is totally unnecessary.

"Okay." Clocks tick, and a door slams in the hallway.

"How did your mom react to the tabloid?"

I sigh. "She wanted to talk about it in front of the cameras. That's what Chuck was pushing for, anyway."

"Chuck?"

"The head producer. And I didn't want to do that. So we didn't talk about it."

Diane nods. "It must be hard not to have much access to your mom."

"I don't know. It's . . . just how things are. How they've always been. There are thirteen of us, you know?"

"Your mom called and said you were upset about this week's episode."

I don't care. Not having Patrick in my life is all I can think about right now.

"Why don't you usually watch the episodes?" she says.

"I don't like seeing myself on camera." But that's not it—that sounds shallow, like I'm worried I'll look fat or something. "It's like somebody is walking over my grave. TV immortalizes you. The episodes are what my family would watch if I died."

She asks me more questions, all vaguely trying to ascertain if I really, really truly am not pregnant. When the bell rings, she gives me a candy cane.

"Merry Christmas, Chloe."

I feel bad I didn't get her anything.

"You too."

I walk out, and Patrick's standing there. He has dark circles under his eyes, and when he sees me, he steps toward me with slow, tentative strides.

"Hey."

I'm standing there like an idiot, clutching a candy cane in my hand and looking like death. Seriously, I haven't seen the inside of a shower since yesterday morning. He opens his mouth, like he's going to say something, but I hold up my hand as if the candy cane had the power to protect me from people who take my breath away.

"Patrick. I can't."

I blink my eyes to keep from falling apart in between sixth and seventh periods. I know that two steps forward would bring me instant relief. I know exactly how good it will feel when Patrick wraps his arms around me. Am I being brave? I feel like a coward. Maybe Lex is right—maybe it would be braver to admit I was wrong. But I don't think I am. He'll see that. By the time we get back from Christmas break, he'll be over me.

The warning bell rings. Is he thinking what I'm thinking? Exactly twenty-four hours ago he was kissing me outside Spanish class. What little light there is in his eyes dims. He sighs, nods, says, "Okay," and walks away.

Friday is pretty much the same, except that Patrick is absent. Somehow, this hurts even more. Especially because I know I won't see him for at least two weeks. Christmas break starts at 2:40 P.M.

Lunch conversation, a transcript:

Tessa: Chlo, talk to us.

Me:

Mer: We support whatever you want to do, but Patrick is, like, not okay.

Tessa: Even Schwartz noticed. During gov yesterday, he didn't give Patrick any shit for not paying attention.

Mer: And when Michael Ingraham was all, "Hey, where's your baby mama?" Patrick stood up so fast, and if Schwartz hadn't gotten in the middle, Patrick would have—

Tessa: *Mer*.

Mer: What? She has a right to know.

Me: Guys . . . just . . . (sighs and throws away uneaten lunch)

Tessa: What can we do to help?

Me: Nothing. Seriously. I'll be okay.

Mer: Liar.

Me:

Lexie™ Baker @reallexie™baker

Don't believe everything you read, people.

#BonnieBakerIsn'tPregnant!!

Tonya LaChelle @tonilala

Celeb.com says @realbonnie™baker is gay and this is all a

cover up

Phat Boy @phatboy

I'd do her

Lexie™ Baker @reallexie™baker

You're a disgusting human being. She's a 17 year old girl.

Get a life, creep! #BonnieBakerIsn'tPregnant!!

Phat Boy @phatboy

I'd do you too

Denise Vale @denisevale

@reallexie™baker is right. Leave @realbonnie™baker alone!

Anya Fairbanks @anyafairbanks

Who is Patrick Sheldon and can I get his number?!

#hottieoftheday

Casey Freman @caseyfree

@realbonnie™baker had an abortion last week! Check out

the article: www.celeb.com/bonniebakerabortion

Maria Vasquez @mariavaz

Who cares about @realbonnie™baker? There are children

dying in Africa. Open your eyes.

Baker's Dozen @bakersdozen

Bonnie™ Baker is not pregnant. Patrick Sheldon is just a

friend. #BonnieBakerIsn'tPregnant!! Check out her

family's reactions on www.metareel.com/bakersdozen

Jenni Shaw @jshaw

See @realbonnie™baker freak out in her school parking lot:
http://www.youtube.com/watch?v=cfOa1a8hYP8
HILARIOUS

Sara Bithnell @sarbith

WTF? Hasn't this girl gone through enough sh*% already?
Leave her alone!!!

SEASON 17, EPISODE 23

(The One with the Fort)

*a*fter school on Friday, I go into my room, lock the door, turn off the light, and lie on my bed. I don't move for almost twenty-four hours. Various people (Mom, Sandra, Lex, Chuck, Benny, Farrow™) knock on the door, plead, cajole, threaten, etc. I give them monosyllabic responses that I'm sure the camera is picking up. *I'm not dead*, I say, when they ask how I am. On Saturday, I sit up just as the sun begins to set. My eyes are red and puffy, and I'm starving. I put Patrick's notes, a picture of us, and stray packs of spearmint gum in a bag, which I bury in my closet. When I open the door, Benny is sitting against the wall across the hall. His face lights up when he sees me. Without a word, he jumps up and pulls me into his arms.

"What can I do?" he asks.

I shake my head. "I just need to shower and eat."

I do both of those things, then endure an hour and a half with Sandra while we talk to the MetaReel publicist on speakerphone.

"So you're not dating this boy?" the publicist asks, for about the tenth time.

"No," I say. *I'm protecting him*, I think. *I'm keeping the crazy out of his life. He deserves better.*

The publicist goes on and on, and finally I push back my chair and look at Sandra. "I can't talk about this anymore."

She gives me a sympathetic smile. "Okay, *mija*. Get out of here."

How many teenage girls have to do damage control with a publicist when they have a breakup? Me and, like, Miley Cyrus.

I need to keep busy and not think about him. I have to stop wondering how he's feeling, what he's doing, what his parents are saying, and oh my God, if he starts dating someone before we graduate—or *ever*—I seriously don't know how I'll be able to handle it.

It's impossible to keep my mind off Patrick, and I have no one to help me. Lexie™ has a date—Benny too. He was super apologetic, but he couldn't cancel on Matt because he'd spent last night sleeping outside my door. Mom and I are still not speaking to each other, and Kirk generally avoids me, which is fine because I really don't think I can deal with any trite Kirkisms right now. I babysit the triplets while Mom packs for their book-signing thing—an attempt to boost last-minute Christmas sales in the South. This keeps me distracted until I think of the beautiful book I'd bought for Patrick on this architect he's obsessed with, Frank Gehry, and how it's now hidden in the back of my closet. I can't return it because I've already written girlfriend things inside, but I don't have the heart to throw it out.

I can't believe we're not together.

This thought hits me every few minutes, and it hurts like hell each time. I read bedtime stories to the triplets and let them cover me with kisses and hugs and then I'm alone again. I spend an hour reading *1984* and another one researching universities I know I'm not going to apply to. I have five months to figure out what I'm going to do with the rest of my life. Or at least the next year. I sure as hell can't stay at home. When I was little, I wanted to be a doctor, but I don't think I want to be in school for the next decade. I like math, but I can't see myself doing equations all day or—ugh—teaching. *Undeclared.* That's just quantifiably lame. It's like saying I'm majoring in I Don't Know Who I Am.

I'm contemplating watching a movie, preferably one with lots of blood and guts, when I hear a car pull into the drive—Benny or Lex, back a bit on the early side. A few minutes later, there's a soft knock on my door. When I open it, Benny puts a finger to his lips.

I hold up my hands and start to mouth *What?* but then he steps aside and I forget how to blink. Patrick stands in the doorway, a quiet smile on his face and a pile of blankets in his hands. The blood rushes to my head, and my ears start ringing, and I want to cry and laugh at the same time, and it's too much, these feelings are too much, and then Benny pushes Patrick inside and he's standing next to me. So close I could touch him. But I can't—can I?

"Lock it," Benny says, then shuts the door.

I am alone in my bedroom with Patrick Sheldon.

The sound of the dead bolt reminds me of the *click* of a roller coaster car just before it plummets toward the ground. Right now—with this boy I'm so freaking in love with I can hardly breathe—right now is that moment when the roller coaster car stops at its highest point, just before the fall, and I can't stand to wait, but I'm terrified of what's going to happen next.

"How—"

But he doesn't let me get the question out. He drops the blankets on the floor and crushes his lips against mine. Instinct takes over, and I forget all about my self-sacrificial plan to save him from the Vultures, to spare him the embarrassment of being my boyfriend. I press myself against him, matching his urgency. He tastes like spearmint, and everything is perfect; it's the smell in the air after it rains, and laughing till my stomach hurts, and getting everything I wanted for Christmas and his tongue in my mouth and—*what the hell am I doing?*

"Patrick—"

"*Shhh,*" he whispers, leaning into my neck.

Screw it.

I kiss him the way I wanted to in the handicap stall and outside the shrink's office, when everything in me screamed to touch him. And it's like our lips are having this whole conversation, full of exclamation points, every word in capital letters and underlined. Finally, he pulls away and looks down at me, his hands still tangled in my hair.

"I love you."

No preamble, no hesitation. He says these three words like it's the most natural thing in the world.

And I get a little weepy, which makes him smile, and I tell him that I love him, *God, do I love him,* and his lips smear the tears on my cheeks.

"I should have told you sooner," he murmured, "but I was afraid you'd think I was saying it just because it was in the tabloid."

"Hence the grand gesture?"

"Hence the grand gesture."

I pull back from him a little. "But you realize *why* I did what I did, right? I wasn't overreacting."

His hands settle on either side of my waist, and I lean into him.

It's terrifying, caring about someone this much. To allow them to be the air you breathe.

"I know you weren't," he says. I reach up and brush his hair out of his eyes. "But I always knew this was a possibility."

"But Columbia. This could jeopardize—"

"I don't care about Columbia. I care about *you*."

And of course this makes me all shivery, but there's more I have to say.

"Patrick."

He raises his eyebrows. "*Chloe*."

"I just don't know how we can . . ." I keep my eyes focused on the top button of his flannel shirt. "I want to be with you. More than anything, which, I don't know, is maybe pathetic or unhealthy or whatever. But I don't want cameras around, spying on us all the time."

He rubs his hands down my arms. "I don't want them around, either. We'll figure it out."

He's not getting it. He has absolutely no clue how bad this is. Or how much worse it will get.

"How?" I say. "You're going to get tired of this. All the sneaking around and hiding in janitor's closets. I mean, we've never gone on a real date! And how embarrassing is it that your parents probably thought, for at least a second, that I *was* pregnant."

He smiles. "I told my mom we were hoping for a girl, but that if we had a boy, we'd name him after my grandfather. I also mentioned you have lots of experience with children."

"This isn't funny," I say, pushing him away. But when I crack a smile, he knows he's won. He leans down and kisses my forehead.

"When you're mad, your eyebrows do this"—he scrunches his for my benefit—"and I just want you to know that it's damn sexy."

And of course this makes me go all molten lava inside, but I bite my lip and glance away. I don't want to ruin his grand romantic gesture, but there are real reasons why I broke up with him.

"Chloe, look at me."

I'm afraid to look up, because when I do, I lose all rationality. When the Vultures are after you and one of the hugest corporations in America is trying to ruin your good name, the last thing you want to be is a starry-eyed girl in love. He tilts my chin up, his face serious.

"We'll get through it," he says. "I promise. Our friends will help us, just like your brother did tonight. And we'll find a way to get you more protection from MetaReel and the paparazzi. Okay?"

I hesitate, then nod. I think his life was a whole lot better before I was in it, but I can't voluntarily give him up a second time. "Okay."

"Excellent."

His arms wrap around me, and I lean my head against his chest, feeling overwhelmed and grateful and unbelievably happy. We stay like that for a few minutes, just listening to each other's heart and lungs.

He looks down at me, his eyes warm and serious. "We don't have to talk about it if you don't want to—about your past—but I want you to know it doesn't change the way I feel about you. Not at all."

I hope someday I can tell him about the pills, but for now it's enough to know that it doesn't change anything between us. It feels right to have that secret out.

"Good," I say. Then I shake my head and grin. "I can't believe you're here!"

"I couldn't stay away any longer. The past few days were . . ." He trails off, and the look on his face says everything I wouldn't let him say when he was trying to get through to me.

"I know," I say. "Me too."

I hear a door shut downstairs, and even though I know my door is locked, I glance at it, just to make sure.

"How did you get past the cameras and my parents?"

He smiles. "Ben timed it perfectly. The crew's gone, and your parents were watching a movie. No one saw us, and he kept me away from the stationary cameras—which are freakin' creepy, by the way."

"Tell me about it. When did you guys plan this?"

He plays with my hair, twisting it around his fingers. "We've been talking about it pretty much since the moment you broke up with me."

I bite my lip. "Patrick, I'm so sor—"

He puts a finger against my lips. "It's not your fault. Or mine. We're together now, that's all that matters."

I glance at the clock—it's already after eleven. "How are you going to get home?"

"My parents think I'm at Max's. I'll go home after your parents leave the house tomorrow for the book signings. Unless . . ." He hesitates, his eyes so close that I can see the flecks of gold throughout the brown. "If you don't want me to stay—"

There are footsteps down the hall, and I dash over to my desk lamp and turn it off, plunging the room into total darkness. The last thing I need is for my mom to come in for another one of her pep talks. We stand there, our hearts keeping time as the footsteps stop, then move past the door.

"I want you to stay," I whisper. "Very much."

"Excellent."

It's pitch-black, and we're alone in my bedroom, and the door is locked, and he's not going home until tomorrow afternoon. I lean my forehead on his chest and smile into the soft fabric. I can feel his heartbeat against my skin.

I'm the luckiest girl in the world.

"This is kind of a weird way to see my house for the first time," I whisper.

"This room is really the only part I was interested in," he says.

"Except it's sort of hard to see in the dark."

He nuzzles my neck. "I expect a proper tour in the morning."

My eyes start to adjust to the darkness, and I notice the pile of blankets at our feet.

"What's with the blankets? Did you think I'd make you sleep on the floor?"

He shrugs. "I was prepared for anything, but I was fairly certain I'd be able to convince you to let me share your bed." The look he gives me sends a shower of goose bumps down my back. "Actually, I thought we could reclaim your lost childhood and build a fort. Ergo, blankets."

I grin. "You're serious?"

He grabs his backpack, then switches on the flashlight he took out of it. "Tell me you're not thrilled at the prospect of constructing a one-of-a-kind architectural masterpiece with me."

I grab a blanket. "I do have some experience in this arena, you know. In season seven, Benny and I turned our whole playroom into a fort using cardboard boxes and a parachute."

Patrick cocks his head to the side. "Season seven . . . means when you were seven years old?"

I blush. "I told you my life is weird."

"It is a little strange," he admits.

We work by flashlight and a couple of candles I'd had lying

293

around for decoration. I keep jumping every time I hear movement in the house, worried about how I'm going to explain fort making to my mom. Patrick, I've already decided, will have to hide in the closet if anyone knocks on my door. I kick his shoes under my bed to hide the boy-in-my-room evidence.

"What do you think?" he asks.

"Two thumbs up."

Blankets drape over my desk chair, the hat rack in the corner, and underneath some books on my bookshelf. Patrick pulls back a thick woolen blanket with a Southwestern pattern and hands me the flashlight. "Ladies first."

"One sec." I walk over to my closet and feel around in the dark for the book I'd shoved behind a pile of shoes.

"What are you doing?" he whispers.

"I have a surprise for you."

I clasp the book to me and smile at him as I duck inside our fort, my stomach snap, crackle, popping as I take in our hideaway. He throws me the pillows from my bed and a couple more blankets. I look at the side-by-side pillows, and every atom I'm made of flares up. Patrick crawls in, his eyes searching for mine in the dim little cocoon we've created. I bite my lip as he moves toward me, and he doesn't stop crawling until his lips touch mine. We lie sideways on the floor, my head against a pillow, his propped up on an elbow.

I sit up and hand him the book. "Early Christmas present," I say. "To assist in your architectural education."

He looks at the cover, his eyes wide. "*Chloe*."

"You love it," I say, my voice smug. I knew he didn't have it—it was expensive, and one of those things he'd probably always wanted but would never buy for himself.

"I do."

I hold the flashlight as he turns the pages and whispers to me about titanium and deconstructivist design. Coming out of his mouth, it's like he's reciting love poems.

"It's perfect," he whispers, closing the book. "Thank you."

For a while, we bask in being together, making shadow puppets and filling each other in on the past few days.

"Ben said your mom wasn't really helping you deal with all the tabloid stuff."

"We're not exactly on speaking terms right now."

"Because of last weekend, when you got grounded? You never told me what happened."

I groan and lie on my back, staring at the colorful afghan above me. "It's kind of embarrassing."

Patrick reaches his hand to my cheek and gently turns it so that my eyes are parallel with his again. "Please?"

So I tell him about the extra cameras, how I threw the notebook. When I mention the slap and my mom calling me a bitch, his lips go razor thin.

"I'm sorry," he says quietly.

I shake my head. "Seriously, it's . . . don't worry about it."

"I want to get you out of here, Chlo. There's gotta be something we can do."

I scoot away from him and sit up, hands clasped in my lap. "There's nothing *to* do. I'm on the show until I graduate."

Patrick sits up, too, and puts his hands over mine. "Why?"

And I realize just how much I care for him, when I say, "Okay, don't tell Benny I told you this."

I can't believe I'm telling someone something I wouldn't tell my brother.

He nods.

"Chuck sort of . . . threatened me."

"The producer guy?"

"Yeah."

Patrick's fingers tighten on mine. "What did he say to you?"

"I guess the contract my parents signed said that all of us kids would do the show, and that if even one of us drops out, MetaReel can cancel."

Patrick shrugs. "So that's good, right?"

I stare at him. "No. It would be my fault that this show they all love will be gone. And Chuck said he'd sue my family, and they'd go totally bankrupt with a billion kids—this would be *horrible* for them. My mom would never forgive me."

"Do you think you could get a copy of that contract?"

I shake my head. "That's . . . impossible."

Patrick's quiet for a while and then he says, "My dad's a lawyer, you know. I mean, he doesn't really practice anymore because he's teaching so much, but—"

I lean over and kiss his cheek. "You are so good to me, and I know you want to help. But I'm not taking my parents to court." My sigh sounds like an old woman's. "It's my fault we're in this mess anyway."

"What? No. It's not."

I nod. "I know this was really manipulative of Chuck, but when I was a kid and acting up because I was getting tired of doing the

296

show, he told me that my behavior was stressing my parents out and that was why my dad was drinking so much and it would be my fault if they broke up. So I tried to be good, but I kept slipping into being this Bonnie™ that nobody liked. And it was *me* who caught my dad—which, actually, Chuck made happen, but still—and *me* who took those pills. And Chuck was right. They broke up."

"What the hell? He can't just say shit like that to a little girl." It's weird seeing Patrick look furious. All the angles of his face sharpen, and his posture gets perfect.

"I know, it's screwed up. But he was kind of right. I mean, looking back, I can see how my behavior—"

"No," he says, firmly. "None of that was your fault."

I shake my head. "Maybe. Maybe not. But I owe my mom, even if she's being heinous right now. I have to stick this out until graduation."

"Chlo, you don't owe her anything. You're in an impossible situation." Patrick moves closer to me, until I'm practically sitting in his lap.

I shiver, which is my body's way of reminding me that this is the kind of conversation we can have when we're not in a fort in my room late at night. I crawl into his lap, my legs straddling him. His eyes widen in surprise, and I put my lips close to his ear.

"I don't want to talk anymore."

He places his hands on my hips and brings his lips to my collarbone. "Okay," he whispers.

Then it's just lips and hands and skin until the blankets tumble down on top of us and we have to hold our hands against each other's mouths so that no one hears our laughter. It takes a while to get out from under the wreckage, and we freeze, still tangled up, when one of the kids cries out. I hear Mom go up the stairs and open a door at the end of the hall. I know it's her because her steps sound so efficient.

"My little sister Daisy™ gets nightmares," I whisper.

"Are they about cameras?"

"Mine are."

When the house is quiet again, we crawl out from under the mess of blankets.

"We suck at fort making," I say.

"To be fair, we couldn't really see what we were doing. I'm holding out judgment on our true capabilities."

Without warning, he lifts me up and deposits me on the bed. I laugh and he covers up my mouth with his lips, kissing me like it's our last day on Earth. I feel light-headed, drunk with this pressing need to absorb him. If I could, I would melt myself into him so that there is no him or me, just *us*.

Moonlight fills the room, turning his skin silver, seeping into his eyes. The dark is warm and safe and hidden. I want to stay in it forever. We peel off each other's clothing to get closer. Closer. Patrick's lips and hands travel over my skin, and the shadows sway to the sound of his sweet nothings, which should really be renamed sweet somethings—no, sweet *everythings*.

The grandfather clock chimes downstairs, and we both jump, and I giggle into his bare chest. For a minute we just lie there, staring into each other's eyes. He's so *warm*. And it feels completely right to be here, right now, with him. But I won't let this house have too much of me.

"Patrick, I can't—"

He kisses me. "Neither can I."

I raise my eyebrows.

"Your brother only agreed to me coming over if I swore on my mother's life not to take your virginity. And in case that wasn't enough, he also threatened me with castration via butcher knife."

My mouth drops open. "He told you I was a virgin?" Benny has absolutely no sense of boundaries.

Patrick chuckles. "Um. Since I was your first kiss, I thought it was fair to assume."

I blush. "Oh. Right."

He draws me close to him. "It's fine. More than fine. I can't wait to wake up next to you."

This, I think, is a little glimpse of what life could be like without my family. Home could be a place of laughter and love, a refuge. I'm filled with a terrifying weightlessness, like I've jumped off a cliff, but I know that if I don't look down, I'll be just fine.

We fall asleep pressed against each other, our bodies intertwined, each piece of me fitting with each piece of him, like a puzzle that we finally figured out how to put together.

SEASON 17, EPISODE 24

(The One with the Diary)

"Did he deflower you?" Tessa asks, with characteristic bluntness.

"Tess!" I swat at her, but she ducks, her eyes all mischievous and *ooh-la-la*. It's the first day back at school after break, and we'd all agreed to come early and catch up in the stairwell.

"Notice how she doesn't answer the question," says Mer. She licks some of the whipped cream from her mocha off her lips. "He's good, isn't he? I bet he's good."

"Okay, first—don't speculate on my boyfriend's being good or not. Second, *no*, he did not"—I lower my voice—"*deflower* me." I grin. "But he did sleep over during break."

I'd been dying to tell them, but I'd wanted it to be just Patrick's and mine for a while.

"Shut up!" squeals Mer.

My face is ten kinds of red, but whatever. Who cares what color your face is when you're walking on clouds?

"Details. Now," says Tessa.

"Discretion is my middle name." I zip my lip and pretend to go back to flipping through Mer's *Glamour*. I close it when I come across a *Baker's Dozen* ad.

Tessa bumps me with her shoulder. "I can't believe it. You're finally getting naked with Patrick Sheldon—" I give her a look, and she rolls her eyes. "Or *whatever*, and we don't even get to hear about it!"

"I thought caffeine was bad for the baby," Benny says, from the bottom of the stairwell.

Patrick's behind him, and we choke on our coffee at the same time, which is actually kind of impressive.

"Oh my God, that is so not funny," says Mer.

Tessa's lips curl up, but she doesn't say anything. I didn't think it was possible for Patrick to be embarrassed, but he's actually blushing. It feels good to joke about the tabloid, but I can't help worrying about what the next one will say. And the next. And the next.

"Oh! Happy belated birthday, Ben," says Mer.

We'd had a party for him and Lex over Christmas break. Lex had been thrilled about the cameras coming out to dinner with us, Benny not so much.

He puffs out his chest a little. "That's right. I'm officially a man."

"What he means to say is that he can buy his cigarettes without a fake ID now," I say, glaring at him. "I should have turned your ass in to the cops."

He sticks his tongue out at me, and I jump up and gather my stuff.

"Where are you going?" asks Tessa.

Classes don't start for another half hour, but Mom insisted I see the Skittle Lady.

"Morning sickness," Benny stage-whispers.

"I'm not above killing you in your sleep, you know." I hit his arm with my notebook, but he doesn't even wince. I turn back to Tessa. "I have to go see the school shrink."

Mer nods sympathetically. "Secret boyfriend plus possible pregnancy equals major adult concern?"

"To the tenth power," I say. "See you at lunch."

"I'll walk you," Patrick says.

I smile as he throws an arm across my shoulders. As soon as we round the corner, he stops and leans me up against the lockers. His kiss is soft and lingering.

"Monday's looking up," I murmur.

"Despite all that morning sickness?" he teases.

"Not you too."

"Do you have to go? Because we have half an hour, and I know an excellent way to spend it."

His lips are on mine again, and his hand reaches into my jacket and slides around my waist. His fingers brush against my skin, and I shiver, drawing even closer.

"I . . . really . . . have . . . to . . . go." It's all I can manage between kisses.

Patrick sighs. "Okay." He reaches into his pocket and takes something out. "Don't get mad."

"Um . . ."

"I know you said you didn't want to take your parents to court. Which I totally understand. But what about MetaReel?"

I shrug. "I can't really wrap my mind around that."

He nods. "Do you trust me?"

I don't have to think about my answer for even a second. "Yes."

He kisses my forehead. "Good. I talked to my dad, and he got in touch with one of his lawyer friends." He hands me a card that says MELINDA GREENBERG, ATTORNEY-AT-LAW. "She works with the ACLU, and Dad said she could take you on pro bono." The American Civil Liberties Union—Schwartz worships at their feet.

"Thanks," I say. Even I can tell my voice sounds far away.

"You want me to keep it for you?" Patrick murmurs. I nod, and he takes it from me. "I just wanted you to know I found people out there who will fight for you. *I'll* fight for you."

I reach my lips up to his for a second. "I'll think about it."

But I already know I'm never going to ask him for that card. How could I betray my family like that? This is something Patrick just doesn't understand.

He grabs my hand, and we head toward the main office. The halls look so different now that I'm not Patrick-less in them. Our three days of being broken up is a small weight that we'll probably carry around for a little while longer, but I feel like there's something deeper between us, now that we're on the other side of it.

When we get to Diane Finchburg's office, I slip a note in his pocket.

"What's this?"

I smile. "Sweet nothings."

His eyes light up. "Good luck in there."

"*Ugh.*"

He kisses my cheek and then walks toward the gym, putting in his earbuds as he goes. I know that's where Max and Derrick usually hang out before school. I watch him for a minute, admiring his sloping gait and the way he shoves his hands deep in his pockets. He turns around and grins, like he knows I'm watching him, so I blow him a kiss, and he catches it.

My appointment with Diane Finchburg is nonthreatening, except for the part where she says that if I ditch school anymore, the principal is going to suspend me. When I told him about it later, Patrick was a bit disappointed, but considering we're graduating in a few months, we'll live. Throughout the day, people in the halls stared at me, and my name was on too many strangers' lips. I heard some girls in the bathroom speculating on whether or not I'd gotten an abortion over break. I'd yelled from my stall that it was none of their damn business, and their stunned silence kind of made my day. It felt good just to say what I wanted to. One girl asked me to autograph her mother's copy of my mother's book. I took pity on her because she was even more embarrassed than I was. I turned in the paper on *1984* I'd had to write for Schwartz's class over the break and he'd said, "Good to see you back, Baker." I knew he wasn't talking about Christmas vacation—he'd meant back from the abyss I'd been in those days after the tabloid.

"It's good to be back," I'd told him. And, strangely, I meant it.

~ ~ ~

When Benny and I get home, Mom is sitting at the kitchen table, idly flipping through a magazine. Puma Guy is stationed behind her, like he's been waiting for me.

"Bonnie™, can you come in here, please?"

Benny shoots me a sympathetic look, then bolts up the stairs. I trudge into the kitchen and lean against the door frame. The Wild Things run past and clip me on the shoulder.

"Savages!" I yell at them. But I'm smiling, because you can't get too mad at people whose diapers you've changed. I turn back to Mom.

"What's up? I have a lot of homework."

I know it shouldn't matter, but I really need to remember to brush my hair and put on some lip gloss before I come home.

"We need to talk."

I sigh and plop into a chair. "Can we talk somewhere else?"

Mom gives an imperceptible shake of her head. They'll probably edit out my question, making me look like a willing servant of the show. *Why, of course, America, I love discussing my personal life in front of all of you!*

"You saw the guidance counselor?"

I nod, my face flushing. There goes another secret I don't need to bother keeping.

"Bonnie™, I'm . . . concerned about this boy." She'd caught me talking on the phone with Patrick a few days ago, so she knows we're together. Luckily, her book tour had kept her from having this conversation with me. Until now.

"Mom, I—"

"Don't interrupt me, please." She pats her hair, like she's making sure it's still there. "I think you might be investing too much into this relationship with Patrick."

Don't say his name. It sounds wrong, coming out of your mouth.

My heart gets a sick feeling. "He's a really nice guy, from a great family. There's nothing to be worried about."

"I need to meet him—and his parents."

"Mom! That's so unfair. You can't force them to go on camera."

"I'm sure we'll be able to work something out."

There's so much I want to say, all bottled up inside me, itching up my throat. Each word I've kept inside for all these years is straining to break out. So I don't say anything.

"There's something else I'd like to talk about, while you're here," she says.

I stare at the wood grain of the table until my eyes go glassy and the patterns run together like watercolors. She slides something across the shiny surface to me and when I see what it is, my heart stops.

It's my journal.

I grab the leather-bound pages and hug them to my chest. They did it. On top of everything else, they finally got my soul.

Blood pumps into my fingers—I wish I had claws. I've never wanted to physically assault someone so much in my life. She doesn't even have the decency to look ashamed.

"You read it."

Mom coughs a little cough. Nods a little nod. Then she throws her shoulders back, defiant. "I didn't have a choice. I've tried to reach out to you, but you won't talk to me. You avoid Kirk and me like the plague, and your school says you were truant three times this semester—"

"Did they film you searching for it?"

"Of course. This is our *life*, Bonnie™." When she throws up her hands, it almost looks like she's praying. Maybe she's asking God why he gave her this horrible daughter. "I don't know what's gotten into you!"

"This show!"

My voice is shaking, but I don't have the energy to control it and be robot Bonnie™ for the cameras. *Baker's Dozen* has gotten inside me, infiltrated every private place until . . . *Nothing was your own except the few cubic centimeters inside your skull.* My journal says everything—*everything.*

Mom closes the magazine she'd been reading before I came in with an irritated flick of her wrist. "I thought we were past all this."

"What's 'all this'?" I ask.

"The dramatics! The stomping out of rooms and not smiling for photographs and being rude to the crew, who are only doing their jobs. You act like a spoiled brat."

"How could you just go in my room with cameras and look through my stuff and read my *diary*? That's mine! Those are *my* words, *my* thoughts, *my* feelings. How dare you, Mom? How *dare* you?"

She tosses me a self-righteous glare, but speaks with the voice of a wounded woman. So RealMom™ Beth Baker-Miller.

"I did what I had to do so that you wouldn't hurt yourself—or this family—again. You think I don't recognize the signs? I've decided that we need to put you on some medication—"

"I *hate* you," I snarl.

She raises her eyebrows. "I'm sorry to hear that."

I grab my backpack and vault up the stairs. When I open the door to my room, I see the evidence of her investigation right away. Things set down in the wrong place, dirty clothes in the hamper instead of on the floor, a half-eaten Snickers bar gone. My room suddenly feels tainted, like somebody came in and had sex on my bed and tried on my underwear. I look at the walls covered with calendar images from all over the world and the stack of Patrick's intricately folded notes on my bedside table. The shade of the ornate lamp I'd found at a thrift store with Tessa and Mer sits at an awkward angle. I look at my room through MetaReel's eyes, and I see a girl who is desperate to get away, but can do nothing more than tape pictures of the Taj Mahal and the Pyramids to her wall.

Before I even realize what I'm doing, my hands are tearing down the pictures and crumpling them up; the world is at my feet. I reach for knickknacks left over from my childhood: angel figurines, dried roses from my first Emmy appearance (which I kept only because Dad gave them to me), glow-in-the-dark stars that always seemed garish. I rip and tear and throw, and it feels so good. I don't realize how much noise I'm making until Benny walks into the room.

"Whoa." He looks at the floor, full of broken bric-a-brac and shredded paper. I stand in the middle of it, panting.

I hear footsteps on the stairs, and a camera—followed by five of my siblings—pushes through the doorway.

"Holy crap," says Farrow™.

Tristan™ looks around him. "Dang."

Before the others can say anything, I push them out and fix the camera with an angry glare.

"This is not a public family area, so you need to leave. NOW."

The camera slowly backs away, and I slam the door behind me, then lean against it and slide down to the carpet.

"I want to fight back," I say. I'm sweaty, and my hands have tiny paper cuts all over them.

Benny kicks aside some books and sits cross-legged on the floor opposite me.

"What happened?"

I tell him about the diary, and he lets out a very un–Benny-like stream of profanity. He must have learned those choice combinations from his football-playing boyfriend.

"Wow," I say.

"I've been holding that in for a while." He picks up a crumpled calendar picture and smooths it against his thigh. Red Square, covered in snow.

"What are you gonna do?"

I think of the card that Patrick's keeping for me.

"I'm getting a lawyer."

I call Melinda Greenberg the next day. Her voice is crisp and professional, but she seems to genuinely care about my situation.

While we talk, I stare out at the school football field, empty now except for a few kids throwing a ball around. I couldn't call her from home, for obvious reasons. Benny paces a few feet away from me, chain-smoking cigarettes while glancing furtively over his shoulder for teachers.

"So what exactly are my options?" I ask.

It feels weird to be talking to a lawyer on my own. Like I've aged these past twenty-four hours.

"Well, since you'll be eighteen in a few weeks, emancipation isn't something we would pursue. Do you have friends you can stay with?"

"Yeah, but I don't know if their parents would be okay with it." I feel cold, just thinking about those conversations. "It's just . . . I can't bring the paparazzi down on them."

"Of course. And you definitely do not want to live with your father?"

"Definitely not," I say.

"Well, then there's the issue of money."

"Oh. Mr. Sheldon had said you could work *pro bono*?"

"Yes, but I mean for you. How will you take care of yourself on your own?"

I hadn't really thought about that.

"I have a college fund."

"Is this money you have access to, or is it held in trust?"

"It's in my savings account. I can get to it, but . . ."

My stomach turns as I imagine moving out on my own. Using up my college fund on toothpaste and pasta.

"Well then, I think you might want to consider suing your parents for back wages."

"*What?*"

Melinda Greenberg sighs. "I know that's a hard thing to hear, but the fact is, your presence on the show has made hundreds of thousands of dollars for your family. Your mother's book deals, all the appearances you've done on behalf of the show. The Bonnie Lass™ merchandise—"

I shake my head. "But my mom said money was the reason we had to do the show again." I hope we're not back on air just so we can start taking vacations like we used to.

"Well, if we do pursue a suit, both your parents will have to provide financial records."

Dad. I think of his shiny BMW: *We've got one just like it at home.* How can he afford that car?

"I can't sue my parents—I won't. No way."

There's a slight pause on her end, and I hear keys tapping a keyboard, some paper shuffling. I'm sort of annoyed that she's multitasking during the bravest moment of my life to date.

"In that case," she says, "we can go after MetaReel—sue them for punitive damages, stuff like that."

I smile slightly, imagining the look on Chuck's face when corporate tells him I'm suing his ass.

"What exactly are punitive damages?"

"It's sort of the gray area of lawsuits. Basically, you could sue them for millions because of emotional damage or inappropriate behavior on the part of producers." I'd already told her a little about Chuck. "We could also look into child labor law violations."

"I don't know . . . I mean, I'm graduating in, like, four months." And I don't want to spend that time in a courtroom. I just want a life.

"They might settle out of court. MetaReel doesn't want a huge legal battle, especially now that the ACLU is after them."

My head starts to throb, and everything feels hopeless and stressful, and fuck it, I'll just stay on the goddamned show.

"Um . . . this is too—"

I can hear the nod in Melinda's voice. "Why don't I do some research on my end while you take as long as you need to think about how far you're comfortable going with this?"

A couple girls run out of the gym, giggling to themselves. I want so badly to trade places with them—I don't want to be the girl calling her lawyer on the basketball court.

"Chloe, you don't have to decide anything now. Think of me as your ace in the hole. I'll start figuring out what I can, and you just think on it, okay?"

"Yeah, okay. It's just . . . this is really intense."

"I know. You have to do what's best for you, but you also care about your family. Why don't you call me in a week or so with an update?"

My chest feels a bit looser. Nothing's decided. I haven't sold out my family yet.

"Okay. Thanks."

We hang up, and Benny looks over at me. "So?"

"I'm gonna think about it."

He nods. "If I were you, I would do it. But . . ."

He leaves his sentence unfinished, but I know what he means; he's able to fly under the radar a lot. Sure, people at school stare at him just as much, but he isn't the one who tried to kill himself or has tabloids taking pictures of baby bumps. I know Benny hates being on the show, but not enough to move out of the house before he graduates. Suddenly I feel more alone than ever.

"We better motor," he says. "Kaye Gibbons awaits."

"Hell."

We're going to be in LA for the rest of the week because Chuck wants the whole family for a huge PR circuit. Never mind that some of us are in school, trying to maintain decent GPAs. I've been hoping a miracle would occur that would prevent us from being on the *Kaye Gibbons Show*, but so far no luck.

Benny and I walk to the car while I text Patrick.

I don't think I have time to see you before I go. ☹

NO! Really?

Yeah. I haven't packed and my mom's gonna be in full-on crazy
     mode.

Damn. What did the lawyer say?

Stuff that was hard to hear. I'll try to sneak away and call you later.

Okay. Don't take any shit.

I love you.

Love you too.

Benny looks over my shoulder. "Aww. You guys are at the love stage!"

"Do you mind?" I shove my phone in my pocket, flustered.

"Oh, don't be touchy. I'm happy for you. Sheldon's awesome. Trust me, that was nothing compared to the texts Matt and I send each other."

"I don't doubt it," I say drily.

When we get home, Mom is barking orders at everyone, and the cameras are following kids as they try to pack their own suitcases. I'm guessing this is one of Chuck's ideas—I can hear the hokey, circuslike music playing as the kids put ridiculous stuff in their bags.

"There's no way we're going to escape the traffic," Mom says into Old Guys Rule's camera. "We've been trying to get ready for hours, but Deston™'s not feeling well, and the kids made a huge mess during their homeschool art project this morning."

A camera swivels to the front door as we make our way inside and Mom catches sight of us.

"Bonnie™, Benton™. Are you guys packed?"

"Um . . . ," we both begin, but Kirk pokes his head in from the dining room.

"Honey, what do you want to do about dinner? Are we eating before we go?"

Chuck writes something in marker on a pad of paper and holds it up behind the camera for Mom to see.

"Let's do McDonald's," she says.

Sandra puts a shopping bag on my arm. "Pack these. It's your outfit for Kaye Gibbons and then a few things to change into for the different appearances."

"Oh—okay."

"Mommy! Lark™ ripped my book!"

Jasmine™'s lip is trembling, but my little nine-year-old brother from India shoves her aside. "I didn't do it on purpose," he says.

"Liar! Mom, he—"

Mom puts her hands to her eyes and groans. I know they'll keep this bit in. She looks every bit the RealMom™ the MetaReel PR machine says she is. She's even wearing her "Mom x 13" shirt that a fan sent her last week.

"You wanna . . . ?" Benny nods his head toward the stairs, and I follow him as surreptitiously as possible.

I only need a few minutes to pack, so I spend the rest of my time texting Patrick. Our separation over Christmas break is finally over, and we're both pissed about the next few days we'll be apart. Finally, everyone gets corralled into the big black vans with tinted windows that we have to use whenever we go out as a family. I'm squished in the back of one with Lexie™ and Daisy™. It takes us half an hour to get through the McDonald's drive-thru, and Daisy™ throws a fit because they forgot to put her Happy Meal toy in the box.

Things don't settle down until each kid has some technology in their hands. I text with Patrick and listen to my iPod. Lex does the same, though I don't know who she's texting. The smile on her face tells me it's a boy—I hope MetaReel doesn't find out about him. We get to LA around ten, and Chuck, Sandra, and Lacey Production Assistant go around with clipboards and door keys. The nannies are in the rooms with the little ones, Mom and Kirk have their own suite, and I share a room with Lex and Farrow™. I fall asleep as soon as my head hits the pillow, exhausted from the combined stress of the phone call to the lawyer and getting to LA with my family and its entourage. At four A.M. the phone rings: our wake-up call.

~ ~ ~

"Hello, everyone! Thank you, thank you!" On the greenroom monitor, Kaye Gibbons waits for the frenzied clapping to calm down. The audience is full of middle-aged women who adore her.

"M&M's?"

Benny offers me the bowl that's in the greenroom, but I shake my head. I'm too nervous; just the thought of eating turns my stomach. We've already done a spot for a local news station and a couple interviews for magazines, but Kaye's hour-long special is in its own stratosphere of media misery.

"It's gonna be fine," he says. "She was always pretty nice, right?"

Visions of my birthday gift of "triplets" dance in my head. "She likes surprises."

"*Late Night with Jimmy Kimmel* will be cool," says Lex.

I roll my eyes. "You just want to meet Brad Pitt." LPA (Lacey Production Assistant) had told us he was going to be the other guest on the show.

She looks at her feet, admiring her new heels. "Yeah. So?"

Sandra's put Lexie™ in a dress that ends a few inches from her ass. The fact that a producer, not Lex, chose the dress makes me more certain my sister's the way she is because that's the box Meta-Reel has decided to put her in. She's the "sexy" one. Just like

Farrow™ and Riley™ are the bookworms and Tristan™ is the jock. I try to think back to when we were really young. Was she always in skintight clothing? But if everyone in my family has a label, what's mine? I don't think I want to know. Or maybe the problem is that I don't have one, so now I'm just "the difficult one."

A production guy wearing all black and an official-looking badge opens the greenroom door. "Hey, Baker kids. We're going to have you out in a few minutes. Ready?"

"Yes!" says Jasmine™.

The rest of us have the sense to exhibit a little stage fright. I watch the screen in the greenroom. Kaye is giving my mom and Kirk big hugs, and after fifteen minutes and two commercial breaks, Mom's already dabbing her eyes. I don't know how Kaye does it.

"Damn, she's good," mutters Benny.

"I know it."

Every now and then, Kaye introduces a video from some season of our lives, a montage no doubt put together by MetaReel. I know there's footage they're probably going to use—the 911 transcript, me being rushed to the hospital. I go over and over what I'll say in my head if she asks me any questions about that. For luck, I look at Patrick's text from this morning.

They don't own you, just remember that. Also, I love you.

"Okay, everyone, it's time!"

I take a swig of water and swish it around in my mouth, but I can't make the dryness go away. We follow the intern down a long hallway covered with posters of Kaye Gibbons, inmates on their way to their executions. The heels Sandra insisted I wear are pinching my feet, and I'm half worried I'm going to fall flat on my face when I enter the studio.

I can hear Kaye's voice from the wings. "Well, let's see the rest of the family, shall we?"

Cue applause. We walk out according to height, like the freaking Trapp Family Singers. All we need are matching outfits made from curtains and a rendition of "My Favorite Things." The lights blind me for a second, but even after my eyes adjust, I try to make them glaze over the audience. The lighting over them is dim, but I can still see individual faces. Why do they care about us? I catch sight of a glittered sign that reads: BONNIE WILL YOU MARRY ME?

Lex sees it too. "Psycho," she mutters.

My lips turn up a little. Ever since the night of gift-wrapping, something in my relationship with my sister has shifted. I think she's finally realized that I am more than happy to give her the spotlight. But it's deeper than that—sometime between the tabloid going after me and Mom reading my diary, Lex and I realized we were on the same team.

Once we're onstage, we perch on the couches and stools just like we'd practiced before the taping started. The kids are really antsy—a well-meaning intern treated us all to doughnuts about an hour ago. Mom has a blowout and is wearing about a pound of makeup. Kirk is all buttoned up, looking pleased with himself. They make me sick.

"Well, aren't you all grown up?" Kaye says in her plastic voice.

Her too-bright turquoise suit, blond bob, and red lipstick match her personality perfectly. No assembly required—batteries not included. I had really hoped to never see her again.

She does a little back-and-forth with us, and though she tries to draw me out, I don't play along. Neither does Benny. Lex is beautiful and shimmers and is more than willing to take on the extra work. After another commercial break, the screen behind Kaye lights up.

"So," she begins, turning to my siblings and me, "you've all got a ton of fans around the country, and boy, do they have lots of questions for you! Are you ready?"

"Yes!" shouts Daisy™. The audience laughs, and she beams.

Videos of kids pop up on the screen asking questions to each of us specifically. Some are silly, like "What's your favorite flavor of ice cream?" and others more in-depth, like Benny's "What are your plans after you graduate?" I'm wondering why in the world these people wasted their time uploading the videos, but as soon as I think this, I know the answer: a few seconds of fame. I'd be happy to re-distribute mine—I'm totally communist when it comes to fame.

I'm sitting here on the *Kaye Gibbons Show*, and all I can think is that the whole country is sick. Sick with this idea that it's good to be known and seen by as many people as possible, to show every part of our lives to the public at large. Whether it's Facebook photos, blogs, or reality TV, it's like nobody is content to just live life. The worth of our existence seems to be measured in pixels and megabytes and "likes." Those of us whose lives can be downloaded seem to have the most value—until someone more outrageous comes along to claim their time in the spotlight.

"The next question is for Bonnie™."

I swallow and look at the screen as it starts playing a video of a boy around my age with bad skin and a mop of blond hair.

"Hi, Bonnie™. My name is Brent Livingston from Springfield, Massachusetts, and my question for you is: What is your idea of a perfect date, and will you go on it with me?"

319

The audience cracks up, and I grip the couch, too embarrassed for myself—and Brent Livingston—to bother faking a smile.

"Um." I look at my mom, but she just smiles. Either she doesn't realize I desperately need to be bailed out, or she doesn't care. Probably the latter.

"Don't be shy, Bonnie™," says Kaye.

"My idea of a perfect date . . ." I think of Patrick kissing me while wearing goofy glasses at the dollar store. ". . . is being with someone you love. Um. Because no matter what you do, it's perfect. And, no, I can't go out with you. But good luck."

Kaye smiles at me, and a more recent tabloid photo of Patrick and me holding hands in the school parking lot comes up.

"So, is this your perfect date, Bonnie™?"

Damn. It's one thing to tell a boy you love him and quite another to announce it on national television.

I look at the picture. I imagine Patrick watching. I hope I'm making the right decision.

"Yes."

"Look at Bonnie™ Baker, she's a woman now!" Kaye says to the audience. There are a few whistles and some scattered applause from the audience.

My face is on fire.

"What about you, Benton™? Any special girl in your life?"

Benny blanches. "No," he says.

Kaye gives him a shrewd look. "What about a special guy?"

Either Kaye Gibbons has magnificent gaydar, or someone, somewhere, told her about Benny.

"Kaye, that's none of your business," I snap. She ignores me, her eyes on Benny.

Out of the corner of my eye, I see Lex grab Benny's hand. She looks terrified for him. You know it's bad when Lex wants less attention on our family.

I glare at Mom—*fucking DO something!* She gives me her helpless what-can-I-do look. Kirk coughs uncomfortably, but otherwise, the studio is totally silent. It feels like the whole world must be waiting for his answer. I imagine businessmen stopping mid-sentence, drive-thru workers freezing, bags of food clutched in their hands. Children at recess stop playing, and everyone at Taft stands still in the halls and classrooms. And where is Matt? I picture him sitting at his desk, his letterman jacket draped over his chair. Waiting.

"I agree with my sister that it's none of your business. But I'm gay, if that's what you're asking."

The audience inhales in a collective gasp. TV gold. Kaye's eyes widen—she can't believe her luck. She turns to the camera and does her serious voice, her eyes full of fake empathy.

"We'll be right back."

*m*y phone rings as soon as Kaye's closing credits are playing all across America. Lunch just ended at Taft, and gov is about to start. The taping was live, and I know Patrick, Tess, Mer, and Matt were watching it on their phones. I hurry to the greenroom and find a corner to hide in.

"One," Patrick says, as soon as I answer, "I'm going to *kill* Brent Livingston. And two, ask Benny if Matt needs any help. I don't have his number, and he's MIA."

The rest of our time in LA is a blur of interviews on and off camera, book signings, and appearances. Benny's half catatonic for much of it and spends his spare time on the roof of the hotel, going through two packs of cigarettes as he and Matt shout and cry and whisper to each other across the miles. Tessa and Mer (who are surprised about Benny, but take it in stride) and Patrick keep us updated on how people at Taft are taking it all. It's not long before everyone puts two and two together. Why else would a couple of gorgeous guys—one of them on the varsity football team—be single? Apparently Matt was absent the rest of the week, and his parents were trying to get him to talk to one of those fundamentalist counselors who try to cure you of your gayness.

Mom only tries to talk to Benny once after the *Kaye Gibbons Show*:

Mom: Benny. Honey. Talk to me.

Benny: Go away, Mom.

Mom: Please, let me help. What can I do to help?

Benny: (glaring with red-rimmed eyes) *I don't want to talk to you.*

Mom: Don't shut me out.

Benny:

Mom: I'm making an appointment with the school counselor. If you won't talk to me, you have to talk to somebody.

My brother is not ashamed of being gay. He just never made a thing of it because he didn't want to attract more attention than was absolutely necessary. He and Matt took a chance on each other, and they've been together for a year and a half—I've even heard them talk about getting married someday. Their plan had been to come out to their friends and Matt's family this summer, after graduation. They've been saving up money to go to Paris before college—the same college, whatever they both get into.

"Man, Chloe. I don't know what I'm gonna do."

Benny's sitting on the floor of his bedroom, his head in his hands. We just got home an hour ago, and it's Friday night. Normally he'd be out with Matt, but that was obviously not happening.

"What's Matt saying?"

Benny shakes his head. "It's hard for him to get away to call me. His parents took his cell phone. We're still together, but . . ."

He takes in a shuddering breath, and his shoulders shake from the tears he's keeping bottled up inside. I rub his back while he silently cries—we've had to do this for each other too many times.

"Some of the guys from the football team have been posting shit about him on Facebook," he says. "I don't know how this will affect him getting on the team at USC."

Matt was hoping to get an athletic scholarship—I wonder how many gay wide receivers there have been in the history of college football.

There's a knock on the door, and Lexie™ pokes her head in. "Hey, Bon. Mom wants to talk to you." She looks at Benny and walks into the room. "Bens, want some company?"

He looks up, and she draws a bottle of wine from behind her back.

"I don't know if that's such a good—" I start, but Benny reaches his hand out.

"I do."

I know one of these days I'm going to have to tell Benny he might be a little like Dad in this respect, but I'm not stupid; now is not the time to stage an intervention with my brother. I kiss his cheek and stand up.

"Do you know what it's about?" I ask.

Lex shakes her head. "Honestly, who freakin' knows anymore?"

When I get to the kitchen table, Mom and Kirk are having an

argument. Puma Guy is there, keeping his camera trained on them. Another guy I don't recognize is holding the boom.

"—sure you didn't let it slip?" Mom sees me and puts her hand up. "Never mind. We'll talk about this later."

Kirk swears under his breath and brushes past me on his way to the fridge. He pulls out a beer, pops the top, and hurls the cap into the sink. I feel like gloating—*is this what you wanted, Kirk? Isn't fame fun?*

"Bonnie™. How is he?" Mom's still wearing the pantsuit she'd had on for *Good Morning LA*. She's starting to look like a forty-year-old Barbie doll. I could be wrong, but I swear she's gotten more Botox.

I cross my arms. "Not good."

"Do you think he'll talk to me?"

I shake my head. "No way."

"But I don't understand why he's blaming *me*. It's unfortunate that it happened this way, but it was bound to come out eventually. Isn't it better? Now he doesn't have to pretend anymore."

My body starts tingling, my fight-or-flight response kicking in. I could run, like I always do, or I could take her on—right here, right now. Screw the cameras.

"*Unfortunate?*" I snarl. "Your son has just been outed in front of the whole world, and that's the word you choose?"

Mom pales. "Bonnie™, I won't tolerate this tone—"

"Guess what? I don't care." I smile, feeling slightly crazed. I'm a maniac, I'm out of control. "You know why he's not talking to you? Because you just *sat there*. You let Kaye Gibbons push him, and you didn't stand up for him. You didn't protect him. I think you wanted this to happen. I wouldn't be surprised if you told Kaye yourself."

Kirk stomps toward me. "Young lady—"

"Oh, fuck off, Kirk."

His hand flies up, like he's gonna slap me.

I smile. "I'd love it if you did."

His hand drops, and he gives me a look filled with pure hatred. I'm messing up his plans. He wanted the fame and the money, but all he's getting is a televised nightmare. All hail the Heisenberg Uncertainty Principle. There's no telling what anyone will do once a camera's on them.

Mom's voice pushes between us. "Bonnie™, go to your room."

I throw the camera a *you saw that, right?* little glance. Then I turn on my heel, take the stairs two at a time, and get drunk in Benny's bedroom.

When the bottle is empty and Lex has long since crashed, I put my hand on Benny's shoulder.

"Bens. We have to fight back."

He nods. "How?"

I think back to the class discussion we'd had in gov earlier this week. Schwartz had written the word *resistance* on the board and talked about Gandhi and Rosa Parks. He'd said the only way to fight the Big Brothers of the world was to be unafraid to put yourself on the line for what you believed in. *You have to take a risk*, he'd said, *or nothing will ever change.* It felt like he was talking to me. . . . Maybe he was.

When I speak, my voice is firm, resolute. "Let's go on strike."

~ ~ ~

Monday at school is brutal. I'd thought it was bad before, but now I feel like we're animals at the zoo, everyone staring at us and nowhere to hide. There are no made-for-TV movie events, nothing as dramatic as Benny getting pushed up against a locker, but there are a lot of ugly looks thrown his way, especially from Matt's team. Even my teachers are acting weird. Matt is nowhere to be seen—none of us have any classes with him, and Benny hasn't been able to get ahold of him because of the cell phone issue with his parents. Now he's not even sure if they're still together. My heart twists when I see his face after fifth period. I realize with a start that I haven't seen my usually happy-go-lucky brother smile in nearly a week. By the time we near the caf to grab lunch, we've slowed down to a crawl. Almost by mutual psychic agreement, we stop a few feet away from the wide double doors the rest of the school is streaming into.

"Dude, I don't think I can go in there," he says.

I think back to what Diane Le Shrink said to me about ditching. What the hell—it's for a good cause.

"Let's go to the Tower District. I'll get you some gelato from Vicenti."

"'Kay," he mumbles. He doesn't even look up as he turns toward the parking lot. His moping is giving Eeyore a run for his money. I, however, do not have my eyes on the ground. I stop. I blink. I grin.

Matt's striding toward us up the hallway, wearing a bright red shirt with the words I LOVE MY BOYFRIEND on the front.

"Holy shit," I say.

Benny looks up, then just stares at Matt, his mouth half open. Matt doesn't stop as he nears; he grabs Benny's face and kisses him with so much love, so much unrestrained passion, that I can't help but blush. Then Tessa and Mer show up out of nowhere and start whooping and hollering. People gather around, some clapping and whistling, others looking on in disgust or shock. For a second, I clench my fists, ready to take on anyone who's going to give them shit, but the whole hallway starts filling with cheers and good-natured catcalls. The haters are few and far between. Someone—I can't tell who—yells "faggots," but they're drowned out by the crowd. Phone cameras flash, and for once, it doesn't bother me. Because this *should* be front-page news.

Matt pulls away and kisses Benny's nose. "Benton™ Andrew Baker, will you go to the winter formal with me?"

Benny's smile is dazzling. He kisses Matt back.

"Is that a yes?" someone shouts.

Benny pulls away. "Yes!"

I don't even know I'm crying until Patrick's fingers gently sweep across my cheeks. I look up at him, and he smiles his Patrick smile, all crooked and mysterious. He doesn't seem remotely surprised that my brother and his boyfriend have just made national headlines.

"Did you play any part in this?" I ask. His warm brown-gold eyes hold just a tad more mischief in them than usual.

He shrugs. "My dad's friend owns a T-shirt shop."

I throw my arms around him. "I love you so much," I whisper.

He squeezes me tighter. "Damn. I knew I should have gotten one of those shirts in your size."

I pull away. "What about Matt's parents?"

Patrick sighs. "They suck. But Matt basically told them they'd better get used to having Ben in the family."

"That's pretty badass." I watch Matt twirl Benny around, as if they are already on the dance floor. "What'd his parents say to that?"

"That they would pray for him to see his sin clearly." Patrick smiles. "So Matt said he'd pray for them, too, that they would learn to love Ben as much as he does. Then he said he had to—and I quote—'see a boy about a dance.'"

"Amen," I murmur.

Lunch turns into a celebration—I've never seen Benny so happy. He's glowing, lit up from within. After all those months of hiding how they feel about each other, the separate lunches, the rough-guy hand-slaps and what-up-bro's instead of the gentle caresses they give each other now . . . I can already tell the weight of the world has been lifted off my brother's shoulders.

"This is what life could be like without MetaReel," I murmur, watching them. We're outside on the quad, basking in the unseasonably warm weather.

Patrick wraps his arms around me, and I lean into him, my back against his chest. "We're gonna have that, you know," he says. "A life without MetaReel."

I'm not sure if I shiver because of the way he nuzzles my neck or from the word *we*.

"I know," I say. And for the first time, I can actually see that life. It's not so far away. Maybe only a few weeks away, if I can get up the courage to move out.

"After graduation, we can just . . . ride into the sunrise," he says.

"The sunrise?"

His lips twitch. "If we ride into the sunset, we'd wind up in the middle of the Pacific."

"Just my luck," I mutter.

"Screw luck." He leans down and gives me a spearmint-flavored kiss. "We'll make our own."

The last two classes of the day are impossible to concentrate in because I'm more convinced than ever that what Benny and I need is a little pièce de résistance to bring Chuck to his knees. Matt's bravery was a big statement. We need something like that—we have to wake people up. Patrick and I pass notes back and forth all during gov about it, and I tell everyone to meet me in the gym after school for some strategizing.

Once there, I lay out my ideas.

"This is your influence, isn't it?" Benny gives Patrick a pointed look, but Patrick holds up his hands.

"It was all her idea. I just supplied a few suggestions."

"Whatever, Che Guevara," Benny says. I don't buy his grouchiness for a second. For one, he's still beaming.

I can't sit still, so I stand up and pace up and down the empty basketball court. After an hour in the stuffy space, I've already become immune to its scent of blood, sweat, and tears. Tessa is lying on the polished floor, her head resting on her backpack. Patrick is reclining against the bleachers, and Matt's sitting next to Benny, holding his hand. Mer had to leave right after school for her NYU audition, which is unfortunate because I need some of her all-caps exuberance right now.

"This is probably illegal," Benny says. "I mean, we can't just destroy really expensive equipment and get away with it. Plus, Mom would murder us. It would be, like, the first homicide in the history of reality television. And it'll be *live*. Children across the nation will be scarred for life."

This Tuesday, *Baker's Dozen* has its second live episode. We'll be going back to LA for a special red carpet event: the annual Ultimate Reality™ Expo. This is where stars from reality TV flock to congratulate themselves on this year's brain rot performances. Not only will our crew be there for the live episode, but so will all the major news networks and, of course, the Vultures.

"Sabotage during a live show is far more effective than sabotage that can end up on the cutting room floor," I say. I'd been itching to slice through more camera cords for weeks now.

"I'm deeply concerned about having a criminal record," says Benny.

"Chicken?" I ask.

"Um. Yes? I think it's sane to be worried about vandalizing private property when someone's recording your every move."

Patrick drums his fingers against the bleachers absentmindedly, the dull thuds creating an impromptu percussion with the pen that Tessa taps against her thigh.

Tap, thud, tap, thud, thud.

"I think whatever you do, you should make sure to let the press know what's going on," Tessa says.

I hug my arms to my chest. "I really don't want to be in the news more than I have to be."

"But if you guys just pull pranks, people are going to think you're doing it for the attention," Matt counters.

"Says the man with the I LOVE MY BOYFRIEND T-shirt," I say. He blushes, and Benny kisses his cheek.

"I agree with Matt and Tessa," Patrick says. "I think you have to back it up with something. Otherwise, MetaReel's just going to use it to sensationalize the show. No one will know why you're doing what you're doing."

"Hell, no." Benny hits his hand against the bleachers. "We are *not* doing those bastards any favors."

We sit there, thinking and breathing resistance. The gym becomes so silent, it's loud. *Loud.*

I stop pacing. "What if we took a vow of silence?" I ask.

"When?" Benny asks.

"At the Ultimate Reality™ press conference."

Benny's eyes light up. "Like we don't talk the whole time we're there, even if people are asking us questions?"

"Yeah. Pretty much."

"Excellent!" Patrick says. "My girlfriend is a revolutionary genius!"

I can't hide my pleased grin. It's pretty brilliant, if I do say so myself.

"Can't they just edit it out?" Matt asks.

Benny shakes his head. "It's gonna be a live episode during our press conference and book signing and then the rest of the day is streaming live on MetaReel.com. Plus, all the other networks will be there."

"That's so badass," says Tessa. "What can we do to help?"

My stomach's already tying itself into knots, but I ignore it. I have to—otherwise I won't be able to do what I'm about to do in precisely forty-eight hours.

"Do you have any duct tape?"

SEASON 17, EPISODE 27

(The One with the Duct Tape)

check my outfit in the bathroom mirror one more time, resisting the urge to throw up. I know this is right, and it's going to be a defining moment in my life, but I so want to wimp out. I've been hiding in one of the greenroom bathrooms, waiting for Benny to meet me before we join our family for the *Baker's Dozen* press conference. This is our first event of the convention. After this, we have the book signings and then the red carpet before the Ultimate Reality™ Awards. I'm wearing Tessa's anti-TV Hello Kitty shirt for luck and I finger the note Patrick had slipped into my hand when I said good-bye to him after school yesterday. I don't need to read it again, but I take it out one more time, just to see his handwriting.

Gloaming. Paperweight. Yawp. Chloe.

My name added to his list of favorite words reminds me of who I am. I am *brazen.*

A knock sounds on the door. "It's me," Benny says, his voice low.

I open it, and he scurries inside, looking about as jittery as I do.

"I threw up. Just now. I couldn't help it," he says.

"That's okay. I'm nervous too."

"Mom's going to lose her shit." Benny doesn't seem too sad about this.

I bite the inside of my cheek, a nervous habit that has left my skin raw. "I wonder what Dad will do. He's got to be watching."

It shouldn't matter, but I want him to see this. I want him to take responsibility for what our lives have come to.

Benny crosses to my backpack and roots around inside, pulling out the scissors I brought for us. The duct tape is on his wrist, dangling like a tacky bracelet.

His voice is hard and very un–Benny-like. "Well, if he really cared, he would have called."

He hands me my phone. I dial Tessa's number. Tessa—whose internship last summer at the *San Joaquin Times* has suddenly become very useful, not to mention that her dad's a reporter for the *Fresno Bee.* She picks up on the first ring.

"The ads for the show are playing nonstop. It says it's going to be on"—she makes her voice manly—"*after these few messages.*"

I try to laugh, but it just catches in my throat.

"Ready?" she asks.

I pause, a diver poised on the edge of the board.

"Yep."

"Love you," she says.

"You too."

I look over at Benny. "She'll tell her dad now."

I get a text from Mer just as I hang up:

Down with Big Brother, girlfriend.

Only Mer can do a Valley Girl rendition of *1984*. I wonder if she's watching from the airport.

The tape makes a sharp sucking noise as he pulls it away from the roll.

"Any last words?"

I smile. *"Dismiss whatever insults your own soul."* He arches an eyebrow. "Whitman. Not a poem, just something he said. You like?"

"Damn. Raise the bar, why don't you?"

He brings the tape closer to my mouth. "Wait!" I stop his hand. "I have to say it again if they're really going to be my last words." He rolls his eyes and waves his hand for me to proceed. *"Dismiss whatever insults your own soul."*

And then I feel the tape against my lips.

~ ~ ~

The convention center is huge, filled with booths for each show, food vendors, and public audition sites. Screens are set up all around the perimeter, broadcasting different reality TV shows. Loud music plays, the kind you hear before a basketball game, and there are cameras everywhere: an Orwellian hell.

It's eight P.M., and the place is packed. We pass the casts of *Hit Squad* (a creepy show that has former Navy SEALs leading teams of Joe Schmos in paintball wars) and *Birth Mother* (where women who are giving up their babies for adoption look for the "perfect match"). They're both holding auditions in the same area, and it's weird to see a long line of pregnant women and Rambo types chatting with one another. In another corner, a runway is set up and girls from *Model Life* walk up and down it. I can smell something delicious over by the *Head Chef* booth, and there's Jake Pyers, host of *Landlord Wars*.

MetaReel's "press room" is situated in the center of the convention's huge floor. There's a pretty big crowd assembled, full of Vultures, news stations, and reporters from major magazines and newspapers. There are also a ton of fans, some with signs that have our names on them. Hundreds of people. At first, nobody notices Benny and me as we file onto the little stage with our siblings and take our seats behind a long table. There are cards with our names facing out to the press and a small microphone for each of us. I'm terrified to look up. My heart feels like it wants to break through my chest, and I take big, loud breaths through my nose, wanting so badly to rip the tape off my mouth so that I can get some air into my lungs. I can't believe I'm doing this.

"Hello, everyone!" says a too-tan guy at the edge of the stage nearest Benny and me—the moderator. He's got a microphone in his hand and is wearing a MetaReel T-shirt. "Tonight we've got the cast of *Baker's Dozen: Fresh Batch* with us. Give it up for MetaReel's biggest stars!"

As the crowd behind the press goes wild, we both look up. I quickly put my hair into a ponytail so the tape is totally visible. I've never felt so exposed in all my life.

At first, there are just a few gasps in the audience, but as more and more people notice us, the crowd's relative buzz turns into a roar. Instantly, the Vultures congregate toward our end of the table, pushing and shoving one another to get the best shot. Dozens of them call out my name, telling me to look over here, look up, *Bonnie*™! *Bonnie*™! *Bonnie*™!

Lexie™ is sitting three chairs down from me, on my left, and she leans forward and looks toward us, her eyes widening when she sees our faces. "Oh. My. God."

Her mic's on, so it comes out loud and clear. I'd smile, but I can't with the tape on.

The light from the cameras is blinding but, for once, I'm delighted to see them. Instead of shying away, I stare right at the lenses, daring them to capture me. *Catch me if you can.* The fans at the back hold up cell phones like it's a rock concert—*clickclickclickclickclickclickclick.*

I lock eyes with Benny, and he grabs my hand and squeezes it—his palms are just as sweaty as mine. I've never loved my brother so much in my whole life. Seeing that tape across his mouth makes this feel more real to me than anything else; it's a scary image, violent almost. It makes you think of kidnappers.

I can see our camera crew set up at different stations around the press area, each lens representing approximately four million people. That's twelve million pairs of eyes, not to mention the dozens of non-MetaReel cameras. I can almost hear the gasps and cackles in living rooms all over the country. People saying, *Hurry, get in here—you have to see this!* Journalists calling their editors. Bloggers gleefully type-type-typing away. My classmates texting, updating their statuses. Patrick, Tessa, Matt, Mer watching us with clammy palms, their hearts beating almost as hard as mine. *Brazen, Brazen, Brazen.*

Mom's beside us in an instant. "Bonnie™ . . . what's . . . Benton™ . . ." Her voice changes from startled confusion to low growl. *"Take that tape off this instant."*

My mic catches her voice, and I see Chuck make a frantic motion with his hands, but nobody turns the mic off. Lacey Production Assistant stands next to him, looking like she's about to go into cardiac arrest.

Mom's eyes are deer-in-headlights big as Benny and I shake our heads. She shoots Chuck an anxious glance, but he can't do anything from his post by the stairs. It wouldn't be good for our illusion of reality if the producer started stage-managing us. She holds up her hands like, *I don't know what to do.*

We are a PR disaster.

Some of my siblings start to giggle, but Kirk silences them with a hiss. Mom reaches up to rip the tape off my face, but I jerk back, shaking my head hard enough for the people in the back row of the press corps to see. I clutch the piece of paper in my hand and hold it up for the audience before I hand it to the guy who's moderating our press conference. It says PLEASE READ.

The night before, Tessa and I had worked out a press release, basically a letter to the world explaining why Benny and I are taking a vow of silence. It's a pretty awesome manifesto, and I feel a surge of *hell, yeah!* as I hand it over, knowing it's already being sent to the Associated Press via Mr. Lee, Tessa's dad. The moderator hesitates before he opens it, like it's going to bite him. His smile is still frozen on his face, and he looks back at Chuck, but Chuck's too busy yelling into his phone.

"Read it!" someone from the audience yells. The voice sounds familiar, but I can't place it. My skin tingles with anticipation, and I hold my breath, hoping. The moderator puts the microphone to his lips.

His smile gets wider, but I'm close enough to see the beads of sweat bursting out on his forehead. "Looks like Bonnie™ and Benton™ Baker are pulling a little prank." He doesn't open the letter. "It's a little early for April Fool's, though, isn't it?" Cue forced laugh. "All right, let's get started with—"

"What's it say?"

Wait, I *do* recognize that voice. Tessa? I look in the direction it came from, and my heart glows as I catch sight of Tessa, Matt, and Patrick in the audience. We'd told them not to come, but they hadn't listened.

"Read it!"

And there's Matt. I nudge Benny, and his eyes grow wide as he sees his boyfriend.

"Freedom of speech!"

That was Patrick. Of course. Our eyes meet—a long-distance version of a stolen kiss—and he grins before disappearing into the crowd. Security is already moving through the mass of people, searching for them.

The moderator glances at the cameras and then shrugs his shoulders in defeat.

He reads our letter in an increasingly contemptuous tone, but at least our plan is working. We're telling the world how we feel without saying a word.

To Whom It May Concern:

We, Bonnie™ and Benton™ Baker, are taking a vow of silence as an act of peaceful resistance against the continued presence of Meta-Reel in our home and lives. We have decided to abstain from participating in a production we have both, in many different ways, asked to opt out of. This is not a prank or a ploy at getting attention. We have enough attention. We do this not out of disrespect to our family but, rather, out of respect for our rights as individuals. Our efforts to keep our family off the air have gone unheeded—

He stops, but the crowd starts booing him. Chuck throws Benny and me a disgusted look, then turns on his heel and stalks off. The moderator continues.

> —and our most personal stories have been made public without our willing consent. For most of our lives, the word *privacy* has not been in our vocabulary. Being on *Baker's Dozen* was never something we had a choice in. While we are thankful for our family's efforts to provide for us, we strongly object to our lives being used for entertainment purposes. Thank you.
>
> Bonnie™ and Benton™ Baker

Pride—faltering at first, then stronger—surges through me. I'm doing this; I'm finally standing up for myself. There are murmurs in the audience and then—scattered applause. Not everyone is clapping for us: most people look confused. *Snap. Snap. Snap.* More pictures. Hundreds of them.

Mom: "Get up."

She forcibly pulls me and Benny out of our chairs, gripping my arm so hard I wince. As we stumble down the stairs and across the convention floor, the moderator puts his hands up in the international gesture of Everyone Please Shut Up. My siblings follow our departure with shocked eyes—the little ones still don't get what happened, but they know we're in trouble. Lex actually smirks and shakes her head admiringly. I raise my eyebrows as if to say, *See, you've been underestimating me all along.* When we get to the hallway where the greenrooms are, Mom lets go of us; she looks like she's going to have an aneurysm.

"How *dare* you embarrass our family like this," she says. "Do you have any idea what the repercussions of your little prank will be?"

I'm itching to yell back. To say, *Didn't you listen to the letter? It's not a prank!* But I can't take the tape off yet.

Mom throws up her hands as a MetaReel camera comes into the hallway.

"I don't know what to do with you two. Benny, first it's drinking, now this. Bonnie™, you're acting like a child, throwing tantrums, getting violent . . . this is simply unacceptable."

Violent? Oh, right, the notebook throwing.

She pauses, taking us in, measuring her breaths until they are socially acceptable inhales and exhales. "I know you want a rise out of me, but you're not going to get it. Hopefully someday you'll learn there are more appropriate ways to voice your concerns. Excuse me while I go clean up your mess. Again."

I look at my mom for a long moment. I don't know what I was hoping for—maybe I wanted her to drop everything and demand that the cameras be turned off. Or perhaps I thought she'd scream at me so America could see, once and for all, how messed up our family is. I know one thing I wasn't expecting: her indifference.

She turns toward the press conference and says over her shoulder, "Don't even think about going back out there."

The camera stays on us for a while, but eventually drifts out the doorway, returning to the press conference and the red carpet. Benny and I look at each other, and his eyes crinkle up, like he's smiling through the tape. I nod.

It was worth it.

Viewpoints with Eileen Smith
KTOK AM 540

EILEEN SMITH: Good afternoon. If you're just join-ing us, today we're talking about the outrageous protest by *Baker's Dozen* stars Bonnie™ and Benton™ Baker during the show's live taping last night at the Ultimate Reality™ Expo in Los Angeles. I'm here with Chuck Daniels, the head producer of the Meta-Reel show. Chuck?

CHUCK DANIELS: Thank you, Eileen. I just want to say that Bonnie™ and Benton™ have always had my ear when it comes to any problems they're having. As you probably saw on last week's episode, Bonnie™ was pretty upset about her mother reading her diary. I believe she's just acting out with some normal teenage aggression. Both kids are back at school today without tape, and the family has gone back to normal.

EILEEN SMITH: What do you think of the MetaReel boycott the United Parents Coalition is calling for?

CHUCK DANIELS: I think it's great that people are engaging with the show.

EILEEN SMITH: Is MetaReel considering including more protection and benefits for the child stars of your programs?

CHUCK DANIELS: Well, Eileen, I just make the show. You'd have to talk to our legal department about all that. But I'd like to point out that the contracts we have are good enough for the parents in our programs, and last I checked, the buck stops with them.

EILEEN SMITH: Let's get some other viewpoints in here. I've got Nancy Fraser from Boston on the line. Nancy?

NANCY FRASER: Hi, Eileen. Hello, Chuck.

CHUCK DANIELS AND EILEEN SMITH: Hi.

NANCY FRASER: Well, I just want to say that as a mother of three, I can't imagine how hard it must be for Beth. I've been watching the show since the very first episode, and I think Bonnie™ has just gotten a little too big for her britches. If you ask me, what that girl needs is a good spanking.

EILEEN SMITH: Okay, uh, thanks, Nancy. We've got Tim Birch on the line from Phoenix. Tim, what do you think of Bonnie™ Baker?

TIM SMITH: I think that girl needs to run as far away from her crazy family as possible. What Meta-Reel and her parents are doing is criminal. Forcing these kids to be on camera is—

CHUCK DANIELS: Now let me make this clear. MetaReel is in no way forcing these children to be on the show—they have a father in Florida. Bonnie™ and Benton™ are aware that remaining with their mother means staying on the show. Trust me, we're not hand-cuffing kids to our cameras.

EILEEN SMITH: We've got to go to commercial, but don't switch that dial! If you have a question for Chuck about *Baker's Dozen* or a comment about last night's episode, pick up your phone or put on that Bluetooth if you're on your commute. We'll be right back after these messages from our sponsors.

I've never realized how Chuck's face resembles a piece of ham. It really does. It's a big hunk of pink, glistening flesh with a ring of fat around the outside. Put some brown sugar on him, and you've got Christmas dinner. His beady little eyes flash at me when I come down the stairs. It's Wednesday, the day after the vow, and I've been holed up in my room, doing homework. It had been a great day at school. For once it feels good to be a celebrity. Schwartz started a round of applause for me in class, and a few people actually came up to me to say they thought what we'd done was awesome. Diane Le Shrink gave me not two but *three* packs of Skittles, and Patrick dragged me into the janitor's closet for half the lunch period.

I touch my lips as I remember his heat, the way his skin melted into mine.

"Bonnie™, did you hear what I said?"

I look at Chuck, my face flooding crimson. "Uh. No. Sorry."

"I said, we need to go outside for a little chat."

Outside, as in, not overheard by MetaReel. So when he wants privacy, it's okay to ditch the cameras?

"We can talk here."

He looks in the direction of the living room, where Puma Guy is capturing a few of my brothers arguing over a soccer ball. "No, we can't."

Sighing, I get up and follow him out the front door. It's a cold January day, the sky a slab of marble, and I shiver, wishing I'd grabbed my coat. He's silent as we trudge through the dead grass along the security fence. Finally he stops in the middle of the side yard and fixes me with a seriously sinister glare.

"Just what exactly do you think you're doing?"

Annoyance surges through me—who is this guy? He's not my dad, not my teacher, not someone who should have any authority over me at all. So why is he in control of my life? I force myself to stand a little taller.

"It's none of your business what I'm doing, Chuck. That's sort of the point."

He sticks his doughy face closer to mine, his pointed nose inches from my own. "I'm only going to say this once, Bonnie™, so you better listen. I can *ruin* your family."

"You mean like how you ruined it four years ago?" My voice cuts through the space between us. "You knew Dad was in that guesthouse. You knew when you told me to go get him. How do you *sleep* at night?"

His eyes are cold, betraying nothing: no surprise, no guilt. "Push me, and I will make your mother wish she had never signed up for this show. I'm not going to let you and your faggy brother fuck up my entire career because all of a sudden you've gotten camera shy."

346

I stare at him, too shocked to even wipe away the drops of his spittle that have sprayed my face.

"No more stunts," he says. "I've got the goddamned ACLU on my ass, reporters calling night and day. One more prank like this, and we'll pull the plug on the show and sue the hell out of your family for defamation of character and lost revenue. It's your choice. But I'd think long and hard. MetaReel isn't going to play nice."

He doesn't wait for me to respond. By the time I find my voice, he's already gone back into my house—no. He's gone back to the *set*. Cold uncertainty pushes against my ribs, filling me up. Chuck isn't bluffing, that much is clear. My elation over the great day at school evaporates. The statement we made would be meaningless if we just keep doing the show, but if we say anything, then we're responsible for landing my family in the poorhouse.

I've got to talk to Benny.

I trudge back across the lawn, but when I get inside, he's sitting at the kitchen table with two cameras on him, holding the cordless phone to his ear. Mom and Kirk lean against the counter, watching him. When she sees me, Mom points to the table—*You. Sit.*

I sit.

Which doesn't make me feel like a badass revolutionary at all.

"Dad . . . no. No, we don't want—" Benny puts his hand over the receiver. "It's Dad. He's offering to have us go live with him."

I hold out my hand, and Benny places the phone in it.

"Dad?"

"Hey, honey." His voice is fake-happy, tight. "I was just talking to Ben about you guys maybe coming to stay with me. Sounds like it's pretty rough over there for you."

"They put you up to this," I say.

"No!" But even though we're hundreds of miles away, I can tell he's lying. He's clearly under duress.

"Dad, Benny and I aren't going to move to Florida. We only have four months until we graduate."

He sighs. "But—"

I open my mouth to say we didn't do the vow of silence just so that we'd get secreted away by MetaReel, but Chuck catches my eye and gives an imperceptible shake of his head. *Big Brother Is Watching You.*

"Look. Thanks, Dad, but Benny and I have a life here. We have school and . . . friends."

I think of Patrick, of leaving him to go live with my alcoholic father and whatever floozy he's shacking up with in Miami. Or Benny leaving Matt before they can go to the winter formal together. No. There has to be another way.

"Well, okay, if that's what you want."

He's so obviously relieved that I want to beat the phone against the table.

"Yes," I say, trying to control the emotions that are desperate to burst out of my skin. "That's what I want. Benny?"

He nods.

"And Benny too," I add.

"Well, I . . . I love you guys."

Long dramatic pause.

"Huh," is all I say.

I hang up the phone and look at Mom. She shrugs her shoulders and turns back to the soup that's simmering on the stove. Right now, we have a policy of détente—it's Cold War status up in the Baker house.

When Benny and I get back upstairs, I pull him into my room and tell him about the conversation with Chuck.

"You've gotta call that lawyer back," he whispers. He looks at the door. "Like, now."

I think of how Lark™, my little brother from India, still wets the bed even though he's nine. Benny, hiding who he is because he doesn't want his sexual orientation to make national headlines . . . and drinking on the sly because the pressure is too much. Lex, screwing lots of boys because she doesn't get enough love or attention at home. And the others—night terrors, temper tantrums, and God knows what else. I could walk away and let them sort out this mess for themselves. Not have the lawsuit. Just get out, graduate, and move on. Or I could stand up for all of us.

"Yeah."

I pull her number up on the cell phone Patrick gave me. After the third ring, a crisp what-is-it-I'm-saving-the-world voice answers.

"Melinda Greenberg," she says.

"Hi. Uh. It's Chloe. Chloe Baker."

"Hi, Chloe." Am I imagining the undercurrent of excitement in her voice? "I thought I'd be hearing from you. You okay over there? I was watching last night."

"Not exactly. I think my brother and I need to meet with you."

"How's this Saturday?"

~ ~ ~

We spend most of Saturday morning in Melinda Greenberg's cluttered office, building a case out of long-ago hurts and purposely forgotten violations. We talk about things like the incident in season twelve when my dad called Mom a "media whore bitch from hell" on

Dr. Phil during a segment on marriage counseling. Or how MetaReel had organized a trip to a nutritionist when I was gaining a little weight and how I'd had to stand on the scale in front of the cameras while he outlined all the ways in which my body wasn't good enough. A few weeks later, the cameras tagged along when I went back to the same nutritionist after Mom caught me throwing up my dinner.

I try to explain to Melinda how being on camera makes you start watching yourself, not even knowing where the camera "you" ends and the real "you" begins—like having multiple personalities. She tells us we have a strong case and we just might win, but that it will be hard and ugly. She asks us, over and over, if we are sure we want to do this. That it means even more publicity and that MetaReel won't hold back any punches.

We point to the contract on her desk and ask where we need to sign.

*T*wo weeks. In two weeks I will turn eighteen. Thus far, word hasn't leaked about our visit to the lawyer, so we decide not to mention it at home until Melinda gives us the go-ahead. Now I'm at Patrick's, smuggled away there after school in his mother's SUV. I wonder if the MetaReel camera dude who was supposed to drive home with me is still waiting.

We're lying on Patrick's bed, our limbs tangled, my head on his chest.

"So Tessa's parents are cool with it?" he asks. Tessa and her family have agreed to let Benny and me move in with them as soon as I turn eighteen.

I smile contentedly as he runs his hands through my hair.

"Yeah. I told them the Vultures would descend, but I think Mr. Lee's excited about getting to do our story."

I feel Patrick stiffen. "So they're only letting you stay there if you repay him with interviews?"

I sit up and look down at him. "It's not like that." He purses his lips, his brown eyes flashing. He's pretty sexy when he's protective like this.

"*Seriously.* I can't help it if my best friend's dad is a reporter. And he didn't ask. In fact, when I offered to give him the exclusive, he flat-out said no."

Patrick snorts and sits up in one fluid, agitated gesture. "Chloe, when are you going to stop letting people walk all over you?"

I frown at his frustrated tone. "I'm not letting him walk all over me. I *want* to do the interview. It's the only way I can control the message."

I'm starting to sound like my lawyer.

"But he's got to be objective," Patrick says. "Which means he's gonna have to say stuff you won't want him to say."

"Patrick." I put my hands on his knees and catch his eyes. "I trust the Lees. And it's really the only place where Benny and I can both go and feel totally comfortable. It's the best-case scenario in a worst-case situation."

He sighs and wraps his arms around me. "I just don't want anyone else to hurt you," he murmurs against my hair.

I turn my head and press my mouth against his, shivering when his teeth graze my lower lip. We don't talk for a long time. There's no MetaReel, no parents, no lawyers. Goose bumps spread across his arms when I touch him.

"God, I want you," he whispers, gripping my hips.

He pulls the covers over us, and it's like we're back in our fort. My universe shrinks in size; all that exists are his hands, his lips, his tongue, his breath.

I can't think, I just want want *want*, this heat in me turning to fire. Patrick's eyes ask a question, and I nod. I'm so *so* ready for this. He kisses me as his hand reaches to his bedside table.

I think about the last time this almost happened and how I'd written about it in my journal. *Which my mother read.* I still feel Patrick's lips on mine, but it's like I'm not here anymore. A cold wind blows through me, and my body shuts down, scattering the embers of the fire that had been licking every inch of my skin.

I gently slide out from under him. Why did that world always have to muscle its way into everything?

He pulls the blanket back and looks down at me, his eyes searching my face. "What's wrong?" he asks. Soft, low.

I shake my head. "Nothing. I just . . ." I bite my lip in embarrassment. "Um."

He kisses my nose, my forehead, my eyelids.

"Should we slow down?" he murmurs. He kisses my neck and the flat of his hand on my bare stomach makes it impossible to think clearly.

Slow down? No. No. Hell.

I cover my face with my hands. "Yeah. But I don't want to. Slow down. It's just . . ."

I don't know how to explain what it would feel like to be so close to him and then have to return to the MetaReel cameras and the vast desert of uncertainty that is my future.

"I'd have to go back. Like, right after. And the cameras and I—"

He pulls me against him. "I get it." He sighs into my neck. "I really do. It's just . . . damn."

He blushes, and I put my hands on either side of his face. "You are so freakin' cute when you get all bashful," I whisper.

His eyes are glassy, hungry, and he swallows as my arms twist around his neck. "I can say with complete honesty that I have never wanted anything so badly in my life as I want you right now."

It's my turn to blush.

"Now who's bashful?" he teases.

There's the clang of the garage door opening, and he turns around and buries his face in a pillow and groans.

I let out a shaky laugh. "Guess it's a good thing we didn't . . ."

"Yeah." He gives me a wistful look. "Rain check?"

I nod.

"We might want to put our clothes back on before my mother comes up here."

I look at the pile on the floor. "I suppose that would be the proper etiquette."

We dress hurriedly, and I throw my hair into a messy bun. I check my cell phone—time to go.

"Well, I hate to be *that* girl, but I better leave before my own mother gets home."

She'd been doing book signings and promotional stuff in Phoenix, and her flight is supposed to get in sometime in the next hour.

"Okay. But wait." Patrick opens his desk drawer, and when he turns around, he's holding a small jewelry box. His grabs my hand and places the box on my palm. His eyes dance as I stare at the black velvet. "Open it."

My hands shake a little as I pull back the top. Inside is an antique gold ring with a small, intricately cut oval amethyst shining in its center.

I look at the ring. I look at Patrick. I look back at the ring. Patrick chuckles and wraps his arms around my waist, pulling me closer.

"I didn't know how to top Matt, but I thought this could do the trick." His lips graze my ear. "Will you go to the winter formal with me?"

"Um. *Yes.*" I shake my head. "Patrick, this is too—"

He stops me with a kiss. "No, it's not. It's a reminder."

"Of what?"

"That on February nineteenth, you'll be free." He touches the amethyst—my birthstone—then pulls the ring out of its velvet home and slips it onto my middle finger. It's a perfect fit, which isn't surprising; my boyfriend is a details kind of guy. "And it's to remind you that we still have a sunrise to run into after graduation, remember?"

Graduation. Him going to school in New York, probably, and me going . . . I push the thought away and instead stare down at my ring. The purple gem is a shimmering, deep pool of color.

"It's beautiful. You're crazy, but it's beautiful. I love it." I reach up and press my lips to his. "I love *you.*"

He grins. "But the real question is . . . will it match your dress?" He pretends to look very serious as he asks this.

I give him an arch look. "I guess you'll have to find out on February fourteenth." The winter formal is on Valentine's Day, naturally.

"I can't wait." He leans in for another kiss, but I gasp as a horrible thought crosses my mind. "Shit."

Patrick raises his eyebrows.

"My mom," I explain. "Ohmygod. Can't you see her and Chuck insisting that you and Matt pick Benny and me up at the house?"

Patrick heaves a sigh and twines his fingers through mine. "I guess I have to meet her sometime." He takes in my strained expression, and his eyes crinkle up. "Is it true the camera really adds ten pounds?"

"Patrick. Seriously!"

His face grows thoughtful. "Chloe, I really don't care. Honestly.

I spent a year wanting to be with you, thinking you hated me half the time because you hardly ever talked to me. Now we're together, and the way I feel about you . . ." He looks down and absently plays with a lock of my hair. "I'm perfectly fine declaring it to the whole world."

"I hope you mean that in the literal sense," I say.

His eyes meet mine. "I do."

~ ~ ~

"Nice. More than nice. You look amazing," says Lexie™.

This is seriously high praise. My sister would never, ever tell me something this nice unless it were true. I twirl around in my vintage 1920s dress, savoring its snug fit and shimmering beadwork. It's a deep royal purple (to match my ring) with black accents.

"You sure?"

"Oh, yeah. If we were lesbians and you weren't my sister . . . okay, scratch that. I really shouldn't say stuff like that when cameras are right downstairs."

I laugh and, on impulse, give her a hug. Her body goes stiff, but she puts her arms around me. We haven't hugged for at least five years.

"Thanks for getting me ready, Lex."

She pulls away and adjusts the black shimmery beaded necklace that's looped around my neck twice and takes another look at my ring.

"Are you *sure* you're not engaged?"

I swat at her with my beaded evening bag. "Yes! God." My cheeks flush, and she hands me her favorite lipstick.

"Lose it, and I'll kill you," she warns.

I put it in my bag just as the doorbell rings.

"Dude, I don't know what is more exciting—that Matt's actually going to pin a boutonniere on Benny or that I'm *finally* going to meet the enigmatic Patrick Sheldon."

I shiver just hearing his name, and she shakes her head. "Oh, you've got it bad."

We meet Benny in the hallway, and I squeal when I see him in his tux. "You look so hot!"

He grins. "And you look like you're going to a speakeasy. I *love* this!"

"Benton™! Bonnie™! The boys are here," Mom calls up the stairs.

"The *boys*. Classic," says Lex.

We start walking, but she holds up her phone. "Wait! Say 'condoms'!" We start laughing, and she snaps the photo. "Got it. Let's go."

My heart pinches a little as I think about how much closer the three of us have gotten over the past month or so. I know she's going to feel betrayed that we saw the lawyer without her. I don't even want to think about how hurt she'll be.

But first things first; Patrick is about to make his television debut.

"Hi, Matt!" I hear Mom downstairs, fussing over him. "And *you* must be Patrick!"

I don't like the way she says *you*, but when I reach the bottom of the stairs, she's giving him a genuine smile. Patrick looks toward me, and his mouth sort of drops into an O. I'm sure the cameras are zooming in.

I wish MetaReel wasn't filming this moment, but he's so freaking sexy I almost don't care. I rush down the stairs and throw my arms around him, and he laughs into my neck.

I pull back and take in his black suit with its pencil-thin black tie. Wow. "Hi."

He smiles, ignoring the cameras like he ignores 98 percent of the Taft population. "Hi."

I turn to the crowd that's giggling and ogling in the living room. "Patrick, this is . . . everyone. Everyone . . . Patrick."

"Hi, Patrick!" shrieks Jazzy.

He grins, totally at ease. "You must be Jasmine™."

Mom laughs. "Ah, so you've heard all about our resident loudmouth."

"Kirk," says Kirk, holding out his hand. Patrick hesitates for a slight moment—I'm probably the only one who notices—then he shakes it.

"And *I'm* Lexie™, aka your girlfriend's stylist for the evening."

"Hey." Patrick smiles at her, and Lex gives me a thumbs-up. I redden and shake my head. I can't believe I'm saying this, but I'm actually going to miss my stupid sister.

"*Mom*. I like it the way it is."

Mom's trying to smooth Benny's hair with a spit treatment, and he jumps back. Matt laughs, but it's a little bit forced. He keeps his eyes on the ground, his shoulders hunched. He relaxes only when Benny's physically touching him. For a second, my eyes get blurry, watching them adjust each other's bow ties. They are so incredibly brave, being here, doing this.

"Matt! Look what I can do!" Violet™ attempts a cartwheel, nearly bashing Deston™, my nine-year-old brother, in the face.

"Yo!" he says, jumping out of the way.

I don't know what it is, but this is the most fun and family-like we've felt in a really long time. I wonder if I'm seeing my family through Patrick's eyes, or if we're all really good at performing. Chuck leans against the doorway that leads to the kitchen, and I stiffen at the pleased expression on his face. Patrick must have felt that because he looks past Benny and murmurs in my ear, "That's Chuck?"

I nod and turn my back on our resident puppet master. I'm not doing this for him—I'm doing it for my family. "Boutonniere time."

He holds up a clear box with a simple cluster of white and purple orchids. "Corsage time."

"These are so pretty," I say.

The look in Patrick's eyes tells me everything he would say if there weren't nineteen other people squished into our entryway. Wordlessly, I find his hand and intertwine my fingers with his. He gives me a gentle squeeze.

"You two, give me some love," says Lex. We turn and grin at her camera phone.

"Farrow™, go get the flowers out of the fridge," Mom says. She holds up her camera. "Let's get some pictures in the living room before you guys go, okay?"

Farrow™ rolls her eyes at me as she shuffles into the kitchen, and again, I get that pang of guilt and sadness I'd felt with Lex. How can I just leave them? But then I see Chuck whisper something in Kirk's ear, and I feel a sense of resolve roll over me once more.

Pictures take forever because, of course, Chuck is stage-managing the whole thing. I get a sense of smug satisfaction knowing MetaReel can't get into the dance, though. I pin Patrick's boutonniere to the lapel of his suit, and I hold out my hand for him to slip on my corsage. His fingers lightly brush the inside of my wrist, and I flush, remembering his lips in that exact spot when we were in his room. He winks at me when no one's looking. I wonder if people will be able to see how much we want each other, when we're encased in flat-screen televisions in living rooms all over the country. Is the electric current that is forever running between us visible on film?

"Wow, your family is . . . *wow*," Patrick whispers.

I can't even imagine what it would feel like to walk into this, coming from a three-person family.

"I know, right?"

"Okay, now one with Bonnie™ and all the girls," says Mom.

"Dude, Mom, we actually have to *go* at some point," Benny says.

"*Dude*, you only have one winter formal," she jokes. She gestures to me. "Real quick, hon." She grabs my arm and puts me in the center of all the girls.

It's like we have a cease-fire or something. It reminds me of this French movie, *Joyeux Noël*, that we watched in history last year when we were studying World War I. It was Christmas Eve and these French, German, and Scottish soldiers all climbed out of the trenches and hung out and showed one another pictures of their sweethearts. They shared booze and laughter and songs. But then they went back to killing one another the next day.

Patrick watches off to the side, his hands in his pockets. I love the way he looks at me. There's chaos all around him—shrieking kids, a camera crew, my mother. But he's undaunted, calm as ever, just leaning against the wall. It's like he can put the world on mute for me. When we're done I walk over to him, and he slides an arm around my shoulders.

Chuck whispers something into Mom's ear, and she nods. "Okay, guys, we have a special surprise for you. This way."

"Hell. I should have seen this coming," I mutter.

Patrick squeezes my arm. "Almost done," he whispers.

When we get outside, a gleaming black limo is in the driveway.

My heart plummets. I was really, really, *really* hoping to be alone at some point with Patrick tonight. And the last thing I want is to attract the whole school's attention rolling up to the formal as if I'm arriving at the Emmys. Benny looks at me, and I swear he's thinking the same thing; the limo is bugged. There's probably a hidden camera in it, too.

"Mom, thanks, but . . . we'd really rather take Matt's car," Benny says.

Mom pulls him outside. "Just come look at it!"

"Let's just take the damn thing to my house, and we'll switch to my car," Patrick whispers.

"Were there any Vultures outside?" I ask, my voice low.

He shakes his head.

"Okay."

We go down the stairs, and I give Benny a *follow my lead* look.

"No, let's take the limo. This is great. Thanks, Mom."

I so want to flip off Chuck right now. Instead, during the noisy good-byes, I tell Patrick that the limo is probably rigged to Meta-Reel's standards. He says something under his breath that wouldn't be allowed during prime time. We pile into the limo, and Patrick gives the driver directions to his house.

"This is the MetaReel-doesn't-want-to-get-sued-for-underage-drinking minibar," Benny complains.

I grab a can of Coke. "We'll survive."

Benny starts whispering in Matt's ear, and his eyes grow wide. He must be cluing him in to the wonders of hidden cameras. I hear him say, "Seriously?"

Rule Number One of being in the cast of *Baker's Dozen*: never underestimate MetaReel.

Patrick puts his hand on my knee and leans close to my ear. "You are so beautiful, Chloe Baker."

I bite off my pleased grin. "It's all Lexie™." I finger his tie. "You clean up pretty good yourself, Patrick Sheldon."

The four of us, by unspoken agreement, start talking shit about MetaReel in pig Latin for the rest of the ride to Patrick's house. A sampling:

Benny: "EtaReelmae ancae ucksae ymae ickdae."

Matt whispers something to Benny, and even though I don't hear what he says, I blush all the way to the tips of my ears when I see the expression on Benny's face.

Me: "Istersae ightrae erehae!"

Patrick laughs.

Twenty minutes later, the limo pulls up outside Patrick's house. We ditch the driver and jump into Patrick's old Volvo. He opens the passenger door for me as Benny and Matt get in the backseat. Their doors slam, and he leans forward and kisses me.

"More, please," I whisper.

He smiles and moves closer.

"Hey, lovers, we'd like to get one dance in tonight!" yells Benny.

Patrick gives me an Eskimo kiss and then shuts my door after I get inside.

"Whatever. Like you two weren't just doing the same thing," I say.

Matt holds up his hand. "I plead the Fifth."

Patrick backs out of the driveway, and we give the bemused limo driver a little honk and wave, then we're off.

"Patrick, you are an evil genius," says Matt.

Benny hands me his iPod. "Put on my MJ mix," he says.

We get through "Thriller," "Don't Stop 'Till You Get Enough," and "Bad" before we pull into the familiar Taft lot. Suddenly I feel nervous. In my excitement about the dance, I'd forgotten to pick a wallflower gown; instead, I have a one-of-a-kind vintage ensemble, my hair pulled back into a wavy, low bun held together with a vibrant peacock-feather hairpiece.

As if sensing my sudden apprehension, Patrick holds me against him a little tighter as we walk to the open doors of the gym.

"This is *your* night. You belong here. Screw MetaReel," he says.

My eyes sweep over these three elegant guys who have been through hell and back because of this stupid, stupid show. "This is *our* night."

Benny pulls a flask out of his jacket pocket. "I'll drink to that." I give him a look. "But not too much," he adds.

Matt takes a swig. "Okay, baby. Ready to be Taft High's first openly gay couple at the winter formal?"

Benny grins. "Hell, yeah."

SEASON 18, EPISODE 1

(The One with the Beach Balls)

The winter formal was amazing. I became one with the crush of silk, lace, and polyester on the dance floor. I twirled around with Tessa and Mer. I got to see Matt and Benny do the YMCA and witnessed Schwartz attempting to teach Principal Harding how to salsa. When we were tired of dancing, Patrick and I would sneak into a dark corner or he'd pull me onto his lap at one of the candlelit tables and we'd point out hilarious things on the dance floor. Then we'd go back out at the next slow song and create a little bubble of happiness around us. It was bittersweet; Benny and I were teetering on the edge of moving out, suing MetaReel, and creating a media frenzy. This night felt like a last hurrah, like we could blaze our brightest, at the apex of our insane adolescence. This was our Mardi Gras before the dark days of Lent.

"I feel almost . . . normal," I'd whispered to Benny, during a punch bowl break.

He nodded. "It's like Taft has temporary amnesia. I wonder when they'll start remembering we're freaks."

As I looked over the sea of sparkling gowns and slick tuxedos, I realized that, for once, I belonged.

I felt a tap on my shoulder.

"Hi," said a girl I'd never seen before. "Can I, like, get a picture with you?"

So much for temporary amnesia. I opened my mouth, started to say, *Oh, um, okay, sure*, but then I stopped. I could hear Patrick's voice in my head: *When are you going to stop letting people walk all over you?*

"Actually," I said, "no offense, but I don't know you."

Benny grinned and raised his glass to me. "To my baby sis, who finally grew a pair."

The girl had been annoyed, maybe even embarrassed. I'd felt bad about that, but it was nice just to say *no* for once.

Now the morning sunlight is slanting across my body in sharp lines, and the night has taken on the fuzziness of a dream, the memories already soft around the edges. The sunlight on Patrick's ring makes glittering purple stains on the wall, and my orchid corsage is lying on my bedside table, wilting, but still beautiful. It had really happened. I grab my camera and look through the pictures, turning over each memory like a cherished possession. There's me, Tessa, and Mer, our mouths open wide with laughter. Patrick and me, kissing during a slow dance. Benny with his arm around my shoulder. Benny and Matt pre-kiss. And one of me, all by myself. Patrick must have taken this when I wasn't paying attention. My face is in profile; I'm looking at the dance floor, grinning. Happy. Content.

The next photo goes back to the first pictures of the night. Me with my family. My stomach turns, and I shut the camera off. My hair is stiff, full of last night's hairspray, and I pull back the covers and stretch. I'll be eighteen in five days.

This is my last Sunday morning at home.

~ ~ ~

On Thursday, I wake up to the sound of my mother softly singing "Happy Birthday."

"Thanks," I mumble, still half asleep.

She grabs me in a tight hug. "You know, the day you were born was the happiest day of my life. For so long I thought I couldn't have children, but then there you were—healthy, adorable, *mine*." Her eyes are soft in the early morning sunlight, and I think about what my dad said, how sad she'd been. She tucks my hair behind my ear like she used to do when I was little. I stiffen, but I don't think she notices. "I know it's been a tough few months for you, but I want this year to be better. I love you, okay?"

I nod, and she hugs me again. "There're pancakes for when you get downstairs."

Guilt rips through me, and I bury my face in a pillow as soon as she shuts the door behind her. I'm a horrible person. How can I just leave my family like this?

My phone rings—Patrick. The room suddenly feels brighter, warmer, just because his number's on the screen.

"Hey, you," I say.

"Happy birthday."

"Thanks." God, I wish he were here right now.

"Can you do me a favor?"

"Um, sure."

"Open your closet."

"What did you do?"

I can hear the smile in his voice. "Just open it."

I cross to my closet; inside is a vase filled with delicate sunrise-colored roses. "*Oh*," I say. I take out the vase and bury my nose in the bouquet.

I hear Patrick's quiet laugh. "You like them?"

"Uh, *yeah*. Did Benny charge you for delivery?"

"I just told him to bill me later."

"Thank you," I whisper.

"You're welcome. Now, hurry up so I can see you before first period."

When I come downstairs, my place at the table is covered with handmade cards from all the kids. Jazzy puts a crown she made for me on my head, and Lex gives me a shiny gift bag. Inside is a new diary, leather bound, with delicate flowers carved into it. I glance at my sister and she waves her hand, like the perfect gift was nothing, no big deal.

"Just hide this one better, okay?"

"Thanks, Lex." I feel a pang, wondering how she'll feel when Benny and I make our announcement tomorrow.

The birthday love is too much; I shove down the last few bites of my mom's pancakes, anxious to get out of here before I break down and confess everything. I wish Puma Guy would put the camera on someone else, but I know it'll be trained on me all the way to school.

When I get on campus, Diane Finchburg is sitting at her desk, drinking a cup of coffee. I knock on the open door, and she looks up from her newspaper with a smile.

"Chloe! How's it going?"

"Um." I grip the straps of my backpack and stand frozen in her doorway. For a minute, I can't move. I'm paralyzed with an overwhelming sense of dread that's been growing inside me ever since I sat down in the leather chair across from Melinda Greenberg's desk.

Diane stands up and crosses to me. No shoes, as usual. She has cupids on her socks. She puts an arm around me and guides me to the chair I usually occupy when I'm in here. I slip off my backpack and sit down heavily. Diane crosses to a small coffeepot next to her desk.

"Coffee?"

I nod.

"Sugar, cream?"

I nod.

I can't say anything until I've had a few sips. The hot liquid seems to burn away the lump in my throat. We sit there in companionable silence for a few minutes and the only sound is the soft tick of the clock on her wall.

"Today's my eighteenth birthday," I blurt out.

"Is that a bad thing?"

"I'm moving out. Tomorrow."

Diane's face remains expressionless, but I can see the sympathy in her eyes. God, that's not what I came here for. Why *did* I come here?

"That's a big step," Diane says.

"I have to do it. I can't be in that house anymore." I take another fortifying sip of coffee. "But this morning my mom was all clingy and made pancakes for me, and I just felt so . . . so . . ."

Tears swim in my eyes, salt my coffee. My voice finally breaks. "I'm really gonna miss them. All of them."

Diane hands me a tissue.

"Do you want to move out?" Her voice is gentle, a slight nudge.

I think of the camera in my face this morning as my mom piled pancakes on my plate.

"Yes. But I know she won't understand. And every time she's nice to me, it makes it harder to . . . I mean, the night of the formal, it was like suddenly everything was okay. I mean, not okay, because Chuck was there, but she was laughing and taking pictures, and the whole time I just kept thinking about how I'm going to stab her in the back, you know?"

"Have you tried to talk about this with your mother, maybe without the cameras around? It's possible that if she knew how serious you were, she would—"

I shake my head. "No. It doesn't matter if the cameras are around or not. All of our conversations just end up as fights."

"How does that make you feel?" I give Diane a look, and her lip twitches. "Okay, that was a bit shrinklike, wasn't it?"

I manage a half smile, then bury my face in my mug.

"I'm happy to speak with her, if it'll help," she offers. "Or maybe the three of us together—"

"No," I snap at her, wild and skittish. She jolts in her chair a little. "Sorry," I mumble.

"That's okay."

The sounds in the hallway get louder, and I know the bell for first period is going to ring any minute. Patrick's probably looking for me, and I'll need time to explain my red eyes. *Ugh.* I should never have come in here. I put the coffee on her desk and stand up.

"Thanks for the coffee."

"Sure." Diane gives me a look that's somehow half frown, half smile. "Well, let me know if there's anything I can do, okay?"

"Okay."

I stand up and put my backpack on.

"Chloe?" When I look up, she throws me a pack of Skittles. "Happy birthday."

My meeting with Diane takes the edge off my morning. I think part of me wanted to talk to her because I felt like I needed permission to still move out even though my mom was really sweet to me today. Of course, Benny's leaving, too, and that makes it about a million times easier. But "easier" is relative.

At the end of the day I'm walking out to the student parking lot, my hand in Patrick's, when I see the two familiar black vans parked in the loading area in front of the school.

"What the hell?" says Benny.

I get a text from Mom on my MetaReel phone:

Leave your car here. I have a surprise for you and Benny.

I show Benny the text. "This can't be good," he mutters. He gets on his cell phone. "Matt. There might be a change of plans."

Patrick squeezes my hand. "Can I help?"

I shake my head miserably. "No. I better just go find out what this is."

He pulls me to him for a kiss that is long and sweet. I'm sure my entire family can see us, but I don't care because I'm melting and I don't ever want to be more than negative five centimeters away from him.

"I love you," he whispers in my ear. I can hear other things in those three words: *It's going to be okay. Don't freak out. You can do this.*

One of the vans honks, and I let go of Patrick. "Call you later?"

He nods, and Benny and I trudge over to our family.

As we get closer, two MetaReel cameramen sneak out from behind the vans and the doors burst open. Little hands throw confetti and beach balls at us. They're all inside, even Lex. They must have taken her out of school early today.

"Surprise!" The noise of my family's yelling carries across the whole parking lot and the back of my neck prickles. Cars drive past and honk; every student at Taft has their eyes on me.

"What's this?" I manage. My teeth are clenched, and Mom must notice the look of horror on my face because she bursts out laughing and wraps her arms around me.

"It's a birthday surprise, not an alien attack!" She turns and shouts over her shoulder. "Ready, you guys? One, two—"

"WE'RE GOING ON A CRUISE!" A wall of excited, happy sound.

Benny's body stiffens beside me.

"When?" I whisper.

"Right now!" shouts Jazzy.

"*What?*" Benny and I say at the same time.

But they're not listening, they're singing "Happy Birthday," and everyone's looking at me, please please stop looking at me. When they're through singing and Mom tries to usher us into the car, I catch Benny's eye, and he nods. I gently shrug away from my mom's grip.

"Mom, Benny and I have to talk to you."

SEASON 18, EPISODE 2

(The One with the Suitcases)

I see a flicker of irritation in Mom's eyes, but she covers it up with a too-bright voice. "Okay. Let's talk on the way. We have a six-hour drive to San Diego ahead of us."

"Mom. Can you come over here for a sec?" Benny motions toward the student parking lot. Smart. MetaReel cameras aren't allowed on school property.

My palms are slick with sweat, and it feels like someone pumped me full of helium. Everything buzzes.

Lex catches my eye and mouths, *WTF?* but I just shake my head. She'll know soon enough.

"Benny, what's going on?" Mom's still holding a beach ball, and the bright primary colors clash with everything I'm feeling inside.

"Mom, please. Just. Can we talk to you really quick?" he says.

Chuck and Lacey Production Assistant get out of a third van. I hadn't noticed before, but of course MetaReel's going on the cruise, too.

"Beth, kids, let's go. You don't want to miss the boat."

This is so MetaReel. They're purposefully cutting the time close to heighten the drama. *Will the Bakers make it in time? Or will their ship of dreams take off without them? Tune in Tuesday* . . .

Mom throws up her hands. "Chuck, I have no idea what's going on. Kids, either you tell me what you have to say here, or we'll talk on the road. We don't have a lot of time."

Chuck's eyes meet mine, and he gives me a hard look. I hold his gaze while memories of his larger-than-life presence throughout my childhood crumble at my feet. *This*—right now—is reality. If he wants it on camera, so be it. I turn my back on him.

"We can't go with you," I say. My voice is low, but I can hear my siblings repeating what I said to one another.

"What do you mean? Of course you can. Sweetheart, it's your birthday—"

"My *eighteenth* birthday. It's my choice not to go, right?"

The cameras move closer, and now Lex and Kirk are out of the van, moving toward us. Mom's voice gets low, scary.

"Bonnie™, don't do this right now. You have no idea the pressure—" She stops, remembering the cameras. "This is for *your* birthday. We're not going without you, and if we don't go, everyone will be so disappointed. It's already paid for. Sandra packed your bags and got you some really cute new stuff." She sighs when I don't say anything. "Honey, I know you'll miss Patrick, but it's only for a few days, and you're too attached anyway."

Benny puts his hand on my arm just as I'm about to go off on her. He speaks in a Voice of Reason. "Mom. We don't want to go on a cruise with MetaReel."

"Jesus Christ," Mom mutters.

Just then the Vultures arrive. Someone must have tipped them off. Soon we're surrounded by paparazzi.

"Bonnie™, Benton™, get in the van. *Now.*" (Mom)

"Bonnie™, one picture, sweetheart." (Vulture)

"Benton™, how's the boyfriend?" (Vulture)

"Lexie™! One smile, honey!" (Vulture)

"Get away, you mangy beast!" (Lex, possibly stealing a line from a play)

"Get in, kids. We'll talk in the van." (Mom)

"No." (Me)

I shake my head, my eyes filling. This sucks so bad.

"Bonnie™, you heard your mother. You need to obey her." (Kirk)

"We need to talk to our mom, okay? Can you just . . ." Benny makes a go-away motion in Kirk's direction.

A Vulture gets closer, and Chuck steps in front of him. "This is a private conversation," he snaps.

What the hell part of this conversation was ever *private*? Part of me wants to laugh hysterically; the other part is itching to scream.

Mom grabs my arm, but I yank it out of her iron grip. Out of the corner of my eye, I notice Patrick and Matt edging closer. Patrick looks like he's about two seconds away from stepping in. For a split second, we lock eyes. Then I look away. It's now or never.

"We're moving out."

As the words come out of my mouth, time suspends itself. The only sound is the blood pounding in my ears. A bird flies overhead. There's a scratch on the front door of the van closest to me. A tiny stain near the collar of Mom's shirt. Confetti in Benny's hair.

Then:

An explosion of sound. Everyone starts talking at once, and the

Vultures are screaming at us, trying to get pictures, quotes, anything. Patrick's suddenly there and shoves one of them off me and then he's beside me, gripping my hand. The triplets are crying, Lex is snapping at my brothers to shut up, Mom's on a tirade ("You're doing this right now? Here? How can you do this to us? Do you have any *idea* how this is going to affect our family? All you had to do was wait until graduation, but no, of course not, Bonnie™, you only think of yourself."), and Chuck is talking a mile a minute on his cell. Another Vulture tries to grab Benny, and Matt's on him, going off about privacy and a lot of other stuff he's obviously kept bottled up inside.

"Chlo, let me get you out of here. C'mon, let's go." Patrick's voice, soft and gentle in my ear, his hand gently tugging. I look at him as the chaos continues and nod.

"Benny?"

He, Matt, and Kirk are in a heated discussion. Kirk's voice rises higher: "Fine, I told Kaye you're gay. You know what? *Nobody* cares!"

"You piece of *shit*."

For a second we turn, surprised at where this comes from. Lexie™ is standing next to the van, her arms crossed, glaring at Kirk.

"Lexie™?" I think Mom meant to say this in a you're-in-big-trouble kind of way, but it comes out more as a question. It's like she's finally realizing that she doesn't know any of us.

"Beth, we need to get on the road *now*." Chuck's standing next to two suitcases—mine and Benny's. "Give the kids their bags, and you can sort this out after you have a nice, relaxing time on the cruise."

Mom's face is pale as she looks at our suitcases. "But I can't just go when—"

"They're adults now, Beth. They've made their choice. Let's all take a breather, and we'll talk when we come back," Kirk says.

I'm dimly aware of the tide of Vultures receding; school security has finally got them under control. It's quiet again.

"Mom, I'm sor—" I start, but her voice slices through the air.

"Don't talk to me," she says.

She climbs into the front seat of the van and slams the door. My siblings look at Benny and me, their expressions ranging from confusion to terror. Lex comes up to me, and the most shocking thing of all happens—she gives me a hug.

"You're insane, but I love you." She hugs Benny. "You too." When she pulls away, her eyes are dry, but there's disappointment in them. "That doesn't mean I'm not going on a free cruise."

I smile. "Get some sun for me?"

"Yeah."

Chuck shoos her back into the van, then narrows his eyes at me. "Do you remember what I told you?"

"Yeah, I remember." My voice is edged with barely contained contempt.

"Okay, then."

Bastard.

Chuck gets into the third van with Lacey Production Assistant on his heels, and the last MetaReel camera slowly edges backward, the lens still trained on Benny and me. Confetti litters the sidewalk, and students stand around the area, staring unabashedly. Benny, Patrick, Matt, and I are in the middle of it, staring down the camera.

The vans start up and then they're gone.

"Well," Benny says, "that's a wrap."

~ ~ ~

"Chloe. Put down the packing tape." Mer is holding one of the wine coolers she filched from her mother's stock in one hand and a box of brownie bites in the other. It is so weird to see her standing in my bedroom.

"Mer, I don't care that it's my birthday. Seriously. What if they come back early? I need to—"

She gives me an arch look. "Okay, fine. I know when my powers of persuasion aren't enough." She turns and yells down the hall. "Patrick, she won't stop. It's your turn now."

"They're back?"

Patrick and Tessa had gone into town to pick up Chinese takeout for all of us while Benny and I packed.

I hear Patrick come up the stairs, and Mer holds up her hands. "These will be downstairs for you."

I give her a wan smile. "Thanks, Mer."

"Yeah, yeah." She winks and steps aside for Patrick to come into the room. He shuts the door behind him and immediately gathers me into his arms.

"I got your favorite," he murmurs. "And cheesecake might be involved, too."

"Thanks," I mumble against his chest.

He looks around the room. "You got a lot done."

I nod. "Well, there are thirteen kids. Someone's gonna want their own room."

He smooths back my hair and looks down at me. "Not your problem. So."

He reaches up to turn off the overhead light. The room suddenly feels less empty. My desk lamp is dim and casts an orange glow. "I hear I'm supposed to convince you to come downstairs."

I shiver as his fingers travel down my arms. "Um. This won't convince me to *ever* leave this room."

"Hmm. How do you feel about cold Chinese food?"

I pull him to the bed. "Sounds delicious."

Half an hour later, we manage to get downstairs. As soon as we walk into the kitchen, Tessa rolls her eyes.

"I told you it was a bad idea to send *Patrick* up there."

I scowl at her and put my tangled hair into a messy bun. "I had a box to finish packing."

She stuffs an eggroll into her mouth. "Uh-huh."

Benny shoots Patrick a look, and he shakes his head. "I don't break my promises."

"What promises?" asks Mer.

"Nothing," I say. My face grows warm as I pile orange chicken and fried rice onto plates for us. I decide not to mention how close we've gotten to breaking that promise.

"Ohhh," says Mer, knowingly. She gives Patrick a sympathetic look. "Bet you wish you'd never agreed to *that*."

Patrick raises his hands. "No comment."

"*Anyway,*" I say. "Thanks for coming over, guys."

"It's your birthday!" Mer says. She hands me a wine cooler, then lifts hers up. "To Chloe and Ben's independence day!"

"Hell, yeah," says Matt.

Tessa moans after she takes a long swig. "I have drunk Asian face, don't I?"

I take in her bright red cheeks and nod. "But it's cute."

"*Ugh.*" She shoves her wine cooler away and fills a glass with water.

There's cheesecake and presents and a tipsy tour of the house. It's strange to be here with my friends, with Patrick. To walk around without cameras. It feels empty, cavernous. In all my life, I've never been home when there weren't at least eight people around—I don't know what I'm going to do without the chaos. I know I complain about them a lot, but I do love my family. There's something special about living in a house that hums with the energy of so many people. It's certainly never boring. I'm sure I'll love the quiet of Tessa's home at first, but I can already feel the creeping loneliness that's only going to grow each month as we get closer to graduation. Where will I live when Benny and Tessa go off to college?

"Penny for your thoughts?" asks Tessa, linking her arm through mine.

We're in the basement now, and the guys are playing foosball. I check my phone, just to make sure my mom didn't call. Nope. Two missed calls from Lex, one from Farrow™, one from Dad.

"Just thinking about how I'm going to be a lonely old cat lady living all by myself someday," I say.

Tessa shakes her head. "Not if Patrick has anything to do with it."

"What's that supposed to mean?"

I watch my boyfriend score a goal with expert precision. Is there anything he's not good at?

"Chlo, that boy has *forever* written all over his face when he looks at you. A cat lady you shall never be."

I wish that made me feel better, but it doesn't. Everything is going to change this fall. *Everything.*

The grandfather clock in the living room chimes eleven, and people start getting ready to go. Tomorrow is, after all, a school day.

One that Benny and I have every intention of skipping. There is a certain amount of satisfaction in knowing I can write a note to excuse myself.

"You're sure you don't want to sleep at my place tonight?" Tessa asks as she puts on her All-Stars.

I run my hand along the mantel with the thirteen pictures. Will they keep ours up?

"Yeah, but thanks. We'll be there tomorrow. I want one more night to . . . you know."

She gives me a hug. "Happy birthday, friend."

Patrick and I linger out by his car long after everyone has gone. Benny's inside, taking a shower.

"I wish I could stay over," he says, holding me against him. "I really hate the idea of you sleeping all alone tonight."

I'm so drained and buzzed and broken, I know I'll fall asleep as soon as my head hits the pillow. Still, it'd be nice to be in his arms.

"Why can't you have parents who want to be cool and let you spend the night at your girlfriend's house?"

He chuckles. "Yeah, my parents would definitely not be down with that."

"I am so tired of rules," I mutter.

He kisses my forehead. "Good thing we're gonna graduate soon."

"Yeah."

"Happy birthday."

He gives me a long, lingering kiss and then gets into his car. As I watch him drive away, the enormity of what Benny and I have done and the horrible scene outside school hits me all over again.

I'm finally free of *Baker's Dozen*. So why do I feel as bad as ever?

BREAKING NEWS:

Bonnie™ and Benton™ Baker Leave *Baker's Dozen*

BY HAUTE COCOA

Oh, cast of *Baker's Dozen*, how I love you. Whenever I feel like complaining about my family, I just have to TiVo <u>yours</u> and, suddenly, I feel better.

I don't know why last night's news that Bonnie™ and Benton™ Baker have <u>moved out</u> and quit the cast of *Baker's Dozen* is such a shocker. HELLO! Did anyone else see the <u>diary episode</u> or watch the <u>Kaye Gibbons fiasco</u>? Unfortunately, Mama Bear still doesn't get why B&B said sayonara. "My heart is broken," tweeted Beth Baker-Miller. But that didn't stop her from going on a <u>cruise to Mexico</u>.

I swear, *Baker's Dozen* is America'a answer to the *telenovela*. The drama never stops! Not only have B&B moved in with BFF <u>Tessa Lee</u>, they're <u>planning to go to court</u>, too. Rumor has it that the two reality TV stars are <u>suing MetaReel</u> for damages, including unpaid wages and defamation of character. ¡Ai ai ai!

"My clients have the right to privacy and to be paid for the work they have done," said their lawyer, <u>Melinda Greenberg</u>. Not only that, they'll be helping out the ACLU with their lawsuit against MetaReel. I heart the drama!

No doubt MetaReel producer <u>Chuck Daniels</u> is pissed—and not just because he has a <u>mullet</u>. Hey, Chuck, 1981 called—it wants its hairstyle back!

This is what Chuckie said about the show's future: "We're reevaluating if it makes sense to keep on doing the show. This came out of left field."

Oh, *hell* no! You can't cancel—how else will I know that my family is relatively normal? And what would I do without Beth's <u>televised Botox treatments</u>? One thing's for sure: *Baker's Dozen* is more exciting than ever.

Tell celeb.com what you think:

❑ Sour Grapes: Bonnie™ and Benton™ are totally overreacting.

❑ Just Deserts: MetaReel deserves to pay through the nose. Viva B&B!

SEASON 18, EPISODE 3

(The One with the Letters)

*L*iving with the Lees is an adjustment, but I couldn't have asked for a better interim life. Mr. Lee is gregarious and kind; Mrs. Lee is an amazing cook and probably the smartest woman I have ever met. Tessa's little sister, Casey, is sweet, too—but she makes me miss the triplets. Though Tessa wanted me to share her room, I insisted on being in the guest bedroom with Benny. I didn't want living together to affect our friendship, and I knew I'd be underfoot if I invaded her space like that. Besides, it's comforting when I wake up in a strange room to see my brother a few feet away. He and Mr. Lee clicked right away, and for the first time, I realized how hard it must have been for Benny to grow up without a real father figure around. I often walk in on them playing cards, talking politics, or discussing Benny's college options. I'd never seen him like that with Kirk or Dad.

It's been three weeks, and I still haven't heard from my mom. Lex says to give it time, but I don't know if I can ever forgive Mom for the life she chose for us. I'm so angry, so bitter. The day after my birthday, Benny and I were careful to take anything we didn't want to part with out of the house. We didn't say it, but I think both of us knew this was a forever kind of thing. It was hard leaving. I spent half the morning writing notes to my siblings and putting them on their beds with chocolates I'd bought at the gas station up the street, and I left my winter formal dress on Lex's bed—I knew she loved it, and she'd get way more use out of it than I would. Benny and I cried the whole way to the Lees' house. They welcomed us with open arms and pizza.

It's hardest at dinnertime. It's weird, sitting around this little table of six people, calmly discussing the day's events. I'm so used to the pushing and shoving and there never quite being enough food to go around, so you always have to raid the cupboard after dinner for a snack. Not to mention dinner preparations; at my house, the kitchen was an industrial hive, where all of us were put to work and had designated duties. At the Lees' house, each night is a little different, but deviating from a routine doesn't create total chaos.

I watched the show last week for the first time since the notebook-throwing episode. I was so homesick that I had to check in, even if it was only in the way millions of other Americans could. Benny didn't want to, so I went over to Patrick's house, and we watched it in his room. I cried the whole time. They talked about us a little, but the show was all about deciding who was going to get our rooms. Someone from the home improvement network came over and redesigned all the bedrooms, too. I was glad Benny hadn't watched it—part of me was certain Chuck had organized that episode for the express purpose of hurting us.

My dad and I have talked a few times since I left. Suddenly he's part of my life. He's insisted on helping Benny and me out financially, which is something I'm not too proud to refuse. I know my college fund is going to be used eventually, but since I don't even know if I'm going to college, I've stopped obsessing over it.

"Guess what?" Mer bounds into Schwartz's class, looking even peppier than usual.

"You've just won the lottery?" asks Tessa.

"No . . ."

"You found the cure for cancer?" I ask.

"Not quite . . ."

Patrick shrugs. "I've got nothin'."

Mer waves a piece of paper she'd been hiding behind her back. "I GOT IN!"

"Ohmygod!" (Me and Tessa)

Mer starts jumping around. "NYU, NYU! Can't you picture me on the subway? Ohmygod, I'm gonna live in the Village and get a hot poet boyfriend and go to diners at four A.M."

"And be on Broadway," adds Tessa.

Mer starts belting a Broadway tune about her being *one singular sensation*, and we laugh and applaud.

I really am happy for her, but my smile is plastic, a mannequin's too-shiny grin. Any day now, the rest of them will have their letters. They'll be clutching their bright futures and dancing around. Except me.

Smile. Nod. Repeat.

I try to ignore the fluttering in my chest and the beads of sweat that scatter across my forehead—my body's version of an early warning system. Halfway through Schwartz's class, I know I'm about to have a full-on panic attack. I raise my hand, surreptitiously wiping the sweat above my lip on the sleeve of my shirt.

"Can I get the pass?"

Schwartz gives me a concerned look, then nods. "Sure."

I get out of the room as fast as possible and burst into the infamous stall where I first saw the tabloid and slide down to the floor, pressing my back against the cool tile. My chest tightens, and I struggle to catch my breath. I wish I'd had the guts to be honest with my mom back in November and tell her I needed help with these, but I'd been afraid of my panic attacks being the subject of one of the episodes: "The One with the Psychiatrist." So for months now, I've been pretending I don't get them when actually I feel like I'm having a heart attack about once a week. Sometimes Diane Le Shrink's breathing thing helps, but it doesn't always. I count to ten. Exhale.

I check my phone—it feels like I've been in here for hours. Another minute of deep breathing and then I'm back on my feet. The walls are still closing in on me, but I think I'll be okay. I splash some water on my face and dry it with the brown paper towels that smell vaguely of baby spit-up. When I get back to class, everyone's in the middle of some activity with partners. Patrick's eyes follow me with concern, but I smile smile smile and, "So what did I miss?"

The next week it's Tessa. Stanford. Benny and Matt both get into USC by the time spring break rolls around. Each time it happens, I Smile, Nod, Repeat. Patrick doesn't say anything about Columbia, and I'm terrified to ask. But it's no use. I'm living on borrowed time. In a few months, he'll be gone.

"So why didn't you apply to a school?" Diane Le Shrink asks me this a few days before spring break.

386

"I don't know," I wail. "I couldn't think, with all the cameras around. It's like I didn't have the mental capacity to deal with it or something."

"But what about now? I'm sure there are still some schools that would consider you."

I twist Patrick's ring around and around my finger. "I wouldn't even know where to begin. And what would I major in? And how would I pay for it?"

I'm not great at school, but I'm not bad at it, either. I'm sure if I tried I could get into a semidecent one. Something beyond community college. But I'm not ready to do it all again—meeting people, lying about my past. Maybe that's what it comes down to. It's too daunting being me.

Diane gives me a spiel about financial aid and scholarships and don't I have a college fund, but I'm tuning her out. I think she can tell because she switches tactics.

"What about a job?"

"Yeah, I'd love one, but I can't work here because of the show. So then I have to go somewhere, like maybe another country, and find an apartment and live by myself and get a cat—"

"Why would you get a cat?"

"Because it's my destiny."

Diane gives me a long, thoughtful look. "What about traveling?"

I open my mouth to reject this, when something stops me. Out of all the things she's mentioned, I finally feel something lift inside me. A shift. And the burden I'm carrying feels a little lighter.

"Where would I go?"

Diane shrugs. "Anywhere. Do you have a passport?"

"Yeah." In season seven, my family went to Paris, and in season eleven, we went to Costa Rica. My heart falls a little as I realize I'll have to beg Lex to be my go-between to get it.

"Okay," Diane says. "Then you could go abroad—maybe learn a language or volunteer. Or you could travel around the States. Do a road trip with a friend."

"Ride into a sunrise," I whisper.

"Pardon?"

I shake my head. "Nothing. Just thinking out loud."

That night Patrick and I go to the park. Now that it's spring, the weather is mild. A slight chill gives an edge to the night, but the air smells like grass and flowers. We haven't been here together since our very first date, which feels about a million years ago.

"Hey, where are you?" he whispers.

We're up in the jungle gym, cuddling under a thin blanket. My eyes slide to his, and I let myself get a little lost in them. With just a street lamp to see from, they look like two black pools. I already feel like I'm saying good-bye.

"I'm here." I smile, knowing that's not what he meant.

Patrick takes a breath. "I got into Columbia."

And I know, duh, I *know* he did, but hearing him say it is the last nail in the coffin, the icing on the cake, the last straw, and oh, hell, I hate my life so much.

"That's great. I knew you would. I'm so proud of you."

I throw my arms around him, but his muscles are tense. I look up, rest my hand against his cheek.

"What's wrong?"

"Chloe, you're killing me." He sits up, pulling me with him. "You can be fake with everyone else, but not with me, okay?"

I nod. "When did you get in?"

He hesitates. "A month ago."

"*What?*" This comes out a little more forceful than I'd intended. "Why are you just telling me now?"

He throws up his hands, frustrated. "Because I knew this is how you'd feel, and it was sort of a bad time then."

A month ago . . . that would have been the week before my birthday. "Yeah, okay."

We fall into one of those loud silences where there's so much to say but you can't say any of it. The darkness softens the sharp lines of his face, makes him look like a memory. I've never felt so utterly, completely, totally alone in my life.

"You know, I think we have bad luck in this precise spot in the universe," Patrick says.

At first I don't know what he's talking about, but then I realize . . . of course. This is where we first kissed and I freaked out and ran off.

I look down and play with my ring. On. Off. On. Off.

"Yeah, you might be right about that."

He cups my face in his hands. "This doesn't change anything. I wish you could see that."

But it does. Change everything.

I let him kiss me, and just the feel of his lips on mine hurts too much. I feel like each kiss is numbered. I'm renting him until he finds a non-screwed-up, intelligent, motivated girl at Columbia who keeps him on his toes in all the best ways and has zero baggage and a normal family. And I'll be—where, what? I've lost everyone. Benny's going to LA, Tessa to Palo Alto, Mer and Patrick to New York, my family to MetaReel, Dad to Florida. I feel like I've been banished. What did I do wrong?

Maybe this is what I deserve. You can't screw up your own

suicide and then expect the universe to give you presents wrapped in the skin of a wonderful boy. That's just not the way it works.

I pull away. "Patrick, I—"

"I want you to come with me," he says quickly. "We'll get an apartment; it'll be amazing. We can wake up next to each other every morning. We can hang out with Meredith, and you can apply to a school once you figure out what you want to do. And then maybe in a couple years, we can . . ." He pauses, his eyes hopeful as they read the misery in my face. "We can make it official. If you want."

My eyes widen. "Are you . . ."

He brings his forehead to mine and nods. "Someday, when the time is right, yeah." That crooked grin. "I want to make an honest woman out of you."

"Patrick . . ."

"Just say yes," he whispers, his voice rough.

"To what?"

"All of it."

He kisses me again, more fully this time. For a while, I give in to the taste of spearmint and the way his hands move confidently along the dips and curves of my body. I let myself imagine we have that apartment in New York as I run my fingers through his hair and slip them under his shirt.

But it's all a fantasy. That life has too many ways it could go wrong. I pull away, and he looks at me, expectant. I am so in love with him that it physically hurts.

"Patrick, I can't just be your lame-ass girlfriend while you're at Columbia."

He takes my hand. "First of all, you could never be a lame-ass anything."

I sigh. "You know what I mean."

"I know you've been depressed the past few weeks every time someone mentions college. I know you're still confused about what you want." His voice grows softer. "I just thought *I* wasn't part of that confusion."

"You're not! You're the only thing I'm sure about." I bite my lip. "It just feels like everyone's moving toward something, and I'm treading water."

"What do *you* want?"

I shrug, my voice betraying me. "I don't know."

He clears his throat. "Do you love me?"

"I'm crazy in love with you—you know that."

He smiles. "Then we'll figure this out together."

"Patrick, it's not that simple," I say.

Something ugly and familiar is pushing its way up my throat, and it's like I'm right back in the girls' bathroom stall, looking at that tabloid. I push myself against the wall and dig my fingernails into my skin because that tiny, infinitesimal pain feels better than what's inside me right now.

His smile slips off his face. "What are you saying?"

I can't look at him. "I'm saying you have no idea what it's like to . . . to be where I'm at right now. I mean, you have these amazing parents and all these choices and this normal life and—"

"Right. Because being in tabloids that talk about you impregnating your girlfriend is normal," he says. It's like someone stole all the gentleness out of his voice. "And it's no big deal having conversations with your parents in which you tell them you might not be going to that Ivy League school you got into after all because you don't know if your girlfriend will leave the state. Or not telling your friends you got in because you're afraid she'll lose her shit, so instead all you see is the sympathy in their faces because they think, *Oh he didn't get in*. And not telling *her*, even though you're dying to. Never mind the pictures in entertainment blogs or the paparazzi that follow me even when you're not around."

"You deserve better," I whisper. "Maybe we shouldn't be toge—"

"Goddammit, Chloe!"

I jump, my eyes flying up at the anger in his voice.

"Patrick—"

But he's already halfway down the ladder that leads to the ground. "I'm not doing this with you again. You can't just dump me every time it gets too hard. Either we're together or we're not."

I open my mouth and I want to say *together, together*, but nothing comes out. His jaw hardens, and he drops down to the sand below.

"I'll walk home," he says.

And then he's gone.

~ ~ ~

I don't go to school for the next three days because I'm a spineless coward. Instead, I spend hours holed up in the Lees' guest room, writing e-mails to Patrick that I never send, trying out different voice mails that I never leave. Benny tells me he's not going to help me again, that I've got to figure this one out on my own. Still, part of me hopes Patrick will sneak into the Lees' house with blankets and promises of fort building.

He doesn't.

Finally, in an act of desperation, I call Lexie™.

"You're an idiot," she says, when I tell her what happened.

"I know," I whisper.

"Okay, that right there. *That's* why Patrick is pissed."

"What?"

She sighs. "Falling on your sword is not an act of noble sacrifice. It's just the easy way out."

"*Jesus*, Lex—insensitive much?" I mean, there are things you should just never say to someone who has tried to kill herself.

"Whatever," she says. "The truth is, it's easier to push him away than to actually figure out what the hell you're going to do."

When did my sister turn into Diane Le Shrink?

"You need to go over to that boy's house and beg forgiveness, and you need a plan for what's going to happen after graduation, or he's going to go to Columbia and marry some geeky chick with buckteeth and a 4.0, and you'll be miserable and alone and—"

"Okay, okay," I mutter. "Thanks for the pep talk."

"XOXO."

She hangs up.

I glance at the clock—three-thirty. He's probably just getting to Spin. I drag myself out of bed and jump in the shower. The water burns my skin, but it feels good—like it's boiling away all my indecision.

I park in the tiny lot behind Spin and head in through the back door. The place is empty, and Coldplay falls softly out of the speakers. Patrick must be feeling awful. He hates Coldplay. I walk up the Country/Western aisle, my hands shoved inside my pockets, clammy and trembling, and I'm hoping I haven't waited too long. Patrick doesn't see me. He's just staring out the front window, his arms crossed. He looks miserable.

"Hi."

His shoulders tense, but he doesn't turn around. And now I

know . . . I'm too late. Part of me wants to run right back out the door, but I can't give up the best thing in my life without a fight.

I force myself closer—each step feels like I'm walking the plank of our relationship.

"You asked me what I wanted."

Two more steps.

I can see his face reflected in the window, his lips a grim line, hair falling into his eyes.

"I want to see the world and figure out who I am, and I want to do that with you." One more step, the last one. We're inches apart, but there's never been so much distance between us.

"Patrick. I want *you*."

He turns around, slowly. My heart twists as I catch an echo of the look he'd had in his eyes when I told him we couldn't be together, all those months ago. He looks down at his scuffed-up All-Stars.

Ohgodohgod. *Please.*

A smile sneaks onto his face, and he raises his eyes. "Took you long enough."

All the beautiful things I'd meant to say get forgotten when his lips find mine. Or maybe I just say them in a different way.

SEASON 18, EPISODE 4

(The One with the Cap and Gown)

"Wow. So it's official. Bonnie™ is dead." Benny looks at the piece of paper I've just handed him and shakes his head. "Do you feel different?"

"Nope. MetaReel can have Bonnie™ *and* her trademark," I say. "I shall be forthwith known as Chloe Elizabeth Baker the First."

He hands me back the form the judge had signed earlier this morning, and I lovingly tuck it into my backpack.

"Do you think this will really keep people from recognizing you?"

I shake my head. "Not right now. But in a few years, when everyone forgets about us again, yeah, I think it will help."

He picks at the grass in the Lees' backyard and rubs it thoughtfully between his fingers. Benny has always hated the trademark, naturally, but he's very much a Benton. There's no other name that fits him. It's only recently that he's been under the kind of scrutiny I've been dealing with since I was thirteen, so it's almost too late for him to suddenly become someone else.

"Mom know?" he asks.

"Yeah. I called her and left a message. Honestly, I'm glad she didn't pick up. I didn't want our first conversation in three months to be the one where I tell her I've changed my name."

Benny massacres a few blades of grass. "Well, it's what she deserves."

I put a hand on his arm and squeeze. I know he's still hurt about her one-sentence reply to his e-mail telling her he'd gotten into USC.

He sighs and runs a hand through his hair. "I just want this to be over."

I lie on the grass and stare up at the sherbet sky. I wonder if any of the kids at home are doing this, just a few miles away. "Do you think they'll ever cancel the show?"

Benny's phone buzzes, and he snorts as he checks it. "Oh, man. Speak of the devil. No, my dear sister, there's no *way* they're canceling the show anytime soon. Look what Lex just sent me."

He holds up the phone so I can read the text.

Guess what? Mom's pregnant.

Benny and I look at each other for a long moment. I don't know what to say.

I feel a slight, irrational twinge of jealousy. For so long, I've been the only kid in the family that my mom had actually carried in her belly. I feel like another link between us has frayed.

"Think they'll change the name of the show?"

Benny nods. "They'll have to. Maybe it'll be something like *Fourteen Kids, Two Dads, One Mom, Two Nannies, Two Tutors—and a Partridge in a Pear Tree*."

"That's pretty bad," I say.

"Yeah." He grins. "Not my problem, though."

I watch the clouds above me sail by, untethered, going wherever they want to.

"So *Baker's Dozen* really will be a thing of the past."

A warm breeze pushes against the wind chimes hanging on the back porch, filling the air with a delicate melody. I take a deep breath and close my eyes.

My future has finally arrived.

~ ~ ~

"What is the deal with having to wear a sheet of polyester on a ninety-degree day? I swear to God, I'd burn this thing if I wasn't renting it."

Mer's makeup is melting, and she keeps blowing the tassel from her cap out of her face with an irritated *humph*. Though the sun has nearly set, the temperature has refused to drop. Our class is standing around like cattle, waiting for "Pomp and Circumstance" to start playing so that we can enter the football field and take our places on the bleachers under the DREAMS START HERE banner the cheerleaders painted last week. My whole body has a sheen of sweat over it, and my feet are killing me (strappy high-heeled sandals = bad decision), but I'm too happy to complain. A month ago, this would have been one of the most depressing nights ever. I would have looked at everything as the Last _____ (Fill in the Blank). But that was before I figured out what I was going to do with the next year of my life. It seems like forever since my last panic attack.

"Uncomfortable gowns are a time-honored tradition," I say, straightening Tessa's mortarboard. "It keeps us from getting too sentimental."

Patrick steals up behind me and kisses my neck as he slides his arms around my waist.

Mer rolls her eyes. "Says the 'not sentimental' girl in her boyfriend's arms."

I blush, but clasp Patrick tighter to me. "Where were you?" I ask, looking back at him. "You missed our last Pepsi Freeze run as high-schoolers."

"I had to get a few more things together for tomorrow."

"I can't believe you guys are taking off so soon," Mer complains.

"We want to miss all the traffic," I say. Actually, we're very committed to the timing of our departure—we're going for poetic over practical.

"I still think you should wait a day. You're gonna be super exhausted after all the parties tonight," Tessa says.

Patrick shakes his head. "That's what coffee and Red Bull are for."

I nod. "The drinks of road-trippers around the country."

"Patrick, she is so gonna fall asleep. You do know that, right?" Benny says.

He's fanning himself with his mortarboard, and the breeze ruffles his longish blond hair so that it looks like he's got a little halo. I feel a pang as I take in his suit and tie. I wish Mom and Dad could see Benny now, all grown up.

"Which is why *I'm* driving until we reach Vegas," Patrick says.

Mer gets all bug-eyed. "Whoa. Wait. Are you guys getting—"

"No!" I wave my hands in front of me. "It's just sufficiently east."

Matt shuffles over, a yearbook tucked under his arm. "Chloe," he says, thrusting it toward me, "I'm sure I'll be seeing you on major holidays for the rest of my life, but you're not getting out of writing something nice about me in here."

I laugh and grab the book out of his hand. "I'll see what I can come up with, Mr. USC football star." Matt blushes. He still can't get over his full ride to USC.

The conversation slides around me as I flip to my picture. There I am. Chloe Baker. I have a half smile, and my eyes seem a little lost—nothing compared to the candid photo of me in the senior spread. In that one, I'm at the winter formal sandwiched between Tessa and Mer, mid-laugh.

I flip to the page with the picture of Matt wearing the I LOVE MY BOYFRIEND T-shirt, but there're so many signatures around it that I opt for the back inside cover and scribble for a while. I can't really put into words what he's meant to me this year, but I try. I hand the book back to Matt and pull him into a hug.

His eyes get moist, and Benny punches him on the arm. "Don't start with that, or you'll get me going, too."

Schwartz ambles through the crowd of green-robed students, giving last-minute instructions and trying to get people lined up alphabetically.

"If your last name is at the beginning of the alphabet, get in the *back* of the line. Reverse order, people!"

I adjust the gold honor cords around Patrick's neck and give him a kiss on the cheek.

"Are you *sure?*" I ask him, for the millionth time.

Schwartz comes up to us. "Sheldon! What's this I hear about you putting Columbia off for a year?"

Patrick grins and puts his arm around me. "We're going to see the world first."

A road trip across the States. A flight to Australia. Working odd jobs as we move from hostel to hostel. Europe. Africa. India. Asia. South America. It's ours for the taking.

Schwartz narrows his eyes at me. "Baker. You're not too shabby in the brain department yourself, you know. What are *you* going to do after you see this 'world'?"

I roll my eyes. "Don't worry, Schwartz, I'll go to school."

"In New York, no doubt?"

I give Patrick a sly smile. "No doubt."

Schwartz squeezes my arm. "You've done me proud, kid. Never thought someone would take what I teach in gov so literally."

I break away from Patrick and reach my arms around Schwartz. It feels good to finally give him the hug he deserves. For a second, he just stands there, but then he gives me an awkward pat on the back.

"You're the best teacher I've ever had," I whisper, before I step away. And I mean it.

Schwartz blinks a few times and clears his throat. "When you need a letter of recommendation for school, you know where to find me," he says. His eyes travel to Patrick's. "Take care of her, Sheldon."

"I will," he says, looking down at me, his eyes full of the things you whisper in the dark.

The distinctive smell of pot smoke wafts over us, and Schwartz curses. "Excuse me while I go kill someone's buzz."

Schwartz heads off in the direction of the bleachers, and I squeeze Patrick's hand. "See you after."

"Can't wait."

"Benton™, shall we?" I say, linking my arm with my brother's.

He gives Matt a kiss on the cheek, and we go toward the Bs.

"I'm glad you didn't change your last name," he says. "It would have sucked to not sit with you."

"I know, right?"

Benny holds up his camera, and we squish our faces together for a quick shot.

"Lex is out there?" I ask.

He nods. "Yeah. I guess it was, like, *Mission: Impossible*, but she made it. No cameras. We're gonna meet her at the forty-yard line."

"I'm glad one of them is going to be here."

We'd sent Mom an e-mail with all the details, but we hadn't heard back from her. The prospect of graduating without the whole family to cheer us on has overshadowed the past week's giddy senior mania, but I'm trying to just be happy about what I do have.

"We've come a long way, baby," Benny says.

He puts an arm around my shoulders, and I lean into him, basking in the comfort of his Bentonness. I already miss him like crazy—he's always been my true north, and I hate the thought of going through life without checking in with him multiple times a day.

"I don't know what I'm going to do without you," I say.

"Have lots of sex with Patrick Sheldon, no doubt."

My eyes well up. "See? That's what I'm talking about! Who else can turn my sadness upside down like that?"

Benny kisses my head. "I'm only a text away, you know that." But his voice is rough, and I know that he gets what I mean.

Teachers run up and down the line of students, shushing and reprimanding and congratulating. The energy around us is palpable; we're swimming in concentrated expectation. Then I hear it—the first notes of "Pomp and Circumstance." Benny pushes me in front of him, and slowly the long line of students snakes its way onto the field.

The lights bathe everyone in a fluorescent glow, and the stands are packed with people shouting, holding up signs, blowing noisemakers.

My phone vibrates, and I check the text from Lexie™:

Look to your right, at the top of the bleachers.

"Benny."

I tug on his gown and point out Lexie™. She's wearing a bright pink shirt and waving her hands in the air. I grab my camera out of my pocket and zoom in, holding my breath . . .

"It's just her," I say, my voice dull. I don't think I realized how much I'd been hoping my family would sneak into the ceremony to surprise us. The weight of their absence is heavy and strangely final.

"Meh. Who needs parents, anyway?"

Benny forces a smile, and we both wave at Lex. She texts me again.

BTW, that gown makes you look fat.

The text is so *Lex* that tears prick my eyes again. I wish we hadn't spent most of our childhood hating each other.

The ceremony is probably very nice, but I can't really concentrate on it. After a girl from the show choir sings "I Hope You Dance," my row of graduates stands, and I finger the card in my pocket that phonetically spells my name for whoever's calling it.

KLO-EE BAY-KER

When I hear my name and Principal Harding hands me my diploma, Patrick, Mer, Matt, and Tessa howl, and I hear Lex's shriek of "Go, Chloe!" from the bleachers. I see Diane Le Shrink in the front row, and I give her a little wave before I start walking back toward the mass of robed students behind me.

"Benton™ Baker!"

I turn around and snap Benny's picture just as he's shaking the principal's hand. He smiles at me, triumphant. Somehow, the pain and rage and confusion of the past eighteen years dissolves until all that is left is this one perfect moment; unscripted, unedited, it's ours and ours alone.

It won't last forever. There are years of frustration ahead of us—a lawsuit, and who knows what else. But seeing him standing there, looking like he's conquered the world, I know one thing for certain: MetaReel doesn't stand a chance against us.

~ ~ ~

"Hey, you." Patrick gives me a sidelong glance and brushes my cheek with his finger before shifting his attention back to the empty highway.

The desert flies past, cactus and brush and low scrubby hills, and though my body is stiff from sleeping in the car and my head's fuzzy, I've never felt better in my life.

"Hey, yourself."

I sit up and lean closer to him, resting my head on his shoulder. We'd left Tessa's house hours ago, hiding in the folds of a pitch-black night, Patrick gripping my hand as we skirted past dozing Vultures. Now the sky is a pale blue, and the last of the stars are fading. The radio plays softly, and we drive in a quiet, contented silence measured out in heartbeats.

Then suddenly the sky begins to lighten. Blue fades to gray and becomes a pale peach.

"Wait for it," Patrick whispers.

And then it comes: our sunrise. Brilliant yellow and orange streak the sky, and we roll down the windows and let in the cold early-morning desert air because we have to feel it, every bit of it. I grin as the rays of sunlight stream over me and over Patrick and cover every inch of darkness that I've traveled so far to get out of. All that's left is a blinding, brilliant light.

So begins season one, episode one of the rest of my life.

Acknowledgments

First, thanks to God, who somehow has seen fit to ridiculously bless me. Huge thanks to my agent, Brenda Bowen, for making dreams come true, and to Vanessa DeJesus. Thanks to everyone at Holt, especially my wonderful editor, Kate Farrell, who loves Patrick just as much as I do (we'll have to agree to share him), and all the people who wanted this book out in the world. Your support makes this whole experience freakin' great. Thanks to Samantha Mandel for multiple reads, Rich Deas, the whole sales team, and everyone at all stages of the book for boundless enthusiasm. Did I mention I love Holt?

I absolutely must thank the Children's Book Caucus of PEN New England for the 2012 Susan P. Bloom Discovery Award—thank you for the awesome honor and for bringing attention to Bonnie™/ Chloe's story. Thanks to Anna Staniszewski and her Fall 2011 writing class at Simmons College for early comments and excitement. Lots of love to everyone at Vermont College of Fine Arts' MFA in Writing for Children and Young Adults program, especially my Allies, without whom the daily life of a writer would be lonely and difficult indeed. To my Green Line critique group (Shari Becker, Leslie Caulfield, and Jennifer Ann Mann) for always pushing me to be better. Carter Hasegawa, for teaching me how to read like an editor, and Rita Williams-Garcia, for wisdom I will use forever.

For my family, especially Zach, who makes every book I write better and is the greatest partner a girl could ask for in this crazy world (there should be an award for best supporting husband—love you so much). Also, to Meg, Grams, Mom (for buying me books even when we didn't have the money), Jake and Luke (represented by all Bonnie™/Chloe's little brothers), and Dad. Lots of love to my fabulous in-laws for all their support. Huge thanks to old friends who have always spurred me on: Sarah Roberts, who knew I had a voice before I did and is a damn fine writer in her own right, Brandon (Rosa!) Roberts, and Missy Wilmarth (love you, guys). Extra hugs for all my Boston friends, especially Jamie Christensen, Allison Cole, Andie Krawczyk, Briana Woods-Conklin, and Greg Batcheler, my kidlit buddies and cheering section.

Once more, thanks to Menendian, my Schwartz: you're the best teacher I've ever had. You changed my life and I'll be forever grateful.

Finally, for my grandfather Dan Weeks, who was the greatest storyteller I've ever known, and Me-Me Christy, who always believed I was a writer, even when I wasn't so sure. You won't get to read this book, but both of you made it possible in countless ways.